AS IF BY ACCIDENT

as if by

accident

JULIE JOHNSTON

KEY PORTER BOOKS

Library and Archives Canada Cataloguing in Publication

Johnston, Julie, 1941–
    As if by accident : a novel / Julie Johnston.

ISBN 1-55263-691-7

    I. Title.

PS8569.0387A8 2005   C813'.54   C2005-902649-9

The publisher gratefully acknowledges the support of the Canada Council for the Arts
and the Ontario Arts Council for its publishing program. We acknowledge the support
of the Government of Ontario through the Ontario Media Development
Corporation's Ontario Book Initiative.

We acknowledge the financial support of the Government of Canada through the
Book Publishing Industry Development Program (BPIDP) for our publishing
activities.

The excerpts on pages 122 to 125 are from *The Glass Menagerie* by Tennessee Williams,
copyright © 1945 by The University of the South and Edwin D. Williams. Reprinted
by permission of New Directions Publishing Corp.

Key Porter Books Limited
Six Adelaide Street East, Tenth Floor
Toronto, Ontario
Canada M5C 1H6

www.keyporter.com

Text design: Ingrid Paulson
Electronic formatting: Jean Lightfoot Peters

Printed and bound in Canada

05 06 07 08 09 5 4 3 2 1

For Kathy Lowinger

PART I

Val

one

IT IS LATE DECEMBER— the twenty-seventh to be exact. Val is driving along Highway 7, preoccupied, worried about road conditions, knowing she's on her way to do something stupid, but no more able to stop and reverse direction than change the very purpose of her trip. Val has told no one where she is going. Not Millie, with whom she spent Christmas Day and who would only have called her cell phone six or eight times to make sure she hadn't got lost, no one at Dobbs, Kendall, the publishing house where she is the senior (and only) fiction editor, and especially not her friend Denise, whose advice has always been *Get a lawyer to make the inquiries.* She did get a lawyer. She just hasn't taken his advice.

The sky has darkened. Fat flakes of snow splat against Val's windshield like juicy moths. To stop thinking about what lies ahead, she tries to focus on the novel manuscript in her briefcase, brought along to reread once she gets to Falkirk, her immediate destination. She's wondering, now, if it's really as good as she thinks. She has brought it with her to test her judgment.

If only she could loosen up. She feels the car swerve slightly. Breathe, she tells herself. She turns on the radio and scans through a medley of tired Christmas ditties, some thumping rock, a talk show featuring a priest giving marital advice. Bit ludicrous, she thinks, and turns it off. Something familiar, though, in her twenty seconds of listening. Before she can turn it back on three oncoming cars, in succession, splash her windshield with slush. She feels for the moment that she's flying blind. Maybe has been for months. When her windshield clears she turns the radio back on. The talk show has ended and she gets only the news and a recap of the latest political scandals.

The earlier sound bite won't leave her. The voice. She once edited a book by a very young priest. Mind you, she was very young then, herself. How long ago that seems. She mentally subtracts years instead of concentrating on her driving. And then she sees it. *Oh, God!* Something on the road, almost in the middle, a box. She slows, aware that it's just a cardboard carton; she can get by it easily enough and so could someone in the other lane. Better stop, anyway. She slows and pulls onto the shoulder as a transport coming behind her whooshes past the box, sending it up in the air to land in the ditch on the far side. Val is scarcely breathing. It was her duty to pick up that box.

"No need," she says aloud. "It's all right." She forces herself to breathe deeply. Soon she is able to move her car forward onto the highway, accelerating.

She would like to get past this, get it behind her, but even as she thinks this, the events of that day in the summer just past crowd other things from her mind. Part of her punishment is to replay it.

IT WAS A HOT DAY, excruciatingly hot even for July. She minded the heat, panicking sometimes, afraid she'd never cool down. It was her age; she knew that. She could go from room temperature to parboiled in any weather. They had been invited up north, she and Ed, to Robert Kendall's cottage.

On her internal screen Val sees herself before breakfast packing their things in a bag, bathing suits, towels, a change of clothes, night things. Ed didn't want to go. "Book babble!" he grunted. "Why would anyone drive a hundred and eighty kilometres for that? Could stay home and be bored just as easily." Meaning, she assumed, by her.

He hadn't always been this abrasive. When she married him eleven years ago, he had seemed open-minded, affable, proud of her. He liked the idea of her — it appeared to have worn off — the idea of an educated wife, well read, whose workaday world eluded him (he still had no idea what she did as an editor, and told any of his buddies who might ask that she was a librarian), a wife who, somehow, had charmed him initially.

She carried the bag downstairs. Ed had gone down ahead to make the coffee. She inhaled its addicting aroma. She would have one piece of toast with it and if she was still hungry, as she no doubt would be, she'd have grapes. Only a few.

When they had discovered each other, Ed expected more of her — that being intelligent enough to have a couple of university degrees, she would be more understanding of him, would see immediately what his moods indicated, why he sometimes didn't feel it necessary to reply to her questions or share his thoughts. When she mused on the eleven years of her marriage, tried to pinpoint the exact year, month, day when she noticed the frayed edges, she could not. Her editorial prowess did not extend to deconstructing her marriage. But it didn't stop her from trying.

THEY NO LONGER even attempted conversation at breakfast. He was somewhere behind the sports section of the newspaper. She glanced at the headlines without taking them in while she savoured every last crumb of her toast.

She hadn't known Ed Fennel long before they decided to marry, a few months only. She told her aunt Millie about him.

"Ed Funnel!"

"Fennel."

"Like the herb?"

"Well, yes," she had to admit.

Aunt Millie, the only remaining relative of her mother's generation, looked doubtful about the match and asked for details.

Ed Fennel ran his own flourishing business constructing and installing customized kitchen counters and cabinets. He was white, Caucasian, of no fixed religion, never married, leaned to the political right, and was ten years older than Val. They met while Val was house-sitting for her friends Denise and Dan Levy, who had been called out of town while their house was being renovated.

Val arrived at their midtown house after work one day to find Ed, the kitchen guy, haranguing a young plumber's assistant. "This is crap! Do you see this?" Changes to the plumbing were to have been finished the week before, and now they were rushing it. "What do they teach you these days?" she heard him yell at the young man. "Shit don't run uphill; payday's Friday. That about it? Christ!" A little sheepishly, he looked up at Val then, at her briefcase bulging with paperwork, manila envelopes bundled against her chest. She was still working at the time for Mercy

Publishing but becoming restless, she was thirty-eight, after all. She wanted to broaden her horizons.

"I'm Denise's friend," she said. "I'm looking after their place while —" She glanced left and right at the shambles, her long neck out. She was suddenly self-conscious of her owlish glasses. Her fair hair wouldn't stay tucked behind her ear. Ed took a deep breath and clamped his mouth shut. The plumber's assistant lay back down on the floor to continue grunting and clanging under the sink.

"Where does she want the cutting board installed — beside the sink, or over here near the range top?" Ed asked her.

She sensed him watching as she put down her load and shrugged out of her light jacket. She felt insubstantial in her simply cut, pale green dress — like a single long blade of grass. She found the list of instructions Denise had left. Together they studied it, their heads close. Ed straightened. When she looked up she felt herself admired in spite of her serious glasses. Later, Ed told her that her fine features and delicate lips seemed like something painted or carved.

She worked from Denise's place next day. Ed was in and out, keeping an eye on the work. At about four she made a foray through the dust and debris into the kitchen to fill the kettle at the now functioning sink. Plumber and assistant carpenter were packing up to go. Ed was half inside a corner cupboard making adjustments. He emerged and wiped perspiration from his forehead with the back of his hand. She found his thick dark hair appealing, the way it curled slightly, the way it was flecked with grey and sawdust. And his smile, slow, eyes crinkling. While he retrieved papers from his shirt pocket and unfolded them, she used the moment to glance at his shoulders, the dark hair on his wrists, his arms. They filled her with embarrassed longing. Her eye roamed quickly further. She was excited by him, by his narrow hips. She felt like an electrode catching a spark.

They sat, a little crowded, at one end of Denise's dining-room table littered with the contents of the old kitchen cupboards, drinking tea and commenting on exotic packets and jars of unfamiliar concoctions. He read some of the labels: "Garam Masala, Arborio Rice, Powdered Wasabi. They sound lethal, whatever they are," he said.

On the point of enlightening him, Val held back.

Each day thereafter, Val opened Denise's door expectantly, looking forward to chatting with Ed about the intricacies of installing lazy Susans and pull-out shelves, and the best management of space — topics she had never before contemplated. She found herself longing for an efficient, up-to-date kitchen of her own. Eventually they began talking about themselves, guardedly at first, not willing, either of them, to admit to their ever-increasing loneliness.

ED FENNEL WAS UNLIKE anyone she had ever dated. He stepped smartly ahead to open doors, ushered her to the inside of the street, offered his arm as they crossed. These gallantries made her nervous at first, made her wonder whether she was sufficiently ladylike to deserve them. He was quiet, not given to nervous chatter; he smiled more with his eyes than his lips. He seemed, sometimes, to be lost in deep thought.

The restaurant where he took her the first time they went out was not elegant, but the food was good, homey,

Val thought, surprised to find meat loaf on the menu. The movie was an unfortunate choice for two almost perfect strangers — a complicated plot involving plenty of hot and slippery sex viewed at an invasively close angle. Afterwards, they dropped into a coffee shop. Ed hunched forward across the table from her. The place was noisy. "So, you work for a publisher," he said, once they tired of rehashing the movie.

She nodded.

"What do you do there, write books?"

She had thought he was making a joke.

ON THE EVENING PRIOR to the July day in question, before they were to journey north to Robert Kendall's cottage, a client whose kitchen Ed was putting in phoned, claiming a crisis. "You'll have to go ahead without me," Ed said next morning, from behind his paper. "I've got to finish this guy's kitchen. I don't know when I'll get away from here. There's not a lot to do, but I won't know how fast it will go until I get started."

Over the years, Ed had changed, or perhaps it was Val who had changed. They were both touchy now. The slightest off-putting tone of voice or unacceptable glance was enough to ignite a slow seethe with either of them. There were times when Val wondered if the whole point of the wedding had been to prevent each other from coming home to an empty house. And there were times lately, especially after a pointless grudge-bearing argument, when she found herself wishing that he wouldn't come home at all.

"You might miss dinner if you leave too late," she said.

"I'll grab something on the way."

Probably suit him better anyway, she thought. More than once he'd referred to Robert as "that little faggot who likes to cook."

"I could wait for you, if you like, and we could go up together," she said, not meaning it.

"Sure." He hesitated. "Save you driving."

Val turned from him so that he wouldn't see disappointment in her face and opened the dishwasher to begin clearing it of last night's dishes.

"But, no," he said. "You go ahead. More for you to do at a place like that than me." Ed could swim, but didn't enjoy it.

Val let out the breath she'd been holding, finished emptying the dishwasher and reloaded it while Ed drank the last of the coffee. She scraped at a sharp knife, the blade pointing inward. "Watch what you're doing. You're going to cut yourself," he said. Perhaps because he used potentially dangerous tools in his work, Ed was very safety-conscious.

"You probably won't go at all," she muttered. She didn't look at him, but sensed anger radiating. She wiped the knife on a tea towel and put it safely in a knife block.

"Do you want me to go or not?"

"Of course."

"Fine. I said I'd go, so I'll go. Anything to make you happy." He trudged (stamped might be closer to the truth) up the stairs.

Lately, she had been wondering if she could cope with the intricacies of divorce. *He no longer communicates, Your Honour. He lives in a world of his own. He's predictable. My friends bore him, he has no curiosity about me or my work, and he never wants to go anywhere. He sees me only as a warm body to go to bed with.*

Does he beat you? Does he cheat? Does he belittle you?
Certainly not. I'd have left long ago.
So, the problem is?
He lacks imagination.
Divorce granted.

HER OWN FATHER HAD simply walked out. One morning when she was about four, she came downstairs from where she had been playing in her room to see him carrying a cardboard carton filled with books out to his car. His suitcases stood in readiness. In the front hall, weeping, her mother sat on the floor, her head on the hall chair, as if waiting for a guillotine to chop it off. When Val got to the bottom step he came back in, picked her up, gave her a squeeze, no kiss, put her down and said, "Toodle-oo."

She was used to him leaving and coming back a week or two later. He was in some sort of refrigeration business and had to do a lot of travelling. Her mother began to make short, gasping howls.

"Put a sock in it, Lizzie. You'll get over me." He chucked little Valerie under the chin, picked up his gear and went out the front door. A moment later he was back. He'd forgotten his car keys. And then he drove away, never to be seen again.

When the door closed behind him, it was like a book snapping shut before it was half finished, leaving a lot of unanswered questions. Would life go on? Would it be worth it to go on? No more cheerful whistling as he rustled up a little snack for himself and Valerie, leaving the kitchen looking like the aftermath of a hurricane, no more shoulder rides, her hands greasy from his slicked-down hair, no more tickling, screaming laughter, rides in the car with the top down, her mother smiling, wisps of hair blowing across her closed lips.

Bitterly, her mother took to her bed. Val begged her to get up, to go after him, to bring him back. "Do you know how many women there are in the city of Toronto?" her mother asked.

"No," said four-year-old Val.

"He could be with any one of thousands."

Val's mouth hung open. A thousand was more than a hundred, and she could not even imagine a hundred.

She pulled blankets off her own bed and camped outside her mother's bedroom, thinking she'd simply hang on if her mother tried to leave. She'd have to drag her everywhere. When her mother tried to make her way to the bathroom, Val coiled herself like a boa constrictor around her mother's legs. She howled; her mother pleaded. At last her mother slapped her and left the screaming child outside the bathroom door.

Val took her wounded pride and her fear of abandonment outside, where she hid under the back porch joined by her dog, Bix. She heard her mother calling her eventually, heard a neighbour join in. But she clung to Bix and promised him a life of marshmallows and butcher-bones and lying on the furniture as she envisioned their solitary existence in the house above them. At least the dog would stay, she thought, at least she could tie him up. It was a wasps' nest under the porch that finally forced her out in the late afternoon, as its occupants wafted back to their papery home.

The neighbours had to be phoned about her return, the police, Aunt Millie.

FROM TIME TO TIME HER mother roused herself to make sure Val had enough to eat and to attend to matters of business. Aunt Millie helped out when she could. Single, and a schoolteacher, she spent all her holidays urging Val's mother to get a grip on her life. But, Liz Hudson had developed some sort of malady. She bought home-medicine books, pharmacology manuals, medical textbooks to pore over, ticking off her many and varied symptoms and trying to reach a conclusion about them. It took up hours of her time. She could almost have opened a pharmacy or taken up the practice of medicine. By the time Val entered university, her mother had settled on cancer and died of it within a year.

There was no shortage of money at the time, inherited from Grandfather Hudson, enough, at least, to see Val educated. When she and Aunt Millie went through her mother's desk after her death, they found a picture of her young father beaming self-confidence at the camera in spite of a shock of hair that had escaped the Brylcreem helmet. Harry McDaid, it said on the back in her mother's handwriting, and a date — the year of Val's birth. Her mother had never taken Val's father's name, nor had she given it to Val. "The reason for that, if you must know," Millie told her as she tore the picture in two and pitched it in the wastebasket, "is because he never married her."

Val, nevertheless, fetched the pieces out again when Millie went out to make tea. She placed them, without taping them, among souvenirs her father had given her, a stuffed panda from the CNE, a mug from Niagara Falls, and a pink ballpoint pen from a hotel in Mississauga. For years she kept them as a little shrine to his memory.

THE DAY OF HER WEDDING was the first time Val experienced morning sickness. Aunt Millie had fussed over her, not knowing what ailed her, believing that the marriage was all wrong and should be called off. It was a case of history repeating itself, she told Val. "Your mother took on a man impetuously and look what happened to her. It's not too late, you know."

"Oh, yes it is," Val said, sliding palely into the washroom at the back of the church.

After their wedding trip, after the first trimester nausea settled down, she awakened each morning to a state of euphoria. She gazed adoringly at Ed, the father of her child, the author of her newfound delirium. She felt fit, aglow, adored, a born-again woman newly ensconced in her proper state. Her life was perfect. She begged Ed to take walks with her in the evenings. While they walked at a brisk pace, she raised topics such as breast-feeding, toilet training (not a lot of input from Ed there), nursery school, and what colour to paint the baby's room. Hand in hand they walked while she prattled and Ed, for the most part, remained silent.

"Aren't you happy about the baby?" she asked him one frosty evening. The moon was fat and brilliant in the winter sky imprisoned behind interlacing tree branches.

"Happy?" It seemed to be something he'd never pondered.

She stopped in the middle of the street to look into his eyes by the light of the hostage moon.

"Of course I'm happy," he said. "I never pictured myself as a real father, I guess. Hard to get used to the idea."

As she got closer to the three-month mark she found it impossible not to tell people the good news. Her friends at work planned a baby shower for her. Aunt Millie showed evidence of forgiving Ed for being what amounted to a mere carpenter in charge of other carpenters (she had told her friends he was an architect).

On a snowy morning, though, a week later, Val was awakened early by severe pains that made her feel that her whole midsection was in a squeezing, contorting vise. Her inner thighs were sticky. Panicky, she reached out to Ed to waken him. She could not speak.

Ed brushed snow from the windows of his van and took her to the hospital where she miscarried, painfully, bloodily, heartbreakingly. She lay on her back on a hospital stretcher, her eyes spilling over, tears trickling into her ears. She saw herself as an empty sack, shrivelled, gutted — divested of heart, soul, hopes.

"Why would this happen?" Ed asked the doctor.

"Any number of reasons. A fetal malformation. Nature's way of dealing with imperfections. It happens."

Val reached out for Ed's hand. He was pale. He looked ashamed, as if he were somehow to blame.

"My advice," the doctor said gently, "is to wait three months and try again." She left them then to hurry on to another patient whose perfect baby was testing its lungs.

At home Val put herself to bed and mourned. She tried to get the tiny being that had lived inside her for three months out of her mind, but could not. He had taken form, perfect form. She dreamt about him. He survived in her mind where he remained a lisping toddler, bright-eyed, a prodigy, his arms reaching for hers. She had just turned thirty-nine.

AND SO VAL FINISHED up some chores that July morning before setting off for Robert Kendall's cottage. She gave the grass a brief watering and put the garbage into a container inside the garage. At a shopping centre on her way out of the city she chose a nice bottle of wine, worried that it was too expensive, put it back, and then went back and got it anyway. She bought a veggie sandwich in a deli to eat on the way and by one-thirty she was travelling briskly north along Highway 11.

Her car was quite comfortable. Ed had managed to get the air conditioner working again. It was silly of them to travel in two vehicles, but it was done now. It would be equally silly for her to miss the afternoon and dinner. Ed, she had to admit, had always been a very private person, not a communicator. During meals, he ate while Val tried to interest him in conversation. She talked a bit about her work, her frustrations, her successes. He would nod, say uh-huh, and she knew he was not taking in anything. She would ask, "How was your day?"

He would look up from his plate, tongue probing a tooth, and stare at her for a moment as if translating her question into his own language. "Long," he said. She asked him where he was working, what the house was like, what the people were like. "The Beach," he might say. Or, "the Annex." Never any details. The houses he worked in were "Pretty standard," and the people who hired him were "So-so." Perhaps she should have pressed him for details. Perhaps she should have insisted he converse, take part, do his share, or at the very least, let her into some small part of his life, but she didn't. She got her social stimulation from work.

She took her eyes off the road briefly to look for some gum in her purse, looking up in time to keep from steering into the wrong lane. This was how accidents happened, she chided herself. She was not exceeding the speed limit, not by much anyway.

She turned on the radio to find some music, something classical, and this was when she saw it. On the road, angled across her lane lay a long, thick beam, taking up nearly the whole lane and part of the shoulder. There was very little traffic at the moment, although it had been fairly heavy up to this point, and she was going slowly enough that she could change lanes easily. She got past the thing, as did several other cars following her lead and changing lanes. That was dangerous, she thought. Must have fallen off a truck. You'd think the driver might have been aware and stopped to get it. Someone should stop and drag it away. Maybe she should.

She was well past it now. The road bent and the beam disappeared from sight. She *could* stop; she saw a safe place to pull off, but by now she was quite a distance past it. She'd have had to walk back. And it was so hot out there. Two cars overtook and passed her. Ed would have stopped; he was so safety-conscious. On the radio she recognized a familiar aria from a Verdi opera. She glanced into the rearview mirror; only a couple of cars behind her now. Odd how the traffic had thinned. She hummed along to the music, loudly and rather well, she believed, and cheerfully, because if the truth were known she was glad she was travelling by herself instead of with a sullen husband. She was making good time.

The beam on the road was forgotten.

VAL ARRIVED AT Robert Kendall's cottage at about three-thirty, explaining that Ed had been tied up with business. "He should be here by eight," she said. "Nine at the latest."

23

Other people were already there or trickling in — two writers whom she knew well, one with his wife and six-month-old baby, the other Lynnette Appsley, a woman whose novels had never appealed to Val (nor had Lynnette herself, she had to admit), but with whom Robert had worked in the past; he was trying to lure her back into his stable of authors. Also present was Marshall Saul, Robert's friend of long standing. Val suspected they were gay, but hated to make an assumption based only on the fact that they were both single, both in their forties.

As a matter of fact, she found Robert sexually attractive, in a quiet way. His elegant style and manners appealed to her. She had been working with him for six years, and though she had sometimes thought that it might be nice to be wooed away by a larger publishing house (allowing Robert to be struck dumb by her now apparent invaluable worth), she had not, so far, been beckoned. Nor had she felt sufficiently discontented to actually seek other employment. That could all change, of course, the way the market was going, the way the government continued to find less and less money for the publishing industry. She knew Dobbs, Kendall was actually owned by a large conglomerate, Aksfal Corporation, which threatened, from time to time, to sell them, or cut their losses and dismantle them entirely.

Still, Robert and Val muddled along year after year, with the help of a small staff and what government grants they could muster, publishing some pretty good books between them along the way. She believed Robert appreciated her skills, her ability to seek out what was at the heart of a manuscript, particularly a novel — its raison d'être. He was a good friend, concerned about her well-being. He made her laugh, something she hadn't done very often at home lately.

She tried to hurry into her bathing suit in the bedroom she and Ed had been assigned. Robert Kendall had inherited his family's cottage, huge by the usual standards. It was surrounded by a sprawling veranda and perched on a rise of land overlooking the lake — flat as consommé, this steamy day. There was additional sleeping space over the boathouse and in a sleeping-cabin linked to the main cottage by a boardwalk whose view of the lake was through a scattering of maidenly birches. Idly, as she struggled to pull her bathing suit up over her sweaty thighs, sucking in her stomach, and adjusting the top over her rather small breasts, she wondered if Marshall and Robert would share a room. Unlikely. Robert was intensely private. To walk down to the dock at the water's edge she cloaked herself in her long swimming towel in order to postpone revealing for as long as possible the extra flab she had collected around her waist during the last year or so.

The others were spread out on the dock or swimming in the lake. The baby's parents took turns jouncing him naked up and down in the water on the shallow side of the dock. Val experienced a small spasm of not so much jealousy as longing. For the briefest moment, her fair-haired toddler, her fictitious child whom increasing age had not in the least diminished, played in the sun.

She dropped her towel and dove in straightaway, without testing the water's temperature. The lake was suitably cold and refreshing after her long drive. Robert bobbed up, suddenly, beside her, making her start and then laugh. She was aware of the sun's blaze on her wet head, strands of hair on her face. She ducked her head under water to slick it back.

"This is wonderful," she told Robert. "How can you bear to come in to work on Mondays?" They began to swim shoreward beside each other, not racing, each using strong even strokes. They reached the ladder at the same time, and gallantly Robert offered to let her go up first. She refused, pushing off with her feet to swim on her back. Perhaps she was being overly vain to care so much about her figure. At forty-nine people weren't expected to look the way they had at twenty-nine, she tried to remind herself. Instead, images popped into her head of two women she knew who did. Anomalies, of course. And then, disappointingly, she thought of one more.

THEY DINED ON GRILLED marinated tuna, cooked rare, served with a warm potato salad, and a French Sauvignon Blanc, a meal Ed would have had to choke down. Just as well he was delayed. Ed's idea of adventurous dining was any type of red meat not related to some portion of a cow. Marsh made sure her wineglass was filled. She liked the wine, drinking rather more of it than she probably should. She was beginning to feel magnanimous toward Lynnette Appsley, a bad sign. She told them about the board on the road. They all guessed that they probably would have left it there, too. She sat quietly for a moment, practicing holding in her stomach, half tuned in to Robert's conversation with Lynnette about a book, not a novel exactly, but creative non-fiction, memoir-like, set on the French island of St. Pierre off the coast of Newfoundland where she grew up.

"I still have relatives there; they'd never speak to me if I wrote about them," Lynnette said. Robert told her that was beside the point.

The sun set elegantly, clouds leaking pale ink across the tangerine horizon. Outside, they sat or wandered with glasses of port until the mosquitoes became vicious, sending them in. Val looked at her watch — a quarter to nine. Ed should be arriving soon. Robert turned on an outside light to illuminate the path from the parking area. Nine came and went. The baby had been put to bed in the sleeping-cabin with a monitor. They all listened and smiled at his private snuffling sounds, feeling a sort of kinship, a sympathetic connection that seemed to relate somehow to the fact that they were at a cottage. They sat in the dusk amid soft lamps, talking wittily, listening to a faint recording of a jazz group and then a wail from the baby monitor. The young writer, Ivan, said he'd go and check on his son. His wife, Chris, said she would. They both went.

Val noticed herself beginning to feel edgy. At any moment her husband would arrive, tired, grumpy possibly — not in synch with this contented group. She tried to relax. It was up to her to put Ed at ease. They could go to bed early, which would relieve the situation. Tomorrow he could borrow a fishing rod or together they could paddle Robert's canoe. They should leave in the afternoon, maybe around four. *Where the hell is he?* This was ridiculous. No excuse for him being this late. She checked her watch; it was nearly ten.

At ten, Lynnette Appsley asked Robert for a flashlight and toddled off to bed up over the boathouse. She had slept there before, apparently; she said she was looking forward to being lulled to sleep "by the gentle push and suck of waves as they fondle the rock-strewn shore." Val closed her eyes briefly to keep from rolling them. Ivan and Chris had not returned from the sleeping cabin. The monitor was off; they'd settled for the night. And Marsh, too, had already turned in.

Val looked again at her watch. "You don't have to wait up," Val said to Robert. But he insisted.

"Might as well watch the news," Robert said. They moved down to the far end of the veranda into deep comforting chairs. Robert flicked from channel to channel until he tuned in the local news. Various horrors, they discovered, were occurring here and there in the world — bombings, strikes, civil unrest, drug busts, murders, rapes, forest fires, famine. "Closer to home," the newscaster announced, "an accident this afternoon, near Orillia, Ontario, has claimed the life of one and resulted in injuries to four others when a van went out of control on Highway eleven, colliding with a transport truck and forcing three other vehicles off the road. Ontario Provincial Police from the area are investigating the accident, which witnesses at the scene say may have been caused by a piece of lumber lying across the northbound lane. Details are not being released until the victim's relatives have been notified."

Val felt her face go numb. She turned to Robert. He looked at her without expression. "We are not going to jump to conclusions," he said firmly.

Val could neither agree nor disagree. Her throat had closed. Although her eyes were open very wide, she couldn't focus. Instead she saw a beam slanting across the road, heat-hazed, like a mirage in the blistering sun. She heard her heart pounding hollowly inside her head. She was certain that her husband had been involved in a road accident. She was certain that he had left the city early, after all. And she knew that her own indolence had caused the accident to happen.

Robert was in the kitchen talking on the phone to the Ontario Provincial Police. She had followed him; she heard him speak, but could not understand what he was saying.

Val sat on a chair near the table and rested her pounding head on her hands amid the debris of dessert dishes, cheese plates, knives, spoons, coffee cups. She was aware that the dishwasher was finishing its last cycle. She heard a click as the red light went off. A moth banged against a screen, attracted by the kitchen light. She felt Robert's hand on her shoulder. She was being helped to her feet.

two

HEADING EAST, SNOW FLYING, Val returns to the present. She looks again at the clock. She will get to Falkirk before dark. She will find a motel, get a map, take herself out for a solitary supper, read some of the manuscript, and in the morning go looking for Dogwood Station — if it's even on the map.

Several times she has started a letter to the occupant of the house at Dogwood but has yet to finish one. Her lawyer has furnished her with a letter, still unsent. She is beginning to feel that face-to-face contact would be a better approach. After all, it could be some poor, aging relative Ed has been supporting all this time, someone he forgot to mention to her, or felt it unnecessary to discuss. None of her business.

She is aware of an increase in what now seem to be pinhead-sized snowballs flying furiously, horizontally, at her windshield. They mesmerize her, draw her eyes inward away from the road. The farther east and north she travels, the more snow she notices in fields, on trees, on the centre of the road. It's obviously been snowing for some time up this way. If she had listened to a weather report, she might have turned back. She slows down, but keeps going. When she thinks about what she is about to do, perspiration forms on her upper lip and forehead. She has to open a window.

ROBERT DROVE VAL'S car along Highway 11 while she slumped limply in the passenger seat. The headlights of oncoming cars dazzled her. With each one her hopes soared; she straightened, turned her head to stare at the passing car. She longed to shout, *There he is; the police were wrong!*

Marsh was in Robert's car, behind them somewhere. He had said he would inform the others and then join them at the police station in Orillia. Val pictured him with a flashlight going into the sleeping-cabin, calling Ivan outside, whispering so as not to waken the baby.

He would go next to the boathouse. Lynnette Appsley would sit up, the sheet pulled up to cover her more than ample bosom, startled, or more likely, pleased, to have a man enter her bedroom. Val didn't know what words Marsh would use to relay the message, but she imagined Lynnette saying something theatrical in reply and then rolling over and going back to sleep. She wished Robert would drive faster. He should have realized that every minute counted, that the sooner they got there, the sooner —.

Her presence was required, that much she knew. She was a solver of problems, a lateral thinker. Once she put her mind to it, she would be able to find a way for her husband to pull through this ordeal. All is not lost was what she told her writers. The insurmountable shall be scaled. Ahead of them, a haze of light above the horizon beckoned. Orillia.

AT THE HOSPITAL Robert and Val were met by a green-clad doctor. They entered an elevator and went down, not up. There were corridors, a door, lights, voices. This entire scene is wrong, she thought. Trite. How many times must we endure this? Movies, television, books. It must be rewritten. Or omitted. She found herself staring into her husband's face, his eyes half-open, not focusing, his hair plastered against his forehead. He could have done with a haircut, she thought.

Her husband's lips were slightly parted and she could see his gleaming teeth. "He always takes good care of his teeth," she said.

No one answered.

"May I be excused?" she asked as if she were a child wanting to leave the dinner table. Someone led her to a door, opened it, turned on the light and said, "Will you be all right? Shall I call a nurse?"

Val smiled reassuringly. She had been brought into a washroom. As the door closed she was unsure whether she would lose the contents of her stomach or her bowel. She lay on the floor and waited for someone to place her on a stretcher beside her husband.

THE NURSE WHO HAD lifted her head and shoulders from the floor of the washroom, had raised her from the dead, stood beside Val's chair in a small office deep in the entrails of the hospital. Robert occupied a chair on her other side. Beside him was a plastic bag containing odd items from the demolished van, from Ed's pockets — relics. Val sat, stupefied. Her body had gone numb, yet her brain was working overtime. She felt she was experiencing a double load of grief — that if her husband was dead, so, then, was her fair-haired phantom child. She could not at this moment conjure his precious image. She was asked to sign something, but her hand shook. Robert held her hands, squeezed them, and placed the pen in her right hand. Val is left-handed. She had thought he knew that.

ED HAD ASKED HER to marry him only seven weeks after their first dinner together. She had agreed instantly, without a moment's thought — until the next morning when she lay in bed listening to Ed's deep, even breathing, and looked with cold-blooded candour at the unfamiliar vista ahead of her. Wifedom. What had she been thinking? Her present life was entirely satisfying. Yes, she had been lonely before she met Ed, but loneliness, she had always believed, was part of the human condition.

She loved Ed, though; she had felt certain that love was what she was experiencing. She rolled onto her side to look at him. She loved his looks, his body, the way he made love, the way her body responded; she had become used to his presence in her bed, to the way he nestled against her just before falling asleep, to the heat of his groin against her cool buttocks.

But marriage! She had never, even as a child, dreamed of marriage for herself. She leaned over and gently kissed him awake. She tried to tell him that she was having second thoughts, but he merely said, "You worry too much. It'll be fine. People are not meant to be alone."

"We could simply live together."

Ed sat up, swung his legs over the side of the bed, arms resting on his knees. He looked around at her, scowling — a little boy not chosen, rejected by the team. "We belong together; you know that. What is it? Some kind of a class thing? You don't want the world to know about us?"

She had no reply to that, except to pull him back into bed, to cover his body with hers.

IN THE AFTERNOON, Robert and Marshall accompanied her to the funeral home while she delivered clothes for Ed, including underwear and socks. As she handed over a small zipper bag she imagined Ed boarding a single-passenger plane, destination unknown. She had put in the required items, choosing his newest underwear, his most conservative socks, while trying unsuccessfully to erase a vision of strange hands tugging on, pulling up, this intimate apparel over the uncooperative stiff feet and legs of her dead husband. She had tried to choose a tie for him, even though he hated them and rarely wore one. She had put one in the bag anyway, admitting to herself that she was a controller, a perfectionist. She had always wanted her husband to look his best, as if he represented the cover of a good book.

She imagined Ed saying,
Forget it, I'm not wearing a tie.
It's appropriate.
Who will see it? No one.
Why must you always flout convention?
Val, whose funeral is this, anyway?
She removed it.

SITTING IN THE FRONT pew of the funeral home chapel, Aunt Millie on one side of her and Denise and Dan on the other side, Val bowed her head while the minister droned a long prayer. She had not attended a church service since her marriage, although at one time she had contemplated joining the Roman Catholic Church. How long ago that seemed. Not seemed, was.

When she tried to keep her eyes closed for the prayer she felt dizzy and so she stared down at her hands, fingers intertwined, alternately flexing and relaxing her knuckles. She had been in her twenties when she had met religion head-on. Thirty loomed. It was a time in her life when she felt unidimensional and lonely. Depressed. Or, no, not depressed exactly, but certainly a trifle meloncholic. Her entire outlook was undermined by this mild distemper. At one time in her student days she had thought that she would like to write a book. But this hadn't happened. Instead, eventually, she found work with a textbook publisher, inserting editorial corrections into manuscripts, marking them up for the typesetter. The book she felt compelled to write remained shapeless, evanescent, beyond the reach of her imagination.

In this frame of mind she had begun to ponder the mysteries of death and life. She was not toying with self-destruction so much as wondering what made people cling to life against all odds — the terminally ill, for instance, or the elderly. Her brooding took her into the realm of religious zeal, contemplation of belief in a higher being, in a hereafter. She tried time and again to imagine herself making the necessary leap, but in vain. She was unable to ally herself with those sure-footed travellers as they soldiered on, confident of their eventual ascent to a better place. Her leap always seemed to be from one glacial peak of a chasm to another. She was afraid of slipping in. She looked around at the people she worked with, the people she knew, her friend Denise, and wondered what kept them content.

From university days Denise and Val had built up a trust in each other that allowed them to be each other's cheering section or crying shoulder or reservoir for untested theories. With downcast eyes Val asked Denise one day, "Why do we persevere in the face of our inevitable disintegration?" She could easily imagine herself going home, climbing between the cool sheets of her bed and just waiting for the conclusion of life.

"Perhaps we're too busy to notice ourselves crumbling," Denise replied. She loved her new job and loved Dan, her fiancé. She was a travel consultant. Her life pulsed with people to meet, places to go, things to see.

Val said, "Or perhaps we're too involved in the present moment."

"Same thing." They were having a Friday after-work drink at a bar Denise had chosen because of its preponderance of eligible men, one of whom, she believed, would fall insanely in love with Val, once he got to know her.

"We can't see beyond our present stage of life," Val said. "We're young, we're attractive." She peered around at the other thirtyish, attractive people. "We think this is the way it's always going to be."

Denise waved at someone she knew.

"People think life is merely a continuum," Val said, "but it isn't."

Denise polished off her glass of wine and signalled the waiter.

"It comes as individual parcels in plain brown wrappers, and each parcel is *it*, us, the way we are forever — until we take delivery of the next parcel." This was the image of life that ambushed her in the night, pushing sleep aside.

"I think you need another drink," Denise said.

VAL STARTED SPENDING more time in the library, picking up books about saints, visionaries, martyrs, people who claimed to have experienced death, glimpsed an afterlife, been converted, been reborn, people who had something to talk about. Her own life, by comparison, seemed not only starkly linear, but inconsequential. She got up each day, went to work, came home, read, went to bed, put the garbage out on Tuesdays, and vacuumed on Saturdays. She wondered if she should get a long-haired cat, so that at least there would be something to challenge the vacuum cleaner. And then she heard of a job opening with a publisher of religious and inspirational material. She applied for the position at Mercy Publishing and got it.

She felt like a tulip after its long underground coma pushing up through the warming earth. The job was stimulating, carrying with it more responsibility than she'd had so far. At last she was learning the ropes of the publishing business. In her first few months on the job, she beamed at her co-workers, and marvelled. They were kind, she thought, caring, hard-working, bound in brotherly and sisterly love — a different breed of people altogether. She got a kitten that tore her curtains, but it didn't matter. Not really.

The perceived virtue that surrounded her in her new job continued until she'd been there half a year, until her saintly co-workers decided she could be trusted with their petty grievances against each other, their nit-picking jealousies, and their small, conniving insurrections against the despotic rule of some of the principal players. One day, from behind a partially closed door, she heard her immediate boss yell at someone over the phone, "God is love, for Christ's sake! Gimme a break."

At home, the cat, now fully grown, began biting her when she least expected it, drawing blood. She gave it away and wept.

SHE WAS WEEPING now as the minister talked about Ed as if he actually had known him although he had only her notes to go on. Denise put a hand over Val's clenching hands and squeezed.

Following the funeral service the minister announced that everyone was welcome to go back to Valerie's home for refreshments. Aunt Millie had insisted on this and Val had agreed, partly because it was easier than disagreeing, and partly because she wanted to put off for as long as possible being alone.

Her aunt bought squares and cookies for the event and Denise had made sandwiches. Her young daughter, Judith, helped to pass them. Robert had been put in charge of supplying a couple of bottles of good medium-dry sherry.

People milled about, squeezing past each other in Val's tiny dining room, trying not to jiggle the elbows of people sipping coffee. Val bit obediently into a sandwich, but could barely summon the neural command needed to make her throat swallow. "They're very good," she told Judith, who nodded seriously. "I know. I helped make them."

Val had eaten almost nothing over the past three days. Denise drew her attention to a heavy-set woman in her sixties, perhaps, hair dyed a dull black, hovering near the door as if for a quick exit. Val peered. "A relative of Ed's, maybe," she whispered. "I'd better go and speak to her." Denise suggested she sit down first, that she have a glass of sherry, that she eat something more. Robert poured sherry for people, Marsh circulated another plate of sandwiches.

"I don't know what we'd do without you two boys," Val heard Aunt Millie whisper to Marsh, a trifle patronizingly, she couldn't help thinking. She knew Millie's analysis of the Robert and Marshall relationship. "Flaming," she had said once after a dinner party to which Val had invited her. Ed had turned the television on in the living room, trying to catch the last minutes of the game. Val never remembered what game was being played. As far as she was concerned, it was a series of eternal conflicts, not unlike a soap opera.

"Who's flaming?" she asked.

"Robert and his friend!" Millie had not one iota of use for attractive, eligible men who insisted on putting themselves beyond the reach of attractive, intelligent, well-brought-up girls like her own niece, forcing them into less than ideal marriages.

"You think they're gay?"

"Downright ebullient," Millie had said.

PEOPLE WERE BEGINNING to leave the post-funeral reception. Val searched for the crow-haired woman in order to speak to her. Ed had told her years ago that he had no family to speak of. A runaway sister, parents deceased, a cousin or two whom he'd lost track of years before. Val is curious about the woman. His sister returned, perhaps? But a search both upstairs and down proved fruitless.

At the bottom of the stairs she was engulfed by three elderly women who had known her mother, widows, friends of her aunt. They clutched at her hands, squeezing them between their own gnarled knuckles, their heavy rings digging into her, telling her how sorry they were. "It's not fair," one of the women said. "It's just not fair. To

39

be struck down like that in the prime of life. What a tragedy! And in the middle of summer. It's not fair, it simply is not fair." She enveloped Val in a powdery embrace while Val found herself wondering if there were some seasons more acceptable than others for accidental deaths.

When they had left, she was approached by a sad-faced man, a stranger, who introduced himself as one of Ed's clients. Downcast, he mumbled so that Val had to devote her complete attention to what he was saying.

"You know, it was our kitchen Ed was working on that day," the man confessed. "I can't help but feel I'm to blame somehow for the accident. If I hadn't phoned him, if he'd been able to leave earlier —."

"Oh, please don't," Val said, her face creasing, her eyes watering. "You mustn't blame yourself." She said this either magnanimously, or perhaps jealously, knowing that blame was being reserved as her exclusive right. She could not and would not share it with this stranger. When she thought about the morning of that day she remembered resenting her husband's intrusion into her weekend. She remembered contemplating divorce. Her guilt was fathomless.

The man said, "We were supposed to be having guests on Saturday and, well, you know how it is, all that mess and the inconvenience, and we couldn't use the kitchen, and my wife was in tears about the whole thing because the countertop material Ed had been waiting for was actually delivered Friday night, about seven. So that was why I phoned him. You know? I thought if he could come in on Saturday, and get us to the point where we could use the kitchen —."

"It's not your fault," she said.

"We could have gone *out* for dinner."

Val patted his arm.

"And then," the man continued, "once he got started, it didn't really take him very long. He finished up before one."

"Yes," Val said. She knew by now that he had been almost right behind her on the highway — less than five minutes behind her, the police had estimated. *The Toronto Star* had made much of this irony in an article about the accident. The reporter had phoned Val's home, and when she answered, she thought at first that she was talking to the Provincial Police, who were investigating the accident. She couldn't think why, unless she hadn't heard the person properly. He must have said he had been talking to the OPP, and she had misunderstood. In any event, she answered several questions and even mentioned her anguish about not stopping to remove the beam, before she regained her wits and said goodbye.

She relived the stretch of highway, saw again the beam aslant across her lane. She could have pulled her car off the road onto the shoulder, stopped, walked back and yanked it out of the way. If she had, she would have seen Ed's van, he would have seen her pulling it away, saving his life. He would have stopped and got out of the car. *Oh, my God!* he would have said. *That could have been dangerous!* And they would have embraced. And Val might have said, *Let's just go back home and have barbecued hamburgers.*

The man took a handkerchief out of his pocket and wiped his nose. He needed to be comforted, Val could see, needed to be absolved. She leaned closer and said quietly, "Do you know something? Ed didn't want to go away that day, anyway. He would have stayed home working quite happily. He was only going because he thought I wanted him to." She stood back from the man, looking up into his face, offering him redemption. He uttered a shaky sigh and pressed his lips stoically against his teeth. He nodded.

THE MORNING AFTER the funeral, Val drove out to Ed's office to go through his filing cabinet where he kept his personal papers. In it she came across the deed to a house owned by Edward James Fennel in a township and county she had never heard of, in the implausibly named hamlet (she assumed it was tiny) of Dogwood Station. Within his accounts book she also discovered tax and hydro receipts paid on behalf of a house there and the receipts of bills paid for its general upkeep. She had no idea why he had never mentioned the house to her.

Her suspicion, though, was that the woman who came to the house after the funeral but did not stay to introduce herself was the occupant of the house at Dogwood Station, living rent free. Val assumed it was rent free — nothing in Ed's books indicated otherwise. She had a rush of anger that burned with the incandescence of a blow-torch. Val and Ed, both, had stinted themselves to save for their house in Toronto, and had had to settle for something very small, in a pleasant enough neighbourhood, but less than ideal in other ways, something they could afford. "It will be fine," Ed had said. "In a few years it will be up over twice its value. Have you seen the places a few streets north of here they're replacing these old houses with? They're fantastic."

She had seen them and they did look fantastic, but somehow they had never got round to trading their tiny house for a tall, narrow, modern one. Still, Ed should have told her about this other house. She felt even more like an outsider in his death than she had in his life. His will, she knew, left everything to her, including the place in Dogwood.

Now, she had to confront this woman, Ed's relative or whoever she was, and tell her she had no desire to keep the house on under the present conditions. She would kick the baggage out. Into the cold. There is no free lunch.

three

WINTER DAYLIGHT IS beginning to fade. Her eyes feel irritated from staring into the snow still falling, thickly shrouding the road ahead. She rubs them, adjusts her glasses, turns on the radio again but only half listens to the four o'clock news. She seems to be coming to something, a traffic light; she's made it as far as Falkirk, or at least its outskirts. Certain members of CUPE are threatening to strike, the radio says. She looks to left and right for motels, chooses one that looks promising. Workers may walk off the job by midnight tonight, the radio continues.

Her room in the Lucky Stars Motel is large and tasteless. Pinched, she thinks. Starved. A mattress, scantily clad in a tired bedspread faded to a sallow nameless shade, lies prostrate, thin as a cheese sandwich before a headboard constructed of some wood-like material; a slender-legged table cowers against one wall; a chair, minimally upholstered, turns its back on the window. A sign outside promises colour TV, and she wonders if colour is something of a novelty this far east of Toronto. There is coffee available in the front lobby, the desk clerk who shows her to her room informs her, but no coffee shop. There are fine restaurants nearby, he assures her, some of the very best. "You've got your McDonald's, you've got your Wendy's, oh, and one of those chicken places. You name it." She asks him if he has maps for sale, but he hasn't.

"Where do you want to go?"

"A place called Dogwood Station."

"Dogwood Station!" he repeats, looking hard at her as if she has made a somewhat foolhardy choice. "You don't need a map to get to Dogwood. It's just about straight north out of here. You go back to that traffic light there and you turn right. You just follow your nose till you get there."

"How far is it?"

"Oh, well, couldn't say for sure. It's far enough. Take you a good hour. Longer if this snow don't let up. They're saying there's a chance the snowplow operators will go on strike. You might be wishin' you had the four-wheel-drive on that station wagon of yours."

"I have."

"You have? Well, then, you're all set."

Val doesn't bother hanging up any of her clothes. She's taken the motel room only for the night. The elderly television set, the heftiest item in the room, offers two channels, one French, one English, both in colour, both channels favouring a pastel green, a faded gold, and a pinkish orange. She turns it off.

She has removed her stylish boots and lies on the bed wondering how many adulterous trysts have taken place in this cheerless setting. She has nothing against adultery as long as it does not involve sordidness, which it certainly would in this motel room. And as long as it doesn't involve family breakup, which it eventually would, leaving a child lost in the chaos of an adult world and a mother filled with rancour. Religious taboos she doesn't consider. She has

45

floated beyond the tidal wave of religious enthusiasm that once flooded her life. She looks in the drawer of the bedside table and yes, there is a Gideon Bible.

HER FIRST MAJOR editorial assignment at Mercy Publishing had been a self-help book written by a young Roman Catholic priest. It was aimed at young people looking for a guide to making the right Christian choices at school, in their careers, and in marriage. She was excited about the book. It was a trifle dogmatic in places, but that wasn't necessarily a bad thing. For part of that winter she and Father Ryan worked on his book over the telephone, in her cubbyhole office knee-deep in manuscripts, and over coffee at a nearby doughnut shop. "The chapter sequence is awkward," she told him. "The third chapter would make a better opener." Father Bill Ryan made a note and then looked up and into her eyes with a trusting purity that made her heart lunge, made her take a sudden breath.

She couldn't stop thinking about the book. Well, that wasn't entirely true. She had to confess that she couldn't stop thinking about Father Bill Ryan, about the way his whole face seemed lit from within when he smiled, about the one engaging dimple in his cheek, about the way he cocked his head and looked at her quizzically. And also, of course, about his earnest, uncomplicated beliefs.

Val took it into her head, one day, to attend mass at St. Dunstan's, a Roman Catholic Church three blocks from her apartment. She came away feeling good, as though she'd made a positive decision, as though she'd opened a present for herself containing contentment. She took to going to St. Dunstan's at odd hours when no mass was being celebrated. The religion seemed so sensible, somehow, so cut and dried. You sinned, you confessed, a priest listened, you atoned, you rejoiced in forgiveness. A well-structured religion, she thought, everything designed to fall right into place. It even crossed her mind that she could take instruction, become a *bona fide* congregant. She confided this one day to Father Ryan who took her hand, held it, pressed it, looked deeply into her eyes and said, "You must be very certain. It's an important step, but one you won't regret."

Two or three times a week she slipped into St. Dunstan's to sit and contemplate divine love and her feelings for Father Bill Ryan, which, she had to admit, were far from pious. She sat in a pew near the back, thinking, dreaming, observing — not praying, certainly, for the salvation of her wretched soul. How did one pray, she wondered, to not think about something that gave her such a rush? She had yet to reach that level of involvement with the divinities.

Still, she was beginning to have a sense of necessity, of fulfillment. She often caught herself smiling and wondered if anyone noticed.

Sitting at the back of the church she experienced tranquility as her benevolent gaze took in the painted statuary, the colourful windows depicting a cubist's version of Christ among modern-day people, the walls of the nave (an unfortunate salmon pink, not that it mattered), and the ceiling, stuccoed in turquoise, aglitter with flecks of something sparkly. She attended mass regularly, getting the hang of it, shaking hands with Father Bordini, the pastor, who asked her whether she was new to the parish, and she said yes.

By early May, Father Bill's book was ready for the typesetter. "Shouldn't we celebrate this?" he asked. He was sitting across a desk from her, grinning boyishly, leaning on his elbows, head tilted. Val wasn't sure whether it was the innocence of his smile she couldn't resist, or the intense blue of his gentle gaze.

"I'll cook dinner for you," she blurted.

"You'd do that?"

"I'd be delighted to."

He lowered his eyelashes studiously. "I would have to get back to you about this. Do you mind?"

Val did not mind, in fact she didn't really believe he would accept. Nevertheless, two evenings later, by the time he rang her buzzer at seven o'clock, proffering a bottle of wine, she had changed from her skirt and low-cut blouse to tight-fitting pants and a turtleneck, and then back again to blouse and skirt. She had developed feverish red spots on her cheeks. She pressed the start button on her record player stacked with enough chaste music to last the evening, beginning with something divine from Bach, moving through Vivaldi, to Miles Davis, Joni Mitchell, and finally (she couldn't resist) Led Zeppelin.

The dinner did not live up to her expectations. The chicken was overcooked and tasted like papier-mâché; the vegetables, undercooked, were the consistency of bullets, and the dessert was runny. Father Bill dutifully and appreciatively packed it all away. The wine, however, was more than acceptable. They downed it and opened the bottle Val had in her fridge. Meanwhile, Val allowed her brain to slack off into neutral while "Stairway to Heaven" wafted through the speakers.

It didn't really come as any surprise to her — after sharing the better part of two bottles of wine, that just plain Bill by now, humming to the music, told her that the only thing he missed from the secular world was dancing, and that he longed to dance with her — although it did give her pause.

They left the table, kicked off their shoes, and fell a little drunkenly into each other's arms. His lips nibblingly close to her ear, he murmured, "I have dreams about you." She wanted to tell him she dreamt about him, too, but some latent moral instinct must have held her back. She moved her head away to look at him.

"I adore you," he breathed, holding her tightly against him.

It should not have shocked her, either, to hear him whisper next, "I want to go to bed with you."

Hold on! Her mind kicked in. She was sober enough to reason that priests did not do this. Sin now, pay later was only a sidebar. It had not been mapped out in the table of contents.

As he deftly undid the buttons of her blouse she couldn't rid her mind of the near life-sized crucified Christ writhing on a golden cross at the front of St. Dunstan's, raspberry blood gushing from his side, and dripping from a thorny crown into his eyes upturned in tormented ecstasy.

Admittedly, besides her nighttime dreams, she had day-dreamed of this moment, but never, in her wildest erotic fantasies, had she envisaged Father Bill Ryan removing his clerical collar, unzipping his sacred trousers, exposing his cherubic buttocks to her spiritually muddled, half-naked self. She recognized, too late, that what she had wanted was to witness him in the role of martyr in the passion play of her life. She wanted him torn, and, yes, tormented. And yet she always imagined him gently but firmly turning from her, sacrificing his baser needs to the greater glory of God — or at the very least, putting up a bit of a moral battle before succumbing to the magnetic temptation of her charms.

Instead, he panted rapturously as he wrestled his way into her underwear. It was the giddy brink of temptation she had sought, not a willing fuck.

Afterwards, still unrepentant, he asked her if she had any cigarettes. She hadn't.

She never saw him again. He phoned to apologize. He told her that he was being transferred to Kapuskasing, and gave her his forwarding address and phone number. She sent him the galleys. His book came out in the fall to not very significant acclaim. And that was that.

IN THE WEEKS following Ed's death, going from room to room in her house, her feet followed a pattern that took her through each step of the tragic event as if they were Stations of the Cross where, wordlessly, she acknowledged her guilt, hoped vainly for self-forgiveness, dreamed of doing penance.

The days turned into nights, seemingly endless because she wakened so often in spite of the sleeping pills her doctor had prescribed. But eventually day showed up again and the whole march of moments went forward. What wakened her in the night were the phantom sounds of Ed's breathing, his soft snores. And her sense of smell played her up: a lingering pleasant male scent, part sweat, part sawdust, wafted over her in the night, and the smell of coffee in the early morning because Ed had usually been the first one downstairs. She lay there for a moment wondering if Ed had a spirit, and if, in life, it had felt unloved. Would it know what had happened, know that his wife had failed to be a responsible citizen, that her carelessness had cut him off in his prime? She sometimes lay in bed until noon.

Early in September Robert phoned to ask when she thought she would be ready to return to work. "I don't want to put pressure on you — you realize that, I hope — but, in many respects, it would be good for you to have something else to occupy your thoughts." She agreed. She knew he was right. He said, "I've got a manuscript here that might interest you. Shall I courier it over?"

"Well —."

"Let me know what you think of it."

She agreed to get back to him either the next day or the day after that. She sat beside the phone after hanging up and thought she might quit her job. He said he hadn't wanted to pressure her, but that was precisely what he had done. He was no different from anyone else; all he thought about was getting the job done and moving on to the next. She couldn't go back to work. It would intrude. She didn't have time for work. Her days were filled to capacity with grief. Grieving and a need for atonement had become her way of life. In the mirror those mornings she saw a woman bereft of husband, of youth, of her vision of her perfect child. She was a woman who had killed her husband. Nothing more, nothing less.

She found herself wondering if some people were surrounded by an aura that caused or attracted accidents. Maybe she was one of them. There was a memory that stood out in bold relief, that haunted her now when she thought about the state of her marriage. It was of an incident that had happened a few years ago. She had dropped by her husband's shop on a Saturday morning to get his opinion, to make a final decision on something, carpet samples, she thought. His office was in an industrial complex in the west end, in a barn-like structure that housed his supplies, his workshop, his employees. Above it, on the roof, a huge annoying sign declared (she longed to edit it): Kustom Kitchens and Kabinets.

She was greeted by one of the carpenters who worked for him. Through the large glass window that overlooked the shop, she could see Ed in his office talking on the phone, his desk a clutter of blueprints and measurements and invoices, above it a faded, slightly tattered poster advising that accidents don't just happen. Sean, the carpenter, began telling her a complicated story about his son getting blamed at school for something he hadn't done. He enjoyed talking. He liked to make a short story long, and he had to shout because of noise from the router he had been using before she came in but hadn't turned off. Elsewhere, tools whined and a large industrial fan roared.

Val kept glancing toward the office, hinting that she'd like to talk to her husband, but the story dragged on. To be polite she shouted the occasional, *oh, my gosh*, and, *how unfair*. She had never seen the place so busy on a Saturday. Someone operating a forklift had stopped near them to raise a stack of plywood onto a shelf above them.

She wasn't sure whether Ed knew she was there, so intent was he on his telephone conversation. She could see him in profile, gesticulating, glaring at the poster. He was definitely unhappy with the caller. She'd never really seen him so animated. He rarely lost his temper at home and if he did, it was more of a sulk. He was so handsome like that, she thought. Thrilling. She had a sudden impulse to run in and throw her arms around him, seduce him right in front of his workmen.

As this thought formed, Ed suddenly turned to face the window. His eyes bugged; his mouth opened; he pointed wildly at something above her. She turned in time to see the load of plywood tipping off the shelf above, sliding toward her. Sean looked up at the same time and shouted. They both leapt quickly out of the way as the top three sheets clattered to the floor with a crash and bounce landing almost where she'd been standing.

Ed was beside her, anxious, holding her against him, asking if she was okay, scarcely giving Sean a glance. She could feel his heart beating as fast as her own. He searched her eyes to make sure she was all right and at that moment, whatever doubts she might have had about him vanished. At that moment Val knew she was cherished.

The forklift operator was white with mortification. Ed yelled, "You could have killed someone!" He left Val, then, to question the forklift operator. "How did this happen?" she heard him say as, shaking, knees weak, she went into Ed's office to sit down. The phone was off the cradle. She put it to her ear.

"I know you're there, Eddy," a voice rasped, a woman's voice, she thought, but wasn't sure.

"Hello?" Val said.

Click went the line and she was cut off.

Ed came back into his office while she was still holding the dead phone. He took it from her and hung up.

"Who was that on the phone?" Val asked.

"No one," he said. "An unhappy client."

"Whoever it was called you Eddy."

"I've been called worse. You win some, you lose some."

They discussed the carpet samples for a few moments, Ed leaning toward beige. Val wanted something bolder, more vibrant. Looking at her watch, she gave in. She had promised to drop in on Denise.

When she told her friend about the strange voice on the phone, someone who called her husband Eddy, Denise said, "Maybe he's having an affair."

"With an older woman, I suppose." Val scoffed at the idea. She said, "Ed is the last person who would — he's just not the type."

"I didn't know there was only the one type," Denise said.

Val tried to explain what she meant, that Ed was so shy, such an introvert, that she'd never seen him even glance at another woman. "He just wouldn't."

After a moment Denise nodded. "You're right. He wouldn't." The two friends looked at each other, palms up, eyebrows up. In the convenient little house she shared with her husband and their daughter, in the smart kitchen put in by Ed, Denise had made tea and put some chocolate chip cookies on a plate. She put a hand up to ward off Val saying anything about diets. "My theory is," Denise said, "if it tastes good, eat it. Diets should only be undertaken with food you despise."

And so Ed was exempted from the class of men who had affairs. All he had was a cranky client who phoned him and called him Eddy. The cookies disappeared.

four

IN THE LITTLE TOWN of Falkirk, snug and snowy this evening in late December, the restaurant Val happens upon is entirely to her liking — warm, good smells of good food, not busy. She has brought along her journal. She has taken to carrying the red notebook, which fits into her oversized handbag, nearly everywhere she goes. Writing in it has become a solace, something of a confessional. It lies open on the table at a fresh page, dauntingly white. Carefully she writes the date. She has made a pact with herself to put down only her truest thoughts within these pages, although at the moment her mind is a blank. She writes that her mind is a blank. Sometimes she tells her writers that the truth, if it is to sound true, has to be exaggerated for the sake of the story. The bald truth, certainly, is often a little flat. It is one thing, though, to face the truth in all its starkness and then mould it to suit your own purposes, and quite another to come up against the truth and categorically deny it, to invent a new reality for yourself out of necessity, one you can live with. She finds herself writing this into her book as well. As the central character in her own life she is not without practice in the art of self-deception. After Ed's death, she once bought two pork chops, on purpose, not from a memory lapse, and another time two baking potatoes, as if by providing the food to feed him, she would lure back her husband. Later, guiltily, she wrapped the uncooked food in layers of plastic bags, put it in the garbage, and opened a can of soup.

Sitting with pen in hand, her journal ripe for a fresh thought, Val knows when her mental state began to improve. By early September she was able to picture some future version of herself going about her business, returning alone to the house, living moment by moment, one instant piling up against the next, until time constructed a bridge over which she would be allowed to pass from her present grief to something simpler, brighter, where it would be all right to smile. I am going to recover, she thought. It was as if a drain had been opened or redirected.

IT WAS IN THIS FRAME of mind that September day that Val ventured forth and bought herself the coiled notebook. On her return she found the heavy manuscript Robert had sent by courier in a plain brown wrapper. It had been left between her doors. She slit open the package, read the first page and sat down with it, still wearing her jacket. She read the second page and reached for the phone to call Robert. When he came on she asked, "Where did it come from?"

"The manuscript?"

"Who or what is A. A. McNiall?"

"No idea."

The title page said simply: *A Novel by A. A. McNiall*. An unknown entity. No title, no address, no phone number. Picked from the slush pile, the manuscript had been placed in Robert's hands by one of the freelancers who read for Dobbs, Kendall.

"I thought it might take your fancy," Robert said slyly. "When are you coming back to work?"

"I don't know." She turned to page three. "I'll read this first. Maybe tomorrow. Maybe the day after. Hefty little thing, isn't it?" She checked the back of the book. "Five hundred and thirty-odd pages. How do we get in touch with A. A. McNiall? Was there a covering letter?"

"Apparently not. Or if there was, it's gone. It's not bad, is it? I've only read a chapter or two, but it made my ears hum. Needs a lot of work, I suspect."

That is how Robert recognized good or important work — his ears hummed, a characteristic Val felt was more a feminine thing than masculine, although who could say? For herself, when she sat down with a manuscript of great promise, she experienced an instant and tremendous ache around her heart, or at least somewhere deep inside — a longing, a thirst, a hunger — she could never pin it down to any one thing, but she knew when it was there.

"More your type of thing," Robert said.

And it was. Val knew even from the first three pages that it could turn out to be a worthy book, a book with a life of its own — something she would wish she had written. A. A. McNiall, whoever he was, could do more than turn a phrase. Maybe it was a woman. Women often used their initials. Reading on, she tried to get a sense of the author, but couldn't — a good sign, really. The work existed for its own sake.

She stayed up far into the night to read, collapsing into bed, finally, with only a little over a hundred pages to go.

Robert had made himself a copy, she knew, and wondered if he had stayed up half the night to read, too. The story had her firmly gripped, although it was too long. She was already honing her editorial paring knife. Told in part by a reclusive man in his forties, eccentric, bewildered by life, and in part by a woman slightly younger, who goes headlong in all the wrong directions, it was about the way we are tossed this way and that through mere coincidence while we continue to believe that we manipulate our own fate. The lives of the two protagonists ran, for the most part, on parallel but separate planes, except periodically, when through some accident of fate, they collided, with often touching, sometimes disastrous, occasionally comedic results. It was set in Toronto during the Second World War. Reading, Val found herself at times deeply moved and at other times, chuckling. Once she hooted a laugh, an unusual sound in her mournful house. It's good, she thought, although far from perfect. It read like a first novel. There were more than a few problems with time sequence, but it was good. Already she was itching for a second novel by this author. She liked the characters. She felt she knew them, or someone like them. A quiver of excitement. She used to believe that life's phases came prepackaged. If it was true, she might well have just taken delivery of the next portion of her life.

And then a cautionary voice. *Is the book actually that good? Can you really trust your own mind after all that's happened?*

Maybe she was reading into it something that wasn't there. It was a question of judgment after all, and who could say how sound hers was anymore. She flipped randomly through the manuscript, reading passages, skimming. Events unfolded, it seemed, somewhat episodically — not necessarily a good thing in a novel, but she would reserve her ruling on that until she finished it. In any case, the characters were vividly alive. She related to their loneliness, their small embarrassments, their joys and sorrows. It was like one of those novels she remembered from a time before she read would-be books for a living, when she read for pleasure. It was a book she would be sorry to see end.

She had a moment of panic when she reached the final page. Where had she hung her cloak of guilt while she had been submerged naked in this alter-world, this true-fiction? Mentally, she groped. She needed to be able to reach for it still, to know that even if it was wearing thin, even if it was almost transparent, that she could pull it over her, nevertheless, like a camouflage, when life got a little too distracting, a little too enjoyable. The manuscript would become a book, she knew, was capable of becoming quite a good book, she was convinced, and based on past experience, she would during this process live a life full to overflowing. If she chose.

It was the manuscript's potency that drew her back to work. Not only was she under the spell of the potential book and her intuition about its success, but she was also captivated by the mystery surrounding the author. She was enticed by her own curiosity. She had a reason to keep breathing in and out, to be part of the world.

The day after she finished reading the manuscript she made her way, like a stranger to the ways of the city, hesitantly, from her house to the bus, perching uncertainly on the edge of a seat, hanging on to the back of the seat in front of her as she darted wary looks out the windows for landmarks she'd barely noticed in her previous existence as a married woman, a working woman. From the bus she descended to the subway, hunched, ready for and expecting a crisis; sped to her destination, her heart keeping pace with the clatter of metal on metal; ascended to the world of downtown streets, bristling, jostling, alive with every race on the face of the earth. She felt her chest moving with each heartening breath. She plunged into the melee. She thrust her head forward, one arm swinging (the other hampered by her briefcase), feet finding their own path, occasionally zigging when she should have zagged, feeling inexplicably buoyed up now, as though the throng breathed life into her. In this way she marched up the front steps of the building where she worked, a former Victorian house squashed between a high-rise and a parking lot, and pulled open a heavy oak door, beside which a brass plate announced Dobbs, Kendall, Publishers, and began to tackle the business of being in the world.

She flopped A. A. McNiall's manuscript, held together not very tidily with an elastic band, onto her strangely uncluttered desk (Robert had dealt with and finished her last project) with a sense of — she couldn't deny it — exhilaration. Part of her morning was spent trying to trace A. A. McNiall, but no one by that name existed in the city of Toronto. Well, there was one, A. J. McNiall. She let it ring, expecting her call to be picked up by an answering machine. Instead a man came on who spoke in a high-pitched monotone.

She said, "May I speak with Mr. or Mrs. McNiall, please."

"No. No-no-no-no-no. Gone for good. No more ringing the phone."

She phoned the first-reader, who had searched her office, indeed her entire house, for some clue, a letter, a scrap of paper, but nothing was forthcoming. She went to the library, looked through the phone books of other major cities in Canada, found some similar names, with slightly different spellings, but no one named A. A. McNiall.

"She'll phone," Robert said. "Or write."

He was convinced that the author was a woman; Val was almost sure it was a man.

"There's a certain intuitiveness," Robert insisted, "that points to a woman."

"You can't go by intuitiveness. Everybody's intuitive these days. No. I think only a man could have written the male character — Burke. He's perfect the way he has this unshakable confidence in himself even when he mismanages things. And the way he retreats into his own world so easily, without a backward glance. It has to be a man."

"I don't think a man could have been so bang on with the young woman — Annie Carmichael," Robert argued. He had read the entire manuscript by now, too. "The way she thinks she's bent on one mission, when in fact she's hot on the trail of something else, and the way she makes not just both sides of a question look plausible, but always finds a third point of view just to muddy it even more."

"Men have been writing women for eons," Val insisted.

"Don't overlook the humour," Robert said. "To me, it's feminine."

"I think humour is gender-free."

"Maybe you're right. Maybe good writing is gender-free."

"Virginia Woolf thought so."

"Well, who am I to argue?"

And so it went. The discussion, the mystery, her reaction to Robert's analysis, served to sweep her into taking a firm grip on the life they shared, to take a big bite out of it for the sustenance that was in it. "Maybe," she suggested, "it's actually A. and A. McNiall. Raggedy Ann and Andy. A mom-and-pop operation."

Robert went back to his own office, eyes aimed at the ceiling, not deigning to reply.

Thinking about the manuscript, rereading passages when she should have been moving on to the next piece of work kept her spirits up for a time, at least. When she acknowledged her lack of success in dredging up the author, when she admitted to herself that there was nothing further to be done with the manuscript except wait and hope that A. A. McNiall would phone or write, she began, almost imperceptibly to wilt, to return to a state of preoccupation.

MARSH LOOKED IN on her from time to time, dropping by for a drink on the weekends. After a late day at the office, she and Robert occasionally would take themselves out for dinner. Sometimes Marsh joined them. On one such occasion, noticing her inattention to the conversation, Marsh said, "You're brooding. What can we do for you? Out with it."

Her eyes filled up without warning. "Sorry," she said. The tears, she was shocked to admit, were for herself just then. She had become someone who must not be allowed to brood, someone who was deemed to need sympathy. She was pathetic.

Both men looked disconcerted. Robert poured more wine into her glass. Marsh said, "I know a really good psychotherapist. I only mention this because I know from experience how hard it is to get over grief or to stop obsessing over something or someone. This guy is excellent, or, if you would prefer to talk to a woman, I'm sure he would be able to direct you to someone. I'd trust him with my life."

Val sniffed indelicately, swallowed some wine, and tried to smile. She put her hand on Marsh's arm. "Thanks. Maybe you're right. Maybe I should see someone."

He wrote for a moment on the back of one of his own business cards a name and phone number and handed it to her. She took it gratefully. They managed to get through the rest of the meal without incident and Val insisted she was fine to go home on her own. Robert hailed a cab for her.

She thought about phoning the therapist, considered it, off and on, for two weeks. She tried to imagine what such a person might say, how a therapist might diagnose her present inability to come to grips with her loss. She imagined him, or possibly her, using stock phrases: "You have to give yourself permission to grieve. Time is the great healer. Closure won't come until you admit your husband is gone." Or she imagined a more aggressive approach: "You feel guilty. You believe you caused his death. What's more, you parted from him that day in a state of resentment. You must atone."

It was that authoritative voice she ultimately listened to. She had neglected to act upon her better judgment. She must pay the price. She gave up any pretence of seeking professional help. Instead, she acknowledged that she had put herself through a substantive analysis and in so doing had found the root of the problem — as any editor worth her salt would. Through the Provincial Police in Orillia, who still felt a deep and sincere pity for her, she was able to obtain the names and addresses of the other people involved in the accident. She would write to them, perhaps visit them, discover ways to help them recover from the effects of the accident.

There had been four other vehicles besides Ed's van involved. Among the injured were two teenage brothers driving a station wagon, a woman, fortyish, who had been a passenger in her husband's car (he was unhurt), and the driver of a pickup truck — a man in his seventies. The driver of the transport truck had walked away unhurt. Val sent letters to each of the injured explaining that she had lost her husband, and that she thought it would help her to accept his death, if she could do something helpful for the others involved. She did not confess in her letters to neglecting to remove the beam from the road. She would do that in person, she thought.

Her first reply was a kind letter from the mother of the teenaged boys. They were recovering nicely, apparently. One had suffered a broken collarbone and a slight concussion and the other a fractured tibia. The mother sympathized with Val's plight. *"I know just how helpless you must feel. My husband and my boys are so precious to me. I know I'd almost curl up and die if anything happened to them. Thank God they're doing fine."* She offered Val comforting words, advised her to become born-again in the arms of Jesus, thanked her for inquiring, and that was that. Val refolded the letter with a sense of deflation, not that she wished the boys to be worse off than they were, but ever since writing the letters she had felt the great Sisyphean weight she'd been pushing against become lighter. It had not exactly reached the top of the figurative hill, nor did it give any indication of disappearing entirely. It was resting, it seemed, on an unexpected plateau. This gave her time to straighten her back, loosen up her shoulders, look around.

The next day, a Saturday, she received a phone call at home from the woman who had been a passenger in the small car. "Are you that lady that wrote to me?" she asked. Val gave her name.

"Yeah, that's right, well, I just wanted to say that you have more nerve than enough writing a letter like that. Who do you think you are? God Almighty? As if *you* could actually do something to help me when the doctors can't even help, not that they try very hard."

"Oh dear," Val said sympathetically when the woman stopped to draw a breath. "Why? What's wrong?" She was ashamed of the tiniest spark of self-centred hope in her voice and cleared her throat to erase it.

"What's wrong? What isn't wrong? I got pains up and down my legs all night so's I can't sleep and my neck's so stiff from the whiplash that I can't hardly turn my head, and my insides are all jumbled up. Nothing works right the way it used to. And do you think I can get a lawyer to sue anyone? No, sir. Not a chance. They all say it was an accident and no one was at fault, it was that hunk of wood lying in the road and nobody knows where it came from. Well, I don't think anyone made any attempt to find out that little piece of information, so I don't. And then you come along and write me this weirdo letter like you want to help me somehow, and I say to myself, Bunny, I say, she's got something up her sleeve. She wants something."

Val broke in, "But, you don't understand. I don't want anything from you, I just want to make amends, if I can, if

65

it's within my power to do so, for that piece of wood being in the road, causing the accident."

"Do you know where it came from?"

"No, I don't," Val said.

There was a pause. Then: "Right. I just bet you don't. You're covering for somebody, aren't you? That letter you wrote's got guilt written all over it."

Val was shocked into silence. The guilt was real enough. The woman continued to speculate on how the beam happened to be in the road, about why Val wanted to keep it hushed up, and to reiterate the list of each of her many ailments. At length, when she could get a word in, Val, said, "My husband was killed in that accident. Why would I be protecting anyone else when I couldn't even protect him? I saw the beam lying in the road when I passed it in my own car five minutes before the accident. I didn't stop. I didn't pull it off the road." There was a pause as the woman took this in.

"You really are a shit, aren't you?"

"Yes, I am," Val admitted. Being called a shit was something, at least. "Thank you," Val said.

"Right," the woman said and hung up.

five

THE NEW DAY IS crisp and colder than the day before. Val feels invigorated after her deep and uninterrupted sleep on the surprisingly comfortable motel mattress. She forgot to set the clock radio last night, but it's not so late. At the stoplight, she turns right as the motel proprietor told her to. Snow glistens on all sides. The plow and sanding operators must, indeed, have gone on strike, as the road, except for a few car tracks, is pristine. She will take her time and drive safely. The snow on the road is not terribly deep, ten or fifteen centimetres at most. Anyway, with four-wheel drive, she's not worried; she can get through anything. She is less nervous about driving through snow on the ground than she was yesterday driving through snow pelting her windshield, blinding her.

She can see how windy it is, the snow leaping into excited swirls like a cat after a bird, then settling down, crouching, anticipating the next thrill.

She is trying to justify the purpose of her trip. She won't actually kick the woman out into the snow. She'll explain to her that she cannot maintain a second house. She's sorry, of course, but Ed had been far too generous, far too long. She'll make sure the woman has somewhere to go. She thinks, if it came to it, she could put her up in her own house in Toronto for a short time, until she found a new place. Not a pleasant prospect, and she hopes it won't come to that because she dislikes the woman — at least she thinks she would not like the woman who came to the reception after the funeral.

After the reception, after everyone had gone, Val asked her aunt if the woman had introduced herself. She hadn't.

Millie said, "Lord knows, I tried to get information out of her. Lips shut tighter than a car door. I said to her, 'You poor dear, had you known Ed a long time,' to which she wept fresh tears and rooted around in her bag for a hanky. I said, 'Now wait right there and I'll go get some Kleenex,' but by the time I got back to the dining room, she'd gone. I asked Denise if she'd seen her, and she said she thought she saw her going upstairs. Well, I thought, I can hardly hound her right into the bathroom. And that's the last I saw of her. If you want my opinion, I think she's an old girlfriend. Never got over him; carrying a torch all these years."

"Oh, Aunt Millie," Val sighed. "You've been watching the soaps." Nevertheless, she envies her aunt her imagination, her glib chatter, her ready small talk. Val, herself, has almost lost her ability to chat about anything other than books. She hasn't always been so close-mouthed and has sometimes blamed it on Ed and his unwillingness to communicate, feeling that she caught it from him, like a virus.

With people in the book industry, she's fine. In her day-to-day work she is comfortable with facts. She relies on facts, or at the very least, concretely based suppositions. In her work, she has to. Even in a piece of highly imaginative fiction, A and B must add up to C, or something very C-like.

And now she has this woman to contend with, clearly a fact, but a leftover issue that does not fit in anywhere. She had the distinct impression that she looked older than Ed, partly from the layers of makeup she wore, but partly too, from the way she carried herself, as if she were wearing armour, had struggled into an old corset that barely fit.

Thinking about meeting the woman, or at least meeting the resident of the house, causes an excited tremor to ripple just under her skin. She is having an adventure. Actually, she is having a hot flash and puts the window down for a minute or two and waits for the wild tingling sensation that accompanies it to dissipate.

She passes through several small villages, one a crossroads only, another fairly substantial, a population of eight hundred, the sign tells her. She cannot imagine living in a place that small and wonders what the inhabitants do with their spare time; watch their colour televisions in stunning green, gold, and pink, she decides, and increase the population, perhaps, during the commercials.

The road is hers now, hers the only car on it. As the motel proprietor said it would, it runs straight north. She can tell by the position of the morning sun, brilliant in the arc of overhead blue. The sun beaming through the window is toasty. She turns down the heater.

Maybe she should let someone know where she is. It's a question of common sense, really. Not that she thinks anything is going to happen to her. The driving conditions don't really frighten her. She'll be fine as long as she remembers to go slowly. And the prospect of knocking on the door of a complete stranger's house, although daunting, isn't life-threatening. Surely. She really is away out in the sticks, up here, though. Sparsely populated. Here and there she sees the occasional log shanty with rubble and parts of household appliances and parts of cars in front, littering the immediate landscape.

She drives into and out of another hamlet before she really has time to take it in. She glimpses a building that could be an old-fashioned schoolhouse with a big bell in a belfry. It is unique in appearing well kept, painted, in fact. None of the log cabins, apart from having junk in the front yard, has a lived-in look, nothing homey about them. Their windows glower forbiddingly, blind-eyed. She will take the next opportunity to pull off the road to phone Robert on her cellphone and tell him where she is and what she's up to.

But why phone Robert? What would she say? *Just wanted you to know where I am in case of accident.* Isn't that asking for trouble? No, she decides; what that is, is superstition. The road climbs and soon she comes to a signpost pointing left, "Dogwood Station 20 km." She veers left onto a narrower, rougher road, and decreases her speed.

The area is almost mountainous. How little of the earth's surface we really know, she thinks. We travel the same ant-tracks most of our lives. She feels, today, as if she's forging a new inland route to the icy North Pole. The road has been built high along the rise of a valley. To the left, in the distance, she sees a ridge of land parallel to and higher than the one she's on. She wonders if there is a road along that ridge, if log shanties dot its landscape, or if its world is something entirely different, full of trolls and giants and the occasional sleeping castle.

The road runs through dense forests of pine, and in the valley below a river flows, ice forming at its edges. High in the trees, gusts riffle pats of snow nesting on outspread boughs. Christmas card fodder. She wishes she had her camera. The wind, though, is intent on stripping the trees back to their bare essentials, snow flying off like a sudden sneeze.

Snow-filled clouds begin moving in, knitting themselves across the patch of sky she can see through the windshield. Perhaps it's the lowering sky that makes her feel hemmed in, or maybe the forest is becoming more dense. On the left of the road where the shoulder slopes down and away toward the valley, she glimpses a log hut through the trees, no clearing around it, no discernible road in. Something primal in all of this, she thinks, the setting for evil spells and naive young wanderers.

The wind, fierce now, bullies snow from the road's shoulders across her path. She no longer has the tracks of a previous vehicle to follow. She keeps an eye on the outer edges chiselled out of the highland ridge. On her right where the shoulder sinks into a ditch and then meets a rise, she looks up to see between the trees, large stones, boulders really, poised on the slope — eight or ten of them — huge things, the size of Volkswagens. She slows to study them, stops in fact, looking back. They lie, wakeful, on a snowy counterpane. Splotches of snow clinging to their leeward sides, they stand guard above the road. They have an unsettled look as if they still remember the force that moved them ages ago, as if they are waiting for another chance to roll. Shivering, she turns up the heater and moves on slowly. If one of them rolled down onto the road, she thinks, she'd be here the rest of her life, her work cut out for her trying forever to lever it off.

She has no idea how far she's come since the sign that said it was twenty kilometres to Dogwood Station. She has forgotten to keep track. It's beginning to snow, a disheartening turn of events. Her earlier buoyant mood has dissipated; in fact, she is, quite frankly, uneasy. This is a fool's errand, she now thinks. She should have had her lawyer attempt to get in touch with the person. She would like to turn around and go back — although she's come this far; it would be a shame not to carry through with it. But, no. If she sees a place to turn around, she will. She's in a bit of a lather, again. She puts the window down half way, letting snow blow in to cool her face.

The road is so hilly and narrow she doesn't dare risk making a U-turn, even though she hasn't seen a car in the last half hour. She goes around a bend, her eyes scanning the area for a widening, or a driveway, and begins to negotiate a fairly long series of hills. She thinks she sees something on the road ahead of her, just over the next rise. She feels a familiar panic and tells herself to calm down, it's only a dog. She wills it to run off. She's lost sight of it because of the hill she's now climbing, but just over the brow, it's suddenly there, looking at her, defiant, showing no fear. It's not a dog at all, she realizes as she presses on the brake pedal — it's a wolf.

In her excitement over seeing at first hand an actual wolf, and in the accompanying, unexpected childish frisson of primal fear it inspires, she tries to stop, remembering too late to pump the brake lightly. The car begins to spin in what feels to her like slow motion. Inside the car she has become superfluous; the car has a will of its own. Its interior enlarges, it seems, making her feel tiny. She has a sensation of being weightless, as if she's floating, an astronaut launched in space, an insignificant speck inside a vault — or an atom of sand in a boulder.

It takes a moment before she understands that the car has come to rest. Her Alice-like shrinkage has reversed itself, putting her and the car's interior back into proper perspective. The car is nose down in the ditch on the right side (in more ways than one) of the road. Had it gone off to the left, it would have tumbled down, end over end, into the ravine.

She feels very calm inside the car now chillingly quiet, abruptly still. She takes stock of her situation. She knows she can find a solution. Firstly, she is not hurt. The car is still running, so she must turn it off and remove the key. She will try to open the door. It opens. She will get out. Oh — first she will undo the seat belt. Now she gets out and wonders if she should, in fact, get back in, in view of the fact that the forest is teeming, apparently, with wolves. Cautiously, she creeps up out of the ditch to check the road, taking her handbag with her.

She tucks in her scarf, zips up her thigh-length leather jacket, turns up the collar, and pulls her gloves out of her pockets. Dogwood Station can't be too much farther. The wind is nippy. She doesn't have a hat, but she could put her scarf over her head if need be. Up and down the hills she goes, looking left, looking right. Ahead she sees a sign — Dogwood Station. No indication of population. No station. In the distance, she spies a frame house with a sign above the porch roof — General Store — and makes for that.

She enters through the porch, unfurnished except for toppling towers of empty cartons. Above the door someone, festively, has swagged a green and red twist of crêpe paper, a faded memento of Christmas. She tries the door into the house, finds it unlocked and goes in. No one's about. No bell to ring. On half-empty shelves she sees dusty ketchup and mustard bottles and cans of fruit with unfamiliar old-fashioned-looking labels. There is a freezer against one wall. Above it is a sign that commands, "Shut It." She can hear a television behind a door on the far side of the counter and wonders if she should go around and knock. Instead she calls, "Hello?" Her voice sounds timid. She calls again, louder. In a moment an old woman sticks her head around the door, startled to see her, and like a turtle, quickly withdraws it. "Bessie!" the woman croaks with surprising vigour from behind the door, and in a moment another woman, younger, somewhat slatternly, takes her place behind the counter. "Yeah?" she says. "What'ja like?"

Val has not rehearsed in her mind how she will ask directions to her destination, and of course has no inkling of the name of the woman who came to the funeral. Not only that, she has left her briefcase with the deed giving the lot and concession numbers of the house behind in her marooned car.

"Yes, um," she begins, "I'm looking for a house that my husband owned. He died in a car accident a few months ago, and I wanted to get in touch with the person who lives in the house. I'm afraid I don't know much more about her — I think it's a woman — than that she's — well, sixtyish, maybe sixty-five, a little stout and has, um, black, possibly dyed, hair. She came to the funeral, but didn't stay long enough to introduce herself."

"Hmmf!" the woman snorts. The door behind her opens a crack. A hoarse voice whispers loudly, "Ask her what name."

"As I say, I don't know her name," Val volunteers immediately.

"The husband's name, the husband's name," the old crone whispers fiercely from behind the door.

"*My* husband's name?" Val asks the younger woman behind the counter.

"Her husband's name?" the woman inquires over her shoulder.

"Yes, ask her that, ask her that," the old woman returns.

"My husband's name, was Ed Fennel, Edward James Fennel."

"Hee, hee, hee," she hears, as the old one expresses the amusement this information affords her.

The younger woman is not amused, however. Scowling, she grumbles, "You mighta known it woulda been them Fennels."

"Pardon me?" Val feels her protective hackles rising. Her husband's name is known to this woman, it seems. She doesn't like her tone and is not about to take any abuse from this rustic, this hillbilly. "Do you know the house I mean?"

The woman folds her arms, biceps bulging over barrel chest. "If it's the Fennel place you want, you already passed it comin' in. It's out there half a mile almost, up the hill. Y'gotta look up."

"What does it look like?" Val asks. "I don't want to miss it again."

"She's a beaut," the woman says. Val doesn't know whether she's praising it or being sarcastic, but the woman assures her that she can't miss it. "It's the only one between here and the next place."

"Thank you," Val said.

"Ain't nobody home, far as I know."

Val looks bewildered.

"Could be back by now," the younger woman offers.

"That's true."

Val decides she'll take her chances. "Oh!" Val is about to leave but remembers, stunned that she could have momentarily forgotten. "I've put my car in the ditch. Is there a garage or towing service around here I could call?"

The woman stares vacantly, slack-mouthed. "What?"

From behind the door, the old woman rasps, "Rhys, down the valley."

The young woman says crossly over her shoulder, "He'll be gone out."

"Might come out from over Falkirk way, there," says the crone.

Val is relieved to get a straight response. "Do you have a phone book?" She will call a garage on her cellphone and takes it out of her handbag.

"Doubt they'll come today, though." The old woman, tiny and wizened, joins the younger woman behind the counter, which is as high as her shoulders. She nods at a scene behind Val through the window. Val turns to look. A whirlwind of snow greets her eyes. As fast as it comes down, the wind blows it back up. It looks like a solid wall of snow.

"It came up so fast," she says, helplessly.

"That's the way of it," the old woman says.

Val has no idea what she will do. "I think I should at least try to phone someone," she says. The old woman shrugs and looks at her, eyes asquint, her head tilted as if sizing her up and finding her wanting. The younger woman goes through the door and re-emerges with a dog-eared and stained phone book, three years out of date. While the two women keep avid watch she leafs through the tattered yellow pages, finds what she wants and turns on her phone only to discover that she is out of range of a signal. She asks if she can use their phone, but it turns out that they've had their phone disconnected. "She won't put out the money for it," the younger woman says bitterly.

"Hee, hee," the old one chortles. She winks at Val, gleeful in her power.

The only option open to Val, it seems, is to find the Fennel house, phone from there for a tow truck, and hope for the best. She thanks the women for their trouble to which the old one responds with sniggering merriment and the young one with a look of irresolute suspicion. Val puts her scarf over her head, tucks the ends into the neck of her coat, turns up her collar and goes out into the blizzard. She is no longer safe inside a snowy glass ball.

It seems much colder with snow blowing in her face. She retraces her tracks, all but obliterated now by the sweeping wind and snow. It's hard to make out anything distinctly through the fierce whiteness attacking her, biting her cheeks, blinding her, but she plows on, head bent into the wind. She remembers she's supposed to look up if she's to see the house she's tracking down and stops from time to time to check her bearings. She is, quite frankly, worried. She is out of her element. The workings of this part of the world are beyond her ken and there is no usage manual to tell her how to correct this dilemma. No punctuation mark strong enough to put a stop to it.

As she trudges along, though, head tucked into her shoulders, she takes stock of herself. She reminds herself that she is a sensible woman, healthy, strong, and really, she thinks, often quite indomitable, although not without a certain amount of what she thinks of as healthy fear. In the

77

back of her mind, the vision of the wolf takes shape. She pauses to look around, to listen, because she thinks she hears it howling, although it may just be the wind. Up ahead, on the left, she sees a building, but it's only a barn.

As she is passing the barn she looks up the hill, and there it is, a log house, not what she would call "a beaut," in any sense of the word, but she's relieved that it looks a trifle more substantial than many of the houses she's noticed in the area, although it, too, has an unoccupied appearance. Unlike the other log houses, it has an upper storey, stuccoed and half-timbered. A mailbox on the opposite side of the road declares the name "enne."

She starts toward the house thinking, this is it! High noon! She will be very polite, but firm with the occupant, although not obnoxiously firm because she does need help to get her car out of the ditch. Also she has to go to the bathroom. She treks past the barn, breathing hard by now, up the hill between parallel rows of pine trees. Maybe there is no occupant. If this is the driveway, it hasn't been used in a while. The snow is very deep here, over the tops of her boots. Snow filters down to pack around her ankles, so cold it sears her skin. Freezer burn, she thinks. She pulls her fingers out of the ends of her gloves to curl them against her palms for warmth. The gloves look helpless, like scarecrow hands.

The snow is unbroken by footprints. The front window of the house, cut into the huge logs forming the walls, is curtained and not about to give up any secrets. She steps up onto a platform, a front porch of sorts, also deep with snow. No doorbell. No knocker. She knocks politely with her gloved hand making no appreciable sound above the rising wind. She pulls off her glove and tries again, but it's useless.

She tries the latch without success. Look around, she tells herself. There has to be another door. She steps off the low front porch trudging around the side of the house where she spies another window, not very big, high in the wall, unlit. Beyond that is what looks like a snow-clotted screened-in summer sitting area attached to the side of the house. At the back of the house there is a short wooden staircase leading up to a landing and back door. It, too, is locked. She stands dumbly, shivering, beaten, thinking she'll have to pull down her pants and squat bare-assed in the snow. She could easily burst into tears at this point, but she's actually too cold and anyway she has to think. She needs a solution.

The woman will have left a key somewhere. She doesn't know how she knows this, she just knows that that's what she would do. She feels around on a ledge above the door. Nothing. She is shaking with cold. She hunches into her collar, descends to ground level, squeezes her freezing fists under her arms and thinks about the person she believes lives, or has lived, here. She looks under each step and feels up under the supporting framework of the back stoop. A woman in a certain frame of mind, a busy woman, one who has gone away for a few days only, she believes, would hide a key in a place easily accessible, in a fairly obvious hiding place; whereas a distraught woman, a woman who faces a change in her fortunes, might hide it farther away. She remembers the barn she passed down near the road and in desperation plunges through the deep snow, wind whipping icy pellets in her face, trying to blow her off course.

THE BARN DOOR IS latched shut by a rusty nail through a small piece of wood, which she easily flips out of the way. The difficult part is in opening the heavy, teetering door against the force of the wind. She gets a shoulder behind it, forcing it past the midpoint of its swing where the wind takes over, plastering it flat against the side of the barn. Inside, she can barely make out the forms of various nameless pieces of machinery and topsy-turvy furniture. She stands a moment waiting for her eyes to adjust. As they do, Val notices just inside the door what looks like a roughly built corner cupboard. The lower doors are rusted shut, but the upper ones give way to her tugging and inside she finds — besides pieces of rope, twists of wire, a bag of nails, an enamel dish of screws, washers, bolts, wing-nuts — a flowerpot. She pulls it down and hears something rattle. Inside is a key.

She allows the wind to drive her up the lane from the barn to the house, clutching the key in her fist inside her gloves, their fingers hanging like empty teats. There is something compulsive about what she is doing. She wonders if she has played a trick on herself. Could it be that she is looking for another act of contrition? She has a renewed sense of doing something stupid. Apart from her obvious physical need, there is no necessity to get into this empty house, unless she hopes to divine some essence of the anonymous woman by exploring her lair.

One small part of her imagines that this person, whom Ed has been secretly supporting, had him in her thrall, that he would have rid himself of her had he been able. In some half-baked way, she has talked herself into imagining that she can break the enchantment and in accomplishing this, she will bring relief — but to whom? To Ed's soul? She hasn't thought much about souls since her brief infatuation with Roman Catholicism (and Father Bill). In fact, the idea of a soul saddens her. She cannot bear the thought that her husband and her unborn child, in the guise of souls, are in some merry meadow of Heaven cavorting with angels without her. It makes her doubly lonely.

Val stumbles with fatigue up onto the front porch of the house to try to fit the key into the lock, but she's shivering so hard, partly from cold, but also from the discomfort of a full bladder, and her hands are so stiff, that she drops the key into the snow. By now she *is* crying, something she does with less and less provocation these days, and she's swearing as she crouches and removes a glove to search in the snow for the key. It is at this moment that the familiar slow suffusion of excess heat beginning deep inside her abdomen or her chest — her trunk, at any rate — some place where, if she were a tree, sap would emanate, fills her with a harsh tingling, just short of erotic, just short of painful, like electric charges sparking each other and spreading outwards to her limbs and up to her face, warming her, cooking her flesh from the inside out. For the first time since these hot flashes began, almost a year ago, that she has cursed and railed against when they wakened her during the night and embarrassed her during the day, she is overcome with gratitude as she heats up sufficiently to stop shivering, recover the key, and fit it into the lock. She turns it with difficulty, her hands still cold in spite of her personal heat wave, and then she feels rather than hears a click.

She pushes open the heavy door, steps inside, closes it on the wintry wasteland and finds herself enveloped by a different kind of warmth. She is standing in a large room that is barely visible to her. The only light trickles weakly in from the curtained front window and two small ones high up on either side of the room. To her right is a fireplace, further in on the left a staircase. She climbs the stairs, feeling her way in the semi-darkness, praying for indoor plumbing. Her prayers are answered.

Downstairs again, she can now concentrate on her present circumstances. She turns on an electric light. A wall thermostat, she notices, is set a few degrees above the freezing point. She turns it up, and baseboard heaters, clicking and groaning metallically in response, throw out appreciably more heat. She is cheered.

The room is sparsely but weightily furnished with massive pieces — an old-fashioned settee, a couch of immense proportions, a Morris rocker, another clumsy chair or two. One end of the room is dominated by a sturdy-legged table, four carved-back chairs and a monstrous sideboard. Beyond the table is a door leading to a small kitchen, almost an afterthought. It is equipped with all the usual amenities, all old, but clean and in good shape. The fridge is unplugged, the door ajar. Nothing in it but an open box of baking soda. Val is now fairly certain that a woman lives or has lived here. On the wall near the door is a telephone. She picks it up but, disappointingly, there is no dial tone.

Back in the living room she examines the walls. They are made of logs, stripped of bark, stained a warm brown with a lighter brown where the chinking shows in between. To the right of the fireplace, a tattered and faded Union Jack is thumbtacked to the logs. The fireplace is stone all the way to the ceiling and has been meticulously laid with paper, kindling and two small logs ready to be lit. On the ledge of stone serving as a mantel sits an old tobacco tin. She knows before she removes the lid that it will hold matches. Exactly the sort of thing Ed would have done if he were to leave a place like this for an indefinite length of time. Ed was always very organized, always thinking ahead. The woman has not gone forever. She will return this winter, or early spring she surmises, hence the logs laid ready to light.

Val feels very alert, now that she is beginning to thaw. Her brain snaps out decisions and plans. She'll have to go back outside, back to her car, get her suitcase, get the banana she took from the motel and her water. It will suffice. She'll have to act quickly because it will soon be dark, and she must find a house where the phone works — she'll look for lights when she goes out. The snow is letting up.

Not intending to lock up, she carefully puts her handbag in the sideboard. Before closing its cupboard door, she notices something in there at the back, hanging down, as if it has slipped down from the drawer above, a scrap of paper. She'll look later. Right now she has to find a phone.

Outside, as she nears the road, she hears dogs howling in the distance, and then another dog, closer, louder, howls in response. Val stops. She listens, heart pounding. She wastes no more time but turns around, galloping back up the lane, onto the porch, yanks open the door and slams it behind her. *Those aren't dogs, you idiot.*

She will get up early in the morning, she decides, and go looking for a phone by daylight. If necessary, she'll walk back to the last village.

She builds up the fire and thinks about where she will sleep tonight, upstairs on a bare mattress, or on the couch downstairs. She probably won't sleep a wink. Not with packs of wolves howling and slavering outside the windows.

She prowls the house once again, searching the bedrooms for evidence of the resident. There are no pictures or knickknacks that she can see, anywhere, upstairs or down. Upstairs, the three small bedrooms, apart from beds and dressers, have been stripped bare. In the bathroom there is toilet paper on the roll, a sliver of soap on the sink, a larger bar in a wire soap dish attached to the curved rim of the claw-footed bathtub, and a towel on a hook on the back of the bathroom door. The bathtub gleams.

six

SHE AWAKENS AFTER a restless night. It is December twenty-ninth, her watch says, nearly eight o'clock in the morning. She must rush if she's to find anyone still at home who might let her use the phone. She splashes water onto her face, runs her fingers through her hair, pulls on her outdoor clothing and hikes down the lane just in time to see a truck go by and disappear around the bend in the road, going toward the village of Dogwood Station. That's where she'll head, and if she sees another car, she'll try to flag it down.

She hears what sounds like another vehicle. In a moment, the same pickup truck, reversing around the bend steers back to where she is at the bottom of the lane. A man rolls down his window. "Oh," he says. "Thought you were somebody else for a second, there. Are they back?"

"No." Val does some quick thinking. "They said I could use the house." So there's more than one of them!

"That your car I passed, in the ditch?"

"Yes, I skidded somehow and went off."

"Yup," the man said. "Ice under the snow. Nobody come out here to sand. Mind you, they're all out on strike, but there's a few local people out doin' their best to clear things up."

"I'd like to get someone to pull my car out."

"Rhys Fennel, there, he's got the equipment. He'll drag you out."

The place is overrun with Fennels, clearly. "Where does he live?"

"Along the road a piece. Halfway down the valley in 'mongst the trees. You'd miss it if you didn't know it was there. I'll go down and have a word with him."

She thanks the man. A prince of the road. She watches him turn his truck around to go back the way he came, then heads up the lane to the house. She can't believe how hungry she is now that she knows that help is at hand. She'll be back in Falkirk in a little over an hour, grab a bite, and then set off for Toronto. It will be a relief to be home after this little misadventure, and back to work. At least she has her work, she's grateful for that.

She remembers her handbag, left the evening before in the bottom of the sideboard. Reclaiming it, she crouches and spots the piece of paper wedged in behind the drawer above. She tries to free it, but it won't come. She pulls the drawer above it open, but still can't get it. It feels like a photograph. She's desperately curious now and tries to pull the empty drawer right out of its slot. She wiggles it, tilts it, pulls, and finally out it comes in her hands, so surprisingly heavy that she nearly drops it. She reaches into the empty space, feels around for the photo still caught tight by the framework inside the cabinet, and at last manages to free it.

It's a snapshot, badly creased as though someone has folded it up small at some point. There is no date on it, although it looks old, taken with black-and-white film on a Polaroid camera. A young woman lies in the grass — long meadow grass. A young boy lies next to her, his head resting on her abdomen, or her chest, really; his cheek rests against her rather full breast, his eyes are heavy-lidded, suffused with — sleep? The girl's face is blurred as if she turned it quickly from the camera, although she seems to be laughing. The boy looks stunned, like a rabbit cornered. Judging by the clothes, Val places the date of the picture somewhere in the late fifties or early sixties.

The boy is Ed; she's sure of it. She can see elements of him in the squarish jaw. The young woman might be his mother, although she doesn't look much more than eighteen. Ed, if it is Ed, looks about thirteen or fourteen. She can't imagine Ed, especially a teenaged Ed, lying in the grass like that, in what is to Val's mind a rather compromising position, his head almost buried in the girl's bosom. No. She exaggerates. She's not going to think about it any more. It disturbs her. She puts it in her handbag.

Suddenly the outside door at the end of the room bursts open, which sends her into near cataclysmic hypertension. She presses her hands against her chest to quell her racing heart.

"Drug your car back a ways. Can't get her up the lane, for the snow. Awful deep for the time o'year." The man delivers his speech from the open doorway. He's tall and burly, with greying dark hair that covers almost his entire face. His head hair starts low, barely above his brow and continues on to hide his neck and ears. A thick moustache and beard take over, obliterating all but his nose, eyes, and two slivers of pink lips.

Val is now on her feet. "Thank you," she says. "How much do I owe you?"

The woodsman peers at her through his foliage, his eyes like raisins. "Don't know as y'owe me nothin' yet. Got to get her to town first, if that's what you want."

"Oh." Val is surprised. "Has it been damaged?"

"The thing underneath there, she's bent all t' ratshit. You'll never drive her the width of the road."

VAL IS TRAVELLING slowly toward Falkirk in the cab of Mr. Rhys Fennel's pickup; her car, hitched to the truck, follows behind. Rhys tells her that he was out plowing the road at five o'clock this morning. He got as far as the next village, where someone else took over the job. "By rights, the township's supposed to do it, but they don't get here till late in the day," he says, "except when they're on strike, then they don't get here at all."

"Will anyone pay you?" Val asks.

"There's different ones will pay from time to time, but mostly you just do it and then someone else will do it next time, maybe."

"Sounds very civil," she says.

Rhys grunts, which she takes for agreement. He says, "Had a cousin Sybil. Sybil Fennel."

"Oh?"

"Died."

"Oh."

The conversation wilts. Val would like to show him the snapshot she has in her handbag to see if he can identify the boy and the young woman, but she doesn't want him to take his eyes off the road. She looks back to make sure her car is following obediently.

"Did you know Ed Fennel?" she asks.

"Yup. Killed in a car crash last summer."

"He was my husband."

Rhys gives her a quick perusal. "You don't say. Heard he got married some time back. Hope none of your kids was in the car."

"We didn't have any children." She turns away and peers out the window trying to summon her dream child from the back of her mind. He's hiding, she thinks, teasing. A wisp is all she needs, a glimmer from behind the gauzy veil shrouding her fantasy. "We tried, but without luck." Val hopes he won't go on to say something kind-hearted and sympathetic because if he does, her eyes will probably fill. She tenses, waiting for it.

"Just as well," he says. "The Lord visits His wrath even unto the next generation."

She turns back, frowning. She would like to ask him what this means in terms of Ed and their lack of family, but he is concentrating on pulling off onto the shoulder to accommodate an oncoming truck. Only one lane of the road has been plowed. He puts down his window and has a lengthy chat about the snow with the other driver covering statistics concerning record snowfalls going back many years, even to their boyhoods. The conclusion is that this is nothing. A skiff only.

In Falkirk, he tows Val's car into a garage on the edge of town where the mechanic assesses the damage under her car and says reassuringly, "Oh, yeah, we'll get it right for you. Won't take long once we get at it, but there's a few ahead of you."

"How long?"

"Couple hours, three, maybe."

She glances in at the Spartan waiting room, at the three stiff chairs, at the car-racing and body-building magazines and decides she'll get Rhys to take her to the motel where she stayed the night before last. Surely they'll rent her a room for half a day; even if she has to pay full price, it will be worth it to have a hot shower and a snooze. And a bite to eat at a fast food across the road from it. She's starving. At the motel she asks Rhys what she owes him.

"Don't rightly know, now." He reaches up under his woollen toque to scratch his head. "Would twenty be too much?"

She gives him forty and wonders if she's being an ass. He pockets the cash quickly enough, before she can change her mind. Now would be the time to show him the photo. She reaches into her handbag again and fishes out the picture. He squints at it and hands it back.

"Yup," he says.

"Who are these people?"

"Hard to say without my glasses."

"Have you got your glasses with you?"

"Nope. Scarcely ever wear them. Went to the eye doctor there a while back and he tells me my eyes are gettin' dim. 'What age are you?' he says. Well, sir, I can't tell him. Somewhere in the sixties, I know, so I says, 'Sixty-two, or maybe it's sixty-five, never can remember unless I think back.' 'You better have some glasses for readin',' he says. 'Readin'!' says I. 'Are you sure glasses'll help me read?' And he says, 'Yes, sir, they will.' 'Well,' says I, 'give them to me then and make them good and strong for I've never read a word in my life so far.' And I've never read a word since, neither, because about all they're good for is seein' the magazine pictures. 'Specially the fold-out page."

It takes Val a second or two to respond. She thinks of lending him her glasses, but as they have prescription lenses, they likely wouldn't be of much use. "Um," she says handing him the picture again, "I think the boy might be Ed, although I've never seen pictures of him at that age."

"Could be Eddy, all right, hard to say, though."

"Who is the girl — the young woman?"

"Dang!" he says. "The more I look, the more I can't make it out."

"Is it his mother?"

"No, no it wouldn't be his mother. She wouldn't hold with none o' that sort of thing."

He can obviously see enough to call it *that sort of thing*. "Is it someone from Dogwood? Anyone you've seen before?"

"Could be, could be." He holds the picture at arm's length and then up close. "Well, now, I couldn't be dead certain, no, I wouldn't want to place my wager on that."

"Rhys," she says, "can you tell me who has been living in the house?"

"Sure they all lived there at one time."

"But who lived there most recently?"

"The house there's been lyin' empty for quite some time."

"How long?"

"Oh, since back a few months. Time just flies, don't it?"

"But who lived there? Who was the last person to live in it?"

"Always admired Aunt Helen. She was what you'd call an educated lady. Always called her Aunt though she was rightly a cousin on my mother's side, I believe — Eddy's ma."

"But she's dead, isn't she? She can't have been living there up until a few months ago."

"She died a while back, near as I can figure. You lose track after a while, with all them cousins and such. Big family — everybody related to everybody else."

Val isn't about to get any straight answers from this wily hillbilly, she clearly sees. "I've always thought that Ed grew up in Ottawa," she says.

"Ottawa. Now, sure, he did, too. That's right, I recall that now."

"But did he live out there in Dogwood at one time?"

"At one time, yes, he did." Rhys looks at the sky which is becoming overcast. "I'll be gettin' back, now. More snow on its way, looks like."

She asks him to have one more look at the photo to try to identify the girl, but he tells her it's no use, his eyes are playin' him up somethin' turrible.

HER CAR HAS BEEN fixed and Val feels considerably more human after a piece of chicken, a shower, and a lie-down at the Lucky Stars Motel. On the drive back to Toronto she hears on the radio that the strike is over and that the snowplows are once again out in full force. She finds herself driving behind one and decides it's a good place to be even though she has to travel under the speed limit. She cannot get the snapshot out of her mind. It nags at her and worries her. She's certain that Rhys Fennel knew who the girl was but wouldn't say, perhaps out of family loyalty, or loyalty to someone. Or maybe he really couldn't see it properly. Maybe she should go back sometime and confront him again, this time with his glasses. Yet, why, really? Why, indeed. It's really neither here nor there. No, her present concern is with the house, with selling the house, which may not be an easy thing to do. Dogwood Station is neither an urban paradise nor a recreational playground. It has potential, though. She could put that in an ad, if she could decide potential for what.

The snowplow turns off, leaving her to manage the road as best she can. The driving is really not too bad. It's nearly four o'clock, overcast, beginning to get dark. On the road ahead of her she sees a piece of a tire in the middle of her lane. She guesses it's from a large transport truck with many sets of wheels. She pulls over onto the shoulder, stops, puts on her flashers, goes back, looks both ways, and when there's a lull in the traffic runs out onto the middle lane of the westbound highway, yanks it off the road and dashes back to safety. She heaves a big sigh. She wipes sandy grit from her gloves and returns to her car. The remainder of her drive into Toronto is without incident.

PART II

Gus

seven

AFTER THIRTY YEARS Gus is back in Canada to stay. That's one decision he's made. Now if he could just decide to move out of the family home into an apartment, away from his brother Aidan and Audrey, his aging mother, his life might become tolerable.

Christmas has come and gone, a festivity Gus has never enjoyed, not even as a child. The memory he has of his small self solitarily, in this very house, unwrapping his gifts, sometimes three, usually two, all useful or wearable, has never dimmed. But there was always a book, usually with some stranger's name on the flyleaf because his mother was fond of shopping at church rummage sales. He made himself open it last, to savour it. It gave him a little extra time to imagine what it would be about. A war hero, maybe. Or a runaway boy.

Back then his mother had seemed to spend most of that special day upstairs in his brother's room coaxing him to come out, explaining that there was nothing to be afraid of. But Aidan would have none of it. He was sure that hidden under the coloured wrapping paper would be something threatening, something unfamiliar, that would place itself in contact with his person.

Losing patience, eventually, his mother at last would join Gus downstairs beside the three-foot-tall, fake Christmas tree on a table. He would watch optimistically as she opened his gift to her; once, he remembers, it was a glittering brooch that caught the light and made little rainbows. He had spent two dollars and sixty-five cents on it, nearly every penny he had. Embarrassed, he observed her turn it over and over with that little frown she had. "My, my," she said. "Isn't this something."

No, Christmas had been a day to endure back then. Not much has changed, he has to admit. This year his mother gave him two pairs of woollen socks, for which he is thankful. He gave her a cheque as he had every Christmas of his exile in Los Angeles. Aidan spent most of the day in his room, no doubt reading. So had Gus, for that matter.

New Year's Eve was also a non-event. He no longer really knows anyone in Toronto, although he's met a few people since moving back in June. His mother drank a glass of the wine he bought and promptly fell asleep. Aidan said it tasted like shoe polish after the first mouthful and poured it down the sink. Gus wondered how he would know the taste of shoe polish.

He'd forgotten how cold it gets in Toronto. One of these days he'll go out and buy himself warmer clothes, fleece-lined gloves, some sort of outdoor footwear. Gus is astounded at the way everything has shot way up out of sight in the thirty years he's been away. But he's home.

Aidan seems to have given up on life, and Gus believes that he is largely to blame. This cold evening in the middle of January, he tries to lure him out of his room. He knocks on his door, a mere formality as his brother never invites anyone to come in, and pushes it open. Aidan is hunched over his desk, poring over a book, studying it. He looks up guiltily as Gus comes in, deaf to everything but his own spinning thoughts, and shoves the book under the clutter of paper and open books on his desk. He flips open one of the other books and starts turning pages. Gus knows, without asking, what he's doing, has been doing for months, ever since Gus's return — reading and rereading his own poetry. And Gus also thinks he knows why. It isn't mere narcissism. He thinks Aidan's trying to revise his own work, post-publication.

"There's something on television you'd like," Gus says.

Aidan says nothing.

"About books. You'd like that. They have poets on, sometimes." He sounds desperate, even to himself.

Aidan twirls his chair until his back faces Gus and so Gus leaves him to his sulk.

Downstairs he turns on the TV that he bought when he came back home. He should have put it in his own room because his mother can't abide it, but there's little enough space in his room as it is. He sprawls on the couch just as his mother comes into the living room. In honour of the cold weather she has lugged one of the heaters he remembers from his childhood up from the cellar. She tells him, "If you're here to loll about all winter, you might as well make yourself useful and bring up the other heater and the coal oil and fill them both." She wants one upstairs in Aidan's room and one downstairs in the living room. The book-show host is about to introduce his guests for the evening. Audrey turns off the television.

Gus fetches the other heater and the gallon bottle of coal oil from the cellar. It crosses his mind that these may not be the safest contraptions in the world. "Have you ever had these checked out for safety?" he calls to her from the stairs.

"They're a damn sight safer than those electrical ones you can buy that'd blow every fuse in the house. There's nothing wrong with them. They throw a good heat and we've never had a speck of trouble from them."

He continues on upstairs to Aidan's room and places the heater in the middle of the floor well away from his books and his mountains of loose paper. His brother has a corner room and it's pretty drafty, Gus realizes. The house should be torn apart and reinsulated. Maybe he could do that next summer, he and Aidan. Get Aidan to read a book on how to do it, take him five minutes. They could work together. He grunts. Sure.

Aidan is lying curled on his bed, now, reading, oblivious to Gus who fills the tank of the short cylindrical heater and lights it with his cigarette lighter. For a moment it blazes and then burns with a bluish-yellow flame which he can see through the holes up and down its sides. It does throw an amazing heat. He decides that the middle of the room is probably a dangerous location after all. Aidan might trip over it. He turns it down a bit, picks up the handle, and moves it out of the way closer to the window. "There you go," he says to Aidan. "That'll keep you cozy."

Aidan flips page after silent page. "Right," Gus says. "Think nothing of it. My pleasure. Asshole," he says quietly on his way out.

Downstairs, Gus fills the other heater and places it near his mother's chair. He studies its position and moves it back twelve inches. No. He moves it again to where it was, knowing that no matter where he places it, it will be wrong. Audrey clumps into the living room to check on how he's doing. He catches the scowl on her face and a disappointed click of her tongue. "Why would you put it there?" She asks, indignant.

Gus shrugs. He feels himself grinding his teeth.

"Well, it's a fool of a place to put it." She takes it by the handle and moves it back twelve inches. Gus retreats to his room.

He opens his laptop without flicking it on and stares down at the knuckles of his clenched hands on either side of the keyboard. He straightens his fingers. They're long. Hands of a tall man. And he is tall when he doesn't let himself stoop. He straightens his back and gazing into the blank screen, he drifts, sees himself, a boy of seventeen, gawky, a beanpole.

HE HAD FINALLY got his full height, or most of it, back-ordered, it seemed to him, for years. Peanut, his brother used to call him, when he called him anything. Gus always ducked going through the door into Aidan's bedroom. He didn't really have to, he just felt like it. Aidan would be reading on his bed curled up on his right side like a dried leaf, the knobs of his spine tracing a crooked path under his T-shirt. He was so thin back then, at twenty-one, that you could spit through him, as their mother said. Awkwardly, elbow in the air, he held the book on a tilt with his skeletal left hand to allow him to focus on the page, his glasses askew on his face.

There were almost no clear surfaces in his room free of library books, secondhand paperbacks, discarded school books, books with his father's name on the flyleaf that had escaped his mother's purge after the defection of her husband, clothing, junk that he'd dragged in from the street that he wanted to study: a hubcap, a chunk of concrete, a pedal off a bicycle. Audrey despaired of him, doubted that he'd ever grow up or learn the first thing about tidiness. He was no longer a child, but she still had to remind him to go to the bathroom before he went out anywhere, and to wash his hands; she was always sending him back to wash his hands. She had to tell him to shower, to comb his hair, to use a fork, not his fingers, when he ate — a twenty-one-year-old, for heaven's sake!

Neither of them spoke when Gus went into Aidan's room. Aidan wasn't big on greetings or small talk. In fact, he probably wasn't even aware of Gus slouching against the windowsill of his room. About every four seconds he turned a page. It looked as though he wasn't really reading, only pretending because, as Audrey always said, how can you take anything in that quickly? You're just skimming. Nevertheless, he went on running his eyes down the pages of the book and flipping them in fairly rapid succession.

Once in a while he'd let her quiz him. She would take the book if it was one she'd read and ask him about different parts of the plot, who was married to whom, who died, all that sort of thing. And Aidan, in his funny, flat, almost breathless voice, gave her correct answers every time with page references and word-perfect dialogue samples.

Audrey shook her head. She couldn't understand how he could be so clever at reading and so backward about everything else. Audrey herself was a prodigious reader, although not in the same league as Aidan; nowhere near it. It wasn't as if she hadn't tried to do something about him. God love him, he'd been poked and prodded and stared at by every kind of brain and nerve doctor under the sun, and they all had different ideas about what to do with him, and every last one of their solutions cost a king's ransom, as far as she was concerned, and her a single mother trying to raise two boys each to be the saint their father never was. Of course, she could always put Aidan away in one of the big provincial mental hospitals. She went to have a look once when he was going through a long siege of bed-wetting. Eleven going on twelve he was, at the time. All she saw was a big brick warehouse that stank of stale cabbage and urine and floor cleaner, peopled by grotesques and the staff in their stiff grey uniforms.

Gus managed to break into his brother's consciousness by grabbing the book. Aidan let out a howl loud enough to be heard on the street and struggled to his feet to wrestle it back. Meanwhile, with the book in one hand behind him and his other arm outstretched to fend off his murderous older brother, Gus shouted that it was time for his walk, time for some exercise; he could have the book back later. It was his duty, Audrey reminded Gus nearly every day, to take over some of the responsibility for his brother. It was the least he could do.

Aidan, nevertheless, got his hands around Gus's throat as if he'd strangle him, but either he was not strong enough, or not trying very hard, because Gus easily threw him off. Someday, he thought, he might not struggle — to see whether Aidan would actually strangle him. But he'd like to have someone else around to pull him off, just in case.

They went to the park four blocks from their small house on a street crowded with mostly small houses and duplexes a few blocks south of Eglinton. Aidan wanted to hold Gus's hand, but Gus wouldn't let him. He kept his hands in his pockets, so Aidan walked directly behind him, sometimes treading on his heels, sometimes reaching out to touch the tail of his plaid shirt. Gus had a tendency to trip over his own feet and when he did, Aidan's tailgating caused both boys to crash in a heap like some sort of clown act.

The kids that played in the park after school had nearly all gone home for their supper. One or two stuck around to stare at Aidan, who did look pretty bizarre, Gus had to admit, with his thick glasses permanently bent, his hunched shoulders and crooked spine, and with his unevenly cut hair hanging too long around his right ear because his mother could only get near him with the scissors when he was sound asleep. Gus called him Quasimodo when he wanted to get a rise out of him.

"Is that guy retarded or something?" one of the kids asked. The other kid told him to shut up and they both giggled. Gus ignored them and led Aidan to his favourite swing. He pushed him for twenty minutes, started warning him about five minutes before time was up and every minute thereafter until he stopped pushing. Aidan demanded more, but Gus stood in front of him, arms folded, so he'd know that was it. "Time to let the old cat die," he said. Aidan was back in his trance, his eyes staring at nothing Gus could see, but riveted there, somewhere inside his head, until the swing was barely moving. Gus stopped it completely and pried Aidan's hands free of the chain-ropes; then they started their trek back home.

GUS KNEW HE WAS being selfish, but by the time he was twenty-one, the thought of living his whole life cooped inside the family, inside the family house, depressed him. He had to move away from the repetition of days with Aidan, away from the awareness of his mother's hair, suddenly grey overnight, it seemed, and the way it took her several tries to get out of a chair. She had always been a big handsome woman, shoulders on her any man would be proud to own, yet she seemed to have shrunk. Gus could now look down at her, giving him a view of pink skin through her grey hair. He'd never thought of women going bald.

He'd just as soon not be there to witness Audrey struggling to keep the little family together. She had a good pension from the army coming in. She had been in the women's division during the war and for several years after it. She worked three half-days a week now, in a bakery. Aidan had a job walking a neighbour's two dogs twice a day and feeding them. He related to animals in a way he never had to people. He didn't mind if they jumped all over him or licked his face. He rolled in the grass with them and let them tug at his hair and at his clothing with their teeth, in a mock attack. He growled and yipped at them in their language, and always let them get the better of him.

For his job with the dogs, Audrey wrote out a detailed itinerary for him because he couldn't keep spoken plans in his head. *Leave Mr. Warner's house with the dogs. Walk four blocks out to Laird, turn around, one hundred and eighty degrees. Walk back past Mr. Warner's house, past our house, out to Rumsey Road. Turn around, one hundred and eighty degrees and walk back past our house to Mr. Warner's. Put the dogs in the garden. Close the gate.* Everything had to be spelled out for him, nothing complicated, every step a repeat of the time before. Once she thought he might like to go around the block for a change, but he got lost and it took her an hour to find him.

Gus was working in a fish-and-chip shop peeling potatoes, full-time. He got to bring home fish and chips whenever he wanted. What he wanted, though, was a life of his own. He had recently graduated from York University — so brand new that his was only the fifth graduating class — where he had managed to keep his marks high enough to earn him bursaries each year. After graduation his classmates had all gone off to do heroic things such as save the world by living in a kibbutzim in Israel, or working for CUSO, or joining freedom marches in the southern United States. Those who were not saving the world were making it a safer place to live in by going to law school. Others were thinking about breaking into publishing, as soon as they found out what that meant and how you would go about it.

Young Gus was, himself, a little starry-eyed and rainbow-hued. He wanted to write a book, one that would make a difference, that would make people sit up and say, oh my God, yes, that's exactly right, that's the way life is, or could be, or should be. He wanted to write about a noble character, a worthy man. A hero. He bought himself a secondhand typewriter and a stack of paper and got started on it one day. The typing skills he had learned in high school paid off. His brain seemed electric, unlike his typewriter, snapping out words he didn't even know he knew, sending them down his arms and out through his fingers, clackety-clackety-clack-clackety — letters merging into words across the page and down, across and down. It was so easy. He stayed with it until he had to go to the fish-and-chip shop. All through his shift he thought about his writing and thought the way his character thought as if he were the character or vice versa. If any fault could be found with his writing, he was willing to admit, it was that it was a little derivative of James Joyce — mostly stream-of-consciousness — but still, it was his story, and not bad, he decided, on the whole. Not too bad.

When he got home again from Mulligan's Fish and Chips, he found that his brother had gone into his room, had read the pile of printed sheets of manuscript (about fourteen), had stuffed some of them back into the typewriter and had printed all over them: *This is no good. It does not make sense. I do not like this. Write something better.* Gus strode into Aidan's room finding his brother in the usual posture, curled around a book, and stood over him breathing deeply, loudly, clenching his fists, raising one, ready to clout him, bust his eggshell head open while Aidan continued to flip pages. It was at this moment that Gus knew that he had to leave home.

When he announced his plan to go off to seek his fortune, Audrey let out a long, slow, disheartened breath and stared at the floor, downcast. She told the floor that she was not getting any younger, that Aidan was an awful handful for her to manage all on her own, with no one to spell her off. And then she looked at Gus, raising her voice, "He's your *brother*, after all. Where's your sense of family obligation?"

Gus ground his teeth and made his eyes slits to give the impression that he was stonily unmoved.

"Selfish lout, is what you are."

Gus headed for the stairs. He would get a suitcase down from the high shelf in the upstairs closet.

"You're no better than your father was," she spat after him.

After the war, their father joined a company that produced and sold home freezers. It was a tough sell at first, but before long, the idea caught on and he made quite a tidy sum of money. He bought Audrey the house of her dreams, modest though they were, a two-storey, three-bedroom, near good schools and fine churches. The money, though, spoiled him. He began to drink and he began to work late, to be away on business, to simply fail to show up for meals. According to Audrey he went out one night when Gus was three or four and Aidan not much older to buy a package of cigarettes and returned a week later in a car driven by some woman he'd conned with some story or other. When he came into the house to get a few things, Audrey threw him out. Picked him up by the belt and the neck of his shirt and pitched him right out onto the street. As she told it, he just flew. Landed on the hood of his fancy woman's car. Put a dent in it.

"And this is all the thanks I get for all the years I've spent giving you boys a proper home, a good home, in spite of the odds against you." Her magnificent bosom heaved. Her hostile eyes glinted.

After about a week of this, she let it go and started asking him if he had enough underwear, enough matching socks.

It seemed, the way their mother told it, that their father had had a weakness for anything in a skirt. Why she had ever married him she couldn't tell them. Sure they must have brothers and sisters all over the city of Toronto. The schools must be peppered with them. Gus had a habit of looking closely at people in the subway and on crowded buses and walking along Yonge Street, checking for a family resemblance. He wouldn't have minded having a real brother, one he could at least talk to.

He took all his savings and closed his bank account. The teller had a smirky, sexy look on her face as if she figured he was going to use his money for something pornographic. He glared back with his best fuck-you expression. He didn't care. He was through with this town. He really was moving out.

On the spur of the moment, just before he dragged down the stairs an old brown imitation leather suitcase filled with nearly all he owned, he went back into his room, took the typewriter out of the carton in which he had packed it and took it into Aidan's room.

"Here," he said, "write the great Canadian novel, if your literary taste is so damn good." Flip, flip, flip, went the pages of Aidan's book, Dostoevski's *The Idiot*, Gus noted.

eight

IN EARLY JUNE, one year after young Gus had left home, he returned with his bulging brown vinyl suitcase. He'd bought sunglasses and a lot of black clothes — black shirt, black turtleneck, black pants — and a new typewriter in a case of its own. Beyond the smell of diesel fumes, a freshness caressed his cheek, his sideburns, his black shirt, as he struggled off the city bus with his luggage, nearly falling down the bottom step in his eagerness to see his own neighbourhood, his own street. The air had an after-supper coolness in it, but a languid gust now and then promised warmth come morning. He breathed in the drowsy scent of evening grass freshly cut and listened nostalgically to the whirr-pause, whirr-pause of a hand-pushed lawnmower. Kids, somewhere out of sight, between or behind the houses, one after the other, yelled, "Home free!" They argued about who was "it." Gus thought he'd gone backward in time.

He was about to turn twenty-two and he'd packed in a lot of living during his year away. He was sharp; he was wise to the world. He'd been living in New York City, and he was one canny bastard. He'd been writing plays, and they were good. He had managed to get himself some back-stage theatre work in Manhattan and he showed his plays around to some of the stagehands, to an actress who had been pretty taken with him, and to an assistant director. They'd all said his plays were good. He didn't know why he had come home.

While Aidan was having a bath one night shortly after Gus's return, Audrey led him with a finger on her lips into Aidan's room and opened the closet door. Stashed on the floor were three cardboard cartons filled with stacks of paper — a mix of white typewriter paper, pages torn from magazines, from Eaton's catalogues, Simpson's catalogues, the thick Toronto phone book — many of them raggedly trimmed to fit a typewriter carriage. Each page was covered on both sides with single-spaced typing, no margins, no page numbers, right over top of whatever was on the page. Gus attempted to read some of it but it was hard to make out the words typed as they were over top of ladies' half slips and Bulova watches and names beginning with S. On the white typewriter pages he had better luck. These, too, were single-spaced, double-sided, with no margins. It was his guess that Aidan was writing an autobiography, but in the third person. He read:

His mother says no more paper, we cannot afford it, we are not made of money you know, when are you going to get a real job, she is a very parsimonious woman, very stingy, very mean, very miserly, very tight as the paper on the wall. He takes the phone book and he takes a sharp knife, very sharp, very keen, very edgy, very dangerous, very scary to mother, very all right he tells her.

His mother left to answer the phone while Gus continued to read Aidan's work. He looked up and there was

Aidan naked, dripping. He had a bath towel clutched to his skinny cave of a chest. When he saw what Gus was up to he bit on the towel, pulling at it, clenching his jaw tighter, his lower lip stretched and down-turned like a bloodhound's. His eyes behind his crooked glasses were huge — two smoky blue holes rimmed with hope.

Gus knew what words were taking shape as thoughts inside his brother's head. He had experienced this need for connection, the desire for some common bond with the inside of someone else's head. He knew about feelings tumbling over each other, clinging to each other, giving birth to a secret certainty that his writing was worthy, that he himself was worthy because of it, or nearly so, and yet, and yet, his brain, or maybe his heart, at the same time, was heavy with anguish, because what if it wasn't and he wasn't? What if he'd been merely pissing into the wind, his words splattering back all over his feet? And his feet were clay. At least, this was what went on in Gus's head when he was writing.

Gus had never felt closer to his brother.

It was on the tip of his tongue to say, "Great stuff!" But he hesitated. Aidan would know that "great stuff" was not a Gus-expression. Aidan would know when he was being patronized. Gus said, "How did you manage to write all this?"

Aidan shrugged happily. He took the towel out of his mouth and dried his legs.

"How many pages you got here?"

Aidan said, "I didn't count them."

"I'd like to read the beginning of it."

Aidan picked up his pyjama bottoms from the end of his bed and turned them over and over in his hands until he found a white patch on which his mother had written in indelible ink: *The front of Aidan's pyjamas.* He struggled into them, ineptly, like a child of three sitting on the side of his bed, trying not to get both legs in the same hole. He plunged into the closet and dragged out one of the boxes. He turned the contents, white paper only, out onto the bed so that the bottom page was now on top. Gus picked up the first page and Aidan appeared to stop breathing.

Mouth and cheek and nose holes hang over him to blot him out. Aidan is a stone with eyes that shrink inward when everything comes at him and at him too close for comfort. Hair makes him suck his eyes in, makes him cry and cry and cry.

The word "cry" was repeated to the bottom of the page. On the back of the page Gus read:

And hands. He cries because of hands, and they pluck him up and thrust him into the naked weightless air and he can do nothing but cry because he is a stone. He wants to get away from there because although he is a stone he has ears and the thumping and roaring and shrieking crawl over him and threaten to choke off his mouth and his ears and you'll be the death of me yet.

Gus was spellbound. On and on he read leaning back to prop his shoulders against the headboard of Aidan's bed. He said, "Is this really what it was like for you when you were a little kid?"

"Maybe," Aidan said cheerfully.

"You thought you were a stone?"

"Maybe."

Gus took the pages to bed with him and read until his eyes hurt. Next day after breakfast, after a trip to a store for more paper and quickly while he had Aidan's attention, he showed him how to set the typewriter tabs to make margins. He drew marks on the paper, on the top and bottom of each page with messages. *Start here. Start a new page.* On the back of each sheet he wrote: *Do not write on this side.*

Aidan spent the rest of the day sitting at a wobbly card table in his room tap, tap, tapping out his life's story, using one finger on each hand. In his own room, Gus placed his own typewriter (now electric) on the desk he had used as a student. He was about a quarter of the way into a new play about an angry young man going off to seek his fortune, but he wasn't sure, exactly, where he was going with it. He picked up the bit he had already written and reread it. Full of typos, but he types pretty fast, so it was no wonder. He could always correct it in the next draft. He'd like his character to meet up with someone who turns out to be his half-brother. Or, he'd like this guy to find his father who left home when he was a baby. Every time he tried to get his thoughts in order, he became aware of Aidan, tappety-tapping up a storm on the old Underwood.

Gus shut Aidan's door and also his own, but he could still hear letter upon letter, word upon word, hammered onto Aidan's paper in a never-ending stream. It was driving him nuts. He couldn't think; he couldn't write. From his desk he pulled out the manuscript of the play he had written in New York in the closet-like room he had rented in East Village. He took it into Aidan's room.

"Why don't you read this? It's a play I wrote. I think it's pretty good."

Aidan stopped pounding words and took the bundle of pages from Gus. He ran his eye down the page and the next and the next. "No good," he said. When Gus questioned him (he tried not to sound miffed, but he was), Aidan indicated with his hands close together that his play script was crowded, left too many wide margins. Gus tried to explain that that's the way you arrange play dialogue on the page, but Aidan wasn't interested. Aidan brushed him off with a gesture of impatience and went back to his own work. Over his shoulder, Gus read:

Little brother Peanut comes and goes comes and goes comes and goes

(for about five lines).

One day it is very noisy, very shrill, very screamy, very cacophonous, very too much for one person to bear. And Peanut runs to him and opens his eyes very wide, very big, very round, very much the colour of the sky before thunder and sees the stone, very still, very lumpish, very beside himself with fear and says get away from my brother my brother my brother

(which words Aidan continued to type to the bottom of the page). Gus was somehow touched by this. He put a hand on Aidan's shoulder, but his brother shrugged it off.

"Bother," he said. "Bother, bother, bother, bother."

Gus came up with the brilliant idea of taking Aidan to see a play. He looked in the paper and found that one of Tennessee Williams's plays was on at the Royal Alex; also that an amateur theatre group was staging *Arsenic and Old Lace* in the parish hall of some church. Audrey just shook her head. "I have no money for such fripperies as plays, so don't look at me to cough up the price of admission." Gus assured her that he had plenty of money of his own (although it would be economically prudent to go to the one in the parish hall). "Now, if your brother kicks up any kind of a fuss at all," she said, "you bring him on home or we'll be up half the night with nightmares."

Gus tried to smooth his hair down with water because he hated that axle-grease he thinks his father used to use, but it wouldn't cooperate. It needed a lawn-mower taken to it. He put on his black shirt over a black T-shirt and off they went on foot because Aidan hated buses. They were scarcely halfway to the corner when Audrey came calling after them, her apron coming undone, billowing, threatening to sail her off course. Encircling her ankles, for the consumption of the nosy neighbours who seemed never to have anything better to do than to ogle her in moments of disarray, were her lisle stockings, rolled and thick as those foreign sausages the butcher up on Eglinton often had in his window for half price. "Bring him back!" she called. "Bring Aidan back!"

Puzzled frowns on their faces, the brothers shambled back along the street, the setting sun in their eyes. Gus asked, "What's wrong?"

"He hasn't done his duty," Audrey said behind her hand, not wanting the entire neighbourhood to be witness to her son's shortcomings. She shooed Aidan into the house ahead of her and up the stairs to the bathroom. "And don't forget to wash your hands!" Audrey's voice carried out to the street where Gus leaned against a hydro pole thinking he'd like to take up smoking. Then he thought maybe he should go to the bathroom, too.

It took them an hour, but they got to the hall where the play was to be staged and managed to find pretty good seats. Aidan was on his guard. In this unfamiliar building where the chairs were so squashed together that people were in constant danger of touching each other, he felt the life being crushed out of him. He grasped a pinch of Gus's shirt sleeve and hung on tight, much to the annoyance of his brother. Gus kept his hands firmly in his pockets.

When the house lights went down, Aidan tried to escape, but Gus held him down, put an arm around his shoulders, whispered soothing words, and looked around to see if anyone was staring at them thinking they were queer. A few were. Aidan was agitated throughout the whole first act, jumping each time a new actor appeared on the stage, putting his hands over his ears for most of the dialogue. By the second act, he managed to hunker down in his seat and watch the action through half-closed eyes and before the play was over, he was snoring audibly. Gus shook him awake and yanked him to his feet. He pushed him out past people's knees before the curtain call.

"Very scary," Aidan offered, unasked. "Very noisy, very silly, very old-womanish, very soporific." People were clapping loudly enough, Gus hoped, that they couldn't hear Aidan's critique. Although, they were amateurs, after all, what did they expect?

Gus's next bright idea was to buy a paperback edition of Williams's play, *The Glass Menagerie*, the one that was playing at the Royal Alex and to which he would take his brother come Saturday afternoon. He felt that if Aidan were familiar with the story, the play would be more interesting for him. Aidan read all of it — scene descriptions, stage directions, every word — in nine minutes.

Gus had enough money to buy matinee tickets for them in the second balcony. He even asked their mother to join them. She took her head out of the fridge where she was making room for the weekend's groceries, and said, "And wear what? A bedsheet? Do I not spend every red cent that comes into this house on the care and feeding of you two boys and always have without a thought to myself? Not that I begrudge it."

"Wear your church clothes."

"Mind you, I can manage on very little. Some women need sheer stockings not mended to within an inch of being rags, and smart dresses with no sweat stains under the arms, and all manner of frivolities like that, but I'm cast from a different metal. I get by, thank you very much."

"It's just a matinee."

"You two boys go on. Somebody in this family might as well be having a good time." She ran a critical eye over her sons who by this time couldn't wait to bolt. "You both look very nice in your shirts and ties, although," she scowled at Gus's shirt, "black would not have been my first choice."

Gus hunted behind and among the paper bags of groceries for his sunglasses.

"Off you go, then."

He found them.

"I'll be fine." She followed them out the door, standing on the front stoop to see them off, arms like girders folded across her chest. She could pick up Aidan and carry him like a baby if she had to. "Pity the radio is still broken or I could listen to the opera." Gus had rashly promised to fix it, but had not as yet taken the time to do so, mainly because he didn't know a rat's ass about radios. "Anyway, I've the sheets to mend, and the grass needs cutting."

The boys were off down the street out of earshot, which was just as well because Audrey had it in her mind to tell them about a slight pain she had in her chest. Probably nothing. Besides, she didn't want to put a guilt trip on them the way her own mother used to do to her. Anyway, the pain was probably the kind of heartache you get when you see that your children can function without you.

And prefer to.

GUS HAD TO DO A great deal of talking to convince Aidan to take public transportation to get downtown to the theatre. Aidan would cooperate, he promised, but only if he could hold Gus's hand. "Good God!" Gus said. He was having second thoughts, now, and wondered if the experiment would be worth it. "Why am I doing this?" he asked himself out loud.

Aidan, in his flat voice, replied, "He wants to make big brother like little brother."

Gus stared at him. He knew that this was true, and what's more, he knew that he wanted Aidan to appreciate his writing to the same extent that he did himself. He wanted to hear his brother say, "Very good writing, very touching, very excellent, very much like Tennessee Williams." Gus had a suspicion that, in spite of his so-called handicap, his brother was a better writer than he was.

They walked out to wait for the bus. The doors whooshed open for them and Gus took Aidan's hand. Aidan stumbled up the steps because he couldn't see very well with Gus's sunglasses on and his own glasses in his brother's pocket. Gus wished he'd tried to find a white cane for him, but he hadn't known where to look. People on the bus gave Gus sympathetic nods as he led his brother down the aisle and urged him into an empty seat. Gus felt fine.

INSIDE THE THEATRE, the curtain had not yet gone up and Gus had not yet given back Aidan's glasses. Climbing up the last flight of stairs to the top of the house was nerve-racking even for Gus, who wasn't normally afraid of heights. "Step up, step up," he had to say over and over to Aidan. When the usher in the top balcony tore their tickets, she looked concerned. "I'm afraid you're right up in the gods." She pointed to the topmost row in which there were only two seats. "I might be able to find you something better after the first act."

"No, no, this is great!" Gus guided Aidan up the last few steep steps and manhandled him into his seat. He would wait until the lights went down before giving back his glasses. He hoped that the darkness would hide from his brother the sheer drop to the orchestra about four thousand feet below.

The lights dimmed and the heavy curtain disappeared while Aidan fixed the arms of his own glasses around his large and prominent ears. Eyes bulging, mouth agape, he looked down in horror on the minuscule stage, on the rows of bowling balls or cabbage heads far below them. Closer, just below, were the tops of heads and shoulders of men and women sliding, it seemed, down a steep slope. Aidan clutched at Gus. "I'm falling," he whispered loudly, "help me!"

Below them, necks craned, eyes glared upward. Gus put his arm around Aidan and whispered loudly, "You're not falling, you're fine, now shut up and listen to the play."

Aidan hung on to the arm rests to keep from pitching out head first into the laps of those in the rows below. At length he became aware of a tiny person moving about on the stage talking to himself. He turned to Gus and said, "I think that's Tom reading *The Glass Menagerie* out loud." Gus nodded and put a finger to his lips. After a few moments, quietly, in his monotone, Aidan recited Tom's lines along with him in his long opening soliloquy. Gus frowned and whispered to him to shut up.

Aidan had been half holding his breath, but now let it in and out slowly, more evenly. Gus continued to hold him tightly by the shoulders. Aidan was calm, watching the stage, watching the actors, Tom's mother Amanda, Tom's sister Laura. After a moment he said aloud, "That's not right."

Gus dug his fingers into Aidan's shoulder. "Shut up!" he whispered.

"The mother was supposed to say, 'No sister, no sister, not, no sister, no little sister.'"

"It doesn't matter." Fierce whisper.

From the stage at length they heard, "It's almost time for our gentleman callers to be arriving."

"Start arriving!" Aidan called out in stentorian tones. Gus put his hand over Aidan's mouth. People twisted in their seats shushing, glaring angrily. Aidan bit Gus's hand and Gus pulled away in silent pain, thinking that in one second he'd hurl his brother over the balcony to the mercy of whomever he landed on.

Meanwhile, far below, Amanda moved prettily across the stage saying, "How many do you suppose we're going to entertain this afternoon?"

Angrily, dizzily, before Gus could haul him back, Aidan stood up teetering, and called down from the gods, "She flounces girlishly toward the kitchenette, you silly bitch!" and pitched forward with the effort, the need to hear the stage directions recited along with the dialogue. He reached out to catch himself, to keep from hurtling like Lucifer down into the chaos below by grasping the bald head and beefy neck of the man in front of him.

"God-Christ!" the man shrieked, forgetting he was in a theatre, believing he was being strangled by a madman (as indeed he was). A male usher ascended with the alacrity of a Gabriel, taking two steps at a time. He clambered over Gus to free the man's head from Aidan's steely grip. Gamely, and greatly to their credit, the actors carried on with the unfolding drama.

The brothers did not go straight home but walked down to the bar in the King Eddy and ordered a beer each even though it was not quite three in the afternoon. Gus gave the barman a look filled with such anguish that he failed to ask for proof of age (he *was* legally of age in case anyone wanted to know.) "I'm never taking you anywhere again," Gus told Aidan.

Aidan didn't reply. He was still whispering to himself as he had been ever since they had been turfed unceremoniously out of the Royal Alex and asked not to come back. "'Laura: Excuse me — I haven't finished playing the Victrola.... [She turns awkwardly and hurries into the front room. She pauses a second by the Victrola. Then she catches her breath and darts through the portieres like a frightened deer.]'" By the time they were ready to leave, Aidan was pressing his fingers into his eyes. Gus bustled him quickly outside before anyone thought there was something wrong. Out on the street, Aidan spoke his lines aloud. "'...go! Don't think about us, a mother deserted, an unmarried sister who's crippled and has no job! Don't let anything interfere with your selfish pleasure! Just go, go, go — to the movies!

"'Tom: All right, I will! The more you shout about my selfishness to me the quicker I'll go, and I won't go to the movies!

"'Amanda: Go then! Go to the moon, you selfish dreamer!'"

Young women in miniskirts, shoppers laden with parcels, people hurrying to catch a bus, were all staring at Aidan, at both of them, really, as they set out to walk all the way home. Aidan's voice continued expressionlessly to the end of the play by which time he had tears streaming openly down his cheeks. Gus had stopped caring that much about the spectacle they must present. He was thinking about the strength he had in his legs and his arms, loping along half carrying Aidan, an arm around his back, hooked under his brother's prominent shoulder blades, propelling him, thinking his strength might rub off on him, knowing he could piggyback him if he had to. His clothes felt tight, even with his tie undone and collar open. He was bursting through his clothes. He would like to strip to the waist, discard everything that constricted this new burst of growth he was experiencing. At least he thought that's what it was. He wondered if he were metamorphosing into something no one would recognize.

At about Bloor Street he gave in to Aidan's limp, breathless pleas for a rest and hailed a passing cab. He instructed the driver to stop a block before their house. Audrey would be watching for them to come along on foot from the bus stop, waiting to hear how the afternoon had gone, wanting them to repeat every piece of conversation that had passed between them, wanting to be let into the private thoughts of each of them.

Gus ducked going through the front door, looked down at his mother, suddenly frail in spite of her shoulders which he suspected must be padded, and boomed, "Great play! Great stuff!" Audrey looked at him, noticing some change in him, looked at Aidan's red-rimmed eyes, sensed his physical exhaustion. She asked Aidan what he had thought of the play.

"Very dangerous, very dizzying, very short."

"Did you like it?" she asked.

"Very hopeless." Aidan climbed the stairs like a child, slowly, leading with the same foot on each step.

Watching, Gus flexed his muscles, his chest filled. He knew he had to break out of this place of confinement. Already he was planning his next escape. Halfway up the stairs, Aidan stopped as if he'd changed his mind about going to his room. He looked down at Gus, at his mother. There was a fraction of a moment when no one spoke. No one drew a breath.

"'Laura bends over the candles,'" Aidan said in his monotone, although very distinctly.

"'For nowadays the world is lit by lightning!'" His voice took on an unaccustomed resonance. "'Blow out your candles, Laura —'" Through his skewed glasses, his eyes were magnified pits reflecting nothing. "'— and so goodbye....'"

Gus was thinking he'd go to California. He'd write a screenplay. Get rich.

"'She blows the candles out.'"

Clump, clump, clump. Aidan climbed the stairs to his room. Inside, he closed the door.

nine

GUS LEFT HOME AGAIN and spent the next thirty years in Los Angeles and Hollywood. The first few years were bad. Every second guy he ran into was trying to write a screenplay. He damn near starved to death down there until he got a break. It was a fluke, really, but then that's the way these things happen, he's been told often enough. It was during a cab drivers' strike. Kids were driving around in the family car, rolling along curbside offering rides for a flat rate. They'd take two or three customers at a time, some of them. Gus was on his way to a studio to peddle his latest surefire hit and happened to share one of these illegal cabs with another man. Gus had his work out, looking it over self-consciously. He had a pen in his hand as if he might make changes in it even at this late date. He put a strained, concerned look on his face to make sure he looked like a writer. He *was* a writer. He just wasn't a published writer. He wasn't a paid writer.

Without glancing up he knew the man beside him was reading a page of the treatment he'd written for his screenplay. He could almost feel the heat of his eyes on the paper. The man's curiosity made him sweat with pride and hope. He rolled down his window and shuffled to the next page.

"Who wrote this?" the man asked suddenly.

"I did."

"Mind if I have a look at it?"

Gus's pulse quickened. A gust from the open window riffled the pages. Nervously he snatched at them, dropping some on the floor of the car. A page went under the front seat. He bent to retrieve it, his head almost in the guy's lap, and cobbled them together as best he could. Red-faced he handed them over. The man studied his work in silence, flipped casually through to the end and handed him back the sheaf of paper. "Here's my card," he said. "I'll be in my office at two. We can talk."

To Gus's wholehearted satisfaction, the stranger, who turned out to be a producer of some renown, liked the script, paid real American dollars for it, and took a close look at everything else Gus managed to spew forth. It took him months to stop feeling he was playing a major role in some adult fairy tale.

It wasn't great writing, Gus was well aware, but it was lucrative writing. The more he wrote, the more in demand he became. He even did some bit-part acting. He was living pretty well by this time. He had a girlfriend, a bit-part actress herself, looking for her big break. She got to play waitresses, mostly, or barmaids, which was also what she was in her day job, and perhaps, as a result, did it with such great credibility that these were the only roles she was ever offered. Eventually she became bored. She told Gus that if he was not interested enough to marry her she'd leave and go to New York.

Gus was having difficulty delivering himself into a state of mind that he assumed being married demanded. It wasn't the self-image he had initially invented upon his arrival in California. He pondered the question, looked at all the angles, all the possibilities, the advantages as well as the disadvantages of a life married to one woman. He discussed all this with Lily, which was her name (now all but forgotten) far into the night (several nights). He waffled about, teetered on the brink of indecision until, at last, after a long walk along streets he had never before visited, he made up his mind, that yes, he would risk the leap aboard the marriage train, no matter where it took him.

Unfortunately, he had a little vision just at this moment of a train disappearing into one of those long, Hollywood-set tunnels laden with sexual innuendo. In fact, he hesitated again because of this vision, because the train went in and never came out.

Was this evidence, he wondered, that he might suffer from some heretofore dormant fear of fornication? Mulling over this unthinkable handicap slowed down his decision to wed. But, no. It couldn't be sex that worried him. Never had he ever suffered from any sort of disability in all the countless times he'd been to bed with Lily. God, it would be so embarrassing, though, if it came upon him the minute he got married. Not that he had to worry.

There is, of course, always a first time, some voice, not his own, told him. He had a sudden urge to see Lily, to get into bed with her, to tell her how much he needed her. In fact he would agree to marry her. Although, if he did turn out to have this, this difficulty, she would insist he see a doctor. Better not to marry her. No goddamn way was he going to discuss his dick with some doctor. On the other hand, who else would want him? At least she was willing to marry him — in sickness and in health — but, by the time he got around to letting Lily in on his decision to marry her, she had bought herself a one-way ticket to New York City and was halfway there.

His fears were about marriage itself, he decided, ridiculous as this might seem. What had he thought? That the act of marriage would render him helpless? That he would be sucked in, swallowed whole by Lily, and if not Lily, then some other woman, never to enjoy the familiarity of his own skin, the ramblings of his own mind, the pursuit of his own personal pleasure again? Or that Lily, or some Lily-like person might hoist him up by the belt and the collar of his shirt and heave him out the door?

From time to time, he phoned home. He wished he could talk to Aidan, find out how things were going with him, but he knew that Aidan hated talking into a phone, rarely picked it up when it was ringing, and never made calls himself.

His mother always sounded huffy when she first came on, strained, making him wonder whether he was committing some misdemeanour even at the moment of calling, interrupting her train of thought. Or had he missed some important family event, failed to comment on it, said something last time that displeased her that he should be apologizing for this time? Eventually her voice would thaw, especially when she got onto the subject of the neighbours and how they were always peeping out from behind the African violets in their windows to see what Audrey was up to today, dragging themselves away from their television sets that they kept going day and night to peep out at her, and their living rooms littered with newspapers and dirty dishes, and them never pulling their drapes to hide the clutter. So of course she's going to look in, how can she help it? She knew how they pursed their lips whenever they caught sight of that "poor half-witted" son that hangs on his mother's neck like an albatross or some such thing. "Have they nothing better to do?" she would ask. It was not a rhetorical question. Gus would make some inane reply that he hoped was both innocuous enough and sympathetic enough not to rile her.

"Does Aidan still have his job?" Gus asked.

"What job?"

"Walking Mr. Warren's dogs."

"Oh, goodness, they died years ago. I wrote you that."

"The dogs?"

"And Mr. Warren."

"So what's Aidan up to? Still typing his life history?"

"He's had some of his work published."

"What! Who published it?"

"Oh, heavens, I couldn't tell you now. It was a while ago. He made a little money, not much."

He was curious and tried to get her to put Aidan on, but he wouldn't cooperate. Gus wrote to Aidan — several letters — but nary a reply came his way.

He sent money when he could. His mother always wrote to thank him and dutifully reported, to the last penny, where it had been spent — usually on something for Aidan, slippers, a new suit of clothes to wear to church (Aidan always stood at the back for a quick getaway, should someone come too close), books, more books, and scads of paper. Some of it was spent to repair the roof, some to hire a man to cut the grass because Aidan was still afraid of the lawnmower. Never did any of it go toward her own comfort or her own wardrobe. He phoned back to say, "Live it up a little, buy yourself some new clothes. Go to the movies." He would suggest the ones he'd written the script for, not that they were exactly suitable for one's aging mother, but still, he wanted the satisfaction of knowing that she was aware that he wasn't wasting his time down there in the States, "frittering it away." Here was tangible proof, besides the cheques he sent, of his success, there for all to observe, neighbours included.

"I've little enough time as it is. I'm not about to waste it on the show."

By the time Gus's Hollywood life began to lose its glitter, he had had two more lengthy relationships that came very close to resulting in marriage, but as with his first, these romances died of attrition. He was getting fewer and fewer scripts accepted, and finding it harder and harder even to get one read. As for his acting parts, they dried up altogether. Too old. None of the fresh new scripts (except his own) required a burly, bungling, bearded, fifty-something emptying bullets into the cops or into the mobsters, or even for that matter slouching about in the background.

As he lay in bed one morning in his Hollywood apartment, thinking about rolling over and going back to sleep for lack of anything better to do, a word crept into his semi-conscious brain. *Has-been.* It made him feel as if he'd broken out in a rash. His skin itched. He pushed off his covers. He was sweating and wondering if this was what they called an anxiety attack. He sat up and when he was about to stand, the floor seemed a long way off and the inside of his head felt as empty and light as a blown eggshell. He looked way down at his bare toes and reached out to the wall for support.

By the time he'd had a shower, a cup of coffee, a banana, toast, he felt better. His head began to fill up with ideas again and he knew he'd had what they call an epiphany. That's what he decided to call it, anyway. He could not sleep his life away. At fifty-two years of age he still had a few live brain cells. He now knew something. He'd gone as far as the road was going to take him in this direction; it was time he made a ninety-degree turn and marched forward in another direction. And so he took the first step.

All morning he lumbered about his cluttered apartment, looking for something, not quite sure what, searching in half-full cardboard cartons, an old suitcase, files and drawers containing news clippings, containing folders labelled *Thots*, *Possib.*, *Toss* (still quite full), and *???*. He pawed through all of it partly because he couldn't remember exactly what his labels meant, especially the one with question marks, and partly because he was just compulsive enough to not want to leave a page unturned. Late in the afternoon he came across a failed screenplay that he remembered rather liking. Rereading it, it came to him that its major flaw was that it wasn't a screenplay at all. It was a novel.

He shoved something frozen into the microwave and while he ate the mystery food (he'd thrown out the packaging without really looking at it and the contents didn't enlighten him much), he thought deeply about his find. He went for a walk and began to see how it might start. He saw a road leading right into the heart of the work and he was anxious to get there.

For some reason it worked, it felt right, he felt at home with it. Of course he knew the territory of the story, knew where it was going. His characters were old friends. He'd already given his hero a voice, a viewpoint. He saw him stretch out and up in the novel, saw him with an added dimension. And he saw him as a Canadian. Here in California Gus had been aware of his own Canadianness. He had often had a bit of a them-and-us attitude, as though he stood out somehow, that people could tell he was Canadian just by looking at him, or listening to him speak, or reading his screenplays. No one ever mentioned any of this to him. It probably never occurred to them that there was a difference. It was just a perception he had; he felt Canadian.

What Gus hadn't understood when he first wrote his story as a screenplay was that some things are what they have to be. After some thirty years of writing, Gus felt as though he'd entered a new wing of an otherwise familiar house. A window blind had been yanked up, allowing him a view from a different vantage point.

It was time to go home.

ten

HE CAME HOME in June, home for good. It was the old neighbourhood, all right, but it was nearly all new. He marvelled at the changes. He supposed he'd changed, too, although he couldn't see it. Driving along his street in the back of a cab he craned his neck. The trees were bigger, greener, showier. Lots of new houses on the street where old ones built in the twenties and thirties once had stood. He noticed how tall and slender they were, reaching far back almost to the lots behind. Large, colourful plastic toys, most with wheels, littered many of the front lawns, while chunky, expensive cars filled the driveways. His mother's small house looked foreign, stunted, unfashionable. Getting out of the cab he was nearly sideswiped by a half-grown kid on a skateboard whizzing past, cigarette smoke streaming behind.

His mother was remarkable for her age, which he wasn't sure of, but figured she must be in her eighties. She was a bit stooped but still had that facade of brute strength she'd always had. He doubted, though, that she could pick Aidan up if she had to, a feat she used to be proud of. She still had her wits and her ability to make Gus wonder what he'd done to put her in a bad mood. He had grown a beard while he was in California; she called it an abomination whenever they met face to face. Maybe he'd take pains to keep it trimmed.

Aidan had shrunk, if anything. His shoulder blades protruded more than ever, like a small pair of wings. He rarely went outside, never to the park, not even into the back garden. He pretty much kept to his room, which was now lined on three sides with overstuffed bookshelves. Gus checked to see if the books were arranged in any kind of order, but they weren't, as far as he could see. This didn't much surprise him as Aidan's instant recall probably allowed him to find whatever book he wanted from the Alexandria Quartet to *Zuleika Dobson*, from Richardson to Richler and everything in between.

Gus felt heavy-laden at home, as if something in the very air signified failure, oppression, unrequited dreams. His old room was cramped, his bed lumpy, he had to wait his turn for the bathroom. His mother's cooking had deteriorated. He offered to take over some of it, but she wouldn't hear of it. She couldn't imagine that a son of hers would have the first clue about how to work the oven, how to make passable gravy, or even how long to cook potatoes.

He lost no time in getting Aidan to talk about his writing and to show him his published works, about which Gus had long been curious. He sat on Aidan's bed, neatly made by his mother. Aidan was proud of his efforts, Gus noticed, smug even. He sat at his desk, new to Gus, reached for a small paperbound book on a shelf above it and tossed it to him. Gus leafed through the literary journal with contributions from a number of people, none of whom was familiar to Gus. But, what would he know, living in the States, immersed in the motion picture industry for thirty years?

He studied the table of contents for Aidan's name, but before he found it, Aidan shoved a stack of five more journals toward him.

"You're in all these?"

"Very many books. Very postmodern, very erudite, very stylish." His voice was the same flat monotone with staccato sentences. He had more grey in his hair than Gus. He swivelled in his office-style chair to face Gus, tilting back as best he could with his hunched shoulders, hands behind his head, elbows winging out in front of his face, a foot propped on an open drawer of his desk.

Playing the role, Gus thought, smiling wryly, to the bloody hilt. Gus pulled out his cigarettes and offered one to Aidan, who took it, much to Gus's surprise. Gus held out a light. Aidan bent forward, holding his cigarette awkwardly, like a pencil, but he got it lit. "When did you start smoking?" Gus asked.

"Today."

"So, I'm corrupting you, am I?"

"Like little brother, like big brother."

Gus went into his room and came back with an ashtray. His mother hated the fact that he smoked, although she'd been known to indulge herself from time to time. She'd have a fit when she saw Aidan taking it up. He settled down on Aidan's bed to read his brother's contribution to the journal. Out of the corner of his eye he was aware of Aidan practising smoking, angling his head to glance into the mirror above his dresser, flicking ash off the end into the ashtray whenever Gus did.

Gus turned leaves until he found Aidan's offering. It was entitled: *Inside Cloud* and was a page and a half long. He read it twice without getting it. "I don't get it."

Aidan brought his chair down with a wrenching creak. His eyes were wide, disbelieving. "It's no good?"

"No, I'm sure it's good. I just don't get it, I don't understand this kind of poetry."

Defensively, his voice edgy, loud, Aidan repeated, "Very postmodern, very erudite, very stylish."

Gus could see how wide the gulf was, now, between them, although he thought he understood what was going on in Aidan's head at that moment. This work was more important to him than his stacks and stacks of autobiography, because it had achieved the coveted editorial stamp of approval and had become part of what Aidan worshipped, a book.

At this stage in his life Gus knew he'd been guilty of hubris himself, from time to time. Yet, having also felt the despair and uncertainty of trying to make something of his talent, mediocre as he feared it might be, he was not absolutely certain how he should react. He could quell his brother's fears, flatter him, pretend the writing was wonderful. Maybe it was. It must be, he thought. He knew enough about the literary world to know that having something published in a literary journal, American or Canadian, was a mark of true promise. Apparently. Or he could be truthful and confess that it wasn't his bag, and that he was incompetent to judge it. He remembered how Aidan used to get a grip on his throat whenever he was angry with him, whenever Gus tried to take him away from his reading to go to the park. "Let me see another one," he said, dodging the issue.

Aidan opened another journal with shaking hands. His narrow face was a mass of lines, eyes feverish, jaw muscles clenching. Gus was startled to find his own heart beating overtime in response. He wanted to like this. He would like it or lie.

"Great imagery," he said. "Great choice of words."

Aidan was still tense, clenching and unclenching his bony hands, so like Gus's with their knobby knuckles.

Gus read:

> *passion is a promise is a slow need*
> *burning low very blue-lipped*
> *very unforgiving very*
> *like a candle*
> *blown*

There was more. Gus read on, commented on a turn of phrase, nodded, said, "Great stuff!" He looked up at Aidan with what he hoped was enthusiasm. Take it easy, old man, he wanted to say. It's only a few lines of poetry. Did he really expect to become Wordsworth with this, Gus wondered? He opened his mouth, but glanced up from the page at Aidan before he said anything. Aidan's eyes, behind new but nevertheless off-kilter glasses, were little blazing Roman candles. Gus expected to hear an explosion any minute because Aidan was not fooled by his acting. "It's, it's very strong," he said, afraid he sounded as if he was making up his lines as he went along. He was. "Very impressive." He was afraid he sounded like Aidan. "Very earth-shattering."

Gus had never seen his brother move so fast. Aidan leapt at him, pressed him back onto the bed, got his hands around Gus's throat, squeezing, pumping his head up and down. Gus tried to pull his hands away, thrashed with his legs, eventually managed to roll both of them over, off the bed onto the floor. Aidan continued his death-hold on Gus's neck, but his grip was weakening. Seeing his advantage, Gus got his hands on Aidan's windpipe causing him to choke.

"Stop, this instant!" Audrey, red-faced with anger, was in the doorway. But Gus would not release Aidan's scrawny neck until he felt a lessening in his hold on his own. Audrey reached for whatever came to hand and threw it at the warring brothers — books, a laundry bag, a pillow — as if she was trying to break up a dogfight.

It was over. Aidan lay on the floor coughing. Gus stood up, staggered, and sat on the bed massaging his neck. Aidan rolled over, curled himself into a little ball and sobbed — wrenching, racking, man-sized howls of despair. Audrey crouched down unsteadily beside her middle-aged son, her grey-haired boy, nearly toppling over onto him. She smoothed down his too-long hair, making soft mothering sounds, patting his arm and rubbing his back, until he swatted out at her, grunting, gasping. She reached out to her other son, the prodigal, not out of compassion, but for assistance as she tried to stand up. Gus helped her and then crouched near his brother.

"Leave him," she ordered. "He needs to stop on his own."

Gus ran a hand through his own greying hair. "I'll get him some water."

"You've done just about enough already, young man." She marched out of the bedroom, spry as ever.

Gus left his brother, no longer crying, limp, curled on the floor, torpid, like the chrysalis of some insect. He took a few of the literary journals into his own room, switched on the reading lamp beside his bed, and began a small contemplation of modern literary expression, Aidan's included. His brother's efforts were not, by any means, the least puzzling, the least accessible. In fact, one of his poems was quite striking. It was called *Arms and the Man* and was about their mother, Gus believed, and about Aidan himself (an entirely different take from either Virgil or Shaw). He felt that the poem referred to their mother's strength. At first he was not sure if that meant physical strength or strength of character, but upon a third reading decided that it was both. In it too, was the sense that the grown man, not long ago a baby, wresting himself free of his mother's arms, now needed to feel them picking him up.

Or maybe it meant something entirely different.

A FEW DAYS AFTER his return, a steaming hot day, Gus went out for a walk. Actually he was looking for a place to live. He had a list of bachelor apartments for rent, but my God, they were so expensive.

He knew he could no longer stay at home amidst all the tension and resentment and jealousy and rejection. Aidan seemed to have two speeds with regard to his poetry — frantic arrogance, or numbing despondency. He didn't believe Gus when he told him in all honesty that some of his work was good, nor did he believe him when he claimed that some of it was unclear, shrouded in too much mystery. "For me," he always added, as if that took the bite out of the criticism. Stupid of him to think that. His brother probably needed Gus to worship his words the same way Gus had yearned for Aidan's unqualified praise. Aidan no longer even looked at him. He sat hunched over his work, smoking one cigarette halfway down and then another. Gus wished he'd buy his own and stop taking them from the carton he had on his dresser.

He didn't take any of the apartments he looked at. He was afraid of running low on money before he could find a way of making some. He'd live at home. Once he'd found a publisher for his novel, he might try converting another one of his rejected screenplays. Could become a cottage industry. He might just do that, if he could get his powers of concentration to cooperate in that bughouse he had come home to, and if he could keep from getting throttled by his maniac brother.

GUS FINALLY TOOK the bus and then the subway, one smog-laden day, to the Reference Library, where he spent part of the morning looking up publishers who might be attracted to his book. He returned with several possibilities, some right there in Toronto and some in New York, as well as a list of agents, none of them familiar. He'd never had much luck with agents in the States. He had had one early in his career who gouged him unmercifully, and then another more recently who did nothing for him, talked a lot but sat on his ass. Forget an agent, he thought. He'd deliver it to the first Toronto publisher on the list and see what happened.

At home, he trudged upstairs. He was still reluctant to call the thing finished. He itched to do some final touch-up work on his manuscript, to polish it, sharpen some of the images, make sure he'd layered some of the smaller events that add up to something intriguing. He'd do that before stuffing it into the oversized envelope he'd purchased.

Aidan's door was closed. There was no sound of typing. Dozing maybe, Gus thought. He did a lot of that lately. In his own room the light was on, although he knew he had turned it off before he went out. On his desk amid the clutter of pens, pencils, books, a coffee mug half-full of stale coffee, cigarettes, an ashtray, scraps of paper with meaningless reminders on them, there was an empty space beside his laptop where his manuscript had had the place of honour. His heart pounded and he felt sweat seeping through the pores of his head until he remembered that all was not lost. He could make another copy, although he hated the idea of spending more money on paper and a new ink cartridge.

He swept Aidan's door open nevertheless, expecting disorder, pages ripped, scattered, mayhem. Aidan was humped over his desk, flipping page after page of the manuscript. His ashtray was full of half-smoked cigarettes, some still alight. A big chrome coffee-table lighter that Gus hadn't seen for years, that dated back to some time before he was born, sat amid the debris.

Head bent, his little scapular wings protruding through his shirt, Aidan swivelled his chair around for a quick cockeyed glance at Gus and then returned to his task. Gus decided to wait before saying anything. It wouldn't take him long to finish reading it. He sat on Aidan's bed, but removed himself smartly to lean against the door jamb instead, for a quick getaway, if necessary.

Aidan turned over the last page and remained hunched, eyes downcast, hands motionless. Gus cleared his throat. "What do you think of it?"

No reply. After a moment or two, while Gus shifted weight from one foot to the other, rattled change in his pocket, oversized coins he couldn't quite get used to, Aidan's wings began to shake, tears fell on the white over-turned final page, leaving blots, little shrivelled patches.

Gus wanted to go over to his brother, to reach out and put a hand on his bony shoulder, comfort him somehow, but was afraid that if he did he might bring on another murderous attack. "It's not that sad, really," he said quietly, lamely.

Aidan shoved the pile of papers across his desk toward Gus. Never raising his eyes, he stepped over to his bed, lowered himself as if already in a dream, and with his face to the wall drew up his knees. Gus wondered for a tense moment if he'd stopped breathing, if he had actually willed himself to stop living, so still did he lie. In a moment he heard a sniff, then another.

Gus would have gone down on his knees at this moment, if Aidan had requested it, just to hear him say, *Very good, very nice, very like a real book.* "Aidan?" he said. "Is it any good?"

Silence. A sniff.

Gus couldn't believe how needy he felt, how childlike. More than anything else, he wanted approval from this man, this reader, this human repository of the world's literature. He needed to feel reassured, to feel he had not wasted his time, that his brain, although aging, had not gone into retirement. He needed to extract blood from this stone.

Audrey called up to tell her boys that lunch was ready. In a few minutes Gus went down, but Aidan remained where he was. Audrey fretted, went up, coaxed Aidan, but got nowhere. She made up a tray for him and carried it upstairs. When she finally sat down across from Gus she said, "Well, what did you do to him this time?" Gus ran a hand through his unruly hair, not bothering to answer. He put the rest of his meat loaf (left over from the night before) and his undressed salad of rusty lettuce and pale tomato slices between two pieces of bread, and took it up to his room.

On his way out of the kitchen he heard his mother say, to the wall, "So this is what we've come to."

GUS WAS LUCKY TO find a quiet little bar, just a mousehole of a place, Crocker's, on Yonge not too far south of Eglinton, where he could sit all day at a back table with his laptop and finish polishing up his manuscript, reading and rereading it, making changes, adding, removing. He began to feel less like a drone turning commas into dashes, cringing over some piece of triviality that seemed embarrassingly inept, and more like a man doing something worthy, something he loved doing, able to put aside for the time the concerns he had about his brother, about his mother and the rancour she bore him.

His manuscript still didn't have a title, but it was time, he knew, to get the thing off his hands and into the hands of a publisher. The title would come. He had a couple in the back of his mind, but he couldn't choose, not just yet. He was excited about the novel. Sometimes he convinced himself that it was good, a damned fine effort. Sometimes he awakened in the night and thought himself stupidly naive. How could he do something as daunting as write a novel that anyone would want to read. An old screenwriter like him. A hack.

At length, he shoved the whole thing into an envelope and off he went to the first publisher on his list. He decided to walk that July Monday; it was a great day. It was the best he'd felt since Aidan's mute critique of his work.

With the address of the publisher in his pocket, he walked briskly, his heavy packet under his arm, and made for the Art Gallery of Ontario. He knew the street he was looking for was in that vicinity. He found it and the building without much trouble, once an old house it seemed, and left the large envelope with a pleasant young woman behind a desk who told him she'd see that it got into the right hands.

He left in a daze of excitement and then felt a wave of panic. He should go back and retrieve it. It wasn't ready. It wasn't good enough.

It was...slight.

He stood on a nearby corner long after the light had changed and wondered if he had included his name and address. Of course he had. He was forgetful, not stupid.

He moved on with the next green light. His head was hot, and his feet scarcely came in contact with the sidewalk. It would be incredible if it were published. And what if, after it *was* published, it was optioned for a movie? He wondered if he could rewrite the screenplay. He wondered if the screenplay that failed as a film, and was then turned into a novel, could be turned back into a successful film. These little conundrums took him all the way back to Crocker's where he ordered a double Scotch. He'd bought the *Star* on his way and in it read about a woman whose husband was killed Saturday afternoon in a car accident as the result of a beam fallen from a truck onto the road. The woman, apparently, was only a few minutes ahead of her husband in another vehicle. She was quoted as saying "If only I had stopped and pulled it off the road!" If only, he thought sympathetically. He had quite a little buzz on by the time he headed home. When he got there, he clipped the article about the board lying on the road, and the woman who could have saved her husband's life. He liked the irony. He added it to a folder he had of ironic clippings, entitled *Possib*.

eleven

IT IS A COLD FEBRUARY evening, the coldest February in living memory or some such time span, the weatherman had said. Gus turns up his collar and heads for home. It's late. They'll have had dinner without him. Just as well, because dinners are a pretty sorry affair these days with his mother angrily slamming things around and Aidan on the point of tears every time he looks at Gus.

When he gets inside the house, a scorched smell assails his nostrils. He doesn't think any more about it because he's so hungry. He puts his computer, tucked into its carrying bag, on the kitchen counter. In it, too, are his dog-eared and marked-up screenplay and his *Possib.* folder, along with the floppies on which he stores his work. He sheds his coat, heaves it onto a chair and sticks his head into the fridge. Not much there. She could at least have saved his dinner for him, he thinks. God, he would so much love to move out. He grabs a couple of eggs and the milk. What is that smell, he thinks, as he reaches for the frying pan. And then he knows.

Yelling at his mother, at Aidan, he heads for the stairs. At the top of the stairs he encounters Aidan standing in the hall looking calmly through the door of his room as smoke builds and drifts out. "Where's Mother?" Gus yells. He doesn't know why he's yelling because the fire in Aidan's room makes very little noise. Aidan doesn't answer him because he's transfixed by the flames travelling up his curtain.

"Mother!" Gus shouts. Then he notices the closed bathroom door. He rattles the locked doorknob and pounds the door. He hears his mother's angry voice, "In a minute, in a minute."

"We have a bit of a fire out here," he says, forcing his voice to sound calm, not wanting her to panic, even choosing his words with care because she'll be sure to remember them and tell him later that he didn't have to scare them all half to death by saying the house is burning down. He hears the toilet flush. He pulls Aidan away from his bedroom doorway. "Go phone nine-one-one!" He pushes him toward the stairs. He hears water running in the sink as his mother, ever meticulous, washes her hands. The tap is turned off; she's obviously drying her hands. "What's that smell?" she calls. "What on earth are you boys up to, now?"

"It's a fire," Gus calls. He's got to get his mother out of the bathroom. Does she not understand? Aidan has wandered back to stare into his bedroom. "Fuckin' idiots," Gus mouths as his mother emerges calmly from the bathroom, shaking her head.

"Merciful heaven!" Audrey declares. "I can't turn my back for one moment!" She coughs as the smoke reaches her. Gus takes her by the shoulders to hustle her down the stairs. He's coughing now, too.

"Get your coat!" he orders his mother. She is now looking properly terrified. "Aidan!" she screams, "Aidan!" Gus tears back up the stairs and pulls Aidan, clattering, down behind him. Aidan's face is a puzzled mask, as though he can't understand what all this brightness and heat and confusion have to do with him. "Too much smoke," he says.

Audrey hauls Aidan's winter jacket out of the hall closet and helps him into it, rushing her son gently, as if they're on the point of being late for church. She struggles with his zipper. Gus, meanwhile, is on the phone, his hands shaking so badly it takes him two tries to dial the number. He gives the information to the voice at the other end, his name, address, phone number, what else, he thinks. Height? Weight? He hangs up.

His mother is struggling into her own coat now and kicking about in the bottom of the closet with the toe of her shoe, looking for her galoshes. Gus tries to hurry her, but she has never allowed anyone to hurry her and will not begin now. "My gloves," she says. "I think I left them upstairs."

"Tough," he says. "Out." He pushes a reluctant Aidan out the front door ahead of them and then with his arm around his mother's shoulders and bracing her against him, he trundles her down the front steps out into the freezing starless night. In the distance they can hear the fire sirens as help makes its way up a distant street.

Aidan stares open-mouthed up at the house, looking bewildered, shivering in the cold. Smoke is seeping around the edges of the upper windows, one glowing dully orange, and then an explosion with glass flying everywhere. Smoke pours through the front door, which Gus has left open. He should close it, he thinks. Deprive the fire of oxygen. Futile thought. The next-door neighbour, an older woman, opens her front door and bustles out coatless, her arms folded in front of her. "I thought I smelled smoke!" she calls to them.

"We have a fire upstairs," Gus calls back.

She wants to call the fire department, but Gus assures her it's been called as the sirens scream along their street.

"How bad is it?"

Gus doesn't answer. The roof is smoking. He had no idea fire could spread so quickly. He should go back in and try to save something. And then he remembers his computer on the kitchen counter, weeks of hard work on the new story buried within its memory. His finished novel is on a floppy in a pocket of the carrying bag. His screenplays are in the bag, the central nervous system of everything he's trying to do. He heads for the house, pounding up the front steps.

Other neighbours come out now as soon as the first wailing fire truck pulls to a stop. Aidan calls to Gus's back, but Gus doesn't answer, doesn't hear. The coatless woman rushes toward Aidan and his mother, but Aidan doesn't know her name and is frightened of her. She pleads with Audrey, with both of them, to come with her to her house, to go inside out of the cold. Aidan ducks beyond her reach and runs. He sidles behind a big maple on the lawn of someone who lives across the street.

Audrey has never in her life trusted these nosy neighbours of hers, who have nothing better to do than peep out their windows all day at her, in her well-worn coat and old-fashioned galoshes, and at her poor son who can't help being the way he is. "I'm all right," she says to the woman from next door.

"But, my dear, you'll freeze to death out here," the woman insists.

Two more fire trucks arrive. A crowd is gathering. A fireman moves people back to the other side of the street. Another fireman gets an arm under Audrey's arm and with the woman on her other side escorts the unwilling captive into enemy territory. "Aidan," Audrey calls weakly. But Aidan is distraught, on the other side of the street, wringing his hands, turning away from would-be consolers. He is hunched into his coat, arms akimbo to stave off these predators with his elbows. With his lank sparse hair and skewed glasses he looks like a wide-eyed fledgling almost ready for flight. He's softly whimpering his anxiety into the floodlit night. "Gus," he murmurs over and over, "Gus." His whole being is gathered, bunched tightly into one small prayer for his brother. He knows why he's gone back inside.

Gus turns back from the smoke tumbling down the stairs into the front hall. He runs out and around the side of the house under cover of the smoke screen before anyone can stop him. He's splashed by the water spraying high above him. He slips and falls on the wet ice, but by crawling, crab-like at first, he regains his footing and makes his way to the kitchen door at the back of the house. He knows it will be locked. He puts his shoulder through the glass in the window and reaches in to unlock it.

The kitchen lights are out. The power has short-circuited, he guesses. But Gus's way is lit by the ice-blue floodlights shining through from the hall, from the trucks outside and coming through the kitchen window. He can make out his coat on the chair, and his computer case on the counter. The smoke is just beginning to reach the kitchen. He grabs his coat and tries to shrug into it, but his sweater sleeves bunch up inside. He can't bend his arms. Swearing, he pulls it off and starts again grasping the cuffs of his sweater. Upstairs, above him, he hears wood cracking, beams breaking. The ceiling plaster above the stove gives way. He grabs the canvas carrying bag containing his computer and the screenplays with their hieroglyphical notations and heads for the door. He looks back in time to see a flaming two-by-four fall through the ceiling above the counter where his computer bag had sat seconds before. One end of it has landed on his mother's apron folded on the counter, faded blue, much-mended, with tiny white squares all over it like Chiclets. It has a bib front and long wide ties and it's been part of Gus's home life from the time he was a baby. He runs back, grabs it from under the burning rafter, throws it on the floor to stamp out the flames and then exits with it.

He makes his way back again through the side yard to the front of the house where a fireman yells at him to get his ass out of there. He slips and slides like a madman on the ice, but doesn't fall, nor does he trip on the electrical cable that falls two feet in front of him. He is spared; he is all-powerful; he has a talisman. He stuffs what's left of the blackened apron into his coat pocket.

With his skinny legs galloping and his arms swinging wildly, Aidan rushes from the far side of the street toward him. "Gus!" he calls, "Gus!" The relief in his voice is almost palpable.

Gus pulls up short, amazed, heartened. He opens his big arms to catch his catapulting brother and sees his tear-streaked face.

Aidan backs off a little, pulls at Gus's arms, tears at his pockets, the front of his jacket, the computer case hanging from his shoulder. His eyes are narrow with focused anxiety as he searches Gus's puzzled eyes. "Where is it?"

"What?"

"My work! My pages! My books!"

Gus knows, now; he understands.

"Gone, Aidan, burnt to an ash." He knows by the look of pure anguish on Aidan's face where he stands in his brother's affection. Nowhere.

Aidan crumples onto the icy sidewalk. A fireman is yelling at them to get back. Bitterly, Gus tries to haul Aidan to his feet, but he's gone limp. He drags him by the shoulders and yells, "Stand up, you bastard."

Across from their burning house, now, Aidan stands up.

"Very bad brother," Aidan says to him. "Go back."

"Go to hell," Gus replies.

"You go back inside. You go upstairs." It's a fierce whispered croak. "My work, my pages, my books."

Through the front door Gus can see flames at the top of the stairs. Aidan stops croaking at him, knowing now that his brother will not do what he's being ordered to do.

Gus watches as Aidan walks across the street. The firemen's attention is on the roof, which is beginning to collapse. Aidan walks quickly. Gus knows he is going to run into the house and stands there, waiting. Everyone else is watching the roof. There is an explosion, probably from the oil heater in the living room, as windows blow out on the far side of the house. Someone's bound to notice Aidan and get him back out of the way, Gus thinks. I could run after him, he thinks. There's still time.

The crowd of onlookers has grown. Whole families have come out for the spectacle. A woman bundled up with a big scarf around her head has just arrived. She says to no one in particular, "I thought the fire was right on my street!" She asks a woman beside her if they got everyone out.

"I think so. But wait, look!"

Those who had gasped as the roof collapsed, are shocked into silence, now, to see a man run toward the burning house. Someone yells, "Oh my God." Others ask what's happening. All around Gus people are reacting to Aidan galloping toward the steps, toward the open front door. They cringe to see Aidan reach out as eagerly as a lover to the consuming flames.

Gus's entire body is clenched, petrified. But then, he slings the computer bag strap over his head to make it more secure. He puts his freezing bare hands into the pockets of his coat, fingering the scorched apron.

As he watches his brother run, his legs pumping smoothly, like a runner taking off from the starting line, his arms flapping in his usual crazed fashion, nimbly mounting the outside steps, pausing before entering the inferno, Gus has a rush of horror, imagining burnt hair, eyes, lips. He shoots out from the crowd and dashes across the street bounding up the front walk where he is pushed back by a fireman. He strains, fights to get past him.

"My brother!" he shouts.

The flames on the staircase have consumed the smoke and now they reach with yearning toward Aidan as he runs up the staircase to greet them. Arms spread, back arched like a runner at the finish line, he swoons into their warm embrace.

twelve

GUS SLOGS THROUGH freezing slush to the house next door where his mother has apparently taken shelter. The fire is under control; people are yawning, going home to their cozy beds, but not before they check each room in their house to make sure that all is safe and fireproof. Gus knocks on the neighbour's door. He doesn't even know her name.

"Where's Aidan?" his mother asks the moment she sets eyes on him as he enters the neighbour's living room.

He knows he's going to be blunt. It's not in him to sneak up on something as devastating as this. He is a blurter of bad news. "He's dead."

His mother's eyes are on him, disgusted with his reply. She makes a disbelieving sound with her teeth and tongue.

"He ran back in," he adds quietly. Still she says nothing.

Her eyes flit back and forth over his own, sorting out the meaning of what he's said, giving its veracity the benefit of the doubt.

"No," she says.

Gus is looking at the floor now, at the neighbour's, Mrs. Curl's, ugly carpet, the colour of diarrhea. He looks up, his lips down-turned, pressed hard against his teeth.

"Oh, God!" she howls at last. "My baby!" Over and over she calls out for her baby, her darling, her only child. Mrs. Curl rushes to her, sits beside her on the couch, puts her arms around her still bulky, still capable, shoulders and rocks with her while she bewails her loss.

Gus's slouch is no longer that of a youth with newly attained height. He stands there, middle-aged, stooped. He sags in his sock feet, damp from getting his shoes drenched by the hoses; his shirt hangs partway out over his well-worn jeans, also soaked; his sweater is rumpled; his face with its inexpertly trimmed beard crumples in despair. He leaves the room and finds his way into the kitchen where he sits down at the table, his head in his hands, a non-son, a non-brother.

THE FIREFIGHTERS RECOVER what they can of his brother. There isn't much left of Aidan to bury, but they bury him anyway. There is a short service in the chapel of the funeral parlour to which a few neighbours come as well as a small delegation from the church Audrey attends, and a cousin from Oshawa, and the cousin's husband. Gus is surprised to see a priest among the mourners, no one he knows. He turns out to be a hell of a nice guy. Gus can't think of his name, but he remembers that he has a radio phone-in show that his mother liked to listen to. She said once, turning off the radio at the end of the show, "Even though I was raised United Church, I feel like a Catholic, sometimes." Gus didn't comment, not aware that you could feel like either a Catholic or a member of the United Church (forgetting at the time that he had deemed it possible to feel Canadian). "I think my ancestors must have been Catholic and it's showing up in me." Next she'll be wanting a crucifix, Gus had thought.

Audrey goes up to the priest as if she knows him and starts talking, weeping. He holds her two hands and looks down at her with the gentlest, most sympathetic expression Gus has ever seen. He wonders what his mother is telling him: that he, Gus, is to blame for everything?

Audrey has already given Gus the benefit of her musings. An hour before the funeral she informed him that she holds him wholly responsible for his brother's death, from the moment he first taught Aidan to smoke cigarettes, to his failure to prevent him from running back into the house. And, yes, he *is* blameworthy, he thinks. He knew that his brother was careless with his cigarettes, often having several burning at once. He also felt, at the time, that the coal oil heaters were likely unsafe. He had mentioned as much to his mother, but she wouldn't listen. She'd hauled them out every winter for as long as she could remember and nothing had ever happened. He had felt uneasy about them and yet hadn't argued the point. He doesn't think he has ever stood up to his mother. Or, at least, not very often. Leaving home was his only gesture of defiance and by then he was a grown man.

The priest is getting an earful, he expects. He doesn't know why he feels this way, but he'd like somehow to vindicate himself. He would like this gentle-eyed man to nod at him, say, "It wasn't your fault." He walks to the back of the chapel where his mother is holding forth on the multitude and dimensions of his sins. Gus stands beside his mother, head bowed. His mother stumbles over her words. "Well, enough said, enough said, it's over and done with now, and I, I. . . ." She searches her pockets for dry Kleenex while the priest shakes Gus's hand and murmurs sympathetic condolences. He asks Gus what he does for a living and Gus tells him he's a screenwriter working on a novel. They have something in common, the priest says. He's about to have his third book published.

It was nice of the priest to come to Aidan's funeral, though, and to hang around for a while talking to his mother, and to him, too. Interesting that he writes books in his spare time. In some ways he is pleased that his mother *had* phoned in to his show to tell him about Aidan and about his talent and about the fire. Maybe *he* should phone in, tell him he has no friends. Get the name of his publisher.

Maybe he's turning into his mother.

Gus thanks him for coming and says, "Come on, now, Mother, the funeral car is waiting." He turns to shake hands again with the priest and for a moment, the man holds him in his gaze.

"Nobody's perfect," he says.

Gus looks puzzled.

The priest shrugs. "We all have to accept that."

PART III

Val and Gus

thirteen

AFTER HER DINNER, this extremely cold evening in February, Val hears fire sirens sounding as if they are coming right along her street. Feeling lonely, or curious, or bloodthirsty, she decides to go out and take a look. She throws on her coat, and winding a scarf around her head and across her nose and chin, she runs up the street. A fire truck races past her, siren wailing. She can see an orange glow only a few blocks north. She should go back, she thinks, but doesn't. By the time she gets to the burning house three fire trucks are at work with hoses trained on it as well as on the two adjacent houses. There is instant ice everywhere. The street is filled with anxious neighbours, edging as close as they dare, craning their necks trying to see over people's heads, some grimly turning away, saying, "Oh, my God." Others ask what's happening.

"Some guy just ran in."

Through the open front door of the small house Val catches a brief glimpse, just before she turns away, of flames halfway down the staircase. They seem to hesitate as if unsure whether or not to descend. In their midst she thinks she can make out the figure of a man. Sickened, she asks if there were any children. There weren't, apparently.

No pets, either. She wishes she had never left the security, the innocence, of her home.

Back at home, she can't stop thinking about the open door, the inferno on the stairs, the man melting into the flames. She clears up the few dishes she had left and gets ready for bed. Brushing her teeth she imagines ravenous flames attaching themselves to his clothes, to his hair, attracting other flames, beckoning them, until they lick up all of his flesh and grind his bones to ash. There is no use in trying to go to sleep.

She gets a copy she has made of A. A. McNiall's manuscript and sits propped up in bed rereading Part Three, re-entering the spirit of the story, finding an inexplicable comfort in it as if it were reality and everything else fiction. Eventually, her eyes tire, her head becomes heavy, she puts it aside and turns out her light. She wishes the author would write or phone to inquire about it. She would love to be working on it.

Rolling onto her side with the duvet pulled up to her ears she is afraid she will have nightmares about the fire. Instead, she dreams that she is a character in a book, something like the manuscript she's been rereading. There are a multiplicity of characters who drift in and out of the dream, but when she wakens just before dawn, none of it makes any sense, and the few snatches she remembers float beyond the reach of reason. At odd moments throughout her day, mere shadows, tiny hints, the slightest atom of an emotion returns and she thinks, oh, yes, that dream.

VAL HAS SPENT THE afternoon editing, slashing thirty pages from a promising novel. It has left her with a Gulliver-like sense that perhaps she sometimes treads heavily through her life unaware of what tiny, tender sensibilities she might be trampling along the way. Arriving with little time to spare at the television studio for a live interview that Robert has wished upon her, she has trouble ridding her thoughts of this lumbering, unheeding side of herself.

She is in the women's washroom down the hall from the sound-deadened room only a few minutes before she, Robert, and Lynnette Appsley are to be hurled over the air waves and into living rooms across the country. Her various bodily functions are working harder and faster than is absolutely necessary. She is aware of her heart beating loud enough to be heard. Her bladder is making numerous demands. Her face is embarrassingly red. Perspiration dots her upper lip making her look as though her nose is running. Maybe her nose *is* running. As you get older, you don't recognize little things like that until you catch a glimpse of yourself in an unexpected mirror and there you are with a crystalline pendant.

Washing her hands at the sink, she wishes she had done something about her unkempt nails. She'll keep them out of sight, sit on her hands. She studies herself in the mirror. She looks tired, old, in fact. Today is her birthday. Her fiftieth birthday. Apart from her aunt's phone call early this morning, no one has mentioned a thing, although Denise sent her a card a week early because they were going to be in Barbados on the actual day. She knows when Robert's birthday is. On his last she took him out for lunch and gave him a book of Thomas Hardy's poetry she'd come across in a secondhand bookstore — a particularly fine one, leather bound. She knew he liked Hardy. She assumed he knew when her birthday was. Maybe not. Forget about it.

She has frown lines developing, she notices. If she keeps her eyebrows raised, they are not as prominent. She had thought that someone would apply makeup to them before they were to go before the television camera, but this hasn't happened. "Low budget programming," she mutters.

Her eyes are disappearing, or so it seems. She used to have decent eyelashes and rather fine eyebrows, but they must be falling out. Or they're turning grey and invisible. Beside Robert and Lynnette she'll look like a mole coming out of the dark, minuscule eyes squinting myopically through her dark-rimmed glasses. She really should get contacts, except that now her style of eye-wear is becoming the very latest thing. She has some emergency makeup in a small zipper bag in her handbag.

"Three minutes," someone calls, knuckling the washroom door.

She is trying to move swiftly to brush mascara onto what's left of her moulting lashes. She manages to smear it. A black smudge on her eyelid. It won't come off because it's the everlasting kind of makeup. Other eye. No matching smudge. Eyeliner now along the bottom invisible fringe. "Damn!" She's forgotten how thick this brand goes on. She's drawn a bold curve out to and a little beyond the corner of her eye. Both eyes. Cleopatra, she thinks. On her deathbed. She adds a slash of red to her lips, turns sideways, views her abdomen while sucking it in and holding her breath and cheers up because even though she's putting on weight again, she's still not as hefty as that cow Lynnette Appsley.

The washroom door opens and Lynnette's head appears around it. "What the hell are you *doing* in here? We're almost on the air." Lynnette is staring at Val's new face with an air of wonderment.

"Moo," Val says. She closes her makeup bag, returns it to her handbag and follows Lynnette onto the set. Robert, natty in navy and grey, striped tie, hair stylishly trimmed, shoes shined, stands up, pulls out her chair and doesn't even glance at her lady-of-the-night persona.

Suddenly they are under lights and being scrutinized by cameras. The host of the show, Val knows, is one of the media's terribly bright young men who's read everything (and retained all of it) and who, besides, has charm, good looks and wit going for him. He directs his first question to Lynnette and the camera dollies in close. Lynnette replies confidently.

Val is always somewhat overwhelmed by new venues. Often, in an unusual setting, her hearing becomes impaired while other senses take over. For instance, at this moment she smells Lynnette's perfume and for a flickering second admires it and wonders what it is. The host takes her attention and briefly, she is obsessed with the way his nostrils and lips twitch ever so slightly, like a rabbit. She cannot take her eyes off them. Could he be nervous? He's a little less daunting viewed in this light. Robert is adding a few well-turned phrases to Lynnette's. Meanwhile, Val sits with raised eyebrows to obliterate her frown lines and nurtures a gentle smile because her face in repose tends to make her look suicidal.

Concentrate, she tells herself (Aunt Millie will be watching the show). Her eyes widen of their own accord as if that will help her surf the conversational wave of book-babble, as Ed used to call it, and now she begins to hear it. "In other words," the host interrupts, pouncing on something Robert has just said, "what you're saying is that Canadian books have an exotic appeal abroad. Is that in the sense that Canadian writers themselves are a breed apart, or are our stories, our culture, our landscape things to be wondered at?"

"All of the above," Robert agrees. "Because we are largely a mystery to ourselves, we come across — we Canadians — in literature at any rate — come across as arcane, I think I could say, enigmatic, indefinable, if I may use that word."

Lynnette is looking at Robert rather admiringly, Val thinks. She looks as though she might pat him on the head and say, good boy.

The host turns his magnetic eyes toward Val now. "As an editor," he begins, "what do you see as a common flaw, I mean, if we may be so bold, nay crass, as to suggest that Canadian literature is flawed?" He crinkles the corners of his eyes so that she'll know he's being a little bit facetious.

Val thinks he is looking at her botched eye makeup and is not going to take anything she might say seriously. How could he? She is an imposter. She is a person who relies on her literary taste to earn a living. Although she loves her job, she's picked up her skills along the way, hit-and-miss fashion. She is afraid she may not be nearly as clever as Robert or even Lynnette, much as she hates to admit it, in fact she is not even sure why she's here. She's managed to help bring a few books into the world, books that other-wise might have miscarried. But so what? That makes her a midwife. Nothing more nor less. She is not a writer. She does not have a creative cell in her brain. She has yet to open her mouth.

"Or do you, in fact, feel that this small but impressive canon of Canadian literature we are developing, or should I say, they" (he gestures magnanimously to Lynnette) "are developing is without, for all intents and purposes, blemish?"

Val resents his implication that writers alone develop a canon of literature, but decides to leave it where it is. She says, "Certainly not. All fiction is flawed, in a sense, because it isn't humanly possible to set down the truth truthfully. It's impossible, or perhaps I should say enormously difficult, to write life happening, the way it happens." She senses that she's rambling, but somewhere here is the nugget of a point. She would like to say that a life is like a rich dessert, a mille feuille, she thinks it's called, a random scattering of bittersweet flakes of chocolate, haphazardly stacked—"But do we necessarily want to read merely the truth?" asks the young man.

"Perhaps," she says, "we want someone else's perception of what is true to appear truthful to us. Readers want a writer to authenticate their own perceptions. Readers are borrowers," she says. "We borrow emotions, ideas, a sense of the world from books."

A little heat wave causes sweat to trickle down Val's forehead. Perspiration on her upper lip threatens to drool down to her chin. She puts a fist to her mouth to surreptitiously catch the drips. She should have worn something sleeveless and summery. A bath towel, even. "And when readers have borrowed to the extent of their line of credit," she continues, "they sometimes have an urge to give back something. Some take up a pen and scratch out yet another way of looking at the world, another way of bringing the human condition into focus."

"With all due respect," Lynnette says, "I don't think you've nailed it, quite." Lynnette is becoming contentious. "We don't take up the pen in order to give something away, out of some sense of debt or duty. Writers write in order to examine the insides of their own heads. We're a selfish lot." She tosses out more palaver, often beginning with "From a writer's point of view," and — Val gives her full marks for inventiveness — ending by mentioning the titles of all of her books. Robert gets back into the fray with some piece of gibberish about discovering new authors and comparing his job to that of a prospector panning for gold during the gold rush.

"Or, a better analogy," Val says, "might be a trained pig sniffing out truffles in a forest in France." The others beam their eyes in her direction, mesmerized, it seems, by her glistening face; their eyes narrow just the least little bit and make her think of sharp knives. She doesn't know why she said that. It was entirely imbecilic. They experience a moment of dead air. She feels she must go on, say anything, regain her equilibrium, regain her wits. She says, "One of the strangest things to happen recently at Dobbs, Kendall, was the mysterious appearance of an untitled manuscript with no address attached to it, just the name, A. A. McNiall. And it's wonderful in many ways. We have what may turn out to be a publishable, perhaps even valuable, book that we can't publish until someone claims it."

Their host loves this information. He is bubbling over with excited verbiage, while Robert, at the same time, looks as though he might reach into his inside breast pocket, take out a gun and shoot Val through the side of her head. Why, she wonders? It's true. They're waiting for the author to contact them. It's no secret. Lynnette looks mystified and dismal as though everyone else is having all the fun without her.

Their fifteen-minute time-slot draws to a close, not a moment too soon for Val. Collecting their coats from a waiting room, they are able to watch a closed circuit broadcast of their literary replacements, a middle-aged Native poet, a short-story writer who can't be more than fourteen years old, and a non-fiction writer, a man whose boyish dimple and earnest eyes go straight to some little pocket in her heart. He smiles engagingly at the camera and Val's innards make the kind of lunge she thought she would never feel again. The show's host twitches his nostrils at Father Bill Ryan and asks him how he finds time to write, host a radio show, and keep up with parish duties.

Lynnette has to drag Val away by the arm to catch up to Robert, who by now is outside the studio hailing a cab to take them back to Dobbs, Kendall, for some reason, although it's after nine and they should all be heading home.

Father Bill Ryan, Val thinks. That old sinner. Filled to the brim with atonement, obviously. A happy penitent. A rosy-hued media star.

Years after she'd lost track of Father Ryan, she heard that he had several books out with a different publisher, the latest, a book of personal essays entitled *The Worldly Priest*. Val had dashed out to the nearest bookstore and bought it in hardcover for the full price of thirty-four dollars and ninety-five cents, skimming through to see if she'd been mentioned. She'd sue the bastard.

She hadn't. She took it home and read it carefully cover to cover just to make sure. But, no, she hadn't rated even so much as a parenthetic aside. The book did not so much reveal a perceived fall from grace as it did his ascent into missionary work among the disadvantaged. He was now back in Toronto, the back cover blurb said, with his own small, impoverished parish among drug abusers and gun-toters. He sometimes made guest appearances on television and had his own phone-in radio show. His earnings he rolled back into church repairs, a drop-in centre for teens, and alms for the downtrodden.

Long after Father Bill had left, Val had continued her contemplative vigils at St. Dunstan's until she could no longer stand the sight of the place. She had begun to see its interior religious trappings as gaudy, pedestrian. They came between her and any recognition of a divine being. St. Disney's, she had thought, and, at length, had stopped going altogether, settling for open-minded atheism.

She gets into the cab, her mind still on the wonder of Father Bill. Robert twists around in the front passenger seat to scowl at Val. "Well, I expect we'll have every kook and writer-wannabe from here to the North Pole phoning to claim their manuscript. I can see it all now. I can even see a lawsuit in the offing. What in the name of Christ made you blurt that out?"

She doesn't know. He's probably right about the kooks. It may also, if he was watching, trigger a call from A. A. McNiall himself. She tells Robert that, but he merely grunts. She feels badly. She has never before been quite this deeply inserted into Robert's bad books. She has never before felt his scorn. She feels she could cry. But she won't. Her eyes water up anyway. God! What's wrong with her? She turns to her reflection in the window.

Lynnette prattles lightheartedly to break the tension after Robert's little rant, and soon they are within hailing distance of the Art Gallery of Ontario. They wend their way along short, narrow streets and arrive at D, K in

silence. Val says, "It's late. I'll keep the cab and go home."
But Robert claims gruffly that he has something to show
her that won't wait and anyway, he has his car here and will
drive her home. He seems to have granted her forgiveness.

Robert fits his key into the lock and turns on the light
in the foyer. The place feels unnaturally quiet at this hour,
foreign, out of its usual context, no generalized hum of
subdued voices, footsteps clattering up and down stairs,
phones ringing. Val is more acutely aware than usual of the
way it smells of paper and dust and old leather shoes.
Robert steps into the front room on the left, someone's
pleasant living room once, now a kind of waiting-room-
cum-conference-room, home to several pieces of overstuffed furniture, faded but comfortable, and a large, low
conference table. The walls here as well as in the hall and
up the stairs boast mug shots of the writers Dobbs, Kendall
has published over the years, a surprising number now
household names.

He turns on the light to reveal Carol who manages the
reception desk and phone, Lee the book designer D, K
uses, Arthur their financial wizard, two authors she knows
well and likes, two part-timers, two readers, the freelance
copy editor, a couple of book reps, and Marshall. And, of
course, Lynnette. All in all, quite a handy little turnout,
complete with bottles of champagne, flowers, dainty sandwiches, and small cakes, each sporting a candle, which
Carol now lights, weaving with a long wooden match
among the guests. They greet Val with enthusiastic birthday wishes.

She is overwhelmed. Everyone is silent for a moment,
waiting. She would like to say something witty or at least
intelligible, but she has temporarily lost her ability to use

the English language. "How?" she mumbles with a puzzled frown. "Who?" She shrugs. She grins at her friends, shaking her head, and tells them, "This is, it's —." Marsh puts a glass of champagne into her hand. "Cheers!" she says.

She hasn't seen Marshall for some time. He looks unwell, in her opinion. His face is blotched and bloated as though he's been lately on a binge, or not sleeping well. He has become even heavier. Apart from handing her a glass of champagne he rarely meets her glance, or anyone else's for that matter. He's attacking the food like a bear just out of hibernation. She watches as he stuffs a whole cupcake into his mouth. She turns, then, not wanting to stare. She hopes he removed the candle.

When she at last gets home, a little fuzzy-headed, she has a message from Aunt Millie who watched the program. "You were wonderful, dear, very natural the way you kept rubbing at your mouth with your fist. It was a pity about the makeup job they did on you, though. Could you not have just said no?"

ROBERT WAS RIGHT, as it turns out, about getting phone calls from people claiming to be A. A. McNiall. At ten o'clock next morning they start. Robert tells Carol to put all calls through to Val as he is going to be tied up the entire morning with Harold Jacques, an economist whose controversial book forecasting grim economic changes Robert is editing. The first call is from a man asking Val to send him his advance. She asks him if he can prove that he is the writer of the book. "Of course," he says. "I'll send you a copy of my driver's licence issued to Albert Anson McNiall."

She assures him that they will need more than that for proof. "For instance," she says, "if you could give me a brief summary, including the names of the protagonists, I think I might be convinced."

"I don't have to prove anything to you, lady," he shouts. "I know what the book's about. I don't think I should have to explain it to you."

Val thanks him very much and hangs up.

Another call, from a woman this time whose statements seem to be questions. "Yes, I'd like to clear up the mystery of the book? By A. A. McNiall? Like, he was my father? And he left me this manuscript in his will. And I never, like, actually read it. But I thought I would just, like, send it to your publishing company to see what you thought of it?"

"I see," Val replies. This is going to be a little harder. "Would you be kind enough, I wonder, just to spell out your father's name for me?" She believes that extreme politeness along with a tone of voice that bespeaks dominion over empires will cow all charlatans. The woman spells out Alex Andrew McNile. "Sorry," Val says, "the name on the manuscript is spelled differently."

There are three more phone calls, one from someone in Winnipeg who wants her to send him airfare to Toronto so that he can claim the manuscript, another from a woman who maintains that she wrote it so long ago that she can scarcely remember what it's about, let alone name the characters, and another from a man who says, "Forget the manuscript you've got. It's not nearly as good as my second book. I'm going to bring it to you this afternoon and take the old one back to revise."

Val says, "But I like this one, the untitled one."

"No, but wait till you see my new one. You're going to love it."

"I'm sure I will," says Val. "How long is it?"

"The new one?"

"Yes."

"Oh, roughly, I'd say, two hundred and fifty pages, three hundred."

"Longer than the first one, then."

"Oh, yeah. It's got more to it, eh?"

"Mr.—"

"McNiall."

"Mr. McNiall, the manuscript I have here is five hundred and thirty-three pages long." She waits for a reaction, an excuse, a lie, and gets only a click as the imposter hangs up. Soon the calls cease altogether. Val is disappointed. She has been rather enjoying her sleuthing work. Dobbs, Kendall, at last, settles down to the usual routine.

fourteen

IT COMES TO HIM during one more sleepless night lying on top of his covers wondering how he will ever get out from under the guilt that sits on his chest like a boulder, so heavy that it is an effort even to roll over. But something in the deadness of the night calls him to action. Struggling up out of bed, he finds the *Possib.* folder in his computer case and removes from it the article about the woman consumed by guilt for the accidental death of her husband. He devours it. *If only I had…* He grabs a pencil from a mug on his desk and begins to write without stops or checks, freely, almost automatically it seems, until his hand cramps. He is the woman. He knows the inside of her head, understands her obsession, creeps with her through the darkness searching for the one thing she needs.

As the sun rises on this windy March day he puts down his pencil, blunt now, after twenty or so scribbled pages. He opens his laptop, opens to a blank screen and keys, New Novel.

BY ABOUT THE beginning of May, Gus becomes concerned about all the weight his mother has lost and against her wishes phones her doctor. Audrey has no intention of going to see her doctor, however. And no intention of forcing the unpalatable meals Gus dreams up down her gullet, thank you all the same. She eats bananas and yogurt and the occasional bowl of cereal while Gus frowns down at a plate of baked chicken leg and baked potato and peas and wonders what he did wrong. It tastes all right, he thinks.

At length Audrey decides that it is no longer worth her time or energy to be bothered getting out of bed in the morning and getting dressed, if all she has for amusement is the view out the window and a few jackasses on television. She is very frail by this time, her arms as fleshless as turkey wings. Gus again phones the doctor, who this time comes around to the apartment to examine Audrey. He suggests a nursing home, which Audrey flatly refuses. In the end, Gus finds a home care service that will send someone for a few hours every day. He also moves the television into Audrey's room. "What in the world would I want that thing in here for?" she scolds. Without the television in the living room, Gus does a lot more reading, books, magazines, newspapers just to keep up with the world. In the background he can hear the reassuringly Canadian voice of Alex Trebek, which his mother seems unable to resist.

IT IS NEARING THE end of July. He wonders if his mother is dying. The woman who comes in every day to look after her tells him she thinks his mother should be in a nursing home, or else in a hospital. Her diet is down to one meal a day, and even that is scarcely touched. Her gaunt features bear almost no resemblance to his mother's. She seems to be a different type of being altogether. He sits

176

with her in the evenings reading the paper or the books he gets in a second-hand bookstore while she dozes through an assortment of programs on television. If he turns it off before nine she wakes up and gives him a baleful, accusatory look.

The doctor stops in from time to time and says that there is nothing really he or anyone else can do for her except to keep her warm and dry and to keep her skin from breaking down. He makes adjustments to her prescriptions and suggests the caregiver come in three times a day. He pushes up the sleeves of her pyjamas. Her frail elbows and hands are a network of magenta blood vessels, working on slow time, or perhaps not at all. Her circulatory system is shutting down, the doctor tells him. He uncovers her legs and observes the same situation. Gus turns away, shocked by what she has become.

At the front door he quietly asks the doctor, "Is she willing herself to die?"

"Who knows?" he says. "It's a mystery whether the worn-out body simply begins to shut down in preparation for death, or the tired mind prepares for death by allowing the body to shut down. She doesn't feel hungry, so she doesn't eat. And the less she eats, the less she needs to eat."

Gus sits with her whenever the caregiver leaves. He can get her to open her eyes and to say a few words occasionally, but the effort is great. For some reason he has kept the burnt apron he rescued from the kitchen the night of the fire. Only about half of it remains. It's been folded, not very neatly, and sits on the shelf of his closet. It still smells scorched. He takes it in to show her. He doesn't completely understand why he does this. Maybe he wants to take her back to a happier time in her life, although *happy* is not a word he automatically associates with his mother. Or maybe it's a burnt offering. "Look," he says. He starts to hold it up and thinks better of it. He holds it in such a way that she can't see the blackened edges. "Do you remember this?"

He sees that her eyes are focusing on it. She is lying on her side and stretches one skeletal arm beyond the blankets covering her and weakly makes an effort to touch the apron. Light as a shadow her fingertips brush the blue patterned cloth before she draws her hand back into her warm nest. Her mouth is dry. She has lost the ability to swallow. "Gus," she whispers. He leans closer. "Thinks." She looks right into his face. "Chiclets."

She knows me. He smiles. He thinks he sees a ghost of a smile play across her shrivelled lips. She knows me and she's forgiven me. Her eyes are closed now. He picks up the apron and takes it back to his room to put away, but stops before he gets there. If she knew me, he thinks, she would have said *you*, not *Gus*. He looks at the bit of cloth in his hand. An old singed apron. He takes the apron out to the kitchen and puts it in the garbage under the sink, *Let it go. Let it all go,* he tells himself.

The next day, Myrna, the caregiver, calls him into his mother's room, away from his computer where for the past few days he has written no more than a paragraph or two. "She isn't going to last another hour," she says.

Audrey lies on her side, the blankets pulled up high. Her breathing is short and shallow. With each incoming breath her upper lip rises slightly as if she's about to smile — or sneer. The movement causes a tiny sound. Gus puts his ear close to her head. Snick...snick...

snick, he hears. He also hears a faint rattle deep in her throat. He straightens and as he looks at her she ceases to breathe altogether. He wills himself to comprehend what has happened, to be overwhelmed by the passing of his once vibrant, all-powerful mother into a state of non-being. Instead, he slouches, hands in his pockets, dry-eyed.

There is something anticlimactic about death.

fifteen

IT IS MID-JULY and the dreaded anniversary of the car accident is at hand. The day is muggy, the atmosphere so thick with smog Val thinks she could almost chew it. She goes in to work as usual, feeling jittery and close to tears. She looks haggard from lack of sleep. She's been forgetting things lately, the simplest things — keys, sunglasses, appointments. She makes lists to jog her memory and lies in bed half the night trying to remember what she has forgotten to put on the list. As she pushes open the heavy door at Dobbs, Kendall she worries that she'll be unable to hold back tears if anyone speaks kindly to her concerning her loss of a year ago.

Behind the reception desk, Carol says, "A Mr. Inkpen phoned to say you've had his manuscript for nearly a year and could you please let him know what's up with it."

"I'm sure he's exaggerating," Val says. Business as usual she is relieved to note, although she had thought Carol, at least, would remember the significance of the day. Just as well, though, she thinks. As she climbs the stairs to her office on the second floor, a former bedroom with a fireplace in it, non-functioning, she tries to remember something about this Mr. Inkpen's manuscript and can't. Unusually appropriate name for a writer. She marvels that even the name had slipped her mind. She hunts through a batch of manila envelopes on a shelf and finds his, dated last year, a week after the accident. She sits down with it, heavily. She takes it out of its yellow envelope and begins to read, putting it down only when her phone rings. Marshall says. "You were trying to get me?"

She makes an attempt to brush away her memory's cobwebs. "Yes, about a month ago."

Marshall apologizes for taking so long to reply. "What was it you called about?"

She can't remember.

"Let's have lunch one of these days." he suggests. "I'll phone you."

Not a word about the events of a year ago. She puts the phone back and contemplates the human race, at least the small portion of it that intersects with the path of her life. Self-involvement is the ruling passion of most people, she decides. We are really just minor characters in someone else's badly structured, poorly written, autobiographical novel. She picks up the manuscript she was reading and continues to look for evidence of talent.

Close to noon, Robert comes into her office. "How are you doing?" In his face she reads concern and sympathy and it is entirely too unexpected and too much for her. Tears flood. Robert goes over to where she sits at her desk and puts an arm around her shoulders. "I know, I know," he says. "It's hard not to think about it." He pulls her close to his side gently, squeezes her against him and hands her a box of Kleenex. "I've made a reservation for lunch for just the two of us at that new place on Beverley. Simple, not too upscale, dimly lit. You can bawl your eyes out if you want."

She gives her nose a graceless honk. She looks up, grateful, gives him a return squeeze, and takes back every shortcoming she has ever accused him of having.

Upon her return to the office after an entirely satisfying and comforting lunch she finds that her aunt has left her a message. "I know this is an especially hard day for you, dear. But take heart. Time will kiss it better." Good old Millie, she thinks. Good old sentimental, exasperating, ridiculous, matchless Millie. A moment later, a call comes from Denise inviting her to have dinner with them. She is beginning to rethink her theory about the human race.

That night as she lies in bed, her eyes feeling puffy from all the crying she did during the day, waiting for her breathing to become slower, deeper, indicating that sleep is on the way, a mean, wayward thought impinges on her still conscious mind. She has a niggling suspicion that she has not been crying only for Ed's untimely, painful death, nor even for her own loss of a husband who she knows loved her in spite of everything. She's been also crying for herself. She thinks her tears are for the inconvenience of having to look after household repairs, for the uni-directional cash flow when she has to hire someone to cut the lawn and trim the hedge; for deciding whether or not the roof needs new shingles; for having to go up a ladder to clean the eavestroughs. Regretfully, she's afraid that this is true.

AFTER A FITFUL NIGHT, Val takes herself off early next morning to Kustom Kitchen Kabinets. She lets herself into the empty shop and then through the unlocked door to

Ed's office. She's been putting off this chore out of sheer lethargy. Ed was always so neat that it seemed there wasn't much to do. Now that she has a buyer for the business, however, she needs to get rid of the scraps of paper and paper clips that collect in the bottoms of drawers. Ed's former employees tidied up the shop and swept it before they went off to new positions.

There's really not a lot to do. The new owner wants the tools, the sample books, and the stack of kitchen design books filling the bookshelves. In the desk are notepads that would be useful to her, a few pens and pencils, stamps, paper clips. She scoops these into her bag. She throws out some scrap paper, old receipts, a chocolate bar wrapper.

There are typed sheets of paper that look like instructions for operating something. She looks closer, reads the title. *Patient Care Following a Vasectomy.* That's odd. She turns the paper over. It's from the medical building where Ed's doctor has his practice. She reads on. *Patient should rest for 24 hrs. following the procedure. Acetaminophen is recommended to relieve any pain. Slight bruising of the scrotum may....* She stops reading and sits down in Ed's swivel chair. She realizes that she's taking big, angry breaths, that her mind is flashing backwards and forwards through time, that tears have spurted suddenly into her eyes — tears of anger, not grief, not self-pity. They dry up before they can spill over. When did he do this, she needs to know, although she knows. She might have been fertile into her forties. She might have conceived and given birth to a child. How could he have done this when he knew how badly she — ?

Val begins to calm down. It's too late for anger, but not for bitterness. She's been robbed, made to play the fool.

After her miscarriage he was so sympathetic, seemed so hopeful himself as each month passed them by. A scam. A sham. She throws the pamphlet into the garbage, slams the desk drawer shut and locks the building behind her.

sixteen

GUS HAS TO GET away from the apartment, from the city, from everything that connects him to his life. He needs to be someone else for at least two weeks.

In his second-hand car, a bit of a rattletrap, he passes through a village of sorts. The road has become even more tortuous and hilly, a dirt road, the kind that demands much honking of the car horn. It is the beginning of September. Crows call this information to each other, laughing outrageously. There are no mosquitoes, no deer flies. The sun warms without blistering. All things considered, he thinks, September is the kindest month.

His brakes squeal as he follows a trail inching down a steep curving slope to a small clearing among the trees, just big enough for his car, although not quite big enough to allow him to unstrap the canoe on top with any great ease.

As he crosses the lake, his canoe packed with supplies — fishing rod, tinned and packaged food items, a bag of oranges, a bag of apples, eggs, a canvas carry-all stuffed with pads of paper, pens, pencils, two books by Graham Greene, several by William Trevor (he is systematically rereading the works of both), the news clipping and scribbled notes to himself, a backpack of clothes, a ten-pound reference dictionary-cum-thesaurus, his lap-top, a case of beer, and sundry potables from the liquor store — he wonders why he chose to rent an island. It was cheap, he reminds himself. It has electricity and a telephone that reach it via underwater cables, and it has running water. It was one of three possibilities, all about the same price, so he left it up to chance, closed his eyes and stabbed with a pencil.

It takes him about half an hour, he judges, to reach the island, which is bigger than he thought it would be. From the lake it looks like some huge rock-faced beast newly emerged from the lake bottom. Like a dog, it seems to have just shaken its crest of misshapen pines and birches, bowing, many of them, in memory of recent ice storms. The farther out from the mainland shore Gus paddles, the more the wind catches the bow of his canoe. He has to work hard, dig deep with the paddle, to reach a sheltered cove at the other side of the island with its heaved dock beside a tired boathouse. The boathouse looks about ready to end it all by falling forward into the lake.

He hauls everything onto the shore, including the canoe, not about to trust the boathouse in its slow demise. He turns the canoe over and ties it to a nearby tree for fear of high winds. It takes him three trips to carry his supplies uphill along a path strewn with brown pine needles and veined with tree roots to a weathered clapboard cottage. It has been built on the highest point of the island, half hidden among the pines and arching birches and cedar underbrush. He makes a fourth trip to pick up all the items he dropped along the way from the over-filled boxes.

Unlocking the back door with the key the owner has mailed him, he hauls his stuff inside and is struck by the closed-up cedar chest smell of the place. He walks through the cabin to the front, opens a door, and emerges onto the veranda protected from wildlife by huge screens that run almost floor to ceiling.

Now he takes a deep breath, inhaling a mixture of pine gum, baked earth, and juniper. He flexes his arms, fists on his shoulders, chest out. "Paradise!" His voice resonates in the clear air, although no one is there to hear him. He has a good voice. He thinks he should have been a singer. The view from his rocky hill includes the beginning of a meandering path that disappears into the trees and undergrowth but must end, he assumes, at the water's edge. Both shores of the lake seem about equidistant from his rock. Down the lake, white-crested waves tumble over each other in the sunlight as a sailboat in the distance tilts ahead of the wind. If there are other cottages, they are too far away to be seen. He would like to sit in the red rocking chair on the veranda and look out, dream, think. He would like to throw on his bathing suit and walk down the hill for a swim. He would like to explore the inside of the cottage and the entire island.

The stony path is a little treacherous in places. He slips on pebbles and shale more than once as he follows it down to a rickety pier sticking out into the water ten feet or so. It rests on stilts on the rocks near the shore. Beyond the pier there's a sheer drop-off. The wind is strong. He decides to dive in without feeling the water first. It'll be cold, he knows that, a shock, but he tends to be a plunger. "Whoo!" he yells when he surfaces, shaking water from his hair and close-cropped beard with a single flick of his head. It's cold enough to take his breath away. He's heard that people can have heart attacks by diving into cold water. It's the shock. He treads water for a minute to make sure he isn't having a heart attack. He isn't.

He plows through the water with quick, even strokes, swims on his back for a while, flips over, face in, and does a slow, studied crawl, something he learned to do as a youngster at the Y. Back to where he started, he hoists himself up with reasonable ease onto the dock and dries off in the sun, smiling to himself, pleased with the place, pleased that he discovered it.

After he's surveyed every inch of the cottage, chosen his bedroom, and explored much of the island, he sets up a little work station at one end of the dining table on the screened-in veranda. He'd like to get right to work, but, of course, he won't. He pulls things out of his canvas carryall: a notebook; a few loose scraps on which he's written cryptic messages to himself, the meanings of which now elude him; an extension cord that he uses to plug in his laptop; finally, a newspaper. He reads the first page, is about to turn to page two but instead folds it up quickly, tossing it out of reach to the far end of the long table. He sighs, calls up his work from a short cut on the screen, rubs his hands back and forth over his thighs five or six times, and reads page one, which is pretty good. He always starts off rereading page one no matter how far into his work he is. It's almost the way he wants it. He changes a comma to a dash. He looks at his watch. God! No wonder he's starving. It's almost three. In the kitchen he paws through a box of canned goods. Probably easier if he took them out and lined them all up on a shelf. Instead he pulls out the next tin he closes his hand around — baked beans — opens it, takes down a battered saucepan hanging over the electric stove and dumps them in.

THE DAYS ARE noticeably shorter now, but Gus forces himself to write until the sun reaches a certain point. The work is going fairly well.

Today he senses that the point has been reached without even looking. He finishes a convoluted sentence that he thinks should be broken up, but he leaves it. A job for tomorrow. He pours himself a Scotch and sets it in front of him while he reads over what he's just written and lights a cigarette. He has brought only a few packs of cigarettes with him, planning to quit up here, but not exactly cold turkey. Although, face it, he's never going to quit unless he quits completely. He's never been very good at fooling himself.

He's well into this, his second novel. He does a lot of revising each day and a lot of walking around while thinking about the book, about its shape, about the way he's chosen to tell the story, about how he's going to get his characters from here to where he wants them. Whoever said writing was a sedentary sport was wrong. Sometimes he thinks about his brother and his mother. He scrolls back quite a bit before today's work.

He frowns as he reads. He's moving things forward too quickly in this scene, or chapter or whatever you want to call it. He wants to see more of her background before zooming in on her anguish, on her guilt. Grief, he knows he can do, but he wants to ease up a bit here. Pile it on later.

It's the sensation of guilt he wants to pursue, the framework of remorse, the whole quivering edifice. The article has been in his *Possib.* file since last July when he cut it out of the paper. At the time he had envisioned a far different story related mostly to the irony. But now, after all that has happened — the fire, his brother, his mother — he finds himself attracted to it in a different way. It speaks to him, addresses his own state of mind. Writing about it, he hopes, will allow him to look clearly at his own very present, devastating guilt. He wishes he could use an alternative word for guilt, but his thesaurus offers nothing as affecting, or as straightforward.

Sometimes, on dark days, unfruitful days, he thinks he's just marking time, that nothing will come of this manuscript, or of the other, his first. Probably make-work projects, both of them. Maybe he should go back to screenwriting. He drinks his Scotch and stares at the opposite shore.

He has the story worked out in his mind and in his hen-scratched notes, except for the actual ending. He knows what he wants at the end, he's just not sure he can express it adequately. He'll have to wait until he gets there. This much he knows. There is an accident. A preventable one. A teenaged child is the victim, not a husband. Gus is trying to change the facts as much as possible to avoid whatever nastiness might arise from people recognizing themselves in his story. The son dies.

He has called his heroine Petra, although he wishes he could have used the name of the woman in the article. Petra is a writer living in Toronto, completely wrapped up in her work. Beside herself with grief, anguished over her carelessness, she must suffer her husband's anger and blame. He had her leave her husband, but didn't like it, so now he has the husband leaving her. It works better.

Gus will keep her in Toronto for a while to work out how she will live with herself. Let her try to get back to writing. Her novel is about a guy called Simon who has a mentally disturbed brother. This brother, who is very intelligent in some ways, walks straight into danger. Simon is aware of the danger, could, could, prevent an accident from happening, but instead, he, he, he turns his back. That's exactly what he does. Figuratively, he turns his back and, and, and now, and now — Gus can't do this. Even though it's a story within a story, he still can't do it. He takes out another cigarette, searches his pockets again for matches. When he finishes this cigarette, he knows he's going to light another one.

seventeen

HER HOUSE IS NO longer an alien space missing its full complement of inhabitants. Val has spread out to fill it. She has done some modest redecorating, painting mostly, colours that Ed would never have approved — egg yolk in the dining room (she painted the second-hand dining table and chairs plum), a lighter, lemony shade in the living room and in the small kitchen she moved along the food chain to ripe peach. She has added decorative cushions to the living-room couch, and a floor-to-ceiling bookcase. She would like to invite both Robert and Marshall to see her handiwork, but she's no longer sure about their relationship. The last time she saw them together — on her birthday — they barely spoke. Of course it was difficult with Lynnette there. Robert had hovered. She phones Marsh anyway. He's extremely busy at work, he tells her. "Come for a drink on the weekend," she says, but he's too busy, he has to meet with a client, has to visit his therapist.

In her fresh new living room she dumps her work wherever she feels like it. Books she's reading lie open, face down, on various pieces of furniture. A new skirt she's hemming straddles the arm of the couch, a cardigan is hung on a dining-room chair. There are no sports magazines, no tool catalogues, no sample books of countertop shades. She feels that she is slowly squeezing out the ghosts.

Val looks around at her egg-yolk dining room, her cluttered lemon living room, at an oversized vase standing on the floor filled with straight black sticks and thinks, this is mine. I have made my own choices. She almost hears Ed's comments. *"Black sticks? Is that supposed to be a joke? How much did that set us back?"*

Yet she is no longer accountable to him for her extravagance, for her wayward decorating schemes, for the way in which she conducts her life. She seems to be sitting on an uncomfortably pointy fence of ambivalence. She is allowing herself one horribly unrepentant moment of smugness even as she admits that the black sticks might be used to flagellate herself when her darker mood takes over.

VAL'S LAWYER IS AT last able to track down the occupant, or former occupant, of the house in Dogwood, Ed's sister, as it turns out, the person she has always envisioned as a nomadic, aging, hippy. The lawyer writes to her informing her of Val's wish to sell the house.

Twice, now, she knows, she's been duped. She doesn't know which of Ed's shams is worse. Neither is forgivable. It still rankles that her husband lied to her about his sister, or at least misled her. She decides to write to her sister-in-law (she feels suddenly uncomfortable with this designation, with the closeness it implies), explaining that she can no longer afford to keep the house. *"When,"* she asks, *"can you conveniently vacate the house? Or, would you, in fact, want to buy it from the estate?"* She receives the following reply from Elsa Fennel.

"... I have no money to buy the house, and have a handi-capped son on my hands. I lived out there all my life until I got word from a cousin we have in Toronto that Eddy was killed in a car accident, which was a terrible blow to me as he and I were always so close as youngsters. My mother left that house to Eddy my brother because we never saw eye to eye, Mother and me. It was through the kindness of my brother that we had a roof over our heads at all. By rights the house should of come to me and little Eddy, my son, but it seems he left everything to you. So if you want to sell it there's not much I can do. I moved my things out last fall because I had a feeling this is what would happen. I and little Eddy are living in town right now with an aunt, but I don't know how long this is going to last as she's a begrudg-ing old woman. I don't know if you own the furniture out there too, but I had an idea I could sell it and have the money as I have very little to live on except for some money from an uncle of mine now passed on."

The letter ends with a postscript saying that she has heard by the grapevine that: *"Ed's wife come out one day in the winter and stayed over in the house. Guess that was you. Well, I suppose you had every right in a way, but it seems a little sneaky."*

Val muses on the name, Elsa Fennel, and wonders if she is divorced, or a single parent, or even married to someone of the same name — none of which has any bearing on the present situation. Val doesn't want to push a poor woman with a handicapped son out into the cruel world, but... She's not sure how to handle this.

She realizes she can no longer keep this entirely new and unwelcome subplot in her life to herself. She has coffee with Denise and spares none of the details.

"Be careful," Denise says. "Do you really think this is something you can handle only a year after Ed's death?"

Val isn't sure. She'll put it on hold for the time being, she says.

ON A RAINY DAY SHE visits her aunt and presents her with a copy of the lawyer's letter and the letter from Elsa Fennel. Millie hunts for her reading glasses and then moves closer to a lamp in the living room to read the letters. "Oh, dear," she says. "I knew something like this would happen."

Val says, "How could you possibly know something like this would happen? I was married to the man, and I didn't know." She doesn't mean to raise her voice.

"I don't know, it's something I felt, some little undercurrent I sensed. I felt that things were not all they seemed. You know how sensitive I am to people."

"You never liked him."

"That's not fair, and it's not true. I grew to like him. But, at first, well, there was just something about him. And of course there was his name — Fennel. Now what kind of a name is that?"

"Oh, Aunt Millie!" Val can't keep exasperation from her voice.

"Well-l-l-l!—" Millie changes the topic. "So, what do you want to do about this, if anything?"

Val frowns, perplexed. What she probably wants is for Aunt Millie, or Denise and Dan, to read her mind, the contents of which she doesn't fully understand herself, agree with her subconscious thoughts, and advise her to take the course of action she suspects she wants to take anyway, which is based almost wholly on curiosity. "I don't know," she lies.

"Well, as I see it," Aunt Millie says, "you don't necessarily have to do anything. Sell the house, give her the money from the sale of the furniture, if you like, and wish her well. And that, I should think, would be the end of it. It's not as if she made any effort to welcome you into the family." She looks at Val over the tops of her glasses, knowing full well it isn't the end of the story, and that her niece, just like her mother before her, will do precisely what she wants.

On her way out to the kitchen to check the oven Millie says, "She's just as fraudulent as Ed was."

"Fraudulent?"

"Well, what would you call it?"

Secretive, for no apparent reason, perhaps. Underhanded. She's thinking now about the health instructions she found in his desk. How, she muses, does her guilt fit into all of this? Is it no longer part of the equation? Does underhandedness cancel out guilt? Val stokes a hot coal rising within her, a no-longer-dormant volcano threatening to gush forth and rain down torrents of fiery anger into this intermediate space where she now finds herself, this no-man's-land of the emotions where the past is not to be trusted and the present meaningless.

From the kitchen Millie calls, "Ed was a man who minded his own affairs and expected others to mind theirs. This is not something I find admirable, necessarily, but there it is." Val knows this is true. During dinner she decides to drop the issue. Driving home, however, she thinks she might see what Robert has to say on the subject.

Accordingly, on Monday morning she tells Robert about her northern adventure last December and shows him the letter from Ed's sister. He reads it and hands it back, disconcerted, skeptical. "She's trying to gain your pity," he says.

"Why did Ed keep her a secret, the house a secret?"

"If he'd wanted you to know, he'd have told you. My advice is leave it alone. He would not have knowingly subjected you to anything unpleasant. Let's just assume he felt the need to protect you."

"But from what?"

He pulls at his chin with thumb and forefinger. "I have never been accused of having supernatural powers, as you may be aware."

Val lets out a suspended breath and tells him she intends to visit the woman. It is now the inevitable next step. "Want to come with me?"

"Val, Val, Val," he says. "Don't do this. Let your lawyer handle it. Keep your distance."

"Am I to take that for a 'no thank you'?"

He continues to sit, tight-lipped, shaking his head. "It sounds like a can of worms I can't afford to think about right now, nor can you. You know how busy we are presently, and how precarious our situation here is. Look, I'm advising you to be cautious. That's about the best I can do for you right now. Don't get drawn into something you'll later regret."

She takes back the letter, lets him know with a deeply drawn sigh that she is displeased with his response, and goes back to her own office. God, she thinks, he can be such an unfeeling jerk when he puts his mind to it. She had only wanted his moral support. She phones Marshall and is invited to leave a message, which, grudgingly, she does. What's the use? For the moment she will do nothing. She's not sure why she has this urge to meet the woman anyway: simple curiosity, she guesses. Answers. Explanations. And, too, there is the wrinkled photograph she took from the house in Dogwood. She thinks Elsa Fennel might be able to fill in the blanks.

eighteen

GUS'S FISHING ROD bends almost double, whips up, and then bends again. Son-of-a-gun, he thinks, bloody whale. He plays it, gives some slack, a bit more, reels in, shows him who's boss, a little fight for supremacy going on. He hopes he won't tire of this before the monster on the end of his line does. He doesn't know why he thinks he's a fisherman, because he's not. For two cents he'd cut him loose. How the hell is he going to land him without a net?

The fish gives up seconds before Gus. He reels him in, yanks him out of the water onto the dock where the fish jumps and arches in one last stand until Gus gets a foot on his tail. A bass. It's actually not that big. Two meals. Maybe.

By the time he finishes cleaning the damn thing with a dull carving knife he found in a kitchen drawer, it's getting dark. And there's barely enough flesh for one meal. He gets down a frying pan and hunts through the fridge for butter to fry the fish in. He knows he's running low on butter. Must be here somewhere. Surely he hasn't used up the last of it. He finds the small pat wrapped in foil and decides he'd better economize. He has a few more days before his time here runs out. He starts thinking about future meals, about breakfast, and decides he'll save it for frying eggs. So, how is he going to cook this thing without butter?

He could boil it.

HE SITS SMOKING, digesting, watching a candle burn down, finishing the rest of the wine. He'd poured some over the fish to cook it, and it wasn't half bad, either, with a little salt and pepper. There's that little settlement, hardly a village, he drove through at the other end of the lake. He thinks he recalls seeing a sign for a general store. Besides butter, he's running low on cigarettes. He'll go tomorrow.

This is very pleasant. He enjoys his own company when he has a few glasses of wine. Moths bash insanely on the other side of the screens, attracted by his candle. Water laps drowsily at the rocky shore. Beyond the candle's sphere the darkness wraps him in mystery. His youth feels like something he read about once in some book, dated now, naive by today's standards. In front of him on the table, his candle flickers as it becomes a puddle of wax. He blows it out.

Beyond the smell of burnt wick and melted candle wax, he smells rain. The night is moonless, overcast, close, a tent draping him in its folds. He reaches out a hand to push futilely at the cloying atmosphere. Absurd, he knows. He can't even see his hand in front of his face. It's just the dark, he tells himself. His mother used to say that to Aidan when he awoke screaming. "It's just the dark."

Behind him on the rough-hewn buffet sits an electric lamp made out of a crockery jug. He turns it on. Rain patters lightly on the roof reminding him of some fleeting moment in childhood, snugged up in flannelette sheets and a wool blanket in his narrow bed, in his striped pyjamas, listening to the rain and distant thunder and feeling smugly safe in what seemed to be his never-ending boyhood. He tilts back gripping the table for support, listening to the wind rise, a sudden gust fretting the tree branches. He's getting wet sitting near the screens. Wind chases the rain madly across the roof and back, a wild and lonely sound that makes him feel lost and alone. He brings his chair forward with a crack just as lightning sears the dark beyond the screens. For a moment he believes he caused it.

The wind goes down as quickly as it came up. He should read over his last bit of work. There's something about rain in the night, though, that removes all immediate ambition. Just listen, he tells himself. He is no longer lost but connected to it as it pebbles the roof. He fancies he can hear individual raindrops. He imagines each one dropping, bouncing, sending up a minuscule spray, making a splash in the world. Drops whisper through leaves on trees, giving them a reason to dance, to nod this way and that in some courtly gavotte; raindrops spit on a carpet of pine needles and leaf debris, making it shiny, slippery. Drops converge in eavestroughs and pour out recklessly onto stones, sand, rutting out tiny canals going nowhere.

He's thinking about his work again. He likes his female character. He is completely in sympathy with her, mourning with her. Eventually he hopes to climb with her up out of the quicksand of grief and loss and guilt. He is beside her as she marvels that the world goes on. He knows, as she does, the salty taste of remorse. He is there to help her move beyond it and hopes she will drag him along with her. He is tempted to fall in love with her.

BY MORNING THE RAIN has washed the sky clean of clouds, polished it to a brilliance seen only in fine gems, and revived the primordial scent of earth. It is a new day, a cold one. For the first time he feels the need of a jacket. He turns over the canoe, slides it into the water, and gets in, a little heavily, gracelessly, in fact he loses his grip on the dock and nearly tips it. He should have put the paddle in first. Now he has to paddle with his hands back to the dock. His watch gets wet. It's an awkward stretch to reach the paddle, but he does it without dumping himself in the lake. He hasn't always been this disorganized and ungainly, he would like to think. On the other hand, he can't remember a time when he was a really smooth operator.

It takes him about twenty minutes to paddle with the wind at his back to the village end of the lake where he ties his canoe to somebody's wharf and hopes they won't mind. He hasn't seen many cottages on the lake, only a few, boarded up, awaiting winter. He's removed his jacket and tossed it onto the cane seat in the bow. Even though it's nearly the middle of September, there's still a vestige of summer warmth. The road curves around the perimeter of the lake. Nearby are four substantial cottages, or perhaps they're permanent homes, situated on a rise of land on the other side of the road overlooking the lake. Beside the wharf he's claimed for the length of his stay are two others in varying stages of disrepair, probably the property of the homeowners. No one's about. He won't be here long, anyway. A dog barks to let him know that it's not a ghost town.

The sun warms his back as he walks along the road toward where he thinks the general store is. There it is. A big sign up over the porch of what looks like a house. He pauses a moment, swearing under his breath, because he thinks he's left his wallet in his other pants back at the island. But, no. He has it. Inside the store a somewhat slatternly woman is talking to a customer, herself no gift to the fashion world. Her clothes are of the shiny, satiny variety that look too tight, too hot, and altogether too lacking in comfort to serve any purpose other than to shield the woman's uncorseted rolls from eyes used to more decorous sights.

Gus surveys the scanty provisions on the shelves with little interest. Against a wall stands a large chest freezer. Opening it, he paws through an assortment of frozen desserts and treats, TV dinners, bread, and sundry other staples until at last he finds a frozen brick of butter. He takes it over to the counter where he waits his turn.

"Shut it!" the proprietress demands. Gus looks up, wonders briefly if she is addressing him, realizes she is, and turns to where she is pointing. Good God, he thinks, I've made this woman angry. "I'm sorry," he says and goes back to the freezer to close it, noticing as he does, the sign above it in brazen letters urging patrons to "SHUT IT."

Someone else comes into the store, a small man with a deeply lined, elderly, almost gnome-like face. His pear-shaped body is unhealthily pudgy, in fact he reminds Gus of a punching clown he and Aidan had as children, which, every time it was knocked to the ground, would pop up for more abuse. He calls the other customer Momma and asks for a Popsicle. His look of naivety reminds Gus of Aidan.

The gnome gets a Popsicle from the freezer (and shuts it), struggles to tear off the paper, succeeds, drops it on the floor, and goes outside through the screen door. "Get back in here and pick that up!" Momma yells at her offspring.

Obediently, he returns, picks up the paper, and hands it stickily to his mother, who shakes her head as if sorely tried.

She says to the woman behind the counter, "So, I don't know. I mean what are we supposed to do? Every stick of furniture's been in the family for years, generations. I used to think I'd pass it down to my little guy, there, but what's the use. He's such a child."

"He's all right," the shopkeeper mutters without conviction.

"A child, and always will be. And what'll become of him when I go, I don't know."

"Someone'll take him in."

Gus barely disguises the fact that he's eavesdropping. What the woman has just expressed is what his own mother used to say regarding Aidan. The woman glances over at him, and then turns back to the woman behind the counter. She shifts her head in his direction. "Wait on the gentleman," she says.

Is she being sarcastic, he wonders, or is he just a trifle paranoid? He asks for a package of cigarettes. He reconsiders. "Make that two."

"Cheaper by the carton," she says.

"No thanks," he says. "Two'll be fine." He'll be leaving for home soon. He puts the butter on the counter. It's burning his fingers.

"I can give you a deal on a carton."

He considers for a moment, then shakes his head. "I'm trying to quit."

She rings up his butter, which seems to Gus a bit expensive, and his two packs of cigarettes, and says almost under her breath, "You'll be back."

He ignores her, pays, pockets the cigarettes, picks up the butter, and leaves, turning right (he doesn't know why except that a flock of geese is flying over and he has, for the moment, joined ranks with them, admiring their precision), instead of left toward the wharf where his canoe is tied. An old woman, tiny, a crone, bent over her stick, makes her way along the road approaching him. She stops in front of him. "You've come about the house, no doubt."

"What house?" he asks, feeling as though he's been transported from his real life into some Disneyesque movie.

"You'll find it soon enough," she says. "You gotta look up."

GUS WALKS ALONG THE dirt road carrying his pound of butter, first in one hand and then the other. It feels greasy, besides being ice cold. He wonders why she didn't give him a plastic bag. Before long he sees cars parked by the side of the road and lining a driveway sloping up to a house. A *Sold* sign is nailed to the fence. Up in a field in front of the house items of furniture bow and list on the uneven ground, as if abandoned in a sea of grass, while nearby, small clusters of people listen to an auctioneer under the shade of a tree. Gus can hear his singsong spiel, but can't make out any words. He has half a mind to go up closer. Why not?

He has no intention of bidding on anything. People standing in the shade turn to stare at him with his pound of butter, which he lobs from hand to hand, but soon look away, returning their attention to the auctioneer. Some are wandering among the pieces of heavy oak furniture and Gus joins them. Nothing he would want anyway. Pretty ugly, most of it. People are bidding, though. He hears little spurts of sound in response to the auctioneer's patter, sees the occasional hand going up.

Back up under the tree he stands behind the bidders just in case he has an urge to scratch his ear or otherwise unwittingly draw the auctioneer's attention to himself. He glances toward the house. Near it sits a woman in a car, both doors open to catch the breeze. She turns her head toward Gus just at this moment and their eyes meet. Does he know her? His hand is up, now, shading his eyes. He looks away from her, quickly, and back at the auctioneer. He hopes he hasn't just bid on something. The auctioneer brings down his gavel with a crack. Gus looks back at the woman. He would be unlikely to know anyone in this area. He doesn't even know the owner of his island paradise. He made all the arrangements over the Internet and by phone. She looks at him again, too, but immediately looks away. He'd better get out of here, before some bruiser of a farmer comes after him for flirting with his wife.

He skirts the back of the crowd and heads down the long slope of driveway. He can still see that woman in his head.

nineteen

SHE IS ON HER WAY to Falkirk, nearly there, in fact. It is Friday, almost the middle of September, warmish. A fresh breeze flirts with the tops of trees. The fall colours are further along up here. Distant hills look tufted, as though they've been worked in needlepoint in shades of dusky rose, mulberry, muted carmine, burnt orange. She wishes Marsh were here to wallow with her in these visual delights.

Weeks ago she had managed to make contact with him and had attempted to persuade him to go with her to Falkirk.

"Why me?" he had asked.

"I thought you'd like the outing. It's a pretty little place. Besides, you've been ignoring your friends, hiding yourself away like a hermit. I'm sure the only human being you ever talk to any more is your therapist."

"Appropriately enough," he had said. At length he had agreed to go with her provided she wouldn't try to psychoanalyze him. This had been fine with Val. Her analytical powers would be devoted wholeheartedly to "the woman" as she had begun to call Ed's sister.

As it turned out, Marsh had only let her know that morning when she had pulled into the loop in front of his apartment building that he wouldn't be going. She had watched him come out, empty-handed, no overnight bag, looking enormous. Since the last time she had seen him, he had ballooned to unbelievable proportions.

Val had got out of the car. "Where's your luggage?"

"Something's come up." He had apologized, then, and told her that he had tried to call her, but that she'd already left. He hoped she'd understand.

"Oh, Marsh." Genuinely disappointed, she'd been counting on his company.

Studying him as he pressed his lips together, grimly, Val gained the distinct impression that he was trying to suppress excitement. Just one of those things, he said, an important meeting, something he couldn't put off. He smiled at her winningly, asked her not to be cross.

What could she say? She softened, smiled back, asked, "What about after your meeting?"

"Impossible," he told her. The meeting promised to be a lengthy affair.

She got back into her car and told him he was forgiven — this time. "I'll call you when I get back. Maybe you could come for a drink and I'll tell you all about my adventures."

"Absolutely."

She had headed onto the road, waving, watching Marshall wave back with a cheerful salute. Whatever his meeting involved, Marsh was looking forward to it. He looked positively gleeful. Through her rear-view mirror, she had watched him march smartly up the steps of his building, taking them two at a time.

On the highway, heading east, she couldn't remember the last time she had seen him so animated. The last face-to-face conversation she'd had with Marshall had been back in early spring after a dinner with Robert and Lynnette. They had shared a taxi. She remembered asking him how his therapy sessions were going.

"Fine," he had said. No elaboration.

"You've been going to this guy for quite a while."

"Yes." He had looked at her quickly and away. She had detected a challenge in his attitude.

She said, "You once encouraged me to go to a therapist. Do you remember? I probably should have taken your advice."

"Why? It's not for everybody. In fact, most people get along just fine." He looked out the window on his side. Val started to say something in reply, but he interrupted. "People tend to just sail along, you know? As if their lives are tight little ships, even in a typhoon. Somehow or other they seem to right themselves and just bob along."

"Maybe they just give that impression."

Marsh hadn't listened, hadn't heard her. "I tend to run aground. Or bump into things and sink."

Val had wanted to elevate the mood, but at the same time, she wanted to know what was eating Marsh or, more to the point, what it was that was making him overeat. "I've never seen you this troubled, Marsh," she'd said. "I'd be glad to listen, if you want to talk about it."

"I'm not troubled," he'd said irritably. "I know, I know, I've put on weight and you're concerned and the first thing you think of is that I'm unhappy. Let me assure you that I'm not. At least not any more unhappy than the next joker. I'm genetically predisposed to body fat, that's all. I come from a long line of overeaters." Val had looked over at him as sweat ran down the side of his face and had opened the window on her side of the taxi a couple of inches.

What she is remembering right now, driving toward Falkirk, is that she'd said something about Robert being concerned about him, too. The street lights had changed his pallor to a mottled fuchsia. She had definitely gone too far. "I don't seem to be able to mind my own business," she'd said. "Sorry."

In a moment Marshall had turned his face toward her. His eyes, thick-lidded, lost a little behind the flesh of his cheeks, were still the same compassionate eyes he'd always turned on Val. "It's okay," he'd said. He had reached out and patted her knee. His hand had radiated heat even through the wool of her skirt.

SHE REACHES FALKIRK IN time for a late lunch. Sitting over a cup of coffee recently replenished, she takes a scrap of paper from her purse on which is written the phone number where Elsa Fennel can be reached. She lets the phone ring five times, six, and is on the point of hanging up when an elderly woman, by the sound of her voice, comes on the line. "Elsa ain't here!" she shouts.

"When will she be back?" Val finds herself almost shouting in turn.

"She's gone up there to Dogwood."

"Will she be back this evening?"

"Dogwood!" the woman screams. "Up there at the house."

"When will she be back?" She can't yell, really, not in a restaurant.

"Ain't no phone up there," the woman bellows.

Val hangs up.

SHE REACHES THE SIGN that says "Dogwood Station 20 km" and knows she must pay attention to her driving. The road seems curiously different from the way she remembers it. Last winter she had infused it with something of the fantastic, with the notion that it was unlike any place she knew, as though she'd made it up to scare someone, herself, in fact. There had been something surreal about it, as though it were part of some giant, cosmic unconscious creeping up toward the light. Now, without its blanket of snow, it lacks the element of menace she'd been aware of in the winter. The road is straighter than she remembers and less hilly. The other ridge of land running parallel to the road she's on can scarcely be discerned through the rainbow assortment of trees. The valley between the two ridges, what she can see of it, is not very deep, not the canyon she had thought it. The log shanties look much the same, landscaped with about the same amount of trash, perhaps even more. There are a few children about, goats, chickens, dogs. No wolves.

The Falkirk real estate agent she had hired to list the property had phoned at the end of August. "There's a buyer," she'd said. "Wants to tear down the house log by log and rebuild it at a new location." Val had been jubilant, although barely able to imagine such a painstaking endeavour. They had agreed on a closing date. "And as far as the furniture goes," the agent had said, "my husband is the best auctioneer in the entire county. Don't you worry about a thing."

When the date for the auction had been set, Val had written to Elsa Fennel to tell her of it and invited her to keep what furniture she wanted. She had added that she was welcome to the proceeds from the sale of the furniture, as she was sure that that was what Ed would have wanted. She hadn't been sure of that at all, but it had sounded polite and a humane thing to say. She was no longer sure about any aspect of Ed's life.

SHE IS ALMOST BEYOND the hillside boulders before she recognizes them. Stones, that's all they are, really, fairly large stones. Considerably smaller than Volkswagens. She does not stop to stare, but notes that they are not even as big as the stove in her kitchen. She feels let down. Under its winter camouflage these highlands had seemed rife with the possibilities found only in folklore or dreams or nightmares. She'd had a sense at the time that anything could happen up here, and frequently did. Now, in the pure, clear, three-o'clock-in-the-afternoon light of early autumn, she is quite sure that nothing happens here, that nothing has ever happened, that it is a backwater forgotten by both good fortune and bad.

Before long she spies the barn and above it the house in question. She drives up the long drive and parks in the shade under a tree near the front of the house beside an old car rusted out in spots. The house looks more squat than she remembers, even less a "beaut" than she had originally thought. She gets out of the car and sees a figure standing in the screened-in area tacked onto the side of the house. For a moment, from either side of the patched screen, she and Elsa Fennel each stare as if the other is a foreigner, immune (as is often assumed) to the rudeness of such a frank gaze.

VAL SITS IN AN aluminum-and-plastic lawn chair, somewhat wobbly, inside the screened porch. Her sister-in-law stands across from her, a small metal table between them. They did not embrace when they met; they did not even shake hands. Val fusses, shifts her weight in the creaking chair, is aware of Elsa's probing eyes, believes they are searching for clues to her personality, for some hint of what on earth could have attracted her brother to this city woman, a woman in a crisp white blouse and ironed chinos. It's as if, accepting their dissimilarities as a given, she seeks some hidden side of Val with which she can communicate.

Val breaks the silence. "We've had a letter from the buyer of the house," she tells Elsa. She does not know why she uses the inclusive *we*. Elsa's eyes dart over her face, dwell on her eyes. She says nothing. She's taller than Val, nearly as tall as Ed was. Val says, "He wants to dismantle the house and rebuild it somewhere else."

"Why not?" Elsa says. "Best thing that could happen to it." Her voice is deep, smoky. At close range Val is not at all sure that this is the elusive woman who attended the funeral and then mysteriously disappeared from the reception. She watches the woman go through the connecting door to the kitchen and decides, finally, that it is. She returns with two small tumblers and a bottle of what looks like homemade wine. She pours it and puts a glass in front of Val who has it on the tip of her tongue to say *no thank you*, but instead wraps her fingers around it. They each drink. Under other circumstances, Val would have said "Cheers." Their eyes meet in what could be construed as a silent toast to Ed's memory.

"So you're Eddy's wife. Widow, I should say."

"Why didn't you introduce yourself at the funeral?"

Elsa looks away, out through the screen at a riot of colour caught in a shaft of sunlight. "Why didn't I? I was too"— she searches for the word —"heartsick."

Heartsick is what Val felt when she learned of Ed's vasectomy. She feels a lump in her throat and against her will feels empathy with this overblown woman. There is strength or perhaps pride in the woman's features, giving her face a hard, rich beauty when she speaks.

"I was five years old when Eddy was born," Elsa says. She glares at Val as if she expects an argument. Val nods. She will encourage this woman to spin out a childhood story for as long as she wants. She knows little enough about her husband's early years. Indeed, she has made the trip out here today to have the blanks filled in, some at least.

"I saved his life. He was more precious to me than my own life."

It is Val's turn to stare. She sees a woman, once voluptuous, who has given up the struggle to keep her figure, who has bowed to the inevitable pendulous breasts with a roll of flesh bulging just under them like a spare set. She has hair in abundance, wavy, too long in Val's opinion, badly dyed, much grey showing, slung back out of her eyes with a plastic barrette. She reaches into the pocket of a man's shirt she wears unbuttoned over a silky, skin-tight T-shirt and withdraws a pack of cigarettes. She offers them to Val, who declines.

"I don't know what was wrong with Mother's head at that time," Elsa says through a veil of smoke. "There was a baby boy before Eddy, but he died for no good reason. I guess I must have heard something, Father telling her off after she buried it in a clearing way back beyond the house, this very house, telling her she didn't have the right to do that, to take a pillow and crush the life right out of a child, like that. I guess, that's what I heard because it's certainly what I came to believe. 'Delivered of the will to live,' was all she'd say to the few neighbours who got up the nerve to ask."

"But," Val can't help breaking in, "that's horrible! It's criminal!" The thought of a mother, any mother, enduring nine months of pregnancy, the pangs of labour and the risks of delivery, and then to, somehow, weeks or months later, take a pillow and... "Didn't anybody ask questions? Didn't the neighbours get suspicious?"

"The neighbours were more than a little afraid of Mother, and with good reason, I expect. We had a hog we were raising for slaughter and it took off one day. Mother chased it with a knife all over hell's half-acre before she ran him to ground. She cut off his balls to teach him a lesson, slit his throat right then and there, and dragged the carcass near a mile to get him home. Blood running like a river."

Val is fascinated. The editor in her appreciates that Elsa Fennel is a born storyteller, and not only that, that she won't spare anyone's sense of outrage or decorum. Nor does she show any desire to make a long story short.

"When Eddy came along, I was five and I wanted him for my own. I had nobody else to play with. Oh, there were cousins here and there and families up and down the road, plenty of kids, I'm not saying there weren't, but they weren't my type. I don't know why. Low-lifes my father called them.

"I watched over Eddy like a mother cat, all claws and hiss. Never took my eyes off him even while she nursed him. She made a big play of showering love on him like she did with the other wee boy, but I didn't trust her for a minute, not a fraction of a minute. Soon as he started in to wail in the evenings, I'd pick him up, small as I was, and I'd rock him in the big rocker we had, and still do have as a matter of fact, and I'd get him to calm down. But then, in time, I sensed Mother starting to tire of him, starting to get annoyed by his noises and his smells and his dirty diapers, and I'd take him into bed with me so she wouldn't put a pillow over him in the night. I don't know if she would have, but I was all for playing it safe."

Elsa pauses briefly. She rustles around in a shopping bag beside her chair, draws out two balls of wool, one bright orange and the other a pale blue. Out comes a block of knitting attached to the balls, rolled around thick needles. She extricates the needles, pulls at the strands of wool and frowns into her knitting, her fingers dexterously plying the needles. "You ask about the neighbours. Well, I should tell you that folks around here in those days kept pretty much to themselves. Ask me no questions, I'll tell you no lies, was the motto in these hills, you might say. The fewer church and government noses poking around under beds or back up in the bush the better. There's no family on the face of this earth that hasn't got a black secret or two. Especially up here in the highlands." Elsa rests her knitting on her abdomen for a moment to drink her wine.

"After a while, of course, Eddy got big enough to fend for himself, not that he needed to, because by the time he was five or six, Mother stopped looking at him like the one that got away. She got used to him. She loved him in her own way. It was just that she was so forceful about it. She just meant to touch him or pat him, I think, but it came upon him almost like a wallop, knocking him off his little legs. She used to hug the breath clean out of him, and I'd wrestle with her to get him free."

Val cannot imagine what Elsa means by love, or what passed for love in that outlandish family living back in the forties and fifties beyond the glare and righteous composure of a *Father Knows Best* civilization. She sits spellbound through all of this, by the story itself, and by the rhythmic clicking of the knitting needles. She doesn't mind the cigarette smoke, doesn't even notice it. She sips at the wine, which is rather sweet. She asks, "Was your mother ever taken to a doctor, a psychiatrist?"

"Hell, no. We were Fennels, much too good to be accused of having a mental illness. No, we never took her to a doctor except once when she cut her arm with a knife and it looked like an accident. It was an old doctor in Falkirk, there, sewed her up. Dead now. Can't even remember his name. Nope, we were Fennels through and through. My grandfather and great-grandfather owned a lot of land around here. Lumber barons they were. Not as rich as some I've heard tell of, but no slouches. Granddad passed on some fine things to my father. Silver jugs and Persian carpets and whatnot, and a bunch of silver knives and forks. We had them all the time we were growing up, and I just sold them a couple of years ago to buy the Pontiac.

"Nope, we thought we were God's rare old gift in those days. My father worked for a while back in the bush. He'd help get the logs down the river and on into the lake, just to make sure they did it right, because a lot of them were logs from Fennel property. There used to be train tracks along here near the lake and they'd haul the logs out and onto flatcars and then away they'd go by train to wherever they went. Lumbering dried up, though. Father looked around for a job of some sort, but to hear him talk, they were all beneath the likes of a Fennel. He wouldn't work at any old joe job.

"I don't really know for sure how we lived. Father hunted. We always had meat, and mother had a garden, so we didn't starve at all. I guess he sold off the finery he was left by the old man and most of the land.

"There was a school a couple miles off. I started when I was about eight and took Eddy with me because I didn't trust leaving him with Mother. The teacher didn't mind because he was so good. Never kicked up any kind of fuss. Mother had taught me to read and do arithmetic, so I was right up there with the smartest of them at school. Mother was an educated woman. She had a few books that she read over and over until I swear she had them memorized. Religious stuff as I recall, uplifting poetry. She'd spout that stuff at us any time of the day or night. She had her beliefs, and if they didn't fit alongside the preacher's beliefs, well, that was too bad.

"There was this one bothersome chap, the preacher from over Mount Reba way where there was this Holiness Movement church. He was a regular missionary, came every two weeks to try and get us into that church with the holy rollers. Sometimes Mother told him we were Catholics and would he please be kind enough to mind his own business. She'd get down on her knees with her hands pressed together and say, 'Forgive him, Father, for he knows not what he does.' And she'd cross herself in a haphazard way, never the same way twice because she wasn't Catholic at all and didn't know the first thing about it.

"The minister was a bald little man with a bad case of the pitted face. The work of pimples likely, or the chicken pox. He'd be all overcome with mortification and beg her to please get up, Mrs. Fennel, and not be making a mockery of religion. Other times, she said we had our own religion based on the harvest moon or some damn thing. He'd come out after his own church service and Mother would sit him down and get out one of her books and make him listen while she read to him without even looking down at the page. And it was the worst load of holy-bless-my-soul claptrap you ever heard. God in each and every tree and blade of grass and even in the stones you kick from underfoot until you wouldn't know who was trying to convert who. And you know, she always managed to look properly elegant the days the minister came. She could be quite grand when she put her mind to it, hair done up high on her head, and wearing a low cut dress that showed off her figure, and she'd cross her slender legs just so with the skirt of her dress hiked up just far enough to make baldy blush. Father took himself off somewhere because he couldn't stand the act she put on. She was a lovely woman on those Sundays and made her voice as charming as anything you might hear on the radio. And the minister, he'd be all fidgety and looking around and he'd catch sight of Eddy and me, our arms around each other sitting in the same chair." Elsa's eyes softened with the faraway memory.

"Even when we were too big to fit in the chair, Eddy'd be on my knee and I'd hug him and rock him. 'Aren't you a little too big a boy for all that cuddling?' the minister said, once. And Eddy, he just twisted around and looked at me and laughed and I kissed him hard on the mouth and the minister got all red in the face and asked us to please leave the room so he could have a few words with our mother."

Val feels uncomfortable. If she tried to stand up, her knees would be too weak to support her. Perhaps it's the wine. She focuses on the woman's knitting. The intermingling of the coloured wools reminds her of an old cardigan of Ed's.

"Father wanted me to go off to high school at about that time and board in town with an aunt, for I guess I was going on fifteen, but I didn't want to leave Eddy on his own. I could never be sure what Mother would take it into her head to do, and by now, Father was becoming a little odd, staring at me, staring at me and Eddy. 'Get to hell out this house!' he'd yell at me, with eyes ringed red as embers. But, I never went. I couldn't leave. I didn't want to leave Eddy. As he got older, I didn't want him going around with any of the shanty boys from down the road. He was a good boy and a smart boy, Eddy was. He was an angel and he was mine."

Val rubs her arms. She feels cold even with the still strong four o'clock sun slanting across her shoulders. She wants to get up and leave, but she feels sapped of the strength it would take to bring herself to her feet. She has a sudden memory flash. She has sometimes felt, since Ed's death and since her discovery of this house, that the person who lived here must have had Ed in her thrall. She believes now, in a way, that the idea was less fancy than truth. It is what she wants to believe, that Ed was somehow mesmerized.

Elsa offers more wine, which Val hastily declines. She fills her own glass and continues to recall the past. "I remember it was about this time that Father took to playing with rope. He'd get different lengths of rope and he'd tie knots, different kinds of knots. And Mother'd beller at him to get outside and give her a hand with the weeds in the garden and leave his knots alone or else go hang himself and be done with it.

"One day at about the end of June, Eddy came home that last day of school with a note from the teacher. Mother read the note and said, 'My, my, son, the teacher just thinks the world of you. She says you are a bright lad and should go on to high school in town next fall.'

"'Is that a fact?' says I. 'Well, we'll just see about that, won't we, Eddy?' Eddy, he just stood there with a look on his face, black as the Holy Bible. Mother and I glared at each other, ready to do battle. But Eddy stood up tall, and I swear I saw him grow up in that very instant. You could see how his shoulders were getting broad and the silk on his lip was getting dark. He stood with his arms folded and said in this croaky voice that was halfway between a boy's and a man's, 'I want to go to the high school, and that's all there is to it.' Well, I don't mind telling you it was quite a blow to me. I felt burned, singed like a chicken, all mottled and prickly, like I was going to fall down in a faint. High school wasn't in my plans. I wanted him to finish growing up right here, at home, and take over the farm when the parents passed away. I thought the two of us could live here forever, happy as could be. He was all I had and all I ever wanted to have. I saved his very life. He owed me every inch of his skin, every hair of his head, every part of his body. We were like two in one.

"But that was one godawful summer. Just godawful. Eddy and me fought, sometimes for real, to hurt each other, and sometimes just to wrestle, which was the only time Eddy'd let me get near him any more. And Father's eyes'd be on us as if he was making a difficult calculation. So we'd sneak away.

"Sometimes Eddy would run away from me and hang around with kids down the way, so I started hanging around with our cousin Rhys who lived a half mile or so down the ravine, way into the bush, still does. He always used to come up to the house to get me to help him with his homework, and just kept on coming all that summer. Spent two years in every grade, that lad, and the teacher never found out he couldn't read. He used to stare at my bosom whenever he was over at our house. I got so sick of him leering, finally, I said take a picture, if it'll make you happy, and by golly, didn't he get himself one of those Polaroid cameras and follow me and Eddy everywhere. Of course, by the end of the summer everything changed."

Val waits, but Elsa is lost in thought. Her shoulders rise and fall as a sigh escapes her. She puts her knitting down on the table and asks Val if she'd like to stay for supper. Val explains that she has to get back, that she's brought work with her to do. "That's too bad," Elsa says. "Don't let me hold you up with all my blathering. I know about the auction tomorrow, which I don't plan to sit around watching. The auctioneer came out and looked at all we have and I told him what I'm keeping. He'll have some lads out first thing in the morning to carry the pieces that are to be sold outside. We're selling most of it for I need the money."

Val sees that she is being dismissed and leans forward, hands on her knees about to stand up, but doesn't. "You said that everything changed at the end of that summer. What happened?"

Elsa draws a long breath. She sits back, picks up her knitting, but instead of working her needles, she rolls it back up and puts it away in the shopping bag. She glances at Val and then looks away.

"The day before Father finally hanged himself was the day Mother looked at me sideways and said, 'I'm guessing you're pregnant, not that I'm surprised.'" Elsa squints into the setting sun. Her mouth is a tight straight line. "There used to be a man out this way made coffins, although he's been dead himself for years. We got him, next day, to hammer together one for Father."

Val waits, not wanting to breathe.

"A lot of people came for the funeral, most of them related to us somehow, either through Father, or on Mother's side, although I believe Mother's grandmother was a Fennel, too. They all knew how he died. Things like that have a way of seeping out into the open. A few people looked at me and Eddy as if we were fiends from hell, as if we'd knotted the rope and strung him up. I guess maybe they were right in a way. And when they all left, Aunt Corrine and Uncle Stan made Eddy pack up all his clothes and stuff so they could take him in their car back to Ottawa where they lived.

"Eddy just stood away from the car, not moving. When he looked back at me, he had tears running down his face and I thought, *He's going to stay*. He's going to haul his stuff out of the car and stay. I reached out my arms to him. And then quick as lightning he slid into the back seat and off they drove."

Elsa looks at Val with such deep sadness that she, herself, experiences pain. Elsa's face seems to collapse in on itself. She pulls in and lets out such a long, heaving breath that it is as though she has taken on the heartache of the universe. Val has to turn away from the enormous loss expressed in her eyes. Elsa gets up and looks out at the glorious sun behind the trees, her back to Val, until she gains control of her voice.

"I only saw him once after that, almost two years later. Mother had pneumonia and we all thought she was going to die. He had almost nothing to say. I asked him things like, 'How's school?' If he answered at all, he'd say, 'So-so.' I asked him how he liked living in Ottawa. 'Not bad,' he'd say. And never a glance in my direction. It was sickening. It was like my Eddy shrivelled up and died inside and left this husk that sort of resembled him. 'What do you think of the baby?' I asked him. Little Eddy was sitting there in the middle of the floor throwing his toys at a cat we had. 'I don't know,' he said. I said, 'Isn't he cute?' 'No,' he said. And he wasn't either. Little Eddy was the homeliest baby I ever laid eyes on. 'Well, take a good look at him,' I said before he got back into the car and left, 'because he's just as much yours as mine.' Eddy yelled at me then and burst into tears, a big, almost fully grown boy. He said, 'It wasn't my fault. I didn't know any better. You drove me wild.' And I did, I guess. He was so young. What did he know? You have to understand that I wasn't just playing with him. I truly believed it was a way to keep him with me."

Val has her hand over her mouth, swallowing, staring at Elsa and then at the concrete floor of the screened annex.

"They drove him away and I never saw Eddy again." Elsa's next breath is as much a moan as a sigh. "So, Little Eddy's all I've got in the world that I can call my own, even if it sometimes feels like he's a great weight of a stone crushing all the life right out of me." Her voice cracks unexpectedly. Conflicting thoughts fly through Val's brain. She almost feels sorry for the woman, for her losses. She almost envies her her freedom from feelings of guilt. She would like to strike her, beat her for the damage she has caused. She is to blame, Val believes, for her own childless marriage.

Elsa brushes the heel of her hand quickly across one eye and again stands up resolutely, pride or stubbornness in her bearing, and Val stands up too. She must go, she says. But before she does, she removes the picture she had freed from the sideboard last winter from her handbag and gives it to its rightful owner. Elsa stares at it, frowning.

Val lets herself out through the screen door and walks to her car. She looks back before she gets in. Elsa's head is still bent over the picture.

twenty

THE LAST FEW DAYS slide into each other under cool September nights and weakening daytime sun until at length Gus's island retreat is over. He would have liked to stay beyond the two weeks, but the owner is coming soon to close the place up, to drain the plumbing, to put up the shutters. His canoe is lighter going back, although it contains a bag of empty bottles and tin cans. His other garbage he either composted or burned on the island. In no time, it seems, he is back on the mainland where he has parked his car. He stows his laptop and his manuscript in the trunk, a first draft almost half finished. He should be further along with it, but it's been slow going. There were days when he just couldn't get into it, days when he sat, smoked, relived his own life, parts of it causing him to wish for numbness so he could be free of it. He's in that frame of mind right now. Maybe it's because he's been having such vivid dreams lately, usually a sign of heightened creative ability. His dreams, though, are of the struggling variety, of the past, of his brother, his mother.

It's no easy trick getting the canoe back up onto the roof of his car, but he manages. He doesn't think he's left anything behind on the island, although that kind of lapse is not entirely foreign to his nature. He has a brief moment of frustrated swearing until he locates his car keys in the pocket of his jacket, which he has heaved into the back seat. With difficulty, he eases the car out of the parking spot, up onto the gravel road, and off he goes, passing, eventually, the houses with their wharves where he tied his canoe once, the general store, the house with the neon-green *Sold!* banner across a sign in front of it. This reminds him of the woman in the car whose face will not fade from his memory.

He's driving along the highway, now, not too much beyond the speed limit, his mind a jumble of past events, mainly the fire. If he could sort them out, look at them somehow, frame by frame, he could understand what happened. Look at his role in it. Assess his guilt. Figure out how much of a bastard he really is. Yeah? he asks himself. And to what end? Is he actually going to let himself off the hook?

GUS IS NOW SPEEDING along the 401 toward Toronto with his canoe on top of his car. The day has turned grey. He checks his speed and moves into the slow lane. He doesn't want his canoe to go flying off in the midst of this hectic end-of-summer traffic. What an obstacle in the road that would be! No end of cars piling up, spinning out of control, overturning in the ditch. Could put that in his novel. He has a lot of nerve, he thinks, writing a second novel when he has yet to hear from the publisher about the first one. He should have got an agent. This is ridiculous, not to have had one word back about it, not even a letter saying: *We hate your manuscript; stop bothering us.* He'll phone them when he gets back. Although, he thinks, what the hell was the name of the place I took it to? He remembers handing it over to a very pleasant woman at a desk who smiled and nodded, covered the mouthpiece of the phone into which she had been speaking, and said, "I'll see that it gets into the proper hands." Where was that? It's been over a year. A lot has happened since then. Maybe if he looks at the list of publishers he got from the library, it will come back to him. And then he remembers the list was destroyed along with everything else.

Maybe it will come to him if he stops trying so hard to remember. He'd like to get it back and take it someplace else. It's not such a bad story. He's not surprised that it never got off the ground as a screenplay back in California when he first wrote it. It wasn't as shiny as a Hollywood movie needs to be, not as tightly plotted. Maybe it doesn't work as a novel either, otherwise he'd have heard. Or else maybe they're still thinking about it. A long delay could be a good thing, no news is good news. On the other hand, fourteen months is a long time for a publisher to make up his mind. Still, what does he know? He's never sent anything to a book publisher before.

He's thinking about Aidan's reaction last winter when he'd left his finished draft on his desk in his room and Aidan read it and went into some sort of decline. He thinks he knows why, although Aidan never actually said anything about it. He believes that Aidan thought it was good, that it had some sort of literary value. Gus wishes his brother could have said, simply, *Pretty good*. Or, *Not bad*. He recognizes that that was a vain hope, knowing his brother, sensing now how fiercely competitive he had become over the years while Gus had been away writing screenplays and acting.

He dreads going back to his apartment, empty except for the disquieting sense that his mother is still there somewhere, eyeing things with suspicion, looking around to find fault, and that his brother is in another room, weeping silently, his face to the wall.

It occurs to him that there is something he could do that might help to make his brother's life — and death — seem less futile. He could contact the publishers of every literary journal in the country and buy the editions in which Aidan's work appears. He will get some bookshelves, put them on it. That's exactly what he'll do. Show them to people. Sure, he chides himself, like who? He thinks about the people he knows in Toronto. His mother's doctor, an old guy (probably not that much older than Gus. He takes back "old"). The insurance guy. And of course the funeral director. He was pretty caring and friendly, but you don't phone up the person who buried first your brother and then your mother and say, hey, how 'bout a beer?

On the other hand, why not?

And there's that priest. Maybe he should become a Catholic. Beg absolution.

As Gus drives into Toronto from the east, he meets a funeral heading north. He stops at the corner, the engine idling raggedly while he waits for it to pass.

It's not a huge funeral, but big enough. It's certainly bigger than either his brother's or his mother's. He sits waiting, thinking about his lack of family. He can see the bow of his second-hand canoe curving over the roof of the car above the windshield. He'll store it in the basement of the apartment building. He turns right and follows the last car in the funeral parade for a few blocks.

His mother never really got used to living in an apartment. And she had never actually recovered from Aidan's death. He can't say that he has either, really. He still dreams about the fire. He wakens sweating, burning hot. Always in his dream he has gone into the blazing house after his brother. He runs up the stairs to Aidan's room, through gold-tipped flames, through choking smoke, in a wild-eyed search. Sometimes he discovers Aidan lying curled up on his bed reading a book, untouched by the flames surrounding him, sometimes he sees him still on the stairs heading up to his room and reaches out to pull him back, but the fire is tugging him forward and Gus is too weak to pull him away. He awakens usually to a golden sun streaming through the window piercing his eyelids and to his morning smoker's cough.

He parks in front of the apartment long enough to unload his gear. The superintendent gives him a hand with the canoe and together they manoeuvre it into the basement. "Any chance of a one-bedroom coming up in the near future, one that comes with a parking spot under the building?" he asks.

"Might be," the man says. "I'll let you know."

Lying on the couch in the dark little living room of the apartment, Gus can't stop thinking about funerals. The procession he stopped for had a little purple flag on the hood of each car. He lies still, his arm slung across his forehead.

twenty-one

VAL SITS IN HER CAR with both doors open under the tree where she had parked the day before. The auction is in full progress. Elsa was there earlier with her son, a stunted, sad-eyed boy — man, really. He would be somewhere in his mid-forties, Val had calculated. There was something pale and alien about him, she thought, as though he had grown out of the earth like a mushroom.

As the auction time got closer, Elsa had said, "We're not going to stick around to see our furniture sold to the riffraff." Down the lane she strode as the first pickup trucks arrived, little Eddy, splay-footed, slip-slapping behind her like a pet penguin. She has told Val that her cousin Rhys has asked her and her son to live with him. "Wants me to keep house," she said. "Suits me fine. The place is a pigsty. Been wanting to get my hands on it for years. Nothing I like better than a neat house."

The auction has attracted a large and varied crowd. Besides the household effects, there are pieces of machinery and a few less than perfect antiques from the barn. Val watches curious neighbours, bargain hunters, antiques buffs wading in among the items to be auctioned, studying joins, fingering upholstery, opening and shutting drawers.

Shortly after the auctioneer begins his nasal, monotoned spiel, her attention is drawn to a man standing back behind the crowd lobbing a pound of butter from hand to hand.

Their eyes meet briefly before he turns toward the auctioneer. He shades his eyes, and then quickly puts his hand in his pocket as if he doesn't want his hand on his forehead to be mistaken for a bid. In a moment he starts off down the lane with an easy sort of gait, playing catch with his pound of butter. An odd duck, she thinks.

She leaves before the auction is over, anxious to get back to her home territory, back to the city, grounded as it seems to be in rock-hard concrete. It is late afternoon by the time she arrives back in Toronto.

AFTER A SHOWER SHE picks up her phone messages, her wet hair dripping onto her terry-towel bathrobe. The last message is from Robert. His voice is low and gruff. "Phone me at home," he says.

Worriedly, she dials his home number. She can barely hear him when he says hello. "Robert?" she inquires. She hears him clear his throat.

"I've got some sad news," he says bluntly. "Marshall is dead. He choked on something. And he died."

Val has the sensation of sudden numbness, that her hands, feet, her limbs have gone to sleep. She feels as if she's in a void. She can't grasp what he's said, can't believe it. "No," she says. But she knows it's true. Robert is still trying to clear his throat. He tries to speak again, but his voice cracks with emotion and he stops.

Val is immediately shocked out of her temporary paraesthesia. Robert is in bad shape. She is aware of him blowing his nose. "I'll come right over," she says.

She hears a barely audible, "Okay."

"I'll be there in fifteen minutes."

The phone rattles in its cradle as she replaces it. She jumps when it rings a moment later. Picking it up she hears a woman's voice saying, "This is Ruth Murray. I'm phoning from my brother Marshall Saul's apartment. I found your phone number in a book here, and I'm phoning a few of the numbers. I, I wanted to let you know that"— the voice hesitates —"that my brother, that Marshall died last night after choking on, on, something he was eating and he, he just...."

Val interrupts at this point to tell her that she has just heard the news from Robert, another friend of Marshall's. "Yes," Ruth says. Both women are in tears now as they try to understand what has happened. *Choked on...complete obstruction...the panic...living alone.* Ruth tells her about the funeral arrangements and they hang up. It feels somehow as if they are old friends.

She should have told Robert half an hour. She has to get dressed, dry her hair, make herself look...*Marsh is dead, you idiot!* She doesn't have to look any way but the way she feels — stunned, wretched, flattened, as if she's been run over. She sheds her bathrobe, throws on a pair of jeans, a sweater, and is soon in her car heading up Yonge to Robert's house a few blocks north of Lawrence.

She is, somehow, not surprised to find that Lynnette Appsley is nowhere lurking about the premises. Robert looks a mess. His eyes are red, his hair uncharacteristically disorderly, as if he's been driving his fingers back through it. He's been drinking Scotch and offers her a drink, which she accepts. She had been about to embrace him when she arrived at the door, but he had stepped back, ushering her into the living room.

He takes a handkerchief from his pocket, blows his nose, puts it back. They sit in his well-appointed living room, formerly his mother's, like something from *Architectural Digest*. There are no words, trite or otherwise, to fit this occasion. "I can't make my brain believe this," she says. "What happened? How did you find out?" Her hands are in her lap. Her drink is on a table beside her.

Robert attempts to pull himself together enough to answer her questions. "We ran into each other the day before yesterday, quite by chance, really. I suggested we have dinner sometime. He seemed agreeable to that and then thinking I had nothing else on, I said, 'What about tomorrow night?' He agreed. He said he had something on but could free himself." He stops to blow his nose, again. "And then the next day I was swamped with work and in a rotten mood, and so I phoned him in the afternoon and cancelled." He looks away for a minute. "Well, today I felt badly about it. His line was busy when I phoned him, so I went to his apartment. He didn't answer his buzz. His paper had been delivered but not picked up and his line was still busy. I was worried, because, you know, he rarely goes out and he would never leave a phone off the hook. So I got the superintendent and we went into his apartment." He takes a breath. "We found Marshall dead, sort of crumpled on the floor. The television was on. A small table was overturned, food all over the place, wine, broken glass, the phone on the floor. He must have been frantic to dial someone for help." Robert stops talking.

Val shakes her head sorrowfully. What can she say? *You should have ... you should not have ...* She can't take this train any further.

"We called the police. They said he'd choked."

She waits for Robert to say something more, but he's up pacing the room. She sips her Scotch and soda and finds it oddly soothing. Another few swallows and she may not be accountable for anything she says or does. "Is that when you called Marshall's sister?"

"Yes," he says, his voice still low. "She and her husband came immediately from Burlington."

Val feels she's not being of any help to Robert. Her intuition tells her to put her arms around him, offer him — what — motherly comfort? Sisterly? She wants to cry with him. She's his friend, his business associate. She's known him for going on seven years, and yet she doesn't know him at all.

"Did he have any family besides Ruth?"

"Not close by. Only me."

"And me," she says. She waits.

"It's all my fault," he says.

Robert has his back to her and is leaning an elbow on the elegantly carved mantelpiece massaging his forehead with the ends of his fingers. She wonders if he isn't, just the tiniest little bit, striking a pose. Guilt, she thinks, is not so much inflicted upon us, as sought by us.

"You mean if you had gone out for dinner with him he wouldn't have choked."

Robert still has his back to her. His voice is muffled, but she hears him say, "I believe he wanted more from me than mere friendship. That's more or less why I cancelled."

She gets up and goes over to Robert. She puts her arms around him and gets him to turn toward her. When she releases him she says, "I think he was a very lonely man. He just wanted someone to love him. He had a lot to give, and no one to give it to." She doesn't know how she knows this, or even whether it's true, but it seems true, it seems to sum up Marsh. And then she thinks, how sad! To have a friend sum up your life in three short sentences. "Oh, what am I talking about?" she says. "He was much more complex than that. He was sensitive and kind. That much I do know."

Robert goes back to where he left his Scotch on a gleaming marble-topped table and sits down. He sighs. He looks down at his long legs stretched out in front of him. "I wish he were still here. I wish I could go back, to explain, to talk it out. I should have been kinder. I should have met him for dinner. I could have."

"I know," she says. "If only we could go back and do things differently, we'd end up being perfect. But no. We are meant to have blood on our hands, I think." Is guilt, she wonders, the big irony in our lives? Do we really think that we are the cause of every effect, that we have that much control over ourselves and every living creature that comes into our lives? It's when we come face to face with our frailties and our own mismanagement that we have this need to be the scapegoat. She will not tell this to Robert because she isn't at all sure he will agree.

AT THE FUNERAL, VAL and Robert and Lynnette Appsley take a pew near the back of the funeral home's synagogue. There is a modest turnout — Marsh's legal associates, a few clients, a few neighbours from the apartment building where he lived, men from his synagogue. By far the largest contingent is his family — nieces and nephews from Burlington, cousins from Montreal, along with their own large families, as well as a number of elderly men and women dressed in black.

Just before the service is to start a man hurries in and sits fussily at the end of the pew beside Val. He is elderly, dapperly dressed. She watches as he crosses and uncrosses his legs, straightens a handkerchief in his breast pocket. He peers back at Val with piercing dark eyes from under his bushy grey eyebrows. She looks down, wondering if he is Marsh's therapist, wondering if he holds all the clues to her friend's inner workings.

After the funeral, cars move sedately north to the cemetery. Robert, his eyes red-rimmed, takes his turn when the shovel is handed to him and covers with earth the casket of his friend. Val, Lynnette, and Robert join many of the others back at Marshall's apartment. Lynnette makes herself known to Marshall's family, offers condolences, manages to keep up a conversation with his mother who is from Montreal, with two of his cousins who look enough alike to be twins, with a teenaged girl. Lynnette is good at funerals, Val thinks, a trifle jealously, whereas she herself is awkward and wordless. Val and Robert cling to the edges of Marshall's living room, sipping coffee from rented cups, pale wisps of humanity, Val thinks, compared to his robust family. Marshall's sister Ruth takes pity on them, offering them a plate of devilled eggs.

They find themselves near the man who had sat at the end of their pew and Val engages him in conversation. He is indeed Marshall's therapist, a Dr. Stein. When she introduces herself she looks closely into the man's face for any sign of recognition, imagining that Marshall might have mentioned her as a friend. He blinks not an eyelid. Robert then introduces himself, and the doctor nods benignly, without awareness. "Marshall will be missed so much by his friends," Val says, thinking as she says it, how lame she sounds, how uninvolved. Can she not come up with something more personal, more heartfelt? Robert does better. He talks about how long he's known Marshall, going back to their student years. They were both in the same year at law school. Val hadn't known this, hadn't known even that Robert had once been a lawyer.

Dr. Stein says, "I think I can speak for Marshall to this extent, that he never gave up on his friends. No matter how troubled he was in spirit, the trust he had in his friends buoyed him up and gave his life direction." He takes himself off then to speak with Marsh's mother. Val feels let down. She expected more insights from Dr. Stein. If anyone understood Marsh, it would be him. Marsh trusted his friends, he said. Maybe he was actually mocking her and Robert. Perhaps he had meant just the opposite of what he said, that with careless friends like them, who needed enemies? By "them" she thinks she actually means Robert. Not something she wants to discuss with him, though. Maybe she's just being paranoid on his behalf. She sees that he is talking to Ruth right now.

The day after Marshall's funeral, Val cannot rid herself of an urge to call him on the telephone just to hear his sincere and courteous voice on the answering machine. When she at last gives in and dials his number, her heart pounds so hard she can hear it. Marsh, still alive in the machine, explains with an endearing warmth that he is unable to take her call and invites her, with that resonance she knows so well, to leave her name and number and promises to return her call as soon as possible. For a wild moment she is tempted to leave him a message, harangue him for skipping out on his life before it was half over. But she doesn't. She hangs up and sits there. It's as though we believe it will never happen to us, she thinks. Or maybe it's our imperfect memories. We forget from moment to moment that delivery of our final package is on its way.

Still afraid of letting Marsh's voice slip from her memory, she phones a day later. After a series of tones a disembodied voice, not Marsh's, tells her that that number is no longer in service.

Later, at home in bed that night, she remembers how Marsh had offered his help after her husband's accident. She remembers seeing tears in his eyes, tears for her loss. She remembers the way he had looked almost adoringly at her last winter when he was sick with the flu and she had made soup and taken it to him. We need more words, she thinks, to express how we feel. There aren't enough words.

twenty-two

IT IS A RARE DAY in early October, stage-lit, it almost seems, to give a theatrical impression of a golden autumn morning. The mood at Dobbs, Kendall is less than bright. There have been rumblings over the summer that if no one comes forward with the cash to buy them by the end of October, their corporate owner will, in all probability, dismantle them and hurl them into the void. Robert breezes through the front door looking confident, as if he hasn't a worry. Carol who sits at her desk in the wide downstairs front hall passes on a message for him. The brass at Aksfal have scheduled a meeting at ten-thirty and would like him to be there. Carol has anxiety written all over her face. She needs answers. She needs the job. "What will this mean for us?" she asks Robert

"It doesn't mean anything," he says soothingly. "Somebody will buy us and we'll go on just as before, only better." He goes on up the stairs to his office, worry furrowing his brow. He composes his face before poking his head into Val's office. Val peers over the tops of her owlish specs. "What do you think the Aksfal meeting will be about?" She's been talking to Carol.

"Nothing," he says. "The usual blather."

Val shakes her head. He doesn't fool her. She knows him well enough to see the whirlpool beneath his calm surface. Dobbs, Kendall isn't perfect, but it's pretty damn good for its size. They do a great job on the books they publish. Surely they wouldn't let this "little Canadian gem," as they have been labelled in reviews and news articles, die, simply drop dead from lack of nourishment. She chats with him while he picks up some papers from his office, sombrely, their voices almost whispers. They go downstairs together and Robert continues on out the door to his meeting. She and Carol exchange a gloom-filled glance.

She has a meeting to attend herself in a few minutes with the sales and marketing people. She pauses before going into the conference room, straightens her shoulders, breathes. In spite of the uncertainty of their future, she's looking forward to discussing the spring list now that the fall books are out of the way and doing fairly well. The fall list is strong and includes Lynnette Appsley's latest tome. She chastises herself for being cynical. It's actually quite a good piece of work. It will sell. She has a stack of manuscripts and notes in her arms to take into the meeting.

The others are there already. She leaves the door of the room open. The sun filtering through the brilliant leaves of the large maple outside the front window drenches the room in light and unnecessary heat. She removes her suit jacket and drapes it over the back of her chair, knowing her face and neck look as hotly pink as they feel. She sits near the open door ready to close it if the foyer becomes noisy or too distracting. People are quietly chatting, waiting for her to begin. Instead, she leafs through her notes as if looking for some important piece of information, waiting for the tingling sensation that accompanies her rise in temperature to dissipate. She feels like a cheap electrical appliance about to short-circuit and begin to smoke. She calls the meeting to order.

ON THIS DAY IN OCTOBER, Gus reminds himself that it is almost three months since his mother died, and nearly a year and a half since he deposited his first manuscript with a publisher called Dobbs, Kendall. The name of the publishing firm has eluded him until recently, but now he has it solidly imprinted, he thinks. He had liked the sound of the name and he'd liked the look of the place. An old house. He imagined that the people working there would be kind, would care, would treat his work with respect and even if it wasn't quite ready for publication, would be interested enough to offer him a few suggestions. And now he has another manuscript half-completed about a woman suffering the guilt of feeling responsible for the death of her teen-aged son.

He's waited long enough to hear about the first manuscript. He will confront the publisher in person. Or an editor. Or the girl at the desk. He will demand some sort of explanation. What other business would keep a potential client waiting that long? He can't think of any.

He tries to keep his disgruntlement topped up, but finds the autumn sunlight shimmering amidst the yellows and oranges of the city's trees too distracting. He doesn't realize that he's almost smiling as he strides along the street. His car would only have been a nuisance to park. There it is, the old house. Big maple in front crowded between sidewalk and house, and a scattering of sun-yellow leaves blanketing exposed roots. Brass plate gleaming beside the door. What the hell is he going to say? He tries out a scowl, but has trouble making it stick.

He opens the front door and walks in. On his left is a room with some people sitting around a table, straight ahead a desk, and on it, besides a computer monitor, are stacks of manila envelopes, one of them probably his, untouched, much less read, he's willing to bet, since he dropped it off last summer. No one about. He glances again toward the room. Some sort of meeting going on, he supposes. He's wondering what he should do now. No place to sit, to wait. He could go up the staircase, see if he can rouse anyone. Maybe all the employees are attending the meeting. He could go out and grab a coffee somewhere and come back. He could interrupt the meeting and demand they give him back his manuscript. Half-assed little set-up like this. Serve them right. Serves him right. Should have got an agent. He should have taken it to a bigger outfit, one he's at least heard of. American-sounding. He paces for a moment. He looks through the open door again and, my God, it's her. That woman. She's looking at him, too.

AT THIS PRECISE MOMENT, looking through the open door, Val recognizes the man she saw at the auction sale at the house in Dogwood station. For one wild instant she thinks he's stalking her, that he's even gone so far as to find out where she works. But that's silly. On the other hand — it happens. She gets up to close the door even though the meeting is essentially over.

"Wait!" he says, rather louder than he has intended. He puts out a hand to prevent the door from closing. "Have we met?"

"Um," she says with a hint of anxiety. "Is there something you want?" Where on earth is Carol, Val thinks, peering around the man at Carol's vacant chair behind the desk.

Gus looks over his shoulder following her eyes. He's aware of her tone, barely polite, dismissive. He'll come right to the point. The fact that they have bumped into each other (more or less) before is not as fascinating to her, obviously, as it is to him. "You've had my manuscript for over a year. I'd like it back."

She looks at him blankly. "Manuscript?" She attempts a polite but friendly smile. "I'm in a meeting right now. And, I'm afraid we would have to look for your manuscript. It could take a while. Could you leave your name and phone number at the desk with Carol when she comes back and we'll..."

"No. I couldn't."

She stares at him.

"I'll wait."

"Oh, fine," she says. "Carol will be back in a moment." She closes the door feeling more rattled than she needs to and wondering why.

IT MUST BE THE SAME the world over, Gus muses, thinking he'd like to kick the door open again and frog-march this snippy woman to the location of his manuscript. Producers, directors, publishing people, they all behave as if they're working to a strict deadline that will run out in three minutes, so please don't hold them up for longer than twenty seconds. Once they discover you have something they covet, however, time is irrelevant. There is no sign of the woman named Carol. He looks at his watch for no very good reason other than that he's been thinking about the value of time. He has nowhere to go, no one to see. No meetings. He could go back to the apartment and write, but he doesn't feel like it. Writing has lost its appeal somewhat.

He grabs a pad of Post-it notes from the desk, scrawls on it: *Forget the ms. I'm taking it elsewhere. A. A McNiall.* And off he goes. He doesn't need the copy they have. It's no longer on his hard-drive, but he's saved it to a floppy. He'll reprint it. And about what comes next, he's not sure, maybe inquire into agents. Or forget the whole thing. Stupid bloody way to try to earn your living. Whatever made him think he could do it? A well-dressed man approaches Dobbs, Kendall just as he's leaving. The man nods worriedly, quite a dapper fellow really. Gus nods back, sullenly.

VAL, HEAD DOWN, comes out of her meeting and nearly collides with Robert returned from *his* meeting with Aksfal. The others gather their notes, their jackets, sweaters, chatting, not in any hurry, and make plans for lunch. Carol has just returned to her desk after trying unsuccessfully to get the coffee maker to work. On her desk, written on a Post-it is a message from A. A. McNiall. After a sudden intake of breath, her voice up about an octave, she exclaims, "McNiall was here and I missed him." She's nearly in tears.

Robert says, "It doesn't matter." Carol says, "I'll go after him, he must have just left." Val, says, "No, no, I'll go." My God! the inside of her head shrieks. That was A. A. McNiall! Aloud and loudly she says, "I know what he looks like." Carol asks what he looks like because they had better go in different directions.

"He has a beard," Val says.

Robert intones, "Ladies!" They pause, frowning; they hate to be called "ladies."

"It matters not a whit if William Shakespeare himself was here. We no longer exist."

They both turn to look at him, to take in the significance of his pronouncement, and then dash out anyway — Carol because she is guilty of abandoning her post and has to do something to make up for it, Val because she doesn't want to believe that their publishing house is on its deathbed. Something as good as Dobbs, Kendall can't just end. She remembers, though, that there had been a time, and not so long ago, when she had almost wished that it would go belly up. She had thought that something that drastic would push her to do some writing of her own, force her to actually confront blank pages day after day, month after month. And yet a not inconsiderable impediment to all of this would be that she doesn't know what she could possibly write that would pass muster in her own exacting judgment. The very thought of a meagre attempt at fiction fills her with dread — self-doubt would be a constant companion, failure an ever-threatening black pit.

Carol hurries down the street to the right and Val to the left, turning to stare rudely, both of them, into the faces of beardless strangers.

Val flies along three or four blocks, looking left and right up and down cross-streets before turning back out of breath. She returns at a walk, slowly, fruitlessly, head down, deep in thought. She ponders the future. She will not write. She knows that. There will be a job for her somewhere. She has both talent and not a bad reputation.

BACK IN THE APARTMENT he looks through the drawers of the beat-up old desk he was able to buy in a second-hand furniture store. There it is, the diskette labelled *novel #1*. He turns on his computer and shoves it in. Nothing on the screen. A message only, informing him of some sort of fatal error. "Christ!" he says. He feels sweat coming out all over his entire scalp. He takes the diskette out and jams it in again while his machine merrily clickety-clickety-clicks to no avail. He can't believe this is happening. He has no novel. He has an early hard copy version somewhere he thinks, lacking about two hundred and fifty pages, much marked up. His head in his hands, there is only one word for this, which he uses quietly, repetitiously. He's thinking of picking up the laptop and heaving it through the window. He's thinking of heaving himself through after it. He's thinking about buying cigarettes even though he quit smoking thirteen days ago. He snatches the floppy from the snide little mouth on the side of his laptop and goes out.

He lights his second cigarette in the computer store he discovered not far from the apartment, where they not only buy and sell, but repair. The guy behind the counter takes the floppy from him doubtfully, tries it out in a variety of computers, shakes his head.

"It happens," the computer guy says. "Every once in a while you get a dud. Maybe it got too close to a magnetic field."

"What am I going to do?" Gus doesn't mean to shout. "This represents a year's work. I'll sue the bastards."

"Nothing's perfect," the computer guy says. "We live in an imperfect world."

AS LUCK WOULD HAVE it, an hour and fifteen minutes away on foot from where Gus is contemplating pasting the owner of a computer service shop, or twenty-five minutes using public transportation, the mailman who includes Dobbs, Kendall in his route has just dropped off the day's allotment of letters. Both angry and polite, they inquire about the fate of certain precious manuscripts, and there is a bundle of several more manuscripts, both solicited and unsolicited, a handful of business letters, and an important-looking envelope from a prominent legal firm addressed to Robert. Robert turns it over in his hands, frowning, wondering, what on earth? Is he being sued? That's all he needs at this point, now that Aksfal has announced definitely that if a buyer cannot be found within the next week, Dobbs, Kendall will cease to exist. One week. That's all. He takes his marble-handled letter opener and slits the envelope. He reads its contents slowly, carefully, and immediately looks up the phone number of his own lawyer. He dials.

ON LINE TWO, Val, still irked at not managing to capture A. A. McNiall, and about to dive into a healthful fruit salad in her office, takes an incoming call. Carol has gone home for the rest of the day with a migraine brought on, Val believes, by the stress of feeling guilty over abandoning her post at the very moment of McNiall's incarnation. "Dobbs, Kendall," Val says. On the other end of the line, a man mutters his name, Gus, it sounds like. *Did he say McNiall?* "Mr. McNiall?"

"Yes." He hesitates. Is this that woman, he wonders? Christ. He clears his throat. "I find I'll need my novel back, after all. I don't have a copy of it."

"A. A. McNiall?"

"Yes. Uh. Would you mind taking a look for it? I want to place it somewhere else. I'll leave you my phone number."

"Oh, no!" Val moans as if he's just mentioned that he has a fatal illness. "I'm so sorry," she says. "We have some bad news."

What now, Gus wonders. They've lost it. Inadvertently put it out with the trash. Shredding it first. Warily he asks, "What's wrong?"

And then the whole story comes flowing out through the phone lines, about how much they love his novel, how everyone who works for Dobbs, Kendall has read it and loves it, how they really wanted to publish it, how they had felt that it might even win a few prestigious awards. Val pauses and says, "Except that —"

He knew it was too good to be true. "Uh-huh?" He waits for it.

"We're no longer in business."

"No longer —"

"No longer a publishing company."

"So, what are you?"

"Nothing. We're defunct. Jobless."

There is a long pause. Gus thinks he should say something sympathetic, like sorry you're out of a job. "Sorry you're out of a job," he says.

"It isn't as sudden as it seems. We just never really believed it would happen."

Gus is wondering what to do about his manuscript, where to send it, whether he should start canvassing agents. Just because this freak of a little publishing house likes it, probably doesn't mean a whole lot in the grand scheme of things. He feels a great weight settle on him, a great grey blimp of depression. He's right back where he was thirty years ago, waiting to find someone to take an interest in a story he wants to tell, waiting for a break. Except that this time round, he's fifty-three years old. Wearily, he says he'll come back tomorrow and pick up the manuscript.

Val says, "Would you like to have lunch? Maybe we can work something out. Shall we say one o'clock?"

He thinks, why would she want to have lunch with me? And, more to the point, why would he have the remotest desire to have lunch with her? "Sure, fine," he says. As an afterthought, he announces, "But I have to be somewhere at two."

"That doesn't give us much time," she says.

"Well, two-thirty then." He doesn't have to be any-where any time, but he doesn't relish the idea of being stuck with this unreliable woman for half the afternoon.

twenty - three

VAL HAS AGREED TO meet Angus McNiall at the little bistro that Robert favours. She made a reservation under Dobbs, Kendall, requested Robert's usual table, and told them the name of her guest. Even if she were to be a minute or two late, the headwaiter would nab him, seat him, and, she hopes, hold him captive until she gets there. She had hoped that Robert would join them. However, he left her a voice message this morning saying something's come up and that he won't be in until about three today. He is, in fact, calling a meeting at that time for all the staff, full, part time, and occasional.

She's about ready to leave the office when one of her writers phones to say she doesn't know why she ended her manuscript the way she did, that she's thought of a better ending and needs more time to work on it. Val gropes through her mind to the woman's manuscript, to the ending. She can't recall anything awkward or misplaced about the ending. It just ends. "I think it's fine," she says. If she had thought otherwise, she would have said so when she began editing it.

"No, but," the writer continues, not convinced that Val's judgment is infallible. She goes on at great length, back and forth from pivotal scene to ending, another pivotal scene to ending, until Val feels dizzy. She looks at her watch.

"Can I get back to you?"

The woman is not ready to release her. Val tells her she's late for a meeting, but still the writer bleats on.

"Yes," she says, finally, "you're quite right about the ending. Send me your revisions and I'll get back to you."

GUS GETS TO THE restaurant ten minutes early. He walks around the block, briskly, and kills three minutes. He's starving. There are a number of restaurants in the area. Maybe he could grab a quick bite somewhere and have a second lunch with madam queen. He doesn't even know her name, he realizes. He goes into the restaurant at five to one. There are a few people ahead of him which gives him a moment to glance around. Popular place, pretty well packed. Maybe they won't get a table. A waiter is giving him the eye, even though there are still people ahead of him.

"Dobbs, Kendall?" the waiter asks. He leads Gus to about the only empty table in the place, a little away from the general hubbub, seats him, and asks if he'd like a drink. He would like a drink, but declines. He thinks he should call the guy back; say he changed his mind. But he doesn't. Gus looks around, drumming his fingernails on the cloth. Nice place. Someone fills his water glass and he drains it, looks at his watch. Maybe she's not going to show up. They've given him a menu to stave off the pangs. Not cheap. He thinks he has enough, or will she pay? He's never been asked out to lunch by a woman. He's going to give her five more minutes and if she doesn't show, he'll get up and leave. He'll go back to the publisher's, can't be very far from here, lean on whoever is there, and demand his manuscript. He'll haunt the place until they hand it over.

SHE'S NEARLY TWENTY minutes late. The restaurant is fairly full, but she doesn't see him. She sees a man seated alone, but it's somebody else — but isn't that Robert's table? She knows the waiters, she'll ask. He's probably left. Once again Dobbs, Kendall (that was) will have let him slip through their careless corporate fingers. A waiter takes her in and seats her at the usual table with a beardless stranger who looks instantly familiar, once she adjusts. He gets awkwardly to his feet, nearly upsetting the table. She pulls at her chin. "Your beard!"

He looks sheepish, shrugs. "Shaved it off."

"Valerie Hudson." They shake hands and sit. "It's nice to meet you finally," she says. Her cheeks are pink. "I mean properly meet."

Gus is looking at her with blank amazement, studying her, in fact. Valerie Hudson is the name of that woman who, according to the *Star* a year ago, slightly more than a year ago, failed to pick up a piece of lumber lying on the road, and.... No. He's not sure. Yet, he thinks that was the name. He knows it was Valerie, at any rate.

Val looks up to see Angus A. McNiall observing her, making a mental note of her and their surroundings as if he's going to be a material witness in some complicated court case.

"How long have you been with Dobbs, Kendall?" he asks.

"Seven years," she tells him, although it may only be six. She's lost track. She wonders whether he's doubting her skill, thinking she's a fraud.

253

He wants to find out if this woman has a husband and a bunch of kids and hoping she does because he doesn't want it to be the Valerie of the traffic accident. He could not bear to have lunch with a woman whose life he has stolen and transformed, but stolen nevertheless, and put into his second novel, resurrecting her tragic loss, exploiting her fatal mishap. But he can't ask her that, because what if she says she lost her husband in a car accident a little over a year ago. Instead he asks what she reads in her spare time, if she has such a thing as spare time. He hopes she'll confess that her large vibrant family takes up her spare time. But while she's still mulling his question, he asks her what films she likes. And then, does she read poetry, does she prefer novels to short-story collections? At last she puts up a hand to quell the barrage of questions. "Aren't we supposed to be talking about you and your novel?"

"Mmm," he says looking at his hands folded on the table, at his big knuckles. He'll look into his files (a brown paper shopping bag) when he gets home to see if he still has the article from the *Star* with the name of the woman.

She's got his manuscript. He saw it sticking out of her briefcase before she sat down. He doesn't know why she would want to have lunch with him when they could easily have just met in her office.

The waiter brings their orders: a salad for her; for him, steak and onions. His looks good, she thinks, although she seldom eats meat any more. He notices her eyeing his plate. "Let me give you a little," he says.

"Oh, no, no," she says. "Thanks anyway." But he cuts a small portion of his rare beef for her topped by an onion ring. She wishes he hadn't. It's a rather intimate thing to do. It puts her in almost an infantile role, like a baby bird. He passes it over to place on her bread and butter plate, nearly knocking over her water glass. "Sorry."

"It's all right," she says. The waiter hovers, hoping everything is all right. Val forks up the offering of beef he has deposited right on top of her little curl of butter. "It's very nice," she assures him.

Gus loses a couple of french fries down his front. He's not usually this inept, he thinks. But no, on consideration, he probably is.

The man's a hazard to himself, she thinks, pretending not to notice. She keeps her eyes on her salad, nibbling like an anxious guinea pig. Raising her eyes, she sees him, chin down, look up, almost penitently, through tufts of eyebrows. He should have left his beard. It suited him.

They eat in silence for a moment. "About your manuscript," she says. "It really will make a remarkably fine book."

His eyes, when he looks up from his plate, glow, shimmer, actually. And he blushes. She's never seen a man his age blush. She goes on to tell him about the plight of Dobbs, Kendall, about the fact that at this late date, with less than a week to go, it's very unlikely that anyone will step in to buy them. "In spite of this, Robert and I will try to find a publisher for you."

"Thank you," he says. "That's very kind."

She explains that the reason they didn't get back to him was the lack of a return address or phone number.

He frowns and then nods. He should have gone back and checked. He can't rely on his memory. Of course he has a different address, now, different phone number.

"How's your salad?" he asks.

"Not bad." (He needn't hope for a taste.) "Do you have a title in mind?" she inquires.

He's polished off his lunch before she's even halfway through her salad. He wipes his napkin across his mouth, and fingers his beardless chin, surprised by its smoothness. "Still thinking about it," he admits.

She smiles at this oddly likeable man. "Tell me how you came to write the book."

He tells her that his novel started off as a screenplay that never quite made it to the screen. She quizzes him further, he talks, spills the abridged version of his life story. They have coffee. "And then what?" she wants to know when it seems that he's about to stop. "When I began to run low on money I was able to get some bit parts in a couple of films. And now, I have a new novel on the go."

He likes the way she smiles. He even likes her funny glasses; they suit her.

Val wants to hear about his second novel, but she has just sneaked a peek at her watch. She has her meeting with Robert at three. She has to run, but not before she gets his phone number and address. "I've really enjoyed hearing all this," she says. "I brought along your manuscript in case you want to try placing it somewhere yourself."

"No," he says. "I have faith in you."

She gives the waiter her credit card and Gus gets out his wallet. "Lunch is on the company," she says. When it's time to go, they shake hands, pleased with each other.

Outside she calls, "We'll be in touch," and walks smartly back along the street, not wanting to be late for her meeting. She expects Robert will want to give them details of the company's demise, give a little eulogy, probably. She expects they'll all end up in tears.

Gus watches her go. She's not so bad, he thinks, not bad at all. He scratches his itchy chin, thinking he'll let the beard grow back. He walks rapidly up to Dundas and waits at the corner to let a taxi pass. The passenger in the back seat looks vaguely familiar. He wonders what's on his mind to make him look like that, as if he's responsible for the way the world is going.

ROBERT HAS TAKEN a taxi from his lawyer's office across town to his own office. He looks at his watch. He's going to be late for the meeting he's called, and, as one might expect, the driver is in no particular hurry. They are held up on Dundas by construction work. He wishes he felt happier than he does. He should be excited. Val will be excited. But he feels sick at heart, actually. Feels as if he's kicked his best friend in the gut. And been rewarded for it.

The driver is fiddling with the radio, tuning in some talk show thing. Robert hates these shows where idiots phone in with their stupid, inconsequential questions or their bigoted, uninformed opinions. He'd almost rather have heavy metal rock. That, he can block out. The show's host says, "Don't be so ready to lay blame. We're like noodles in a pot of boiling water. We move randomly, brush against each other briefly, accidentally, ceaselessly. We're not perfect."

"You mean nothing's our fault?" asks the caller. "Or anyone else's?"

"I didn't say that. I meant that we are in control only of our choices. But how they'll turn out is another matter altogether."

The driver opts for a baseball game and Robert tunes out.

He looks through the window at traffic on the other side of the road crawling past the construction site, hears the racket of pneumatic drills. It brings to mind an incident from his student days. He and Marsh were walking past an excavation site somewhere along Bloor, he can't remember exactly where. There were windows in the boarding so that passersby could pause and watch the work. They'd watched for a while, Marsh behind him, taller, watching over his shoulder, marvelling at the heavy equipment, watching the workmen expertly manoeuvre it to do their bidding. "Like watching giant robots," Marsh had said, "their every move planned." He leaned his arm on Robert's shoulder, pointing, and said, "Watch this one." Robert doesn't even remember what he was pointing at. He only remembers the feel of Marsh's arm on his shoulder and the way it both attracted and repelled him. He stood his ground, not wanting to flinch or move away. Marsh was so close he could feel the heat of him along the length of his whole body. Years ago, that was. An invitation. He'd even known that at the time. Marsh wants me, he'd thought. But at the corner of the street he'd said, "I'm meeting my girlfriend. See you later." He'd gone off, then, running, in fact. He knew that if he stopped and turned around, Marsh would still be there watching him, waiting for him to come back.

But he didn't stop; he kept going until he could run no further. He went into the nearest subway station and phoned a girl he'd taken out once, about a month ago, to see if she'd like to meet him later, go out for a drink, go back to his place, maybe.

Later, back at his tiny excuse for an apartment with the girl whose name he can't remember now, he'd offered her another drink, swilling the booze back himself, until, instead of becoming amorous as he had hoped he would, he became sarcastic and insufferable and she got up and went home.

He'd had plenty of invitations from Marsh over the years, at least, he took them to be invitations, although they were very slight, innocuous, sometimes just a glance held a little too long, and he'd turned them all down.

Marsh knew, of course. Even though he, Robert, had had a variety of girlfriends over the years, Marsh somehow knew, sensed what attracted him, must have decided it was just a matter of time before he broke, admitted. But he hadn't. He never did give in to it. Never gave anybody the satisfaction of knowing. He hates the word gay. Nothing gay about it. He remembers how his father talked about those goddamn queers. Should all be gassed, he used to say. A disgrace to the male gender (his father would never use the word sex).

Right now Robert loathes himself. How could he have treated Marsh so badly? Why couldn't he have —.

Robert's narrow, well-put-together face lengthens into a mask of sorrow and remorse as he recalls what he'd sooner forget. It all seemed to come to a head last winter. Marshall actually made a pass at him, at least, he thinks it was a pass, and he had reacted badly. He can barely remember the details. He doesn't even want to think about it. He'd had a lot to drink, they both had. He remembers phoning him the next day or the next and saying he was sorry, and Marsh, coolly had told him not to be ridiculous, had said he had no idea what he was talking about. And Robert had let it go, and it had essentially spoiled their friendship. Had he called Marsh a goddamn queer? He thinks he had, and had said it sneeringly as if *he* wasn't.

And then they met, Marsh coming out of the bank as he was going in and he'd suggested dinner. He didn't know why. Maybe he was lonely, wanted their old camaraderie back. And then he'd got cold feet, afraid he might give away something of himself that he would never get back. He wonders what would have happened if he hadn't backed out of dinner at the last minute. Marsh would still be here, he's pretty certain of that. At least if choking had been in the stars for him, he wouldn't have been alone. He would have had a friend to rescue him. Robert knows he is unworthy of the name friend.

He thinks Lynnette Appsley has figured him out. She becomes less and less attentive each time he sees her, and less and less available each time he calls. He likes good-looking women, he knows that. He admires them. And there will be others. He prefers to think of himself as asexual, on hold until the perfect lover materializes.

Robert pays the driver and hurries inside. He's a little late. He wonders if the rest of the staff will be here on such short notice, but there they are in the conference room, awaiting his arrival. Val and Carol and the readers, and freelancers, the typesetter, all the people essential to Dobbs, Kendall. They all look so serious. They think it's going to be a wake, but it isn't. He's starting to feel excited, but then that little trickle of guilt begins to dampen his spirits. He hangs his overcoat on a rack near one end of Carol's desk. We're not perfect, he thinks. He is cheered enough to smile and rub his hands together when he goes in to tell his staff that he has just found out that he has been left a very large sum of money and because of that, along with a substantial loan, he just might be able to buy the company back from Aksfal.

twenty - four

AUTUMN GRADUALLY turns to winter. Val spent Christmas Day with Aunt Millie, who commented that she seemed to be in exceptionally good spirits. Val told her about the book she's editing, and about the author, dwelling on his idiosyncrasies, laughing at them a little fondly. Millie smelled romance and sighed inwardly.

"I'm going to do some housecleaning during the holidays," she told Millie. "Old clothes, some of them Ed's. That ratty old striped cardigan he could never seem to part with. And a lot of other stuff that's just taking up space."

True to her word, she hauls out boxes and bags of stuff she hasn't looked at in years, Bix's dog collar and leash, childhood birthday cards, old essays and reports and yellowed photos of people she had never known or had forgotten, among them her treasured mementoes — the pink pen and the panda bear and the torn picture of her father. She puts the picture aside, debating about whether to pitch it. Once she finishes she feels better. Feels she's done one of the jobs she was put on this earth to do. And yes, the picture of her father might as well go, too. She wonders whether he is even still alive.

THE WORK IS GOING well on Gus's book. Val asks him to
come to her office from time to time to discuss the work,
people running in and out, nerve-racking, he finds it. She
invites him to her house where they sit at her dining-room
table discussing the second half of his book. He likes this
arrangement better once he gets used to it. There is a small
picture of her husband on a bookshelf in the living room.
A nice-looking man, he thinks, an openness about him
you could trust. There are bags and boxes in the living
room of stuff she is throwing out. Some for Goodwill, she
says, and some she thinks she might as well just put out for
the garbage pickup. When she gets around to it. On top of
a box crammed with childhood things, a ratty panda bear,
old photos, is a torn picture. He can just make out that it is
of a man. He wonders why it's torn in two, but he doesn't
go close enough to snoop.

His mind is on Val often throughout the weeks when
they are not meeting, while he toys with paragraphs, considers dropping a non-essential character, whittles the
manuscript down to its nerve roots. He wonders how long
it will take her to get over her husband, and whether she
will ever want another. He sometimes finds himself wondering what she thinks of him, personally, not just as a
writer. He wonders if their work relationship precludes
any other kind of relationship. She has never really
encouraged him in any way; he's just wondering.

He likes her hands and her neat nails, polished a dull
shade of pink; sometimes the polish is chipped. He likes the
way her hair falls forward when she bends her head over his
manuscript, half hiding her cheek, and then the way she
impatiently rakes it back behind her ear. There is something very down to earth about the way she sometimes

takes off her jacket when she gets too warm, forgetting, he guesses, that she must have undone the button at the back of her skirt. Everything looks right about her, somehow, everything belongs. He likes the way minuscule beads of sweat appear on her upper lip, from time to time, and she hunts through her pockets for a handkerchief to mop it.

IT IS NOW THE END of February. Gus remembers that he left his moderately expensive fishing rod in the boathouse on the island he rented last summer. "I'm going to drive up there to get it," he tells Val. "Would you have any interest in coming along? We can walk across on the ice?"

Val's thoughts in order are: Walk on the ice! Are you mad? A fishing rod in the middle of winter? Long way to go just for a fishing rod! "Sure," she says, sensing that she is about to be swallowed by something larger than her own pre-packaged existence.

The highway has been bare and dry all the way from Toronto, which they left fairly early in the morning in order to have plenty of time in Dogwood. It's an easy drive, a bit of traffic, but all of it moving well. They plan to spend the night in Falkirk. What the sleeping arrangements will be have not yet been worked out, let alone discussed.

By this time in their friendship, they have exchanged life histories, more or less. Gus has filled Val in on large portions of his life, but not all of it. He keeps his feeble, belated attempt to rescue his brother from the flames under lock and key. Val has relinquished highlights in her own life, holding back only Ed's dark secrets.

Riding along, getting close to Dogwood Station, Val is thinking about Gus's second manuscript. He was reluctant to give it to her at first, saying it wasn't finished. She couldn't imagine why he seemed so nervous about it. It's perhaps not quite as successful as his first, but she thinks it will get there. It needs work, and Gus believes in it, which is important. She has every confidence that he'll get it in shape. It's a strange book. It's about a woman who loses her son in an accident for which she feels responsible, and is overcome with guilt because of it. She sees parallels with her own experience. A curious coincidence, she thinks. It's not upsetting to read, not as disturbing as it might have been a few months ago. She almost sees shades of herself in the protagonist, although she's probably reading more into it than she should. She hasn't got to the point of discussing it with him, yet. She hasn't quite finished reading it, and she wants to keep her focus on the first novel.

They pass a grove of maples, sap buckets slung about their trunks. "I thought it was all done scientifically these days, with pipe lines," she comments.

"Apparently not. I'd like to collect sap and boil it down, someday." He grins at her.

She likes his grin. She can't imagine what he'd be like collecting sap. He'd accidentally spill it; he'd trip; he'd fall into the fire. Sometimes, she thinks of him as a large, friendly, but clumsy animal. If he were ever to put his arms around her it would be in a bear hug. She thinks Ed would have liked him. It surprises her that she can think about Ed in the context of her present life. She knows now that Ed's past cannot stand for his present, or at least not for the present she knew until it was snatched from them both. Ed himself had surely buried his past in order to function as an adult. Buried all but one aspect.

Her own life has changed. She would probably still stop to remove obstacles from the road ahead should the occasion arise. However, and she finds this curious, there are fewer and fewer opportunities for her to do this. Now, more often than not, the road is perfectly clear.

There are still many things she doesn't know about Gus. She knows that his brother died in the fire that she went out to see one extremely cold night, and that he still can't talk about it, but that is almost all she knows. The place where he grew up is only a few blocks away from her house. The small burned storey-and-a-half has been carted away, the lot sold, and a new, rather attractive house built, tall and narrow, similar to many of the other houses on the street.

They actually walked up from her place one day to look at it; he'd never been to see it and she had talked him into going. "I watched that fire," she had told him. "I thought it was in our block."

He looked at her, trying to imagine her and the fire in the same place in time and could not. He viewed the changed site from across the street, arms crossed, chin on one fist, as if he were looking at an artifact in a museum. She asked him if his ghosts were buried.

He had sighed, shrugged. "Almost."

ONLY TWENTY KILOMETRES to Dogwood Station. The road is plowed, still hilly with many dangerous curves. Gus drives slowly, taking in as much of the landscape as he can. Val wishes he would keep his eyes on the road. The boulders remain steadfastly fixed to the hillside. The log house has been carted away, they notice, although the barn remains. A truck approaches just past the barn. Gus slows, rolls down his window, and signals to the driver who stops. It is Rhys Fennel. "Do you know if the ice is safe to walk on?" Gus inquires.

"She's safe, all right. Good two feet thick. Won't rot out now till the beginning of April." Rhys pulls at the peak of his hat, nods at Val's friendly smile without recognizing her, and drives off. Didn't have his glasses on, she tells herself, but is a little put out anyway that he didn't remember her. Maybe some things are best forgotten.

They would like to go into the general store for old times' sake, but it has a closed sign on it and so they park the car and set out on the ice heading in the direction of the island. The ice is solid underfoot, a little slippery where the snow has blown off. Gus takes her hand sometimes and sometimes lets it go. In this way they slip-slide toward the sun, its slanting rays throwing purple shadows against the snow, as they contemplate the evening and its mysteries.

acknowledgements

I AM INDEBTED TO Michelle Berry for reading the manuscript, for her enthusiastic encouragement, and for pointing me in the right direction, and to Charles Foran for his kind and thoughtful comments. I am also grateful to my agent, Hilary McMahon, for her cheerful diligence on my behalf.

I also thank Anna Porter and Jordan Fenn for their generous thumbs-up, and a special thank you to Janie Yoon, who deserves a medal for both her patience and her keen editorial instincts. To Ingrid Paulson, thank you for the inspired and haunting cover. Also, thanks are due to Marie-Lynn Hammond for her skillful copyedit.

I am grateful to the following for their encouragement, advice, and much-needed comfort and cheer: Mary Breen, Jane Collins, Lea Harper, Patricia Stone, Betsy Struthers, Florence Treadwell, and Hugh Conn; and to John Johnston who provided me with one of my favourite expressions. A special thanks as always to my ever-supportive husband, Basil, and to Leslie, Frank, Nicolas, Rebecca, Lauren, Kevin, Samantha, Katherine, Andrea, David, Mackenzie, Adam, Charles, and to Melissa for her suggestions for the manuscript.

I also thank New Directions Publishing Corporation for their permission to use excerpts from Tennessee Williams's play *The Glass Menagerie*.

about the author

JULIE JOHNSTON IS THE author of five novels for young people, including *Hero of Lesser Causes,* winner of the Governor General's Literary Award for Text in Children's Literature, the IODE National Book Award, and the Joan Fassler Memorial Book Award; *Adam and Even and Pinch-Me,* winner of the Governor General's Literary Award for Text in Children's Literature and the Ruth Schwartz Young Adult Book Award; *The Only Outcast,* shortlisted for the Governor General's Literary Award for Text in Children's Literature, the Ruth Schwartz Young Adult Book Award, and the Geoffrey Bilson Award; *In Spite of Killer Bees,* shortlisted for the Governor General's Literary Award for Text in Children's Literature, the Mister Christie's Book Award, and the Red Maple Award; and most recently, *Susanna's Quill.* Her work has received starred reviews in such publications as *Publisher's Weekly, Quill & Quire* and the *School Library Journal. As If by Accident* is her first novel for adults. The mother of four grown daughters, Julie Johnston lives with her husband in Peterborough, Ontario.

AMIRI
BARAKA

AMIRI BARAKA

Bob Bernotas

Senior Consulting Editor
Nathan Irvin Huggins
Director
W.E.B. Du Bois Institute for Afro-American Research
Harvard University

CHELSEA HOUSE PUBLISHERS
New York   Philadelphia

Chelsea House Publishers
Editor-in-Chief   Remmel Nunn
Managing Editor   Karyn Gullen Browne
Copy Chief   Juliann Barbato
Picture Editor   Adrian G. Allen
Art Director   Maria Epes
Deputy Copy Chief   Mark Rifkin
Assistant Art Director   Noreen Romano
Manufacturing Manager   Gerald Levine
Systems Manager   Lindsey Ottman
Production Manager   Joseph Romano
Production Coordinator   Marie Claire Cebrián

Black Americans of Achievement
Senior Editor   Richard Rennert

Staff for AMIRI BARAKA
Text Editor   Marian W. Taylor
Copy Editor   Philip Koslow
Editorial Assistant   Michele Haddad
Picture Researcher   Patricia Burns
Designer   Diana Blume
Cover Illustration   Donna Perrone

First Printing

1 3 5 7 9 8 6 4 2

Library of Congress Cataloging-in-Publication Data

Bernotas, Bob
   Amiri Baraka / by Bob Bernotas.
      p.   cm.—(Black Americans of achievement)
   Summary: A biography of the black poet, playwright, and po-
litical activist (formerly Leroi Jones), who was a leading member
of the 'Beat Generation.'
   Includes bibliographical references (p.   ) and index.
   ISBN 0-7910-1117-8
         0-7910-1143-7 (pbk.)
   1. Baraka, Imamu Amiri, 1934–   —Biography—Juvenile
literature. 2. Authors, American—20th century—Biography—
Juvenile literature. 3. Afro-Americans—Biography—Juvenile
literature. [1. Baraka, Imamu Amiri, 1934–   . 2. Authors,
American. 3. Afro-Americans—Biography.] I. Title.
II. Series.
PS3552.A583Z56 1991   90-2649
[B]   CIP
[92]   AC

Frontispiece: *Poet-activist Amiri
Baraka (center, with microphone)
addresses hundreds of black high
school students at a 1968 protest
rally in Newark, New Jersey.*

CONTENTS

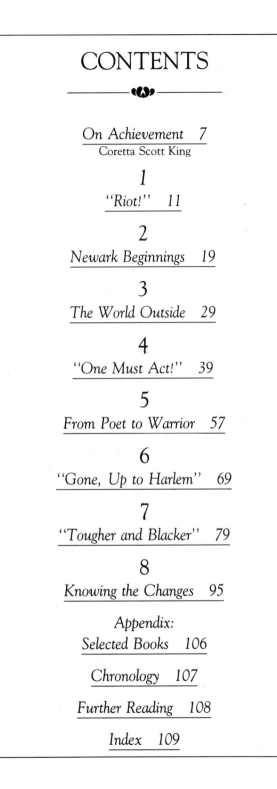

BLACK AMERICANS OF ACHIEVEMENT

Ralph Abernathy
civil rights leader

Muhammad Ali
heavyweight champion

Richard Allen
religious leader and social activist

Louis Armstrong
musician

Arthur Ashe
tennis great

Josephine Baker
entertainer

James Baldwin
author

Benjamin Banneker
scientist and mathematician

Amiri Baraka
poet and playwright

Count Basie
bandleader and composer

Romare Bearden
artist

James Beckwourth
frontiersman

Mary McLeod Bethune
educator

Blanche Bruce
politician

Ralph Bunche
diplomat

George Washington Carver
botanist

Charles Chesnutt
author

Bill Cosby
entertainer

Paul Cuffe
merchant and abolitionist

Father Divine
religious leader

Frederick Douglass
abolitionist editor

Charles Drew
physician

W.E.B. Du Bois
scholar and activist

Paul Laurence Dunbar
poet

Katherine Dunham
dancer and choreographer

Marian Wright Edelman
civil rights leader and lawyer

Duke Ellington
bandleader and composer

Ralph Ellison
author

Julius Erving
basketball great

James Farmer
civil rights leader

Ella Fitzgerald
singer

Marcus Garvey
black-nationalist leader

Dizzy Gillespie
musician

Prince Hall
social reformer

W. C. Handy
father of the blues

William Hastie
educator and politician

Matthew Henson
explorer

Chester Himes
author

Billie Holiday
singer

John Hope
educator

Lena Horne
entertainer

Langston Hughes
poet

Zora Neale Hurston
author

Jesse Jackson
civil rights leader and politician

Jack Johnson
heavyweight champion

James Weldon Johnson
author

Scott Joplin
composer

Barbara Jordan
politician

Martin Luther King, Jr.
civil rights leader

Alain Locke
scholar and educator

Joe Louis
heavyweight champion

Ronald McNair
astronaut

Malcolm X
militant black leader

Thurgood Marshall
Supreme Court justice

Elijah Muhammad
religious leader

Jesse Owens
champion athlete

Charlie Parker
musician

Gordon Parks
photographer

Sidney Poitier
actor

Adam Clayton Powell, Jr.
political leader

Leontyne Price
opera singer

A. Philip Randolph
labor leader

Paul Robeson
singer and actor

Jackie Robinson
baseball great

Bill Russell
basketball great

John Russwurm
publisher

Sojourner Truth
antislavery activist

Harriet Tubman
antislavery activist

Nat Turner
slave revolt leader

Denmark Vesey
slave revolt leader

Madame C. J. Walker
entrepreneur

Booker T. Washington
educator

Harold Washington
politician

Walter White
civil rights leader and author

Richard Wright
author

ON
ACHIEVEMENT

———— ❦ ————

Coretta Scott King

BEFORE YOU BEGIN this book, I hope you will ask yourself what the word excellence means to you. I think that it's a question we should all ask, and keep asking as we grow older and change. Because the truest answer to it should never change. When you think of excellence, perhaps you think of success at work; or of becoming wealthy; or meeting the right person, getting married, and having a good family life.

Those important goals are worth striving for, but there is a better way to look at excellence. As Martin Luther King, Jr., said in one of his last sermons, "I want you to be first in love. I want you to be first in moral excellence. I want you to be first in generosity. If you want to be important, wonderful. If you want to be great, wonderful. But recognize that he who is greatest among you shall be your servant."

My husband, Martin Luther King, Jr., knew that the true meaning of achievement is service. When I met him, in 1952, he was already ordained as a Baptist preacher and was working towards a doctoral degree at Boston University. I was studying at the New England Conservatory and dreamed of accomplishments in music. We married a year later, and after I graduated the following year we moved to Montgomery, Alabama. We didn't know it then, but our notions of achievement were about to undergo a dramatic change.

You may have read or heard about what happened next. What began with the boycott of a local bus line grew into a national movement, and by the time he was assassinated in 1968 my husband had fashioned a black movement powerful enough to shatter forever the practice of racial segregation. What you may not have read about is where he got his method for resisting injustice without compromising his religious beliefs.

He adopted the strategy of nonviolence from a man of a different race, who lived in a distant country, and even practiced a different religion. The man was Mahatma Gandhi, the great leader of India, who devoted his life to serving humanity in the spirit of love and nonviolence. It was in these principles that Martin discovered his method for social reform. More than anything else, those two principles were the key to his achievements.

This book is about black Americans who served society through the excellence of their achievements. It forms a part of the rich history of black men and women in America—a history of stunning accomplishments in every field of human endeavor, from literature and art to science, industry, education, diplomacy, athletics, jurisprudence, even polar exploration.

Not all of the people in this history had the same ideals, but I think you will find something that all of them have in common. Like Martin Luther King, Jr., they all decided to become "drum majors" and serve humanity. In that principle—whether it was expressed in books, inventions, or song—they found something outside themselves to use as a goal and a guide. Something that showed them a way to serve others, instead of living only for themselves.

Reading the stories of these courageous men and women not only helps us discover the principles that we will use to guide our own lives but also teaches us about our black heritage and about America itself. It is crucial for us to know the heroes and heroines of our history and to realize that the price we paid in our struggle for equality in America was dear. But we must also understand that we have gotten as far as we have partly because America's democratic system and ideals made it possible.

We are still struggling with racism and prejudice. But the great men and women in this series are a tribute to the spirit of our democratic ideals and the system in which they have flourished. And that makes their stories special and worth knowing. ❧

AMIRI
BARAKA

1

"RIOT!"

———— ❦ ————

THE TROUBLE STARTED at 9:45 P.M. on
Wednesday, July 12, 1967. White policemen in Newark, New Jersey, arrested a black cabdriver for a traffic
violation, then brought him to the city's 4th Precinct
station house. The angry cabbie, insisting he was
innocent of the charge, exchanged blows with two
police officers. A report—inaccurate, as it turned
out—quickly reached the street that the detained
man had been beaten to death. No one, in fact, was
seriously injured in the melee.

Nevertheless, rumors spread rapidly. In that city,
at that time, they were easy to believe. The nation
had recently been racked by urban disorder in its
metropolitan ghettos. A combination of rising demands and frustrated expectations among blacks had
produced a violent revolt in Watts, a black ghetto
in Los Angeles, in 1965. In the aftermath of Watts,
other inner-city districts had exploded. During the
summer of 1967, rifles, clubs, and homemade bombs
had become commonplace sights across the country,
from New York to Atlanta to San Francisco.

Newark was next. Its largely white police force
had gained a well-deserved reputation for brutality,
particularly against the city's 208,000 black residents.
Grimy and overcrowded, Newark had the nation's
highest crime rate, the largest number of condemned
houses, the most cases of venereal disease. The city's
unemployment figures were twice as high as the nation's; among the unemployed, blacks outnumbered
whites by two to one. Newark, in short, was dynamite
waiting for a spark.

*A defiant LeRoi Jones (later
known as Amiri Baraka) heads
for prison after his arrest during
the 1967 ghetto uprising in Newark, New Jersey. Convicted for
illegal arms possession, the poet-
playwright was acquitted following
a second trial.*

Copyright 1990 by Fred W. McDarrah
(7/14/67)

The day after the cabdriver's arrest, a crowd of blacks gathered outside the 4th Precinct station house to protest his alleged mistreatment. An officer came out to talk to the demonstrators, and a peaceful dialogue seemed possible. Then someone threw a bottle. A brick followed. Suddenly, a wave of blue-uniformed policemen burst from the station house and waded into the crowd, nightsticks flying.

The spark had struck. Breaking into small groups, the demonstrators fled and began looting stores. By 11 o'clock that night, Newark resembled a war zone. Glass from shattered store windows littered the streets, snipers fired from rooftops, and hundreds of buildings blazed in the night. When the city's 1,400 policemen proved unable to handle the pandemonium, New Jersey's governor sent in 2,600 National Guardsmen. The reinforcements met the embattled blacks with tear gas and gunfire. Newark, said the governor later, was "a city in open rebellion."

Into that rebellion stepped LeRoi Jones. A 32-year-old poet, playwright, and jazz critic who would later go by the name of Amiri Baraka, Jones had earned a formidable reputation, not only as a writer but as an uncompromising black militant. He found the Newark mayhem exhilarating. "In rebellions," he wrote later, "life goes to 156 rpm and the song is a police siren accompanying people's breathless shouts and laughter."

During the height of the uprising, Jones jumped into his new Volkswagen bus and, with two friends, drove through the city. Reveling in the sight of black crowds fighting for control of the streets, Jones and his companions also spent much of the night picking up the wounded and delivering them to hospitals. The police had beaten or shot scores of people they had lacked time to arrest.

But they had time for LeRoi Jones. As he and his friends moved down Newark's South 7th Street, a group of police officers stopped the van and dragged them out. Jones heard one of the policemen say, "These are the bastards who've been shooting at us!" Another demanded, "Where are the guns?"

A strange feeling came over Jones when he recognized one of the officers: He was a former classmate of Jones's at Newark's largely white Barringer High School. "Hey, I know you," said Jones. At that moment, he recalled in *The Autobiography of LeRoi Jones/ Amiri Baraka*, "the barrel of [the white officer's] .38 smashed into my forehead, dropping me into half consciousness and covering every part of me with blood." As policemen rained nightstick blows on his head, Jones feared they would beat him to death.

Instead, they tossed him into the patrol wagon and took him to the police station. There, he was confronted by Newark's police director, Dominick

National Guardsmen prepare to search suspected looters during the rebellion that rocked Newark in July 1967. Among the most violent disturbances in a summer of unprecedented urban chaos, Newark's black revolt took 27 lives, injured more than 1,500 people, and led to 1,397 arrests.

Spina, grinning with satisfaction at the sight of the city's best-known black citizen. "They got you," chortled Spina as his men dragged the poet away. After hospital attendants treated Jones's wounds, policemen took him to the Essex County Prison and placed him in solitary confinement.

With Jones safely behind bars, the Newark police took care of other matters. Assisted by members of the National Guard, they fired a hail of bullets through the windows of Spirit House, the building in which Jones and his family lived and in which he had established a theater and a small printing shop. To escape the gunfire, Jones's wife and baby hid in a closet. The following night, the police broke into the house, ransacking and destroying Jones's possessions as his wife and child crouched in darkness on the third floor.

Meanwhile, dazed and in pain from his beating, Jones stared at the cell walls. "This was it," he later recalled thinking, "the real America, the America of slavery and lynching. I could feel an absolute kinship with the suffering roots of African American life." Jones soon learned that his bail had been set at the unusually high figure of $25,000; that, he said, was "a blatant ransom." He made bail with the help of some of his parents' friends, who allowed their homes to be used as security.

Charged with resisting arrest and unlawful possession of firearms—two revolvers and a box of ammunition were found in the Volkswagen, the police claimed—Jones and his friends pleaded innocent when they went on trial a short time later. The guns, they swore, were not theirs but had been planted by the police. Before the jury began its deliberations, Judge Leon W. Kapp told its members, recalled Jones, "that the 'boys in blue,' the police, who were the state's principal witnesses against us, 'would never lie.'" The verdict of the all-white jury: guilty.

At the sentencing, Judge Kapp read "Black People!"—a Jones poem published by the respected literary journal *Evergreen Review* shortly before the trial.
Kapp omitted what he considered "obscenities," replacing each with the word *blank*. Among the lines
Kapp read were these:

> you can't steal nothin from a white man, he's already stole
>   it he owes
> you anything you want, even his life. All the stores will
>   open if you
> will say the magic words. The magic words are: Up against
>   the wall mother
> [blank] this is a stick up!

Kapp called the poem a "diabolical prescription
to commit murder and to steal and plunder."

Jones replied, "I'm being sentenced for the poem.
Is that what you're saying?"

The poem, said the judge, "causes one to suspect
that you were a participant in formulating a plot to
ignite the spark on the night of July 13, 1967, to
burn the City of Newark and that—"

Jones interrupted: "You mean, you don't like the
poem, in other words."

Later, when the judge told him he was convicted
of "the unlawful possession of two revolvers," Jones
snapped, "and a poem!" Kapp sentenced him to two
and a half to three years in prison and a fine of $1,000.
His two companions each got a one-year sentence.

Jones was taken to Trenton State Penitentiary,
where he received a hero's welcome from the largely
black inmate population. After a week in prison, he
was released on appeal. Largely because of Kapp's
reading of the poem and his prejudicial instructions
to the jury, the convictions of Jones and his companions were reversed at a retrial.

Jones's arrest and trial, he believed, confirmed
everything he had written and said about white
oppression of black people. His anger hardened, his

hatred crystallized. "The hottest rage," he noted in his autobiography, "had become a constant of my waking personality."

Jones's grim experience also changed his attitude toward art. The Newark uprising, he wrote, "was a canvas, a palette no painter could imagine. A scale no musician could plumb." Jones was not saying he considered art irrelevant to politics; he meant that art alone was not enough to reach people and put them in motion. Art, he decided, might inspire people, but only organized political action could liberate them.

To Jones, the uprisings in Newark and other cities prophesied momentous changes. Although it was still disorganized and unfocused, the fight against racism had entered a new stage, militant and intense. But

An aerial view of downtown Newark's Springfield Avenue reveals burned-out buildings and littered streets, the aftermath of a second night of rioting in New Jersey's largest city. The 1967 upheaval produced more than $10 million in property damage, most of it in Newark's predominantly black Central Ward.

if blacks were going to win that fight, reasoned Jones, their attitudes and actions would have to be given a clear political direction. "The Black Liberation Movement was raising full up," he wrote later. "It was a war, for us, a war of liberation. One had to organize, one had to arm, one had to mobilize and educate the people."

Already a well-known literary figure, Jones became a kind of political celebrity after his much-publicized arrest and trial. The new role thrust him into a position of leadership in the most militant wing of the black movement. Over the previous few years, he had occasionally involved himself with politics, but his priorities had shifted. From this point on, the poet and playwright would be a full-fledged political activist.

2

NEWARK BEGINNINGS

EVERETT LEROY JONES was born on October 7, 1934, in Newark, New Jersey. (He would later change the spelling of his middle name to LeRoi.) His father, Coyt Leroy Jones, worked for the post office; his mother, Anna Lois Jones, was a college-educated woman who, her son recalled, "started out working in sweat shops before they started giving black women jobs." The Jones family belonged to the lower middle class, a group poised between dreams of success and the harsh economic realities of depression-era America.

Jones's maternal grandfather, Thomas Everett Russ, had owned several businesses, including a prosperous funeral home, in Dothan, Alabama. After fires—set, many people believed, by resentful whites—twice burned his undertaking parlor to the ground, Russ and his wife, Anna, decided to leave the South with their daughter, Anna Lois. They moved first to Beaver Falls, Pennsylvania. The Russes sent Anna to high school at Alabama's Tuskegee Institute and then to Fisk University in Nashville, Tennessee. In 1925, the family moved to Newark, where Russ opened a grocery store.

A small Newark grocery store, much like the one owned and operated by Leroy Jones's grandfather, Tom Russ, attracts shoppers in the 1930s. An Alabama undertaker, Russ had left his native state after suspicious fires twice destroyed his funeral parlors.

Like Tom Russ, Coyt Jones also came to Newark, as his son would later put it, "running from dee white folkz." A native of Hartsville, South Carolina, Jones had hastily headed north after punching an abusive white movie-theater manager. In Newark, where he found work in a barbershop, Jones met and married Anna Russ.

Anna Russ dropped out of Fisk upon marrying Coyt Jones. She found a job doing piecework in a clothing factory; her husband, by then a postal employee, drove a mail truck and delivered packages. (In 1941, when the United States entered World War II, Anna Jones would land a job in the government's Office of Dependency Benefits, then begin a career as a social worker. Coyt Jones, who earned several promotions, was to become a postal supervisor by 1951.)

The Joneses—Leroy; his parents; his younger sister, Sandra Elaine; his mother's parents; and his uncle, G.L.—"were always in motion," Jones remembered. The family often moved from one part of Newark to another, but despite frequent changes of address, young Leroy felt little disruption. "There was a security to my home life," he recalled. "That's the only way I can describe it. A security that let me know that all, finally, was well. That I'd be all right."

That security sprang from his family's supportive warmth. Leroy Jones was surrounded by caring adults: a mother who would go to school to investigate a teacher's attitude toward her son; a father who taught his son to stand up for his rights, even in a losing battle; a grandmother ("my heart and soul," Leroy Jones called her) who tried to impress upon him her religious convictions and sense of respectability; a grandfather who preached self-reliance and courage; and an uncle, a railroad porter and a "race man" (in the 1930s, a black with a special interest and pride in black culture) from whom the young Leroy Jones learned his first, only half-understood lessons about black pride.

The ever-moving Joneses settled in several racially mixed neighborhoods, and Leroy grew up playing happily with children of Irish, Italian, and other European backgrounds. But all too soon, the youngsters picked up on the fears and tensions that divided their parents. "Adults," Leroy Jones said later, "fed us various poisons that pushed us apart as we grew, naturally. And by high school, almost miraculously, the relationships we'd had on the street level and in grammar school had disappeared."

Leroy proved to be a natural student. While he was in kindergarten, he was struck with whooping cough, then with measles. He used the long periods at home to teach himself to read. "Nothing in grammar school was hard (to me)," he wrote later. "Except keeping quiet. Otherwise, it was just something you did because, well, you did it."

Leroy's parents, who recognized him as a gifted child, did their best to nurture his intellectual growth. He devoured the books they gave him, particularly those by British writers Charles Dickens and Rudyard Kipling. His son, Coyt Jones once told an interviewer, "read everything that there is worth reading."

Leroy had a prodigious memory and an active imagination. At the age of eight, he surprised his family with a word-perfect recitation of Abraham Lincoln's Gettysburg Address, which he had memorized with no adult encouragement. And when his father gave him an American history book, Leroy voluntarily learned the names and dates of all the presidents from George Washington on.

So bright that he skipped a grade in grammar school, young Jones often impressed his teachers—and frightened his younger sister—with bizarre stories of his own invention. In Theodore R. Hudson's 1973 book, *From LeRoi Jones to Amiri Baraka*, the author tells of the day a group of grade-school teachers un-expectedly arrived at the Jones home. They had come, they said, "to see the snakes." It turned out that Leroy, late to school, had told his teachers that a horde of serpents had invaded his home and that he had been required to protect his mother from the fearsome invaders. What happened after the teachers' visit is unknown, but it seems safe to guess that Le-roy's parents had a few words with him.

The Great Depression of the 1930s took its toll on Americans of all races, including Leroy's grand-

Leading his quintet at a Manhattan nightclub in 1947, legendary alto saxophonist Charlie ("Bird") Parker shares the spotlight with trumpeter Miles Davis. Young Leroy Jones, who idolized these great musicians, would grow up to become one of his era's leading jazz critics.

father, Tom Russ. "For all the bourgeois underpinnings on my mother's side," Jones noted in his autobiography, "the depression settled the hash of this one black bourgeois family." Russ's grocery store, like thousands of other American businesses, fell victim to the economic collapse triggered by the stock market crash of 1929. After his store folded, Russ found a job as a night watchman.

Although his income and status had dropped sharply, Russ remained the dignified family patriarch, active in his church and politically well connected.

"My grandfather," young Jones later recalled proudly, "was a big important man . . . in middle-class black Newark." One day, however, a freak accident (a falling streetlamp struck him squarely on the head) crippled Russ permanently; he spent his last years silent and almost paralyzed. He died when Leroy was 11 years old, but he left his grandson with fond and respectful memories. Leroy Jones would one day dedicate two published plays to "Thomas Everett Russ, American pioneer."

Perhaps mindful of his grandfather's advice, Leroy never got into any real trouble as a boy. "There were no real gangs at my age group," he said of his early teenage years. Fights were mostly of the one-on-one, school-yard variety. But, he added, "There were the gang clashes later that I knew about and almost got mashed up in several times." The operative words here are *knew about* and *almost*; Leroy rarely took part in gang battles.

To young Jones, he wrote later, "the world was mysterious, wondrous, terrible, dangerous, sweet in so many ways." He loved to run, he said. "I'd just suddenly get it in my head and take off. And I dug that, the way running made you feel." Jones, in fact, loved all sports, especially basketball and baseball. Looking back on his days as a slight but wiry playmaker in Newark's municipal basketball leagues, Jones wrote, "I was never a great shooter, but I could move the ball and connect with those passes. I got big off assists. But if I got matched with a small man I would go into my scoring act—such as it was."

Leroy particularly enjoyed trips to Newark's Ruppert Stadium, where he and his father cheered for the Newark Eagles, the city's all-black baseball team. (While he was growing up, blacks were barred from playing major league baseball.) "There was a special grandeur to going someplace with my father and having all the 'you look just like your father' folks identify us as such," Jones wrote later. "There was a pride in that."

There was pride, too, in supporting the Eagles. Jones and his friends followed such baseball teams as the New York Yankees and the New York Giants, "just to keep up with being in America," he said. "We had our likes and dislikes. 'Our' teams. But for the black teams, and for us Newarkers, the Newark Eagles was pure *love*."

Like most of his friends, Jones enjoyed the comics (he created his own strip, "The Crime Wave," when he was in the seventh grade), movies, and such popular radio programs as "The Shadow" and "The Lone Ranger." The radio thrillers, noted Jones in his autobiography, "taught us that evil could be destroyed . . . that evil needed to be destroyed. And I believed that—impressionable as I was at those young

Barringer High School students attend a senior prom during the 1920s. Always predominantly white, the Newark school made Jones feel like an outcast. "I put up with many nigger callings," he said of his years at Barringer.

Jones won a scholarship to Rutgers University in Newark (above: the school's Newhouse Law Center), but he left after one year, calling Rutgers "even whiter" than Barringer High. In 1952, the restless 18 year old transferred to largely black Howard University in Washington, D.C.

ages—but the trick is that I still believe it! (And this, I was later to find out, can get you killed!)"

Jones's lifelong passion for music started early. Even as a little boy, he found himself drawn to gospel, blues, jazz, rhythm and blues: the music of black people. He came to regard black music as a personal tie to the culture and history of his people; it was, he once wrote, "the great definer and link, the extension cord of blackness in me." As a teenager, Jones flirted briefly with the trumpet, but he was not inclined to follow the "square" instructions of his classically oriented teacher. Interested only in playing jazz in the manner of his hero, Miles Davis, Jones gave up the lessons, a move he would later regret.

After eight years in a predominantly black grade school, Jones entered a largely white junior high school. He found himself completely unprepared for a social and academic environment dominated by white teachers and students. "I was now all but invisible," he recalled later, "and when not that, the butt of something unpleasant." It was a frightening and intimidating year. Nevertheless, he did well and went on to Barringer, a nearly all-white college-preparatory high school.

Every morning, Jones took the long, lonely bus ride from Newark's growing black ghetto, Four Corners, across town to the last stop, Barringer. He excelled academically in high school, where he also made his first stabs at writing (science fiction stories). But as one of only a tiny number of black students at Barringer, he remembered, "I put up with many nigger callings and off-the-wall comments and intimidations."

Jones would never forget the loneliness and alienation that plagued him during his high school years. "The straight-out teenage joys, the simple concern," he said later, "was never mine. . . . Most of the time, I was just passing through, even as words were coming out of my mouth or doing whatever I was doing. I was not wholly there, I felt, but the part of me that was, suffered."

Graduating from high school with honors, Jones received scholarship offers from a number of colleges: Seton Hall, Holy Cross, Lincoln, and Rutgers, Newark. He chose Rutgers, to which he could commute from home, but soon found it "even whiter" than his high school. He felt, he wrote later, "completely isolated" at Rutgers.

After a year at Rutgers, Jones told his parents he wanted to transfer to Howard University in Washington, D.C. The Joneses consented, and the renowned black institution accepted him. Armed with a bag of biscuits and fried chicken lovingly packed by his grandmother, Leroy Jones boarded a train for Washington. For the first time in his life, he would be living apart from his family, his source of security and strength.

3

THE WORLD OUTSIDE

LEROY JONES ARRIVED at Howard University in the fall of 1952. He was in a hopeful mood: Howard, often called "the capstone of Negro education," would surely offer him more than largely white Rutgers. Quickly accepted by the "Jersey boys"—Howard students from his own area—Jones became part of what he called "a little mob," a group that was "something else again."

Like college students everywhere, Jones and his gang developed their own vocabulary: A well-dressed, self-confident person was "down"; an intellectual was "heavy"; pretty women were "phat"; unattractive women were "bats." The highest compliment was "way," as in "Oh, man, that babe is way." To "punch out" was to fail; "over you" meant, loosely, "go to hell." Jones, short and slender, was universally called "that little cat."

"I was a member of the mob, of really great guys, in the sense of those times," Jones reminisced in his autobiography. Great talkers all, he and his friends "spent hours, months, years" in conversation about the future, women, sports, clothes, music, and books. The mob's priorities, said Jones, were to "tell jokes, lie, insult people, and try to get out of schoolwork."

Some schoolwork, however, appealed strongly to Jones. Although he detested his required science courses and made a habit of tormenting their instructors, he deeply admired several of his professors. Among them was Nathan Scott, the distinguished scholar of religion and literature. Scott's humanities

Jones found much to criticize at Howard University, but he enjoyed the company of his "mob" and their endless conversations about books, music, women, and sports.

Copyright 1990 by Fred W. McDarrah

29

classes introduced Jones to the works of the Italian poet Dante Alighieri (1265–1321), who would be an important influence on his own writing.

Jones found Scott's boundless enthusiasm irresistible. "Nathan Scott's preaching about Dante," he recalled in his autobiography, "conveyed an *intellectual* love for literature that I hadn't seen. It was like some minister pushing us toward Christ, but Scott was pushing us toward Dante Alighieri. And it was directly due to this that I later went back to Dante and read what I was able."

The "high point" of his Howard education, said Jones, was his exposure to poet and literary critic Sterling Brown. A "heavy" professor of English literature, Brown also organized informal classes in black music, usually held in a student dormitory. Jones credited Brown with "opening us up to the fact that the music could be studied and, by implication, that black people had a history. He was raising the music as an art, a thing for scholarship and research as well as deep enjoyment."

Brown's approach to black music would deeply influence Jones's later work as a jazz historian and critic. But taking jazz seriously ran counter to Howard's prevailing attitudes. The professor's repeated efforts to organize jazz concerts on campus met with repeated failure; jazz, said the head of the music school, would never be heard in *his* Music and Art Building. While Jones was at Howard, the university finally did sanction an "official" jazz concert; it featured Stan Kenton, a white arranger-bandleader who concocted a watered-down version of the genuine article. Jones's reaction to Kenton's concert: "AAAAHHHHGGGGGGG!!!!!!"

Despite his social circle, his several girlfriends, and his favorite professors, Jones found much of Howard's atmosphere incompatible with his tastes and ideas. He saw the university as a training ground for

A 17th-century engraving depicts Italian poet Dante Alighieri and his conceptions of earth, hell, and paradise. As a Howard sophomore, Jones fell in love with Dante's masterpiece, The Divine Comedy, a work he would later use as a model for his own fiction.

the "black bourgeoisie," a place that taught aspiring middle-class blacks how to imitate whites and how to integrate themselves into the white world. Howard helped blacks to become doctors or lawyers, professors or politicians, generals or government officials; but fundamentally, according to Jones, it helped them learn how to work for powerful whites.

In Jones's opinion, this renowned institution lied to its eager black students, glossing over the fact that mainstream America, that promised land they were trying to enter, was riddled with discrimination and racism. "We were being taught integration," he recalled, "and nothing of the kind existed. . . . We

Sterling Brown, the eminent poet, literary critic, and Howard English professor, won Jones's respect by treating jazz as a serious art form. Brown's conviction that black music "could be studied," said Jones, implied "that black people had a history."

were readied for a lie as a lie." Howard, he said, was "an employment agency at best, at worst a kind of church."

Jones was also repelled by what he saw as racial discrimination among the Howard students themselves: Many of them, he said, evaluated people by their skin shade or type of hair. "There are some who think that being light-skinned is preferable to being dark," he noted. "It's weird, especially if you are dark, to think like that."

Jones asserted that Howard fostered "the Negro sickness." This deep-rooted sense of inferiority, he said, "is another burden, something [whites] have put on your back to carry around, so that you can't straighten up and confront them as man to man, but rather as man and something else."

While he was at Howard, Leroy Jones changed his name: Between his sophomore and junior years, he became LeRoi Jones. "My justification," he explained in his autobiography, "was that my father's name, seeing his birth certificate named him Coyette Leroy, was French, so why wasn't the 'y,' 'i'? But also I'd read that summer . . . Roi Ottley's *New World A-Comin'* and I think that's what did it." Jones must also have been aware that in French *le roi* means "the king."

Thanks to Professors Scott and Brown, Jones was becoming increasingly interested in philosophy and literature. Utterly bored by his science courses, however, he cut classes and ignored assignments, bringing his grade point average to the disaster point. At the end of his junior year, LeRoi Jones—the young man who learned to read early, who amused his elders by giving speeches, who sailed through grammar and high school, who won spelling bees and scholarships—flunked out of college. "I made my various goodbyes," he said, "and went reluctantly on my way. (Which was where?)"

"Where," for the time being at least, was Newark. Jones spent the following summer at his parents' home, making occasional trips across the river to Manhattan. Hearing that an old high school friend was living a "weird" life as a writer in Greenwich Village, Jones went to see him. "I did not know what this weirdness manifested," he recalled, "but I was vaguely interested."

He was also at loose ends, "drifting," he said, "with nothing really to do." In the fall of 1954, the 20-year-old ex-student looked into his future, saw nothing, and felt a combination of panic and despair. "I was completely unslung. Disconnected," he recalled. "So, for some reason, I joined the Air Force."

Jones's basic training began on a cold, gray day at an upstate New York air force base. "No one sang 'Off we go into the wild blue yonder,'" he noted wryly, but they did go out of their way to see "how quickly any self-esteem [could be] erased." The young recruit viewed his grueling 10 weeks of basic training as a kind of "payback" for his "stupidity and lack of seriousness" at Howard. "I set a new base record for [kitchen patrol]," he recalled, "pulling it some 20 times before we got out of there."

After training, Jones went to weather school at an Illinois air force base; he turned out to be its only black student. "As isolated and lonely as I might feel among bloods [other blacks]," he wrote, "to be the lone spot in the buttermilk is totally a drag." He spent all his free time in Chicago, where he began his intellectual development in earnest.

Glancing into the window of a Chicago bookstore one day, Jones noticed books by such giants of 20th-century literature as James Joyce, Ezra Pound, T. S. Eliot, and Dylan Thomas. "I suddenly understood," he wrote afterward, "that I didn't know a hell of a lot about anything. What it was that seemed to move me then was that learning was *important*. . . . I vowed, right then, to learn something new every day."

Jones started buying books by the armful, devouring words and ideas the way a hungry person attacks a hot meal. "I needed to learn. I wanted to study," he recalled. "But I wanted to learn and study stuff I wanted to learn and study. Serious, uncommon, weird stuff!"

Finishing at the top of his meteorological class, Jones was allowed to choose his permanent assignment. He selected Puerto Rico's Ramey Air Force Base, largely because of its "country club" reputation (which he quickly discovered to be undeserved). At Ramey, Jones enrolled in gunnery school, where he would be trained on a B-36 bomber. "We were the Strategic Air Command," he later told an interviewer, "right out of [the film] *Dr. Strangelove*. I spent most of my time reading, in the air and on the ground."

Airman Second Class Jones soon acquired a small circle of like-minded friends: whites and blacks who shared both his interest in books and music and his growing distaste for military life. Gathering in Jones's room, they indulged in what Jones called "our record and booze and nonstop rap sessions." After several months, he said, "we became a kind of defensive unit for ourselves, a kind of salon. . . . We all were unified by our hatred for the Air Force."

During his stint at Ramey, Jones began to keep a journal. At first, it was merely a place to describe what he called his "effusive self-pity"; later, he used it to list the dozens of books he read, everything from current best-sellers to the works of Herman Melville, Fyodor Dostoyevsky, and Henry James. "I read constantly, almost every waking hour," he recalled.

Jones also started subscribing to the nation's leading literary journals, the *Partisan*, *Hudson*, and *Kenyon* reviews, to which he submitted the poetry he had begun to write. "I got rejection slips from all the quality magazines," he recalled with amusement. "They all showed the good taste and consistency to turn me down flat and very quickly."

Visiting San Juan one day, Jones sat down in a park and began to read a poem in the sophisticated *New Yorker* magazine. The verses, he recalled, "spoke of lawns and trees and dew and birds . . . of a world almost completely alien to me." Suddenly, Jones found himself crying. "I realized I could never write like that," he said later. "[I] knew somehow that it was correct that I be myself . . . [but] myself could not deal with the real meanings of the life spelled out by those tidy words." Nevertheless, the young airman kept on writing poetry.

Jones's "new intellectual life," he wrote, "made soldiering harder and harder," but he got halfway through his four-year hitch with no major problems. Suddenly, however, he received disturbing news: His security clearance had been withdrawn. Someone, it

Stan Kenton (standing, at left) leads his band at a college dance in the late 1940s. Although Kenton's stylized form of jazz won wide approval from white audiences, Jones considered it a joke. His response to the white band-leader's 1953 appearance at Howard: "AAAAHHHHGGG-GGGG!!!!!!"

With his Strategic Air Command colleagues, Airman Second Class Jones (back row, second from left) poses for a group portrait at Puerto Rico's Ramey Air Force Base. Jones, who hated almost every moment of his two years in what he called the "Error Farce," was delighted to receive an undesirable discharge in 1956.

turned out, had sent an anonymous leter to Jones's superiors, accusing the young man of being a Communist. This was a very serious charge in the cold-war atmosphere of the 1950s, a period of intense American fear and hatred of communism. As a result of the letter, Jones was taken off flying status and assigned to menial duties.

He heard nothing further for many weeks; finally, he was called in and questioned by a panel of officers. They asked him whether he belonged to certain organizations, then showed him a list of "evidence" against him. "Among the artifacts the air force was amassing as to my offense were copies of the *Partisan Review!*" reported Jones, incredulous that anyone could consider the highly respected literary publication an organ of the Communist party.

Months after the interrogation, the air force handed Jones its decision: He was to receive an undesirable discharge from the service. In spite of the absurd and unfounded charges against him, Jones could not have been happier; he had wanted out, and now he was out. Sent to South Carolina, he underwent two weeks of processing, then boarded a bus for the 20-hour ride to Newark.

The "Error Farce," Jones commented later, "was my graduate school or maybe it was undergraduate school." In the air force, he had continued to practice the role he had first assumed in junior high school, the role of outsider. At Barringer and Rutgers, he had been a black student in the midst of indifferent or hostile whites; at Howard, he had been an introspective, alienated youth in the midst of career-oriented, middle-class blacks; in the air force, he had been a budding intellectual in the midst of unimaginative, highly conservative militarists.

Jones was delighted to be free of the service, but now what? A 22 year old with no college diploma or marketable skill, he was out of work and short on prospects. He often found himself thinking about the visit he had made to his friend in New York. He "was a writer!" mused Jones. "The idea of this made me drunk with wonder. A writer! What a thing to be— so weird—so outside of the ordinary parade of gray hellos and goodbyes. . . . A writer. In the mysterious jumble of Greenwich Village."

4

"ONE MUST ACT!"

❧

Iℕ EARLY 1957, LeRoi Jones headed for Greenwich Village, the roughly mile-square Manhattan district that had long magnetized the young, the creative, and the rebellious. Here, the sound of music, laughter, and serious conversation spilled into narrow streets from dozens of small cafés and coffeehouses; here, poets and playwrights, actors and singers, classical and jazz musicians practiced their art; here, residents set their own standards, ignoring conventional styles of dress and behavior.

The young rebel from Newark decided that the Village, "where Art was being created, where there was a high level of intellectual seriousness," was where he had to be. Establishing himself in the only apartment he could afford—a $28-a-month, cold-water, walk-up flat on the nearby Lower East Side—Jones found a job in an uptown bookstore. He quit impulsively soon after he started, and for several weeks survived on unemployment insurance and the generosity of friends. Then, in March, he responded to a want ad: A small magazine, the *Record Changer*, needed a shipping manager. Aimed at jazz fans, the publication featured advertisements for old 78-RPM records along with reviews, interviews, and essays about jazz and folk music.

Jones dressed in a button-down shirt, neatly pressed pants, and a pair of desert boots and applied for the the job. At the *Record Changer*'s tiny storefront office on Sullivan Street, he met the magazine's subscription manager, a short, dark-haired young woman named Hettie Cohen. She was reading a paperback

Looking every inch the "cool dude," Jones strolls through his newly adopted hometown, Manhattan's Greenwich Village. The young Newarker arrived in the Village, he said, "looking, trying to 'check,' being open to all flags."

edition of *Amerika*, a 1927 novel by the Austrian writer Franz Kafka.

A great admirer of Kafka's, whose fiction dealt with the alienation and anxiety of 20th-century Western society, Jones immediately sat down and started talking with Cohen. She later described her first impressions of Jones: "He was smart and very direct, and for emphasis stabbed the air with his third—not index—finger. . . . But his movements were easy, those of a man at home not only in skin but in muscle and bone. And he led with his head."

The two became so engrossed in their conversation that they almost forgot to discuss the job, but Cohen finally explained that it involved packing and mailing records ordered by the magazine's readers and that it paid one dollar per hour. Jones became the *Record Changer*'s new shipping manager.

Although he was clearly overqualified for the job, Jones found it a valuable experience. Going through the magazine's stock of records, he studied the musicians and bands of different eras, learning about jazz trends and their leading practitioners. "I began to understand when and how the music changed," he recalled. "Later I would do my own deeper research to find out *why* it changed, which remains to me the most important question."

Jones's job brought him into daily contact with Hettie Cohen. She admired what she called "his pleasantly dependable nature" and his typing speed, developed during his air force days. He introduced her to his favorite books, including E. Franklin Frazier's new *Black Bourgeoisie*, and asked her to call him Roi, the name used by his good friends. (Jones pronounced his name le-ROY.) Jones and Cohen read Shakespeare aloud together, told each other their life stories, and spent evenings at the Village Vanguard, the Five Spot, the Half Note, and other local jazz clubs. They soon fell in love.

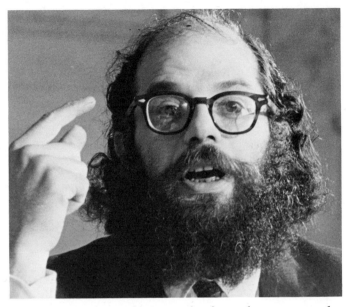

Poet Allen Ginsberg, a charter member of the Beat Generation literary movement of the 1950s, made a deep impression on Jones. After reading Ginsberg's work, the aspiring young poet said, "I now knew that poetry could be about some things that I was familiar with. That it did not have to be about suburban birdbaths and Greek mythology."

Interracial couples were far from the norm in the mainstream America of the 1950s. Although the U.S. Supreme Court had declared school segregation illegal in 1954, blacks and whites still kept their distance, and few mingled socially. Even in liberal, unconventional Greenwich Village, the sight of a black man with a white woman could draw second glances and sometimes more.

One evening, as Jones and Cohen strolled arm in arm down the Village's Bleecker Street, they heard loud catcalls, obviously directed at them. Cohen, she recalled later, felt outrage: "Nobody called *me* names." She turned on the group of jeering whites, "ready to fight or preach." Jones grabbed her arm and said, "Keep walking. Just keep on walking."

"It was his tone that made me give in," Cohen recalled, "and only later that I realized we might have been hurt, or *killed*—and him more likely. . . ." Her "ignorance," said Cohen, embarrassed her. "The dangers became more obvious. Also, and most important, to live like this I would have to defer to his judgment."

His relationship with the white, Jewish Cohen "had its tentative aspects," Jones wrote later. "I was open, naive, in the sense that I did not know what such a relationship involved—i.e., the black-white thing. I don't think [Hettie] knew much either." Jones and Cohen discussed the terrible damage inflicted on minorities by bigotry. "White supremacy, and anti-Semitism," noted Jones, "not only work on the victims to deprive them of material and spiritual ease but they can convince them that they are hated for correct reasons, and the victims take up this same view, only, of course, it is now self-hate."

Because the *Record Changer* was about to cease publication, both Jones and Cohen began to look for other jobs. Cohen later recalled the day she entered the *Changer* office to find Jones on the telephone, obviously talking to a potential employer. Jones, pretending to be his own boss, said pleasantly, "Yes, I'm well aware that he's a Negro, but he's been a fine employee." Making faces at Cohen while he talked, Jones continued, "He hasn't stolen anything, if that's what you mean. We'd be glad to vouch."

As he spoke, wrote Cohen, Jones's "jaw muscles jumped, repeatedly and noticeably, as if he were gnashing his teeth while the rest of his face remained calm. It was a look I would come to know."

Cohen got a job on the *Partisan Review*; Jones supplemented his $38 weekly unemployment check by working as a part-time proctor, or guard, during examinations at New York Law School. In April 1958, Jones and Cohen launched *Yugen*, a magazine devoted to "a new consciousness in arts and letters." The title of the publication, its founders somewhat cryptically explained, meant "elegance, beauty, grace, transcendence of these things, and also nothing at all." Typed, designed, and pasted up on Cohen's kitchen table, the magazine comprised 24 pages, hand-stapled together by editor LeRoi Jones.

"Slice of Life," Jones's first published poem, appeared in *Yugen*. Set in the railroad station in his father's hometown of Hartsville, South Carolina, the poem features an angel who sees three toilets, "one marked MEN, one/ Marked WOMEN, and the third marked OTHERS." Assuming that the third bathroom is for him, the angel thinks, "I wonder, could they have known?" Commenting on the poem, literary scholar Werner Sollors has observed that its "apparent lightness points to a deep-seated and serious sense of alienation. All God's chillun may have wings, but those who are *aware* of their angelic quality become outsiders."

Not long after the appearance of *Yugen*, Jones published his first essay, a defense of the young writers collectively known as the Beat Generation. The "Beats" scorned wealth and material possessions, political conservativism, and thoughtless conformity. In their place, these free-spirited bohemians advocated spontaneous expression, mysticism, travel, folk songs, sexual liberation, and sometimes the use of drugs, particularly marijuana. Leading Beat Generation writers included Jack Kerouac, whose best-selling 1957 novel, *On the Road*, became the movement's bible; and poets Allen Ginsberg, Gregory Corso, and Kenneth Rexroth.

The spring 1958 issue of *Partisan Review* carried an article attacking the Beats as degenerate, antiintellectual menaces to society, writers whose work appealed mainly to "dispossessed urban groups (Negroes, bums, whores)." Offended by the article's language and what he called its "moral hypocrisy," Jones responded with a fiery letter in which he denounced its author's taste and intelligence and applauded the Beats for infusing new life into the American literary scene. Hettie Cohen, by now the advertising and circulation manager of the *Partisan Review*, brought Jones's letter to her boss, editor William Phillips.

Jones's friend, Beat novelist Jack Kerouac, authored one of the era's most widely read books, On the Road. "The only people for me," wrote Kerouac, "are the mad ones, the ones who are mad to live, mad to talk, mad to be saved, desirous of everything at the same time, the ones who never yawn or say a commonplace thing, but burn, burn, burn like fabulous yellow roman candles exploding like spiders across the stars and in the middle you see the blue centerlight pop and everybody goes 'Awww!' "

"Hey, this guy's a *writer!*" said Phillips. "Sure we'll print this."

The *Partisan Review* letter was the first of dozens of articulate, passionately opinionated essays and articles that would carry the byline of LeRoi Jones over the next several years. His first full-length article, a piece on jazz saxophonist Buddy Tate, appeared in *Jazz Review* later in 1958. In the same year, his poem "Preface to a Twenty Volume Suicide Note" appeared in *The Naked Ear*, a so-called little magazine (one more concerned with discovering fresh talent than with making money) put together in Taos, New Mexico. "The publication was encouraging," noted Jones in his autobiography, "even though who the hell read *Naked Ear?*"

"Preface to a Twenty Volume Suicide Note," which would become the title poem of Jones's first volume of collected poetry in 1961, explores some of the themes of the Beats: alienation, rejection of material goals, and anger at what the poet sees as America's cultural and moral bankruptcy. The poem's imagery is drawn from Jones's own life, rather than from high-flown "poetic" sources. In one verse, for example, the despairing central character says:

Lately, I've become accustomed to the way
The ground opens up and envelopes me
Each time I go out to walk the dog.
Or the broad edged silly music the wind
Makes when I run for a bus . . .

"I had come into poetry," Jones noted, "from a wide-open perspective—anti-academic because of my experience, my social history and predilections." Jones credited poet Allen Ginsberg with helping him find his own voice. "I had been moved by [Ginsberg's poem] *Howl*," he reported in his autobiography, "because it talked about a world I could identify with and relate to. His language and his rhythms were real to me. Unlike the cold edges and exclusiveness of the *New Yorker* poem that had made me cry, Ginsberg talked of a different world, one much closer to my own. . . . I now knew that poetry could be about some things that I was familiar with. That it did not have to be about suburban birdbaths and Greek mythology."

Jones had discovered that the Beats' disillusionment with American society connected with his feelings as a disaffected black American, and he admired the way they reveled in their status as social outsiders. Like Jones, the Beats were striving to break free of conventions, both literary and social. "I took up with the Beats because that's what I saw taking off and flying and somewhat resembling myself," he recalled. "The open and implied rebellion—of form and content. Aesthetic as well as social and political." Jones also shared the Beats' reverence for jazz, which they regarded as parallel to literature. Jack Kerouac, one of Jones's heroes, called writing an "undisturbed flow from the minds of personal secret idea-words, *blowing* (as per jazz musician) on subject of image." The true poet wrote spontaneously ("without consciousness") and refrained from revising or even correcting his or her work.

Along with Ginsberg and Kerouac, Jones admired and learned from such contemporary poets as Charles Olson and Frank O'Hara. Olson, former rector of North Carolina's Black Mountain College and a leader of the so-called Black Mountain school of poetry, expounded on his avant-garde theories of poetry in his 1959 essay, "Projective Verse." A poem, said Olson, is a "high-energy construct" in which "one perception must immediately and directly lead to a futher perception." Olson urged modern poets to abandon formal rhyming schemes and concentrate instead on the sound of the words themselves. Form, he insisted, is "never more than an extension of content."

Jones's often autobiographical early poetry also shows the influence of New York poet Frank O'Hara. Inventor of what he called "Personism," O'Hara saw poetry as a dialogue between two individuals. Personism, said O'Hara, "puts the poem squarely between the poet and the person." Part of one O'Hara poem—actually entitled "Personal Poem"—contains these lines:

> And LeRoi comes in
> and tells me Miles Davis was clubbed 12
> times last night outside BIRDLAND by a cop.

Jones, who published O'Hara's "Personal Poem" in *Yugen*, commented on it in the magazine. "Anybody who is concerned with the poem will get it on an emotional level," he said. "I don't see what makes it any less valid because it's a casual kind of reference

Marching through Mississippi with civil rights leader Martin Luther King, Jr. (left), are Floyd Mc-Kissick (center), leader of the Congress of Racial Equality (CORE), and Stokely Carmichael of the Student Nonviolent Coordinating Committee (SNCC). To Jones, King's peaceful campaign for black justice moved too slowly: "I was not nonviolent," said the increasingly militant poet in 1959.

or that it comes out of a person's life." Jones credited O'Hara with teaching him that "I could say the things I wanted to say, even about myself."

In Jones's view, the various schools of modern poetry were "all linked together" because "they were a point of departure from the academic," from the stodgy formalism of university English departments. Moreover, noted Jones, all avant-garde poets shared a "common denominator": Their prophets were Walt Whitman, the influential 19th-century American poet "who broke away from England with his free verse," and William Carlos Williams (1883–1963), who helped create "an American speech" for contemporary poetry.

In eight issues published between 1958 and 1963, *Yugen* introduced many readers to Olson, O'Hara, Ginsberg, and Jones. "The magazine," wrote Jones later, "opened up a whole world of back-and-forth correspondence among other young writers." To distribute it, he and Cohen hand-carried copies around the Village, leaving them with bookstores to sell. "I think we did 500 copies of [the first edition]," recalled Jones, "and in a short time they were gone. There was no money in it, of course, but we wanted to get the work out."

After working and living with Cohen for more than a year, Jones heard himself suggesting marriage. "What I said opened a trap door into our deeper feelings," he wrote later. "Married? To who? For what? Forever? . . . [Hettie] looked at me smiling, half smiling, uncertain. She didn't know what to do either. What kind of life would this be?"

Finally, both doubtful and delighted about their decision, the young couple agreed to marry. Cohen's conservative Jewish parents, reported Jones, "nutted out" at their daughter's announcement, but the Jones family "took [the news] in stride." Coyt Jones said, "as long as you're sure," then gave his blessing.

("Such is the disposition and tenor of the oppressed," wrote an older, more cynical LeRoi Jones, "they are so in love with democracy!")

Describing herself as "the happiest and best-loved woman in New York," Cohen joined her "smiling intended" at a Manhattan Buddhist temple in October 1958. There, as she recalled later, "at the ear-splitting sound of a huge brass gong," she and LeRoi Jones became husband and wife. The newlyweds settled into Cohen's one-room Village apartment, but it soon proved too small for their needs. They had decided to start a small publishing company, concentrating on the work of new poets and avant-garde writers. And they were expecting a baby.

In the late fall of 1958, the couple moved to West 20th Street in Manhattan's Chelsea district. The apartment became the home of Totem Press, which would publish volumes by Ginsberg, Olson, O'Hara, Kerouac, and, in 1961, Jones's first collection of poetry, *Preface to a Twenty Volume Suicide Note*. The new place also became a social center for artists and writers, many of whom formed the habit of dropping in for a visit and staying on for days or even weeks. Adding to the cheerful uproar, Kellie Elisabeth Jones, described by her proud mother as a "rogue-faced, tearless baby," arrived in the spring of 1959. "That was the high point of my life, another mystery uncovered. I was a father at 24½ years old," said Jones. "Jones, Cohen, Kellie," said the building superintendent, "What are you, starting your own United Nations?"

Cohen had left *Partisan Review* to stay home and care for Kellie; *Yugen* and Totem Press, while much admired, brought in no money. At this point, recalled Jones, "I had to go out and look for a job." He found work as a technical editor for an uptown publisher. "This meant," he explained, that "I had to read the deathless prose of some semi-literate engineering majors and try to put it in readable scribble-scrabble."

Jones's office, he said, "was filled with real characters, mostly suburbanite, lower-middle-class whites
whose vision of the world is so narrow the very look
of them can suffocate you. Just as I was getting into
the literary life, I had to drag off to labor and I
resented it." Nevertheless, Jones conceded grimly,
"it was a must."

Whenever he was not at his "slave job," Jones
worked on the magazine and entertained friends.
"The whole weekend, we whooped it up," he recalled. "Nonstop rap sessions, putdowns, literary
councils. . . . Poetry, literature, was our undying
passion. . . . The magazine and [Hettie] and I were
at the vortex of this swirling of new poetry."

In the mid-1960s, Jones would be known as one
of the nation's most unapologetically political—indeed, radical—contemporary writers. In the late
1950s, however, he considered himself nonpolitical.
Despite his rejection of middle-class values and his
anger about racism, Jones incorporated few political statements into his writing. He and his fellow
Beats were engaged in a rebellion of the alienated
intellectual, not the committed revolutionary.
They wanted to drop out from the system, not over-
throw it.

But world events soon began to alter the way Jones
viewed writing and ultimately his relationship to the
literary avant-garde. "This was 1959," he recalled,
"and the civil rights movement was rising with every
headline." Civil rights crusader Martin Luther King,
Jr., had won a landmark victory over segregation in
Montgomery, Alabama, in 1956. The black leader's
nonviolent campaign for social justice was moving
toward success, but Jones saw King's progress as too
slow and his methods as too gentle.

"Perhaps the intensification of the civil rights
movement, the daily atrocities which fat sheriffs in
Dumbell, Georgia, could run on blacks, began to
[enrage me] much more deeply than I thought," re-

called Jones. "I rejected Martin Luther King's philosophy. I was not nonviolent." He made his sentiments clear in "A Poem Some People Will Have to Understand":

> We have awaited the coming of a natural
> phenomenon. Mystics and romantics, knowledgeable
> workers
> of the land.
> But none has come.
> (Repeat)
>   But none has come.
> Will the machinegunners please step forward?

His militant lines, Jones reported in his autobiography, drew heavy "static" from other members of New York's avant-garde: "The general line being that poets and politics ain't cohabiting."

Jones's position on international politics earned him even more disapproval. Like millions of other Americans in 1959, Jones had followed the progress of Fidel Castro, the tall, bearded revolutionary then leading a guerrilla army against the forces of Cuban dictator Fulgencio Batista. When Castro entered Havana in triumph, Jones proposed that Totem Press publish a pamphlet in honor of the Cuban revolution. His friends' negative reaction, he said, made him see "certain real differences" between himself and them: They insisted that politics and art should remain separate; he was beginning to believe they should go hand in hand.

Jones's pamphlet about the revolution brought him an invitation from the new Cuban government; in 1960, he joined a delegation of black scholars and artists on a visit to the Caribbean nation. "The Cuban trip," he declared later, "was a turning point in my life." Surrounded by young Latin American intellectuals, he found himself under attack for his nonpolitical stance. "And so you want to write your poetry and that alone," they sneered, "while most of the

Advancing on Havana, Cuban rebel leader Fidel Castro (center) leads his troops in a cheer. Jones's glowing tribute to the 1959 revolution earned him an invitation to visit Cuba and marked a turning point in his life. "It was not enough just to write, to feel, to think," he wrote on his return, "one must act!"

world is suffering, your own people included." Jones returned to the United States with a new perspective. "It was not enough," he decided, "just to write, to feel, to think, one must act! One *could* act."

During the next few years, Jones did just that. He started a "political consciousness" organization for black writers, musicians, and intellectuals; he helped establish a defense committee for a militant black activist who was being prosecuted on trumped-up kidnapping charges in North Carolina; he joined the Fair Play for Cuba Committee.

At this point, Jones felt that he was leading two distinct and increasingly separate lives—one artistic, the other political. "I continued meeting people other than the sequestered artistic types I'd been running with," he observed, "and the positions and opinions I was beginning to assume were usually opposed by most of my arty world."

Changes were also taking place in Jones's personal world. "Fired from my job for going off to Cuba," he wrote later, "I had to get back on unemployment." The Joneses, unable to pay the rent on their Chelsea flat, moved to what Jones called "a terrible though

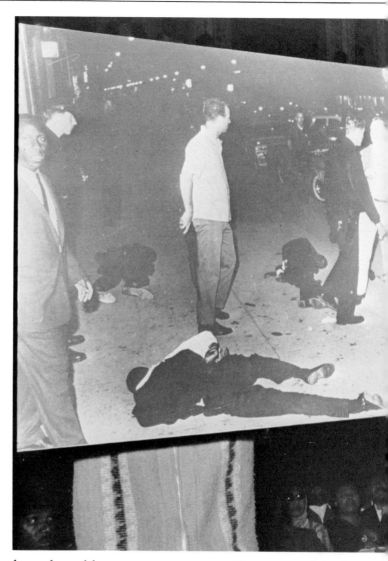

huge barn-like apartment over a Gypsy storefront" on Manhattan's run-down East 14th Street. The following spring, however, brought good news: In June 1961, Jones's first book, the poetry collection entitled *Preface to a Twenty Volume Suicide Note*, rolled off the press. "This book is Hettie's," said the dedication.

Written between 1957 and 1961, the poems in *Preface* are clearly the work of a young man, a poet not yet quite sure how to communicate his feelings:

Backed by a photograph of hand-cuffed Black Muslims on a Los Angeles street, Nation of Islam spokesman Malcolm X urges his followers to respond to violence with violence. His philosophy, which directly contradicted that of Martin Luther King, Jr., strongly appealed to Jones. Malcolm X, said Jones approvingly, "talked bad about nonviolence."

Sometimes I feel I have to express myself
and then whatever it is I have to express
falls out of my mouth like flakes of ash
from a matchbook

Jones nevertheless managed to get off some well-aimed swipes at the values of middle-class life, white and black. In the final section of the book's longest poem, "Hymn for Lanie Poo" (his mother's pet name for his sister, Sandra Elaine), Jones takes the young woman to task for her affectations:

> my sister drives a green jaguar
> my sister has her hair done twice a month
> my sister is a school teacher
> my sister took ballet lessons
> my sister has a fine figure: never diets
> my sister doesn't like to teach in Newark
>   because there are too many colored
>   in her classes
> my sister hates loud shades
> my sister's boyfriend is a faggot music teacher
>   who digs Tchaikovsky
> my sister digs Tchaikovsky also
> it is because of this similarity of interests
> that they will probably get married.

In these early poems, Jones avoids radical politics; that would come later. Here, he rarely departs from the level of amusing irony:

> It's just that . . .
>   Man lookatthatblonde
>   whewee!
> I think they are not treating us like
> Mr Lincun said they should
>   or Mr. Gandhi
> For that matter. By God.

Two months after the appearance of *Preface*, Jones became the father of a second daughter. Lisa Victoria Chapman Jones, noted her mother, had "large brown slanted eyes, skin the color of rare clay, not much hair, [and] a beautiful mouth, usually open."

Hettie Jones hired a baby-sitter and returned to her job at *Partisan Review*; her husband stayed home to write poetry and articles for a wide range of magazines, including limited-circulation "underground" journals such as *Kulchur* and *Wild Dog* and such mainstream publications as the *Nation* and the *Massachusetts Review*. With a writer friend, Diane di Prima, he also produced a new literary magazine, *The Float-*

ing Bear. Consisting of mimeographed pages stapled together, Bear published many new and important writers, including LeRoi Jones. The Eighth Ditch (Is Drama, a play that would form part of Jones's 1965 novel, The System of Dante's Hell, first appeared in a 1961 issue of The Floating Bear.

At about this time, Jones discovered the ideas of Malcolm X, the militant black leader and spokesman for the Nation of Islam, a black religious movement whose members are known as Black Muslims. "He charged me in a way no one else had ever done," Jones said later. "He reached me." Malcolm X's sharp attack on King's policy of nonviolence and on his 1963 March ("Farce," according to Malcolm X) on Washington for Jobs and Freedom struck an especially responsive chord with Jones. King, noted Jones, responded to white acts of violence against blacks—as when four black children died in a 1963 bomb blast at a Birmingham, Alabama, church—by wanting to "kneel in the streets and pray." Malcolm X, on the other hand, "talked bad about nonviolence."

The Black Muslim spokesman, said Jones approvingly, asserted "that those people who had done such a thing and indeed all the white racist Crackers in the world could only be reached if one spoke the same language that they spoke. That language was not peace and love."

LeRoi Jones was moving toward his own war. ✺

5

FROM POET TO WARRIOR

FOR LEROI JONES, the year 1963 started out well and got better. In January, he began teaching courses in modern American poetry and creative writing at Manhattan's New School for Social Research. "Not surprisingly," recalled Hettie Jones, he "proved good at it, and popular with his students." The poet, whose work had recently appeared in several national magazines, was also editing a collection of stories for a New York publisher, checking page proofs for his new book, *Blues People*, and celebrating a payment—of $37—he had just received for a poem in *Evergreen Review*.

"All this success became him," recalled Hettie Jones in her 1990 autobiography, *How I Became Hettie Jones*. "He was fun to be around. Sometimes he sang at the top of his lungs all the songs he knew strung together. To get through the slushy winter he bought huge, heavy boots that left marks like baby tanks all over the house. 'Out of the way, you midgets!' he'd cry, stomping down the hall toward the children who would fling themselves at him in fits of giggles."

Lula approaches Clay in a scene from a Howard University production of Jones's 1964 play Dutchman. *Although some strait-laced theatergoers gasped at the work's uninhibited dialogue, most audiences swallowed hard and applauded.* Dutchman *won the Off-Broadway Award for Best Play of the year.*

Blues People, Jones's study of black music in America, appeared in September to enthusiastic reviews: "A jazz masterpiece," said the *New York Herald Tribune* critic. Writing the book had given Jones special pleasure; it allowed him both to expound on the music he loved and to reexamine his own identity. "I had to study not only the history of African American music," he said, "but also the history of the people."

Jones followed his literary success with a theatrical triumph. "The dramatic form [had begun] to interest me," he noted in his autobiography, "because I wanted some kind of action literature, where one has to put characters upon a stage and make them living metaphors. Drama . . . makes real live people the fuel of ideas. It is also a much more popular form than poetry." In March 1964, Jones's first major play, *Dutchman*, opened in an off-Broadway theater.

Set entirely in a subway car, *Dutchman* presents an encounter between Clay, an intellectual young black man, and Lula, a seductive, bohemian, and ultimately dangerous white woman. Their conversation, at first flirtatious, turns nasty when Lula attacks Clay's middle-class aspirations. When he tells her what he thinks of *her*, she calmly kills him with a knife.

Jones's symbolism is not hard to interpret. Lula represents the white America that entices young, gifted blacks but tolerates them only as long as they accept its abuse. Clearly an autobiographical figure, Clay represents Jones and his own anxieties about attaining "success" in the white world. Clay is faced with two alternatives: He can either surrender his dignity and his manhood to Lula, or he can confront her with the ugly truth about herself and thus force her to kill him. To Jones, Clay's dilemma represents the choice that all black intellectuals must make.

Although Jones had not written the barbed and disquieting *Dutchman* to make audiences comfortable—indeed, quite the opposite—most theatergoers and critics applauded it. *Newsweek*, for example, called it "the most impressive work by an American playwright in the last few years." Some reviewers, however, expressed outrage about the play's "raw" language; others found its theme both disturbing and puzzling. "If this is the way Negroes really feel," said the *New York Times*, "there's more rancor buried . . . than anyone can imagine." *Dutchman* ran for an impressive 232 performances and won the Obie (Off-Broadway) Award for Best Play of 1964.

The critical reactions to *Dutchman*, Jones wrote later, convinced him "that something explosive had gone down. . . . Despite my being called 'foul-mouthed,' 'full of hatred,' 'furious,' 'angry,' I could tell the play had made its mark, that it would not quietly fade away." Hettie Jones later wrote that she

Actors Shirley Knight and Al Freeman, Jr., Dutchman's Lula and Clay, take a bow with the play's author. Despite his gloomy expression, Jones was overjoyed by Dutchman's success: "I could tell that the play had made its mark, that it would not quietly fade away," he wrote jubilantly.

had come upon her husband in his study, reading his reviews: " 'Appreciating yourself?' I teased. 'It wigs me,' he confessed."

Jones's next play, which opened in May, met with less success. In *The Baptism*, a satire of religious and sexual hypocrisy, a black preacher and a homosexual devil vie for the soul of a young, Christ-like black man. Irreverent and raunchy, the play is both shocking and funny, but it failed to amuse most theatergoers and closed after three performances.

A few months later, Grove Press published Jones's second volume of collected poems, *The Dead Lecturer*. Like his earlier work, these poems are fluid, irregular in length and meter, unconventionally punctuated, and packed with fresh, inventive language. Here, however, the political poet begins to emerge. These poems, as Jones put it, "speak of this separation, this sense of being in contradiction with my friends and peers" brought about by his increasing political involvement:

> They have turned, and say that I am dying. That
> I have thrown
> my life
> away. They
> have left me alone, where
> there is no one, nothing
> save who I am. Not a note
> nor a word.

The familiar jibes at America's cultural and moral climate have evolved into sharp-tongued attacks on a racist society that, the black poet feels, is smothering him:

> I am inside someone
> who hates me. I look
> out from his eyes. Smell
> what fouled tunes come in
> to his breath. Love his
> wretched women.

In this volume, Jones begins to express his open contempt for white, mainstream American society; over
the next decade his rage was to grow so hot that some
critics would describe him as more warrior than poet.

In December 1964, Jones presented two more new
plays, *The Slave* and *The Toilet*, as a double bill off
Broadway. In *The Slave*, black revolutionary Walker
Vessels appears at the home of a white couple, Grace
and Bradford Easley. Grace is Walker's ex-wife; their
two daughters live with her and her new husband, a
liberal who was once Walker's professor and friend.
Outside, race war is raging, and Vessels's side is win-
ning. When Walker announces he has come for the
two girls, the Easleys protest; after Walker shoots
Bradford, an explosion destroys the Easley home and
kills Grace. Walker departs to the sound of further
explosions and a child screaming.

In a sense, *The Slave* is the flip side of *Dutchman*;
here, blacks are gaining the upper hand and whites
are the subject of racial retribution. As is true of most
of Jones's work, the play contains autobiographical
elements: a black radical, his white wife, and their
two daughters. Hettie Jones, in fact, once called *The
Slave* "Roi's Nightmare." The play, however, is less
an autobiography than a fantasy that carries white-
black, male-female, and liberal-revolutionary conflicts to their extreme and tragic conclusions.

Although *The Slave* was far less popular with
American audiences than *Dutchman*, the play won
first prize for drama at the World Festival of Negro
Arts, celebrated in the African nation of Senegal in
the spring of 1966.

The Toilet, perhaps Jones's most realistic play, is
less preachy and more naturally dramatic than *The
Slave*. In an urban high school bathroom, a gang of
black students wait for James Karolis, a white homosexual who has sent their leader, Ray Foots, a love
note. When Karolis arrives, the gang punishes him

for this insult with a severe beating. Then, to every-one's surprise, Karolis insists on fighting Foots one to one.

At first, the gang leader refuses to tangle with the battered boy, but the fight finally takes place. When Karolis wins, the gang tears into him, leaving him unconscious on the bathroom floor. In the final scene, a weeping Foots returns and gently comforts his bleeding adversary.

The play's theme is love's inability to survive in a callous, dehumanizing society (symbolized by the toilet). Unable to break free of his macho facade, Foots cannot openly express his true feelings to any-

Cast members perform one of the more harrowing scenes in Jones's 1964 play The Toilet. *Set entirely in the bathroom of an urban high school (designed for the stage by artist Larry Rivers) and laced with profanity and violence, the drama evoked extreme reactions among viewers: "obscene," said some; "brilliant," said others.*

one—his gang, Karolis, or even himself. Foots's spiritual agony makes him as much of a victim as the physically abused Karolis.

Although *The Toilet* abounds with profanity, its language is appropriate not only for its setting and characters but for its subject. To Jones, society's repression of love is the greatest obscenity of all. Not everyone, however, agreed with him: One day after *The Toilet* opened in Los Angeles, the police vice squad closed it on charges of obscenity. Other reactions to the play were mixed. One critic called it "straight bathroom drama with . . . absolutely no uplift"; another labeled it "stunning" as a "study in

Jones reads from his own work during a 1961 Manhattan literary seminar, one of the many public forums at which the poet appeared in the mid-1960s. Despite his undisguised hostility toward the white world, whites doted on Jones, dubbing him a "young, black literary lion" and showering him with praise, social invitations, and requests for articles. "It was as if the door to the American Dream had just swung open," he remarked with wry amusement.

hypocrisy"; a third said it expressed the author's rage in "choreographic terms."

The controversies stirred up by Jones's dramas made him a literary celebrity. *Ramparts* magazine called him "a young, black literary lion"; *Playboy* said he was "the most discussed—and admired—Negro writer since James Baldwin." That Jones "would be heir to the literary baton that had passed from Richard Wright to Ralph Ellison to James Baldwin," said *Ebony* magazine, "became apparent a few years after he set foot on the track. Fools alone doubted his speed and ability."

Ironically, the more Jones assaulted whites, the better they seemed to like him. Instead of recoiling from his ever-growing militancy and rage, the New York cultural world celebrated his anger with cocktail parties and lavish praise. The *New York Times* and *Herald Tribune* asked Jones to write articles for them. A national magazine invited him to cover the civil rights movement in the South. A Broadway producer wanted him to rewrite one of his new plays.

All this newfound fame left Jones amused and bemused. "It was as if the door to the American Dream had just swung open," he wrote later, "and despite accounts that I was wild and crazy, I could look directly inside and—there—money bags stacked up as high as the eye could fly!"

In 1964, Jones agreed to write a piece for the *Herald Tribune*'s Sunday magazine. Entitled "LeRoi Jones Speaking," the article expressed the author's concerns and doubts about the kind of success he was then experiencing. It began, "I write now, full of trepidation because I know the death this society intends for me." Accepting fame on white society's terms, he felt, would mean the inevitable destruction of himself, his art, and his blackness—which he had come to see as one and the same.

But Jones realized that he could exploit his newfound fame as much as it exploited him. He saw the *Tribune* article as not only a confession of personal and professional doubts but as "a commitment to struggle." It was an opportunity "to speak what should be spoken for all of us," he recalled. "I knew . . . my own life, its twists and flip-outs, yet I felt, now, some heavy *responsibility*. If these bastards were going to raise me up, for any reason, then they would pay for it!" He announced to his *Tribune* readers: "This is a fight without quarter, and I am very fast." His statement was, remarked Jones later, "brash, arrogant, sophomoric, but it was smoke from a moving vehicle!"

Jones's eloquent articles, plays, and public statements created an eager audience for his next literary effort, an extraordinary work of prose fiction published in 1965. Drawn from experiences in his own life, this novel-length book is highly personal and, at times, maddeningly obscure.

"I consciously wrote as deeply into my psyche as I could go," Jones noted later. "I didn't even want the words to 'make sense.' I had the theme in my mind. My early life, in Newark, at Howard, in the Air Force, but the theme was just something against which I wanted to play endless variations. Each section had its own dynamic and pain. Going so deep into myself was like descending into Hell. I called it *The System of Dante's Hell*."

In his *Inferno*—part of the Italian poet's *Divine Comedy*, completed in 1321—Dante was a visitor in hell. Jones is a resident. He challenges his readers to join him in the "perpetually gloomy reality" that is his spiritual inferno.

Although usually labeled a novel, *The System of Dante's Hell* lacks all but the slimmest traces of plot or structure. Jones created an intensely personal form to convey his intensely personal message. "I thought of music," he said, "I thought myself an improvising soloist." In various parts poetry, drama, jazz solo, stream of consciousness, and nightmare, the book defies simple classification. It is simply—and not so simply—LeRoi Jones.

More than anything Jones had created thus far, *The System of Dante's Hell* shook up the reading public. Bedazzled, horrified, amazed, or hopelessly confused, reviewers raced to their typewriters, producing a blizzard of contradictory reactions. "It is as if the writer were thinking: I'll be damned if you're going to understand this, reader," snorted the *New York Post*. *Women's Wear Daily* said flatly, "It won't sell because nobody can understand it." The book's only "comprehensive passages," added the influential trade paper, "are perfectly terrible."

Responses from other critics ranged from grudging praise to raves. "This kind of writing can grow tiresome," said the *Saturday Review of Literature*, "but there is a strong cumulative effect." "I don't think there is a single cliché in the book," wrote the reviewer for the *Negro Digest*. Critic Michael Rumaker called *System* "a tortured nightmare, excruciatingly honest and alive, painful and beautiful." According to the *New York Times Book Review*, Jones "has ordered his materials as if man were still the master of creation, and the effect on the reader is close to exaltation."

As the center of a literary whirlwind, Jones now found himself participating in what he called "a dervish of forums, speakouts, intellectual shootouts." More and more often, he used these public occasions to attack whites, lashing out at audience members and even denouncing old friends. At one public meeting in New York, for example, a white woman asked Jones what her race could do to help the cause of blacks. "You can help by dying," Jones shot back. "You are a cancer. You can help the world's people with your death." (Looking back on this episode years later, Jones wrote, "Only people not really serious about making revolution can dismiss sincere allies. But in my fury, which had no scientific framework, I could only thrash out at any white person.")

In this period (1964–65), Jones wrote later, "I got the reputation of being a snarling, white-hating madman. There was some truth to it. . . . I was in a frenzy."

He was also ensnared by contradictions. "I now regularly put down 'whitey,' " he observed later. "I had long done this in my writing. . . . But I was married to a white woman; I still had many white friends." And he was still lionized by the white cultural elite. When he finally resolved these conflicts, Jones would do it in characteristic fashion: by making a giant leap and never looking back.

Addressing a rally sponsored by the militant Black Panther organization, Jones denounces America's racism. By 1965, the playwright's anger against whites had reached a crescendo: "I got the reputation of being a snarling, white-hating madman," he wrote later. "There was some truth to it."

6

"GONE, UP TO HARLEM"

❦

ONE DAY IN 1965, LeRoi Jones recalled, "a feeling of dread descended on me. Like nothing that I had ever felt before." The writer had suddenly realized he no longer felt comfortable with his wife. "It was the feeling that [she] was *outside* of my concerns, that we did not connect up," he said. "I think now I resented her. It was the black-white thing. . . . I had begun to see her as *white!*"

Hettie Jones wrote about this painful period in her autobiography: "In the seven years I'd been with Roi, I'd watched the loosening of what would one day be called 'black rage.' I knew it could turn on me but that was part of the risk and I hadn't imagined how much. Now some people were beginning to say that hypocritical Roi talked black but married white."

Jones's wife had been noticing more and more "sideways" looks directed at her when she went out with her husband. She imagined people asking, Who is that at the playwright's side—Lula the murderer, his white wife, or the former Hettie Cohen? And then, she said, "As I'd dreaded, one day they all became one."

Some months earlier, LeRoi Jones had organized a political movement in the East Village. "We needed a group of black revolutionaries who were artists to raise up the level of struggle from the arts sector," he wrote later. He called the group the Black Arts.

The Jones family—LeRoi, his wife Hettie (left rear) and his daughters Lisa (left foreground) and Kellie—attend a Greenwich Village bookstore party on February 21, 1965. Minutes after this photograph was taken, Jones received horrifying news: Malcolm X, his "maximum leader/ teacher," had been assassinated.

Copyright 1990 by Fred W. McDarrah (2/21/65)

69

"We talked being black, being downtown amidst the white world," Jones recalled. "The fact that we, ourselves, were down there was a contradiction we were not quite ready to act upon, though we discussed it endlessly. . . . So we settled for jumping on people, mostly verbally, and preaching the need to be black and get out of this downtown white hell."

Jones, who had counted scores of white musicians, artists, and writers as his close friends, now saw little of them. "These white men," he recalled with a tinge of sadness, "saw that I was moving away from them in so many ways and there was some concern, because it wasn't that I didn't like them any longer, but that where I was going they could not come along. Where that was, I couldn't even articulate."

At this point, Jones's political philosophy was heavily influenced by the teachings of Malcolm X while he was a member of the Nation of Islam. The charismatic Black Muslim spokesman had believed that blacks would never obtain their rights as human beings in the white, Christian world; to survive and flourish, he had said, blacks must divorce themselves from all aspects of the corrupt white society and establish their own nationalism.

Malcolm X began to modify his position on race conflict in 1964. Not all white people, he said, were necessarily evil; blacks might even benefit by accepting enlightened, progressive whites as allies. Although Jones did not agree on all points with Malcolm X, with whom he had shared the speakers' platform at several rallies, he continued to admire him deeply, regarding him as a potential savior of the black race.

Yet Malcolm X's slight tilt toward tolerance had enraged many black extremists, most notably the members of the Nation of Islam, the Black Muslim group from which he stormily separated in 1964. On the afternoon of Sunday, February 21, 1965, Malcolm

X died under a hail of bullets fired by three black men. Police captured one of the assassins, but no one ever discovered who had ordered the killing.

Malcolm X's murder sent shock waves through the black community. It also transformed Jones from talker to activist. He got the news in a Village bookstore, when a friend rushed in shouting, "Malcolm is dead! Malcolm is dead! Malcolm's been killed!" "I was stunned," recalled Jones. "I felt ugly, stupid, useless. Downtown in my mix-matched family and my maximum leader/teacher shot dead."

A few days later, Jones packed his clothes and prepared to head uptown. The move was wrenching. "For one thing," Jones wrote later, "the little girls, now, were walking around and there was certainly both a deep love and a sense of pressing responsibility there." Five-year-old Kellie, he said, "picked up instinctively a sense of my departure. She said to me, 'You can't go anywhere. You're one of the funny things.' " But, added Jones, "in a minute or so, I was gone . . . gone, up to Harlem. Seeking revolution!" (He divorced his wife the following year, leaving Kellie and Lisa with their mother.)

Jones took the core of the Black Arts crowd along with him to Harlem, the largest black community in the nation. Emerging from the subway uptown, the young men were awash with romantic exhilaration. "We felt like pioneers of the new order," Jones recalled. "Back in the homeland to help raise the race." Jones could not know then just how greatly his optimism would be tested.

In an old brownstone on 130th Street, Jones and his comrades founded the Black Arts Repertory Theatre/School (BARTS). They hoped to create an art that would stir blacks, raising their consciousness so that they might raise themselves. "An art that would reach the people," Jones observed, "that would take them higher, ready them for war and victory. . . .

That was our vision."

To raise money for BARTS, Jones organized a downtown theater benefit. On the bill were two of his own works, *The Toilet* and the new, short *Experimental Death Unit #1*. In *Experimental Death*, a black army unit kills a black prostitute and her two white customers. Reflecting Jones's political thinking at the time, the play's message is clear: Both the evil white society and the blacks who would sell themselves to that society deserve execution.

The benefit proved successful—a nearly all-white audience paid $20 per seat to help finance the planned black revolution—but BARTS needed more money. Successfully applying to a new federal antipoverty program called Operation Bootstrap, Jones received $40,000 for a summer arts and culture program in Harlem.

Federal funds in hand, Jones and his associates organized and sponsored a wide range of Harlem cultural programs. In vacant lots, playgrounds, and parks, BARTS presented free concerts featuring such leading members of the jazz avant-garde (and friends of Jones's) as musicians John Coltrane, Albert Ayler, and Sun Ra.

"Each night throughout that summer," Jones remembered with satisfaction, "we flooded Harlem streets with new music, new poetry, new dance, new paintings. . . . We had huge audiences, really mass audiences, and though what we brought was supposed to be avant and super-new, most of it the people dug." BARTS also offered classes in poetry, playwriting, history, music, painting, and martial arts.

Along with *Experimental Death*, Jones contributed a second original play, *J-E-L-L-O*, to BARTS. A bizarre parody of comedian Jack Benny's popular radio and television show (sponsored by Jell-O gelatin), *J-E-L-L-O* proved immensely popular with its largely black audiences. In this broad farce, Benny's faithful

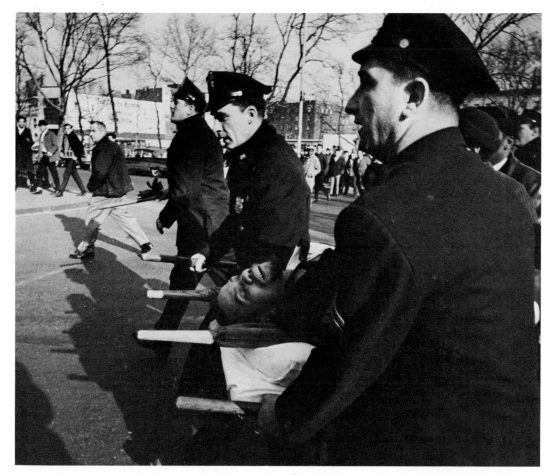

black servant, Rochester, sheds his "Uncle Tom" image and turns militant. After robbing and threatening the life of his astonished boss ("I want *everything* you got," he says, "except the nasty parts"), Rochester howls with laughter and departs, calling, "Goodbye, Mr. Benny. The program's over. I leave you to your horrible lives!"

In *J-E-L-L-O*, Jones employed a time-honored device, as old as comedy itself: the subordinate turning on a superior. But beneath the laughter is Jones's conviction that within every "Negro" is a *black* person waiting for the chance to emerge and take charge. As literary scholar William J. Harris puts it in his

New York City police officers wheel the dying Malcolm X away from the Audubon Ballroom, where assassins had riddled him with bullets. The murder of the Black Muslim leader, said Jones, left him feeling "ugly, stupid, useless." It also stirred him into action: A few days later, he packed his bags, left his "downtown white hell," and moved to Harlem, the nation's largest black community.

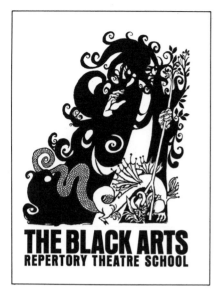

THE BLACK ARTS
REPERTORY THEATRE SCHOOL

To symbolize BARTS, the Black Arts Repertory Theatre/School he established in Harlem, Jones used a drawing of a mysterious, wizardlike figure. "The black arts in the white west," he explained, "were those practices whereby a man could harness the darker forces of the universe to work at his bidding. . . . The black man in this white west . . . needs to realize that these powers are his, are always at his disposal, to be used, the way they were always said to be used, to change the world."

1985 book, *The Poetry and Poetics of Amiri Baraka,* Jones "has turned Benny's happy nigger upside down, creating a new black figure who will act as a model for revolutionary blacks."

Although the BARTS dramatic and educational programs drew enthusiastic crowds, the Harlem organization soon found itself in trouble. It came from several sources. First, conservatives began to accuse BARTS of using government funds to promote racism against whites. One Associated Press story, for example, reported that "each night in a makeshift Harlem theater a group of young Negroes give vent to their hatred of white people. . . . Their leader is the bitterly antiwhite poet-playwright, LeRoi Jones. . . . All the productions seethe with rage against 'Whitey,' an all-inclusive term for whites, who are usually portrayed as homosexuals."

Jones regarded such criticism as bizarre. "So strange, that the victims, once they began to scream and shout at their oppressors, can now be termed the oppressors," he wrote. "We accuse whites of racism so—Presto! Chango!—'black racism' is the real problem."

BARTS was also undermined by the attitude of its own leaders. When, for example, a delegation of federal antipoverty officials arrived at the BARTS office, Jones refused to let them in. "That obviously wasn't cool," he admitted later. With a little bit of intelligent diplomacy, Jones came to believe, BARTS could have succeeded. But, he said regretfully, "We made it easier for them to take us off—we acted so wild and woolly." By the end of the summer, the government had stopped funding BARTS.

"Without the cash flow," Jones recalled, "people started to get more sullen." Most of those connected with BARTS were serious and talented people, but others proved to be greedy opportunists more interested in the project's budget than its commitment to the community. These hangers-on sought to exploit the group for their own political, economic, and even sexual advantage.

Jones found himself spending most of his time and energy in dealing with this fringe element and trying to solve the problems they caused. At last, with the program out of funds and its activities in chaos, Jones gave up; in December 1965, he left Harlem and moved back to his parents' home in Newark. Soon BARTS was no more.

Despite the enormous disappointment of watching his brainchild die, Jones refused to label BARTS a failure. "Bringing art to the people, black art to black people, and getting paid for doing it was sweet," he insisted. "Both the artists and the people were raised by that experience." Several important artists, including poets Sonia Sanchez and Clarence Reed and playwright Ronald Drayton, did their earliest creative work at BARTS. And the project served as an inspiration and model for the many theater-schools that soon sprang up in the black communities of other cities.

During his months at BARTS, Jones had written a number of essays, which he collected and published as *Home* in 1966. The work's title, said its author, "meant coming back to one's self, one's consciousness, coming back to blackness." He ended his introduction with the words, "by the time you read this, I will be even blacker." *Home* opens with "Cuba Libre," Jones's report on his mind-opening 1960 trip to Cuba. The chronologically arranged pieces trace the evolution of Jones's political thought.

In these essays, Jones begins to formulate his radical views on the problems facing blacks. In "What Does Nonviolence Mean?"—a lengthy critique of Martin Luther King, Jr., and the mainstream civil rights movement—Jones indicts American society for crimes against blacks and sentences it to death.

In a 1954 publicity shot for his popular radio show, comedian Jack Benny checks out his ancient automobile as his faithful servant, Rochester (Eddie Anderson), looks on. Turning these well-known characters inside out, Jones wrote a savagely funny 1965 play, J-E-L-L-O.

I advocate a violence, a literal murdering of the American socio-political stance, not only as it directly concerns American Negroes, but in terms of its stranglehold on most of the modern world. The Negro must take an extreme stance, must attack the white man's system, using his own chains to help beat the system into submission and actual change. The black man is the only revolutionary force in American society today, if only by default.

More conventional in form than his fiction, Jones's essays in *Home*, especially his essay about art, "Hunting Is Not Those Heads on the Wall," are nevertheless stylistically distinctive. His wit and poetic sense show up in almost every line.

Deeply disturbed by *Home*'s militantly antiwhite spirit, most white critics laced into the book. But a few reviewers, notably Faith Berry in the *New Republic*, admired it. Noting that Jones had said that "something . . . I aspire to is the craziness of all honest men," Berry wrote: "In certain passages . . . he fulfills it, not only with the craziness of his own honesty, but with moments of truth." In the years since its publication, *Home* has come to be widely praised and often studied in high school and college classes.

The reactions to *Home* could have come as little surprise to Jones, whose expectations of the white press were minimal at best. Besides, as he said in his autobiography, "now I had other things to think about. Like, what was I doing back in Newark?" He knew he would be able to put his confusing, exhausting experience with BARTS behind him. But what lay ahead? Could he learn from his mistakes and establish something positive and lasting? Should he try to build another cultural program, this time with a clear political focus and firm leadership?

At this point in LeRoi Jones's life, questions seemed to outnumber answers. But he had one solid point of reference: "At least I was," he said, "literally Home." ❧

7

"TOUGHER AND BLACKER"

---✿---

LEROI JONES'S BLACK Arts project fizzled in Harlem, but it sent sparks across the nation. In Detroit, Philadelphia, New Orleans, Washington, D.C., and other cities, politically concerned black artists began to emulate Jones, creating their own inner-city cultural institutions. Now resettled in Newark, Jones in early 1966 considered the situation. More than half the city's residents were black; why not try again here? He went to work.

Acquiring a run-down building on Newark's Stirling Street, Jones renovated it with the help of friends and neighbors, then opened it as Spirit House, a theater–cultural center. There, Jones presented plays, concerts, and poetry readings. "We had a small intense audience," he recalled, "an audience that influences others." Spirit House also offered classes, sports, and social activities: "Anything the community wants," promised Jones.

Jones designed Spirit House as a self-help, self-supporting operation that required no funds from—and therefore developed no ties to—government programs or private foundations. Along with the cultural center, Jones founded a publishing company, Jihad Publications; in Arabic, *jihad* means "holy war."

Newark's cultural scene, Jones decided, was "tougher and blacker" than New York's, downtown or up. "There was much less room or tolerance for the 'fake art' syndrome that is so ubiquitous in Manhattan," he observed, "therefore it is much less fertile soil for the maddening and finally vapid 'artsy-craftsy' personality type. Art was literally a lifeblood in a

Jones returned to his native New-ark in late 1965, saddened by the demise of BARTS but convinced that "something had happened that was good." Cultural institutions, modeled on BARTS, had already taken root in Detroit and San Francisco; by the middle of the year, Jones noted with satisfaction, "it became evident that there was a Black Arts movement spreading throughout the United States."

place like Newark and its tenders and developers were . . . dedicated valuable people, with usually a great deal more of a sense of responsibility than their average New York counterparts."

One of those "dedicated valuable people," black actress and dancer Sylvia Robinson, appeared in a 1966 production of Jones's *Black Mass.* Written during his days at BARTS, this short play combines a parody of Mary Shelley's classic 1818 horror story, *Frankenstein*, with the mythology of the Nation of Islam. In the play, a black magician creates a monster, a soulless creature that, says one witness, will "take human life . . . because it has no regard for human life." The monster, of course, is the white man, who "has merely to touch something to turn it into itself. Or else it sucks out the life juices."

Robinson, mother of two daughters and in the process of obtaining a divorce, "always drew applause" in his play, Jones later recalled. He was fascinated by the tall, slender actress, whom he described as "a brown woman with long, straightish-looking hair," and began seeing her constantly. Describing their relationship in his autobiography, he wrote, "There was a fine intensity to it, a dazzling sensitivity to it, of us together, sensuous and alive." Still, Jones and Robinson sometimes fought, especially about his habit of "disappearing late nights into the ghetto to go in and out of the taverns and hangouts." Looking back on these days, Jones admitted, "I was still unpredictable and spoiled and a stomp-down male chauvinist."

Nevertheless, Jones respected—and perhaps envied—Robinson's commitment to the black masses. "People like Sylvia, in the Newarks all over North America, had had that sense of focus and responsibility, because, finally, there was much more of a black working-class underpinning for what they were doing," he wrote. "Such a . . . basis for their efforts was a given. For me, on the other hand, it was something I was still trying to *win*."

Jones continued to write poetry ("A poet writes because he *has* to," he once wrote. "It is like breathing—you can only stop at grave peril"); he also resumed his political activism. He organized a block association, published a neighborhood newsletter, and wrote pamphlets on local, national, and international political issues. Discovering "the concept of Black Power," he began stenciling the image of a black fist on sidewalks and abandoned buildings. "We had not completely focused on the meaning of the term," he recalled, "but we knew it was correct and ours!"

Among the favorite targets of Jones's widely circulated, often inflammatory pamphlets was Hugh Addonizio, Newark's long-entrenched mayor. The hard-hitting leaflets earned the suspicious attention of the Newark Police Department and even the Federal Bureau of Investigation, which claimed that one of Jones's publications had given directions for making a Molotov cocktail (a crude hand grenade). "One thing about the FBI," quipped Jones, "they're always trying to make you famous."

Jones, of course, *was* famous, especially with young blacks. In the spring of 1967, the Black Student Union at San Francisco State College invited the poet-playwright to become a visiting professor and "organize some cultural presence among the students." With Robinson, who was then pregnant, Jones headed west, settling down in San Francisco and organizing a theatrical troupe of black actors and writers. On tour with his group in Los Angeles, he ran into Ron Karenga, a black nationalist leader whose ideas about politics and culture Jones found extremely impressive.

Karenga, head of an organization known as US ("as opposed to 'THEM,'" noted Jones), had adopted

Attending a 1967 conference on black power are (seated, left to right) comedian Dick Gregory, US leader Ron Karenga, SNCC chairman H. Rap Brown, and SNCC official Ralph Featherstone. The teachings of Karenga, who hoped to ignite a black American "cultural revolution," struck a sympathetic chord in Jones.

the title of Maulana, "master teacher" in the Swahili language of Africa. He explained to Jones that US aimed at producing a "cultural revolution, to win the minds of our people." After that, he said, "the political revolution would be a matter of course." Karenga created a set of behaviors, rituals, and holidays—an entire culture—designed to politicize black people by instilling them with "blackness."

Karenga's theories of cultural nationalism fit well with Jones's similar, although less well developed, ideas on culture and politics. Moreover, Jones was impressed by the discipline of US, especially when he compared it with the political chaos that had crippled BARTS. "The fact of the US organization— i.e., that it was an organization and not just a bunch of undisciplined people taking up time mostly arguing with each other about what to do, or what method to use, even about things that most agreed should be done—drew me to US and Karenga," he said.

Full of enthusiasm for Karenga's teachings, Jones returned to Newark in June 1967. Robinson had preceded him by a few weeks. "When I got back," he reported later, "my first son, Obalaji Malik-Ali, was a week old." The boy was named Obalaji ("God or the king's warrior"), Jones explained, after a young friend from Harlem; Malik was for Malcolm X; Ali, for heavyweight champion Muhammad Ali. After the boy's birth, Jones said, "I was full of joy."

Karenga's program inspired much of the work Jones completed at this time, notably his 1967 play, *Slave Ship*, and *Raise Race Rays Raze: Essays Since 1965* (published in 1971). *Slave Ship*, described by Jones as "a historical pageant," stunned audiences; even the critics raved about it. Plotless and sometimes wordless—much of the dialogue is in the African language Yoruba; much consists of sounds such as "AI-IIEEEEEEEEE"—the drama brings slavery's horror directly to the theater. To describe *Slave Ship*, dazzled reviewers used such phrases as "a theatrical phenomenon," "overwhelming intensity," and "absolutely wonderful."

The essays in *Raise Race Rays Raze*, said Jones, were intended to "offer concrete directions for the new black man." Included in the book are "7 Principles of US Maulana Karenga & The Need for a Black Value System" and four other essays about Karenga and his doctrines. While some readers found *Raise* obscure or confusing, most praised it. Jones, observed the *New York Times*, "can make words ignite and burst into flame."

Published in 1967, a banner year for Jones as a writer, were his second book of fiction, *Tales*, and his second volume of jazz criticism, *Black Music*. *Tales* is a collection of short stories, separate but thematically and stylistically connected. Overall, these pieces are more accessible than Jones's earlier work of fiction, *The System of Dante's Hell*. The "tales" are also more humorous. "Answers in Progress," for example, presents the bizarre imagery of space aliens coming to Newark in search of jazz while a black revolution is raging in the streets.

Black Music is an anthology of nonfiction pieces Jones wrote between 1961 and 1966. Some had appeared in such magazines as *Down Beat*, some were liner notes for record albums, and some were new. And many, critics agreed, were brilliant. Jones had rarely been more eloquent than he was in his tribute to the luminous, self-destructive jazz singer Billie Holiday:

> And even in the laughter, something other than brightness, completed the sound. A voice that grew from a singer's instrument to a woman's. And from that (those last records critics say are weak) to a black landscape of need, and perhaps, suffocated desire.
>
> Sometimes you are afraid to listen to this lady.

Jones the poet is never far from Jones the essayist.

As well as producing a new play and publishing two books in 1967, Jones was arrested during Newark's black uprising. "But the thing that most changed my life at the time," he noted in his autobiography, "was marriage." In August, between the arrest and the trial, he and Sylvia Robinson, parents of three-month-old Obalaji, were married in a ceremony conducted in the Yoruba language. "I had thought that I would never get married again," Jones wrote later. "I wanted to avoid those kind of forever ties. But I loved the woman."

Convicted for possession of guns after his January 1968 trial, Jones successfully appealed. Crucial to the reversal of his conviction, he said, was the appearance of a man he and his friends had rescued during the rioting. The man "breezed into the courtroom," recalled Jones, "raised up his pant leg and pointed to the bullet hole," proving that "we were not shooting at people, we were taking them to the hospital. [We] won it going away!"

A handcuffed Jones, convicted of carrying illegal firearms during the 1967 Newark rebellion, leaves a New Jersey courthouse in early 1968. Beaten and thrown into solitary confinement, Jones said he had felt "an absolute kinship with the suffering roots of African American life."

Jones and his father, Coyt, confer after the playwright's acquittal on gun-possession charges. A calm, peace-loving man, the senior Jones had often looked askance at his son's rage against the white establishment, but the trial changed his attitude. "The sight of me behind bars and that beating," said LeRoi, "radicalized my father."

Jones's trial also brought him closer to his father, who had often sharply disagreed with his son on racial issues. "The sight of me behind bars and that beating radicalized my father," Jones reported. "The trial and lockup fired him up in a way I had never seen him before. I guess he knew that if they could do this to his son, whom he *knew* was not a criminal or a bad person, then they deserved his contempt, perhaps his hatred. I heard him use profanity for the first time in my life."

After his acquittal, Jones dedicated himself more seriously than ever to the black political struggle. "I felt transformed, literally shot into the eye of the black hurricane of coming revolution," he said. "If I had been able to agitate and propagandize before, now it was raised up another notch in intensity."

Jones's transformation included a new name. He had been supported during his recent troubles by a group of Sunni Muslims, members of the branch of

Islam to which Malcolm X had converted shortly before his death. Although Jones did not become a Muslim, he was interested in the ideas of his new friends and encouraged them to gather at Spirit House after his release.

The Muslims began to call the writer Ameer Barakat, Arabic for "the blessed prince." The flattering title pleased him; it also made him feel, he said, that he was "literally being changed into a blacker being." He soon modified the spelling, and LeRoi Jones became Amiri Baraka.

The king (*le roi*) was now a prince—but he was a *black* prince. For a number of years, Baraka preceded his new name with a title he received from Karenga: Imamu, derived from the Islamic term *imam* (spiritual leader). Sylvia Jones took the name of one of the prophet Mohammed's wives, Amina, which means "faithful."

The couple, who had named their firstborn Obalaji, would give Islamic-style names to the rest of their children as well. Their second son, born in 1969, was to be Ras (the wise) Jua Al Azia; their first daughter, born in 1971, would be Shani (something wondrous) Isis Makeda. The Barakas' last two children, Amiri (named for his father) Seku Musa and Ahi Mwenge (brother of the masses), would arrive in 1972 and 1973, respectively.

In early 1968, Imamu Amiri Baraka organized the Committee for Unified Newark (CFUN), an umbrella group of black political associations. CFUN called a convention to nominate black candidates for the city council, at that point dominated by Mayor Hugh Addonizio and his well-oiled political machine. Although the CFUN slate lost, the group used the experience to learn and build for the next mayoral election.

Baraka's increasing political commitment reflected itself in his poetry. In 1969, he published *Black*

Magic, a collection of poems written between 1961 and 1967. Included in the volume is "Black People!," made famous by Judge Kapp's censored reading of it during Jones's 1967 trial. Among the other black nationalist pieces in *Black Magic* are "A Poem for Black Hearts," "For Tom Postell, Black Poet," and "Jitterbugs." Laced with rage, most of these poems shocked and appalled white critics. "Black Hearts," for example, calls for revenge against whites for the murder of Malcolm X:

> For Great Malcolm a prince of the earth, let nothing
>   in us rest
> until we avenge ourselves for his death, stupid animals
> that killed him, let us never breathe a pure breath if
> we fail, and white men call us faggots until the end of
> the earth.

Many reviewers, white and black alike, described *Black Magic*—which was anti-Semitic as well as anti-white—as "reactionary," "hate-filled," "inhuman," and "repulsive." In forsaking art for politics, said one critic, Baraka had produced nothing but "shrill propaganda." Other readers, however, looked beyond Baraka's images of violence and loathing and saw the work of a powerful and original artist.

A year later, Baraka became a central figure in Newark politics. In 1970, CFUN picked black civil engineer Kenneth Gibson as its candidate to unseat incumbent mayor Addonizio. CFUN members concentrated on making Gibson's campaign, as Baraka put it, "a juggernaut that plowed into the masses' feelings and used those feelings as fuel." Among CFUN's weapons was a *Life* magazine photograph taken during the 1967 rebellion; it showed a white police officer, smoking gun in hand, standing over the body of a black child he had killed. Reproduced on thousands of posters, the picture carried the slogan Register & Vote! Never Let This Happen Again!

Viewing Baraka, not Gibson, as their main opponent, Addonizio campaign managers tried hard to

Actress Sylvia Robinson appeared in Jones's play A Black Mass *in 1966 and married him in 1967. The following year, when Jones changed his name to Imamu Amiri Baraka, his wife became Amina Baraka. The Barakas, each of whom had two children by a previous marriage, became the parents of four sons and a daughter.*

discredit the black writer in the minds of the voters. "They thought my checkered past and 'criminality'—i.e., being arrested in the rebellions—would turn the masses off," Baraka reported. "It acted exactly the opposite. Every knock was a boost."

The Newark campaign attracted national interest. Eager to help CFUN and its candidates, a small army of liberal celebrities—including Isaac Hayes, James Brown, Leontyne Price, Bill Cosby, Dustin Hoffman, Beau Bridges, the Staple Singers, and Stevie Wonder—descended on the city, riding sound trucks and addressing voters. On election day itself, hundreds of CFUN supporters turned out. With their aid, recalled Baraka, "we could have people at all the polling sites. . . . We had radio cars, walkie-talkies, huge maps in every headquarters, . . . security forces, . . . a steady flow of information."

In a desperate bid to counter the CFUN "juggernaut," the Addonizio campaign sent out sound trucks with a message to white voters: If Gibson won, black militant Amiri Baraka would take over, filling city hall with raging black revolutionists. "Never forget the words of LeRoi Jones," blared the trucks. "After eight o'clock tonight [when the polling places closed] he's no longer welcome in our city."

Despite the opposition's tactics, Gibson won the election handily. "There was much screaming and jumping up and down," reported Baraka. "People were whooping and hollering." The CFUN crowd was gratified—and amused—by televised pictures of Addonizio campaign members fighting with cameramen and reporters. The press, said the politicians, had "sold out the white race" by giving the black candidate too much coverage. "The rage, the running-around frustration and confusion," said Baraka, "was a heartwarming sight, especially to people who themselves were usually in that situation."

After the Newark victory, Baraka focused even more sharply on black nationalism. The title poem of *It's Nation Time* (1970), for example, deals with black nation building:

> time to get up and
> be
> come
> be
> come, time to
>> be come
>> time to
>> get up be come
>> . . .
> It's nation time eye ime
>> it's nation ti eye ime
>>> chant with bells and drum
>>> its nation time

With Gibson safely in office, Baraka turned to a wider political arena. First, he helped found the Congress of Afrikan Peoples (CAP), a national association of black political organizations. (*Afrika* was spelled with a *k*, Baraka explained, because "*c* did not exist" in the languages of that continent.) Baraka and his CAP associates hoped the movement would promote black unity, welding the diverse elements within the black community into a single, powerful force. As a CAP leader, Baraka solidified his reputation as a persuasive speaker and effective political organizer.

A beaming Kenneth Gibson (left center) marches through Newark on the last day of his 1970 mayoral campaign. Accompanying the candidate is singer Harry Belafonte (right), one of dozens of celebrities who aided Baraka and his friends in their successful effort to unseat incumbent mayor Hugh Addonizio.

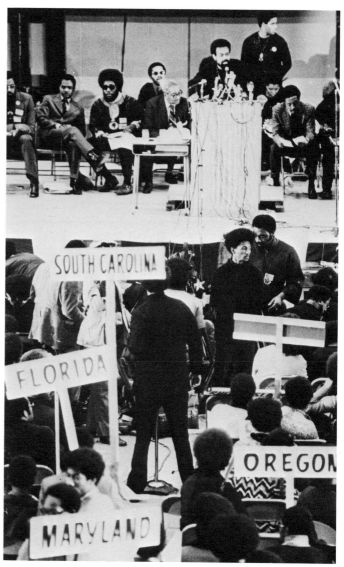

Baraka presides over the National Black Political Convention in Gary, Indiana, in 1972. Attended by 9,000 people from all over the United States, the sometimes discordant gathering finally hammered out the National Black Agenda, a list of black political priorities.

In 1972, black activists from all over the country took part in the first National Black Political Convention, held in Gary, Indiana. The 9,000 delegates represented all degrees of black political opinion, from conservative to militant. Baraka, who served as a co-convener, presided over the often contentious debate on the creation of a National Black Agenda. Proving himself a skillful chair, he kept order and deftly resolved potentially divisive arguments, thus holding the fragile coalition together.

The National Black Agenda consisted of a series of resolutions outlining the concerns of black people. The convention appointed Baraka to represent it at the Democratic party's national convention in Miami; it was his job to make sure that any politician who wanted black votes accepted the Black Agenda.

Miami, however, turned out to be a huge disappointment. "The majority of the black politicians who were talking [militantly] in Gary," Baraka said later, "had reverted to character and were simply scrambling to get on some candidate's payroll. . . . Whenever I raised the question of the Black Agenda, such an idea was openly scoffed at. Hey, that was just for show."

From this point on, Baraka grew increasingly doubtful about the electoral system as a tool for effecting major change: Perhaps no politician could be counted on. During the early 1970s, events in Newark would confirm Baraka's distrust of elected officials, black or white. ❧

8

KNOWING THE CHANGES

B Y 1972, JUST two years after helping Kenneth Gibson win Newark's mayoral election, Baraka had become utterly disillusioned with his choice. Gibson, he complained, "was pulling a disappearing act right before our eyes." According to Baraka, the mayor showed little interest in the concerns of Newark's black and Puerto Rican population. He even seemed embarrassed by his association with Baraka and his "radical" allies. "Word was running around the city," recalled Baraka, "that Gibson was trying to cut himself loose from our baleful influence completely."

Relations between city hall and Newark's non-white residents deteriorated steadily; in 1974, members of the Puerto Rican community finally staged a rebellion against what they described as police brutality. Gibson responded first with force, then banned all gatherings of more than three people. The mayor "was playing 'white boy' to the Puerto Ricans like Addonizio to the Bloods," asserted Baraka.

"I hated the feeling this gave me," he said, adding that he was beginning to understand how white radicals might feel when "white supremacy freaks" practiced "their usual hate everybody oppress everybody" tactics. Soon after the Puerto Rican demonstration, Baraka denounced the mayor and broke with him completely.

Baraka, serving as grand marshal of Newark's 1974 African-American Day parade, acknowledges supporters' cheers with a raised-arm salute. Although he continued to wear ethnic clothing, the poet-activist now insisted that black liberation would require more than "returning to various forms of African dress and learning a few words of Swahili."

At this point, Baraka also began to back away from cultural nationalism. "Merely returning to various forms of African dress and learning a few words of Swahili," he decided, "could not effect black liberation." Just as he had once made a sudden shift from the interracial, bohemian life of Greenwich Village to the world of Harlem and black nationalism, he now took an abrupt swing toward Marxism. "I read more and more Mao Tse-tung [the Chinese leader who had helped establish his nation's Communist party]," he noted later.

Baraka had come to view politics in terms of economic class rather than race. The existing political system, he decided, served only the interests of a particular class; it was therefore a waste of time to try to work within that system. If the needs of the poor of all races were to be met, the system itself required change, even if that meant revolution. "Socialism obviously was necessary," Baraka concluded. "I had come to that, but how to bring it?"

In June 1974, he traveled to the African nation of Tanzania for a meeting of the Pan-African Congress. There, he delivered a ringing speech on "revolutionary culture," calling for a "worldwide commitment by African people to build socialism everywhere and to take up the struggle against imperialism everywhere." The fact that he "stood now clearly on the left," he said, "had now been trumpeted to the four winds."

Baraka's visit provided him with more than a platform to air his new political views; it gave him fresh insight into what he called "the African reality." To go "from the never-never-land Africa of nationalist invention to the real thing," he said, opened his eyes: "Along with the economic and social backwardness and political turmoil, one can see and feel atomic fires burning in Africa, it's in the people's color and faces, the electric roll of their eyes, their franticness and coolness."

Baraka, who began to study the writings of Chinese Communist leader Mao Tse-tung in the early 1970s, made a sudden political leap in 1974. A mere cultural revolution, Jones decided, could never achieve social justice; blacks would attain equality only through a class struggle in which they fought alongside whites.

Baraka said he "could see clearly now how inextricably bound are our fates, the African and the African American, as well as our brothers and sisters in the Caribbean." There is, he added, "an overall unity to our collective plight that we ignore only at our collective peril."

In Africa, recalled Baraka, he lost his "naive cultural delusion" but gained "an even greater hope." Awareness of reality, he said, "no matter how painful, is the only prerequisite for making real change!" Seven-year-old Obalaji, who had accompanied his father to Africa, provided the poet-activist with even more food for thought. As Baraka relaxed on the

SNCC leader Stokely Carmichael (pictured in 1970), who once jokingly described the position of women in his organization as "prone," expressed an attitude common among the men of the black liberation movement. Admitting to his own former "stomp-down male chauvinism," Baraka reversed his views in the mid-1970s; the movement's women, he asserted, had always shown more courage than its men.

beach with the little boy, watching him "romping up and down in the warm water, happier than adults can ever be," he realized "that all black life must finally rise." He gazed at Obalaji, he said, "knowing that he must be readied to take up this struggle at a much higher level than his father."

On his return to America, Baraka's political position continued to evolve. By the end of the year, he had broken completely from Ron Karenga and his abstract notion of "blackness." At this point, Baraka also stopped using the title Imamu, which "master teacher" Karenga had given him. Cultural nationalism, Baraka concluded, was irrelevant to the real lives and concerns of most black Americans.

Baraka replaced Karenga's theories with Marxism, or more precisely, what he called "Marxism-Leninism-Mao Tse Tung thought." Real and lasting social change, he now argued, would come about not through a black cultural revolution, but through a class struggle in which black and white workers fought side by side.

On Baraka's 40th birthday, October 7, 1974, the Congress of Afrikan Peoples declared itself a Marxist-

Leninist organization; it would soon change its name to the Revolutionary Communist League. In keeping with this shift, the Newark CAP publication, *Black New Ark*, became *Unity and Struggle* and switched its motto from Black People Must Unify to Unite the Many to Oppose the Few.

Baraka's revised political outlook included a new racial attitude. For years, he had lashed out against whites indiscriminately, making a special point of denouncing the white liberals who supported black causes. On one occasion, he had even made a speech belittling Andrew Goodman and Michael Schwerner, the white civil rights workers who were murdered with their black colleague, James Chaney, by the Mississippi Ku Klux Klan in 1964. "Those white boys," he had sneered, "were only seeking to assuage their own leaking consciences."

Later regretting that "outrageous diatribe," Baraka wrote. "The willingness of young whites to put their lives on the line for the struggle for democracy *is* a noble thing. . . . If I could have stood some hard truth, Schwerner and Goodman were out there on the front lines doing more than I was!"

In his 1984 autobiography, Baraka discussed his former antiwhite attitude. "To the extent that what I felt opposed white supremacy and imperialism, it was certainly correct," he stated. "But to the extent that I merely turned white supremacy upside down and created an exclusivist black supremacist doctrine, that was bull——." By this point a committed Marxist, Baraka recognized the necessity of political alliances with white radicals. "Any people sincerely interested in making revolution must have allies," he said.

Along with rethinking his position on race, Baraka began to free himself from other bigotries. He came to realize that many of the black liberation movement's male leaders, himself included, had dem-

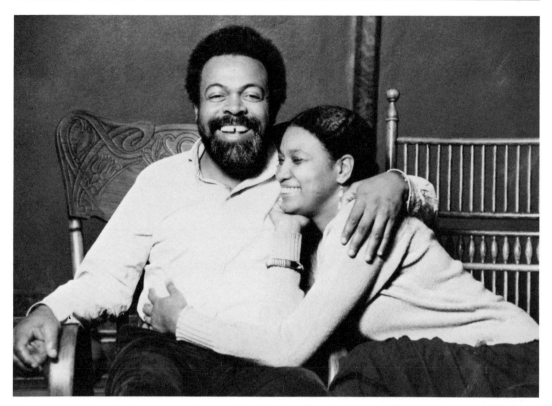

Amiri and Amina Baraka share a laugh in the mid-1980s. "There is no one I have ever been as close to as my wife," Baraka noted in his 1984 autobiography. "Even as the Marxists we both are," he continued, "listening intently to our children's growing songs and pains, we are relieved that we grew up to be even this close to ourselves."

onstrated extreme sexism. Black Power theorist Stokely Carmichael, for example, had once responded to a document entitled "The Position of Women in SNCC [Student Nonviolent Coordinating Committee]" with the quip, "the position of women in the movement is prone."

Looking back, Baraka marveled at the strength of the women within the black movement. "Not only did they stand with us shoulder to shoulder against black people's enemies, they also had to go toe to toe with us, battling day after day against our insufferable male chauvinism," he admitted.

As well as abandoning sexism, Baraka shed the anti-Semitism and homophobia that had once envenomed much of his writing and thinking. "I was acknowledging another change in my life," he wrote. "In my life of changes. (And how can you play the tune, if you don't know the changes?)"

Interviewing Baraka in 1980, literary scholar William J. Harris remarked, "Some people have been concerned about you changing political positions, life-styles, so often." Baraka replied, "I can see people worrying. I just think they should worry about why they don't. I mean because everything is obviously in change. The only constant that I know is in change.

"When I came to New York," he continued, "I got some information, some experience, was influenced by Malcolm X, became a Nationalist. [Then] I saw that Nationalism could not solve the questions that were raised by the day by day struggle. I think that a lot of times when people are . . . engaged in some sort of day to day activism themselves, they will probably find more reason to change."

Baraka had the last word on his own changeability in his autobiography. "I was a child," he wrote, "and growing through zones and degrees until I became who this was when I wrote it (even when this is a book, I'll be gone gone gone gone again)."

Since his political conversion, Baraka has dedicated himself to shaping a revolutionary Marxist-Leninist party in the United States. Just as his earlier writing proclaimed his dedication to cultural nationalism, his recent work supports his new political agenda. *Hard Facts*, published in 1975, includes poems attacking the black middle class, black politicians, and black nationalism. Most of its pieces, however, are "socialist poems," intended to raise readers' political and historical understanding.

Even the poet's admirers found *Hard Facts* hard to take, describing it as "forgettable" and "severely limited." Baraka's "postnationalist, Maoist work," wrote scholar Werner Sollors, "admits only occasional flashes of poetry, which are often overshadowed by hammering political slogans." Here are the closing lines of "A New Reality Is Better Than a New Movie!":

When all over the planet, men and women, with heat in their
   hands, demand that society
be planned to include the lives and self-determination of all the
   people ever to live. That is
the scalding scenario with a cast of just under two billion that they
   dare not even whisper.
Its called, "We Want It All . . . The Whole World!"

Baraka's 1977 play, *The Motion of History*, explores two central themes: "the conscious separation
created between black and white workers who are
both exploited by the same enemy" (capitalism), and
the "recurrent rebellions" that have arisen throughout America's history. When people overcome the
former and learn from the latter, Baraka argues, history will be moved along its inevitable path toward
"the only solution to our problems . . . revolution!"

In the same vein, Baraka's collection of essays
from 1974–79, *Daggers and Javelins* (published in
1984), is spiked with radical slogans and references
to "Marxism-Leninism-Mao Tse Tung thought." Although the book met some sharp criticism (it was,
said one reader, "almost destroyed by its repetitive
phrasing"), it was also hailed as an "important book"
by many reviewers.

Since the late 1970s, Baraka has held academic
positions at some of the country's finest universities.
He served as a visiting professor at Yale from 1977
to 1978 and at George Washington University in the
nation's capital from 1978 to 1979. In the fall of 1979,
he joined the Africana Studies Program at the State
University of New York (SUNY), Stony Brook. He
was tenured (given permanent status) in 1982 and
since then has attained the rank of full professor and
become director of the university's Africana Studies
Program.

On leave from SUNY from 1988 to 1990, Baraka
served as a full-time visiting professor in the English
department at Rutgers University in New Brunswick,

New Jersey. Because Rutgers is close to his Newark home, he decided to seek a permanent position there. In March 1990, however, the English department rejected him. Baraka—and many others—believed Rutgers denied him the post because of his outspoken nature and unpopular political views. "They can act like racists," he told reporters, "but if I call them one, I'm the one who is victimized."

Amiri Baraka—poet, playwright, novelist, essayist, music critic, political activist—has enlivened American social and cultural life for three decades. The heir of Langston Hughes, Richard Wright, and James Baldwin, he is also a wholly original literary phenomenon. Combining radical technique with radical ideas, expressing his own rage, projecting his own dreams, Baraka has given dramatic form to the hopes and fears of America's black community.

Unlike many radicals of his generation, Baraka remains an unapologetic revolutionary. Refusing to moderate his views in exchange for mainstream acceptance, he has continued to work for large-scale social change. Like Malcolm X, he has learned tolerance while maintaining his outrage; like the activist educator and writer W. E. B. Du Bois, he is a distinguished and learned radical whose ideas have evolved but not mellowed. And, like these giants, Baraka has tried to be the political and moral voice of his people.

Nevertheless, as William J. Harris put it in 1985, "Baraka is still an enigma to the American literary establishment, which cannot come to terms with this difficult and brilliant maverick. Possibly the establishment's reluctance to recognize him . . . rests on the real—as opposed to the metaphysical—threat he poses. . . . Baraka's art threatens property and the actual structure of society."

Baraka's rejection by Rutgers certainly indicates that he continues to shock and infuriate conserva-

Graying but still militant, Baraka continues to say exactly what he thinks. "I am a communist, make no mistake about that, a Marxist, a Leninist," he told a reporter in 1990. "The American people are going to be faced more and more with the realization of how they have been had." Nevertheless, he added, "I'm optimistic. I'd say I'm a revolutionary optimist. I believe that the good guys—the people—are going to win."

tives. But he has also inspired many important black artists, including playwright Ed Bullins, filmmaker Spike Lee, and poets Larry Neal, Don Lee (Haki Madhubuti), Sonia Sanchez, and Nikki Giovanni. "Joy to the world," wrote Giovanni. "LeRoi Jones moved uptown. Wrote plays in the vernacular and a people found our voice."

Baraka and his family still reside in Newark, where the poet-activist continues his artistic and political pursuits. The Barakas' big red house on South 10th Street doubles as a headquarters for musicians and poets, who present regular performances and readings there. Family life clearly provides immense pleasure to the graying but still fiery militant.

"But look," Amiri Baraka has written, "the world is still here. There are still things that can be done. And I swear I do understand the world better. We will find out just how well. In words and deeds yet to be written and realitied out." ❧

APPENDIX:
SELECTED BOOKS BY AMIRI BARAKA

1961   *Preface to a Twenty Volume Suicide Note*

1963   *Blues People: Negro Music in White America*

1964   *The Dead Lecturer; Dutchman & The Slave*

1965   *The System of Dante's Hell*

1966   *The Baptism & The Toilet; Home: Social Essays*

1967   *Tales; Black Music*

1969   *Black Magic: Collected Poetry, 1961–67; Four Black Revolutionary Plays; Slave Ship: A Historical Pageant*

1970   *J-E-L-L-O*

1971   *Raise Race Rays Raze: Essays Since 1965*

1975   *Hard Facts*

1978   *The Motion of History and Other Plays*

1984   *The Autobiography of LeRoi Jones/Amiri Baraka; Daggers and Javelins: Essays, 1974–1979*

CHRONOLOGY

1934   Born Everett Leroy Jones on October 7 in Newark, New Jersey

1951   Enrolls at Rutgers University

1952   Enrolls at Howard University; changes name to LeRoi Jones

1954   Enlists in the air force

1957   Moves to New York's Greenwich Village

1958   Marries Hettie Cohen

1960   Travels to Cuba as guest of Fidel Castro's government

1961   Publishes first collection of poetry, *Preface to a Twenty Volume Suicide Note*

1963   Publishes study of black American music, *Blues People*

1964   Writes and produces four plays: *Dutchman, The Baptism, The Slave,* and *The Toilet*

1965   Moves to Harlem in New York City and founds the Black Arts Repertory Theater/School (BARTS); divorces Hettie Cohen; publishes first novel, *The System of Dante's Hell*; produces plays *Experimental Death Unit #1* and *J-E-L-L-O*

1966   Establishes cultural center, Spirit House, in Newark

1967   Produces play *Slave Ship*; arrested during Newark rebellion; marries Sylvia Robinson (Amina Baraka); changes name to Imamu Amiri Baraka

1968   Forms Committee for Unified Newark (CFUN)

1970   Helps elect a black candidate, Kenneth Gibson, mayor of Newark; organizes Congress of Afrikan Peoples

1972   Serves as co-convener of first National Black Political Convention

1974   Embraces Marxism; drops Imamu from name

1977   Produces play *The Motion of History*; teaches at Yale University

1978   Teaches at George Washington University

1979   Joins Africana Studies Program at State University of New York (SUNY)

1984   Publishes *The Autobiography of LeRoi Jones/Amiri Baraka*

1988   Serves as visiting professor at Rutgers University

1990   Returns to teaching post at SUNY

FURTHER READING

Baker, Houston A., Jr. *Black Literature in America*. New York: McGraw-Hill, 1971.

Benston, Kimberly W., ed. *Imamu Amiri Baraka (LeRoi Jones): A Collection of Critical Essays*. Englewood Cliffs, NJ: Prentice-Hall, 1978.

Brown, Lloyd W. *Amiri Baraka*. Boston: Twayne, 1980.

Di Prima, Diane. *Memoirs of a Beatnik*. New York: Travellers Companion, 1969.

Harris, William J. *The Poetry and Poetics of Amiri Baraka: The Jazz Aesthetic*. Columbia: University of Missouri Press, 1985.

Hill, Herbert, ed. *Anger and Beyond: The Negro Writer in the United States*. New York: Harper & Row, 1966.

Hudson, Theodore R. *From LeRoi Jones to Amiri Baraka: The Literary Works*. Durham, NC: Duke University Press, 1973.

Jones, Hettie. *How I Became Hettie Jones*. New York: Dutton, 1990.

Lacey, Henry C. *To Raise, Destroy, and Create: The Poetry, Drama, and Fiction of Imamu Amiri Baraka*. Troy, NY: Whitston, 1981.

Sollors, Werner. *Amiri Baraka/LeRoi Jones: The Quest for a "Populist Modernism."* New York: Columbia University Press, 1978.

INDEX

PICTURE CREDITS

BOB BERNOTAS received his doctorate in political theory from Johns Hopkins University and has taught philosophy and political science at Morgan State University and Towson State University. He is the author of several books on American government and numerous articles on jazz and sports.

NATHAN IRVIN HUGGINS is W.E.B. Du Bois Professor of History and Director of the W.E.B. Du Bois Institute for Afro-American Research at Harvard University. He previously taught at Columbia University. Professor Huggins is the author of numerous books, including *Black Odyssey: The Afro-American Ordeal in Slavery*, *The Harlem Renaissance*, and *Slave and Citizen: The Life of Frederick Douglass*.